By ELLE E. IRE

Vicious Circle

STORM FRONTS
Threadbare
Patchwork

Published by DSP PUBLICATIONS
www.dsppublications.com

ELLE E.
IRE

PATCHWORK

DSP PUBLICATIONS

Published by
DSP PUBLICATIONS

5032 Capital Circle SW, Suite 2, PMB# 279, Tallahassee, FL 32305-
7886 USA
www.dsppublications.com

This is a work of fiction. Names, characters, places, and incidents
either are the product of author imagination or are used fictitiously, and
any resemblance to actual persons, living or dead, business establishments, events, or locales is entirely coincidental.

Patchwork
© 2020 Elle E. Ire

Cover Art
© 2020 Tiferet Design
http://www.tiferetdesign.com/
Cover content is for illustrative purposes only and any person depicted
on the cover is a model.

Mass Market Paperback ISBN: 978-64108-248-8
Trade Paperback ISBN: 978-1-64405-446-8
Digital ISBN: 978-1-64405-445-1
Library of Congress Control Number: 2019955842
Mass Market Paperback published May 2021
v. 1.0

Printed in the United States of America
∞
This paper meets the requirements of
ANSI/NISO Z39.48-1992 (Permanence of Paper).

To my spouse:
my first, middle, and last reader always.
You are my rock and my cushion, my sounding board
and my grounding force,
my best friend and my forever love.

Acknowledgments

PATCHWORK WAS different. Writing the second book in a series, while easier in terms of world-building and character development, is much harder in maintaining the tension, both romantic and otherwise. An author worries about meeting and hopefully surpassing expectations. Will the second book live up to the first? Will readers continue to love the series? And then there is the deadline. When a series is contracted, the first book is usually written prior to signing that contract, over an unlimited amount of time. The second and third books are often not written yet. So the number of people an author can get to critique a book on deadline is sorely limited.

Thanks go first to my spouse—the only one who got to see this in manuscript form prior to being sent to my amazing editorial team: Rose, Yv, and Brian. Between the four of them, hopefully all the misplaced commas and hyphens, along with any plot holes were caught. Any that remain are my errors and mine alone.

Thanks to my writing group: Evergreen, Gary, Ann, and Amy, who did not get to see this but helped keep me sane. Thanks also to the fans who wrote beautiful reviews for the first book, THREADBARE, on Amazon, Goodreads, and elsewhere, or supported me in person with their encouragement and enthusiasm for the series: Bob, Elijah, Arielle, Rob, Jenni, Tim, Lily, the entire Tampa writing community, and if I'm forgetting anyone, please forgive me. Thanks also to my karaoke and teacher friends who cheered me on when I needed it most.

Thanks to my outstanding cover artist, Nathalie Gray, who once again managed to put on the cover what I see in my head. Vick glows because of you. Thanks to the rest of the art department at Dreamspinner Press. You are all awesome! Also thank you to Naomi Grant, social media guru, for your warmth and friendliness welcoming me to the Dreamspinner family and your patience with my online insecurities.

Finally, thank you to my amazing agent, Naomi Davis, and all the folks at Dreamspinner Publications who believed in me and the STORM FRONTS series. None of this would exist without you.

CHAPTER 1: VICK
STORMS BREWING

I AM pissed off.

Fuck, that hurts. I jerk my hand out and blow on singed fingers, then plunge it back into the mass of wires and circuitry.

"This has got to be your worst idea yet."

I spare the minutest of glares for my teammate, Alex, before returning my attention to the open control panel in front of me. "Maybe if you weren't hovering, I'd have this done by now." In the distance, across Girard Moon Base's central hub promenade, I detect gunfire, my enhanced hearing differentiating both the legal-to-carry-in-a-controlled-environment adjustable laser kind and the I'm-a-fucking-moron-getting-desperate projectile variety. A sound like hailstones on a tin roof confirms the existence of the latter. Idiots. If the bullets don't pierce the walls and waste the base's precious atmosphere, they're just as likely to ricochet and hit an unintended target.

"Has it occurred to you that I don't *want* you to be done?" His boots shuffle from side to side across the steel-gray tile flooring.

Yeah, it has crossed my mind.

The fight broke out—I consult my internal chronometer, bringing up the display behind my real-looking, very-manufactured brown eyes—all of fifteen minutes ago. Feels like an hour.

I'D HAD a spoonful of Kelly's delicious vat-grown chicken potpie halfway to my mouth, steam rising off the mixture of crust, sauce, potatoes, and poultry, when the call came in on my embedded comm unit. *Merc disturbance. Alpha Dog Pub. Shots fired. Local law otherwise engaged. Team One respond and assist.*

Kelly slammed her spoon onto the table. "You're leaving," she said. "Again."

I blinked once before remembering that she knows when I "check out" on her. She says my eyes unfocus and I go very still. Like a robot. A machine. My words, not hers. She'd never call me those things, but I can think them, and most of the time she doesn't pick up on it. Maybe. I never am sure.

I also remembered this was the third interruption in our dinner in the past two weeks. First a martial arts demonstration for some potential client. Then a "quick briefing" that lasted over an hour. Now this. "Duty calls," I told her with more than a little hesitation. Anger didn't come naturally to Kel. When it did, it directed itself at me. But I didn't deserve this. Something beyond an unfinished meal was upsetting her, and I didn't have time to find out what. "Stay put. Bar brawl. Shouldn't take long. New recruits probably need reining in. Keep dinner warm for me?" That earned me a fierce glare that sent me squirming backward in my chair before I buried instinct beneath purposeful action. I broke eye contact and stood from her kitchen table, a plastic and metal affair made homey with a red-and-white checkered tablecloth and real linen napkins. Sterile military base or not, she did her best to make her quarters—*our* quarters now that we'd moved into a two-bedroom unit—as welcoming as possible.

Her full red lips parted to argue. Then she clamped them shut, snatched my plate from my usual place, and marched with it across to the disposal unit where she scraped my portion into the hatch.

All I managed was "Why?"

Without facing me, she responded, "Because it's never short. Dinner's always ruined. And tonight...." Her voice cracked. "Tonight I thought we might try again."

"Try... oh." *Try.* As in *sex.* As in that thing we both wanted but I couldn't deliver, because no matter how hard I fought to block it out, whenever she touched me, all I saw was Rodwell groping me, violating me, his cold, callused hands— I shook the image away, swallowing the bile in my mouth and unclenching fists I hadn't realized I'd made. And to make matters worse, Kelly had begun refusing my attempts to take care of *her* needs in exclusion to my own. Not fair, she'd said, that I should keep giving what I desired but couldn't receive.

It's been almost a year and that attack is still as fresh as if it happened this morning.

"You'll never get through it if we don't keep trying," Kelly said.

"We're not having this conversation right now." I crossed my arms over my chest. "I'm a soldier. A leader. I need to be able to function without running to you for help. Eventually I'll work through it on my own."

"But you aren't…," she said in a small voice.

Hence the two-bedroom apartment. Sometimes it's fine, sharing a bed with her. Other times, not so much. If I'm in the middle of a nightmare about what Rodwell did to me and my body comes into contact with hers, things get dangerous for Kelly. I haven't hurt her yet, but I can usually recognize when I'm edgy and need to sleep alone. The fact that that's become more frequent was not something I wanted to be reminded of right then, though.

I whirled and half walked, half ran from the kitchen, aware she called after me, but I was through the archway, crossing the living room that separated our bedrooms, and out the door before she could make me feel any guiltier than I already did.

Not my fault. None of it. She knew that. Frustration talking. That's why we both snapped. Had to be. Her empathic talent meant she felt not just her

PATCHWORK   **5**

own needs but mine, too, and I'd been pretty damn
needy, and edgy, the past few nights alone in my room.
Didn't make her anger and disappointment easier to
take. Not one bit. But I couldn't stick around and hash
things out.

When the Storm orders, I obey. Always. Whether
I want to or not.

In the corridor leading to the promenade dome,
I made two quick comm calls and Alex and Lyle fell
into step beside me. They updated me on the way. Not
new recruits. Not the average bar brawl, but an out-
and-out battle being waged at the Alpha Dog between
our people and the Sunfires, our biggest rival mercenary company.

WHICH BROUGHT me to this moment, peer-
ing into an open control panel just off the promenade
circle and not thinking about Kelly's face when she
yelled at me. Nope. Not thinking about it.

"Where the hell are the local cops?" I growl
through gritted teeth, hands embedded up to my wrists
in older-than-moon-rocks circuitry and frayed and
corroded wiring. This place is one glitch away from a
fatal environmental shutdown.

"Landing bay," Lyle says, coming around to stand
in my field of view. He's got three fingers pressed to
his ear, his own comm just inside the ear canal, unlike the one wired into my mostly AI implanted brain.
"Sanderson reports an explosion in one of the fu-
el-storage drums. Very suspicious. Looks like Sunfire
work. Says we need to get our own damn people in
the pub under control and stop making her officers'

jobs harder." Lyle pauses, cracking a grin despite the intensity of the situation. "And she promises not to charge us for any damages we incur." He moves to stand behind me and Alex.

My lips twitch in a quick grin of my own. Officer Sanderson knows me well. She's got a soft spot for me and I for her. We'll never be more than friends, but I'd trust her at my back, which, including my own team, places her among a very small and elite group of people.

Another cascade of gunfire echoes across the open domed space between us and the pub, followed by a shout of pain. "Hope that's not one of ours," Alex mutters.

"Is it?" I subvocalize so neither of my biological teammates hears me.

VC1, my AI implant, making up 63 percent of my damaged brain, has a twisted sense of humor—*my* twisted sense of humor if I'm honest with myself. She can talk to me in words but prefers to amuse herself and make me work for the knowledge she deigns to give me.

Case in point, some outdated sport's scoreboard pops up in my internal view, green background, loud, clacking, flipping numbers and all.

Sunfires: 1

Storm: 0

I don't doubt her accuracy. VC1 has voice imprints on record in her extensive memory storage of any member of the Storm we've heard speak. Not thrilled with her flippancy, though.

These are human lives, I subvocalize. *This isn't a game.*

It is all a game to me, she responds.

I raise my eyes to the proverbial heavens, knowing she will register the motion since my eyeballs are as mechanical as she is and wired straight into her systems. *Let me put it differently. If this player gets permanently removed from the field, you cease to exist.*

A brief pause.

Not entirely true, but I concede your point.

Huh. I wonder what the hell she means by that, but my functions are far too occupied to devote attention to existentialism.

"We're out of time," I mutter and force my fingers to move faster, rewiring different systems to minimize outages while seeking to achieve the very specific localized results I'm hoping for. With VC1's help, I'm a blur of motion among the circuits and wires.

"What, exactly, is it we're doing again?" Lyle asks, his baritone a little higher pitched than usual. He's more muscle than mechanic, but even he knows that messing around in a panel clearly marked as hazardous and high-voltage with bright orange glow paint is a bad idea.

"*You* aren't doing anything except providing backup, if possible. *I*, on the other hand, am—" I break off as I make the final connection... and the lights in every shop, restaurant, and entertainment venue, along with the overhead illumination panels in the center of the promenade dome leading to them, go out.

This, of course, is followed by added screams and shouts of confusion from those taking refuge in all the businesses.

"Vick...," Alex whispers, leaning in so closely I can feel his breath on my cheek. "You'd better have a plan."

Using my first name. I've really got Alex spooked. At least he's not calling me VC1 anymore. That brings a momentary warmth to my insides. They know VC1 as a separate entity even if the rest of the Storm doesn't. They know I'm my own person.

Acceptance came hard, but it came.

While we've been communing with the base's technological infrastructure, Lyle's been pacing back and forth behind us, acting as lookout for any mainte-nance workers who might object to my activities. The patterned footfalls cease, and his hand brushes my bicep before fumbling and finding my shoulder, then clamping down hard. "What are you up to?"

In response I activate the spotlights built into my eyes, illuminating first the open panel before me, then shifting to the floor at Lyle's feet to avoid blinding him. He jumps anyway, releasing me and backpedal-ing until he bumps the opposite side of the promenade access corridor. So much for acceptance.

"Shit, I hate it when you do crap like that." Lyle places one boot in front of the other until he's within touching distance. But he doesn't touch me again.

I roll my eyes, sending the beams bouncing and reflecting off the metal walls. "You're with me," I tell Lyle, though if he's gonna go all skittery on me, I'm not thrilled about it. I turn to my currently less-freaked-out teammate, the one who held his position on my opposite side. "Alex, monitor the new connec-tions I've made. They may not be entirely stable. I've shut down lighting and emergency backups in this section of the base only. I didn't touch air or gravity or any other sections. Doesn't mean it won't cascade on us. If it does, stop it."

Alex's mouth sets in a grim line. He might not have that much faith in his tech abilities, but I have faith in him. Before VC1 and I worked out the logistics of our symbiotic relationship, he was our go-to guru. After a moment he nods and steps up to take my place while I grab Lyle's uniform sleeve and tug him along with me. We've gone a handful of paces when a thought occurs and I call back over my shoulder, "If Kelly shows up, stall her here. I don't need to be worrying about the Sunfires and her too."

"Stopping a cascade failure will be easier," Alex grumbles. He focuses his attention on the panel's depths and the sparks flickering from within that hadn't been there a moment ago. Dandy.

Into the dark we go, me keeping the illumination from my eyes at the minimum requirement to prevent me and Lyle from falling on our faces. In addition to a perimeter promenade with shops along the outer edge, the dome is crisscrossed with wagon-wheel-spoke walkways creating bridges over the decorative hydroponics gardens below and to the sides. We move along one of these paths, railings and transparent waist-high barriers preventing pedestrians from accidentally stepping off into the delicate foliage. In full light, provided by both stars and sun lamps, the flowers, shrubs, and food-bearing plants bring greenery to folks who rarely experience such luxuries. Now they're seemingly bottomless abysses of murk and shadow to either side.

We hit the open space at the center of the dome, empty curved park benches marking a favorite spot for residents and tourists alike. Nobody here now, though scuttling and scratching around the perimeter indicate survivors feeling their way out of the area. Lyle's voice stops me before we tackle the second half of our journey. "Wouldn't a flashlight have been easier?"

I cock my head at him, knowing he'll follow the path of my eye lights even if he can't see the exact motion. "You have a flashlight on you? Or were you just responding from dinner like I was?" A failed dinner. And an upset girlfriend. And... fuck. *VC1, raise my suppressors to midrange.*

No response from my symbiotic live-in brain-mate, but a cold calm settles over me like new-fallen snow, the worry and guilt buried beneath my emotion suppressors.

Lyle's noncommittal grunt tells me all I need to know about his flashlight preparedness. Still, I reach into a snapped pocket on my uniform pants, remove a small handlamp, and pass it over to him. I can just make out his raised eyebrows in the gloom.

"Paranoid, remember?" I'm known for it. Always ready for a variety of emergencies. I shrug, gesturing at my face. "This is easier for me. I can make adjustments faster with a thought than with my hands. Keep your beam low and switch over to comms," I order, matching actions to words. "We're going in."

"They'll be more prepared than we are," he reminds me, voice crackling over my embedded speakers. "If they set off the bomb in the landing bay, they planned for this."

"They didn't plan on me dousing the lights." I hope. Being the only ones controlling sources of light should give us an advantage. I draw my pistol from the holster strapped to my upper thigh. Kelly's complaints or no, I'm never without it except when we're in bed together, or in the shower, and even then, I hide it beneath her mattress or pillow or keep it on the counter outside the shower door. The XR-7 Safety Net, as its manufacturers affectionately named it, is legal for licensed carriers within all artificially maintained environments including unbreathable atmosphere planetary bases, interstellar vessels, and space stations. Though technically a projectile weapon, it fires blunted rounds, capable of stunning or even knocking out an opponent without risk to walls or domes.

To be honest, I'd much rather be hefting a laser blaster myself, but if Kelly shows up, pacifying rather than killing my objectives is the way to go to avoid triggering her empathic responses. Gas grenades would be nice too. I make a mental note to pack one in my utility belt in the future as part of my personal "crash and carry" kit.

Lyle pulls an identical weapon from inside his jacket. He's not as paranoid as I am, but mercs are mercs. We're always armed in one way or another. Besides the gun, I've got three knives stashed on my person at all times.

"Where's VC1?" an unfamiliar voice shouts from inside the Alpha Dog, followed by breaking glass and the thud of heavy wood hitting the floor—probably one of the tables overturned.

I stiffen. Me? This was somehow about me? What the hell?

"Where's your mechanical lapdog?" the voice comes again.

Nice.

"Beats 'robot bitch.'" Lyle's grin comes through in his tone.

I punch him in the shoulder. "Take the long way around," I order, pointing off to the right. "Circle the perimeter and come in through the pub's emergency exit airlock." I stumble just the slightest bit on the last word. Airlocks and I have bad history. Lyle pretends not to notice, but I'm betting he did. "Don't aim your light at the main entrance. I'm switching to infrared." I do so, cutting our visibility in half, both from our perspective and that of our enemies. Can't have them see me coming.

Lyle heads off, handlamp growing fainter as the distance between us increases. "Don't worry, Corren," he assures me over the comm. "Just get our guys out of there alive. I got your back."

I swallow the sudden, unexpected lump in my throat, then plunge forward.

You want the mechanical lapdog? Better hope you've got a steel leash, you motherfucking bastards.

CHAPTER 2: KELLY
CONTROL FACTORS

VICK IS upset.

"It happened again. Worse this time." My hands over my face muffle my words, and the pause for a response lengthens to the point I'm not sure I'm heard.

Then, "Have you actually *talked* to her?"

I raise my head and meet Dr. Brindle's eyes through the vidscreen. No, not "Dr. Brindle." Linda. She wants me to call her Linda. I'm not a student at the Academy anymore. I'm an adult. With a career and a life… such as it is. "No… Linda."

She smiles knowingly at the pause but says nothing, waiting. Wrinkled fingers with perfectly painted red nails straighten the antique brooch pinned to her shirt's white-ruffled neckline.

I sigh and glance around the so, so empty living room, more spacious than the ones in the one-bedroom quarters, vacuumous without Vick's presence. "I can't." I hate the whine in my voice, but that's how I feel—whiney and petulant like the child I'm no longer supposed to be, debating reality with someone almost three times my age. I stand, pacing away from the desk where the screen sits, then back again, my manners still in place enough that I don't leave the range of the video pickups. "She's got her own problems. Lots of them. I can't pile mine onto hers. And she's on this independence kick. Wants to get through it alone. I understand that. It's part of her personality. But… I don't know what to do."

Completing a second turn, I face Linda again. She nods her understanding, but her expression is serious. She reaches to tuck an escaped strand of hair into the graying bun at the back of her head. "I've read the abridged reports you've shared with me," she says.

I grimace. It's been a point of contention between me and the Fighting Storm that I'm allowed to consult with a more experienced psych-med, but only on the mercenary organization's terms. This means the medical files I've sent to my former teacher don't include some of the pertinent details, particularly those revealing the full impact of VC1 and what having the AI in Vick's head might suggest.

"From what you've sent, it appears Ms. Corren has made great strides in her recovery."

I snort a bit at "Ms. Corren." To my knowledge, no one has ever called the hardass soldier "Ms." anything.

"She's lengthened her autonomously functional periods from minutes to hours to days, to weeks," Linda continues, glancing down as if she's reading from one of the files as she speaks.

I nod. Vick doesn't connect with me nearly as often as she used to in order to purge her pent-up emotions. Except when she's in extreme distress, she's learned to identify and process them on her own, a fact that makes me both proud and a bit sad that she doesn't need me so much anymore.

"And her memories are returning." Linda's fingers tap the unseen table where she sits, then reach to wrap around a mug of steaming liquid, which, knowing the stresses of our shared occupation, likely contains a shot of something stronger than tea or coffee.

I close my eyes for a moment. Yes. Memories. Lots of them. Some of the two of us together, which bring us closer, some of Vick with... others. It's no secret Vick is bisexual and was quite promiscuous before her accident that led to her brain injury. She's not anymore. She's not any kind of sexual right now. But I worry that if she finds those memories pleasant, if she misses that more active lifestyle....

"Stop it," Linda commands, snapping me out of my depressing thoughts. "Right now. Stop it. Whatever you're thinking, it's nothing good. If I could reach through this screen, I'd bop you on the head."

Tales of gentle but firm head bops from Ms. Brindle passed infamously from one class of Academy students to the next and earned her the secret nickname of *Foo-foo*. I smile a little at the nostalgia. "You can't read me from Earth," I say, retaking my seat at the desk. "How did you know?"

Linda takes a long sip of her drink and sets the cup aside. "Sweetheart, you will never be a successful poker player." She claps her hands once and leans in. "All right. Bottom line. Your partner isn't as fragile as you think she is, despite her recent sexual assault."

"Not that recent," I remind her. "Almost ten months. Everything else about her is improving, but *that*… that doesn't seem to fade at all."

Linda waves one hand dismissively. "It will. Some take longer than others. You know that. If I may continue?"

Once my professor, always my professor. I nod.

"Your problems *are already* her problems, no matter how hard you try to shield her from them. The bond between you makes them so. And you snapping at her when it isn't her fault isn't going to make things better."

I wince. Yes, we'd discussed that too. I'd been biting Vick's head off for the past several weeks, and no matter how hard I tried to stop it, I couldn't seem to make the words stay in my mouth.

"You have to tell her what's happening to you. Then you need to seduce her."

I need to—wait. What? The blush floods my cheeks, dipping down to the point of the V-necked T-shirt I'm wearing and rising all the way to the tops of my ears. "Linda!" I am not having a conversation about the art of sex with my grandmotherly former teacher.

"Normally I would recommend continuing to wait until she's ready, but your relationship is, shall we say, unique, and vital to both the happiness and overall mental stability of the two of you, and that relationship is being negatively affected. So you can't wait any longer." Linda peers at me through her screen and laughs at the expression she must read on my face. "You are turning quite the impressive shade of red," she says. "Even in my Empathic Relationships course, you were far more likely to study the floor tiles than the descriptions and images in your vidbook."

I'm avoiding the idea now too. Except it's dark gray carpet in our living room. And it needs vacuuming.

"Look," she says, tone recapturing my focus, "I must run. I have a conference with a student in ten minutes."

Right. Time difference. I glance at the onscreen clock and do the math. It's midafternoon in North Carolina on Earth.

"But you'll be just fine," Linda continues, smiling. "Remind yourself of what attracts her to you. And if you aren't sure, just tap into her emotions when she looks at you. Use what drives her to distraction. No avoidance. Meet her needs head-on. You will work through her traumas together over time as you have been, but her buildup of sexual frustration, her inability to process it on her own, and her projecting it onto you are interfering with that healing process. You have to solve one problem before you can make progress with the others. So. Give her no opportunities to dwell on past events during actual foreplay and lovemaking. Work her up to the point where she cannot resist you.

It may not happen the first time or even the second, but patience, persistence, and understanding are key. If you can get the two of you away for a few days, all the better."

"My annual family reunion is coming up. She said she'd go with me." Reluctantly. Vick's more than a little nervous about meeting my parents for the first time. Again. She has little memory of doing it before. But I talked her into it. It coincides with my birthday, which I don't want to celebrate without Vick. And I spent over an hour convincing the Storm's board that we both deserved some R & R. After all that effort, she practically had to say yes.

I wish she'd agreed more willingly.

"Perfect!" Linda says, clapping once with feeling. "It's settled, then. New scenery, away from the pressures of her job, lots of people predisposed to like and support her. Let me know how it goes. And if you need anything else, don't hesitate to call."

She cuts the connection before I can thank her, leaving me staring at a dark screen, my mind swirling with questions and half-formed plans I discard as fast as they come.

Seduce Vick? Vick had been my first, last, and only. I'd done all right with our first time because she couldn't remember anything better. But now?

Now I'm in competition with every person she's ever been with, not to mention the demons in her head. And I have no idea how to win.

CHAPTER 3: VICK
PRIORITIES

I AM a target.

I work my way to the Alpha Dog entrance, keeping low, letting the walkway's railing shield me until it ends and I must cross the open width of the perimeter promenade. I scuttle across it, dive-rolling the last few feet when gunfire erupts once more from the open hatchway leading into the pub. It goes wide, a beamed shot bouncing off glass, then metal until it scorches longwise across the curve of the dome, leaving a blackened streak and the scent of ozone in its wake.

"Mommy!" comes a plaintive voice far down the row of stores. A glance reveals a tiny figure emerging from the bakery entrance, head turning in the direction of the bar. A pair of hands reaches from the doorway behind the child, grabs him or her, and yanks the kid back inside.

Good. That would be the last thing I'd need.

Panting, I remain crouched, back pressed against the exterior wall of the bar. More shouting, several imaginative curses, and the sound of breaking pint glasses follow, enough that I'm convinced no one spotted me and the shot was a chance near-miss rather than aimed. Several yards away I make out the pinpoint of light from Lyle's borrowed handlamp as it vanishes when he ducks into the emergency side airlock right on schedule. A faint hiss sealing in the breathable atmosphere confirms he's in position. Would've likely been smarter for us to have switched places, with me coming in through the side rather than storming the front door, given I'm apparently the one the Sunfires are all riled up about. Except, airlock.

Fucking airlocks. Holdover tech from two generations past and still in place as "safety backups." We've got shields now. And secondary generators for them. The odds of a disaster large enough to have the locks be our final line of defense between humans and unbreathable air are so slight. Besides, half the doors have been jammed open or closed by the businesses they're attached to for convenience's sake, and of those remaining untouched, few work properly.

A miniscule shudder passes down the length of my five-foot-eight frame, unstoppable even with the emotion suppressors running at half power. I'm tempted to up their output, but it gives me an even more robotic outward appearance and opens up an avenue of control over me that I don't want to risk giving to my AI counterpart.

I shake out the sudden tension in my shoulders, rise to my full height, and slide my way along the metal to the edge of the entryway.

Unusual for the double arched doors to be wide open at any hour, and I now see why: a body lies half in, half out of the Alpha Dog, boots and lower legs extending halfway across the promenade path, the upper portion of the unknown individual still unseen inside. Crouching again, I give a gentle tap to the closest ankle with no response from its owner. I brush the uniform pants leg up, unable to identify the color as Fighting Storm gray or Sunfire copper, and clamp my free hand more firmly around the joint. No pulse.

This the one we're down? I ask my implants. The scoreboard numbers flip on my internal display.

Sunfires: 2

Storm: 0

Well, damn.

I'm not especially religious. Never have been to the best of my knowledge, though that knowledge is pretty sketchy. But I close my eyes for a second and whisper a quick prayer on the soldier's behalf. Maybe his gods will hear it.

"Corren, you in position?" Lyle calls over my embedded comm.

"Yeah. You?"

"Ready to make a scene on your say-so."

"Then get on with it," Alex breaks in from back across the dome. "Things are heating up in the control

box. I've patched a few pathways, but I can't keep up
with it forever."

As if on cue, the ever-present hum of the station's
artificial gravity stutters, then fails. More screams and
shouts of surprise erupt from the surrounding businesses while my own boots leave the floor and I rise
a couple of inches into the air. I slap my palm against
the side of one boot and then the other, activating the
magnetic soles, and instantly I'm reconnected with the
path. After a few moments the gravity returns, but I
leave the magnetization on. It might slow me down a
bit, but I don't want to go floating off in the middle of
a firefight.

"Did that happen everywhere or just here?" I ask,
flicking the safety off my XR-7.

"Just the dome, as far as I can tell. But comms are
spotty in here too. And the ventilation keeps shutting
on and off."

Now that Alex has mentioned it, it does seem a
bit colder than usual. A check of my bio-stats shows
VC1 is raising my body temperature to compensate.
Around the promenade dome, lights flicker on and
off—a neon in a lingerie storefront, an interior overhead glowtube in the throwback Earth diner, some of
the heat lamps in the hydroponics gardens—like some
kind of bizarre holiday display.

Alex curses over the comm. The dome plunges
back into darkness.

We're out of time.

Muttering epithets of my own, I crawl on hands
and knees over the dead body, arching and twisting at
unnatural angles to make as little contact with the still
warm but lifeless flesh as possible and avoid bumping

the doors on either side. He's young, this former member of the Storm, a new recruit. Infrared doesn't quite allow me to make out specific features, but he's familiar. I probably trained him in one of my martial arts classes, or maybe marksmanship. Regardless, I count him as one of mine, and I intend to avenge him with every power I possess.

Inside, the scene is controlled chaos. Overturned tables and chairs, broken glass everywhere, including a shard that makes it through my uniform pants and cuts deep into my shin. I swallow a yelp while VC1 increases platelet production and rushes a stream of them to the affected area. Warm wetness seeps into the pant fabric, then stops, leaving a circle of darker material against the already deep gray.

Though it resembles the aftermath of a tornado, nothing currently moves, everyone having taken cover of one sort or another. I follow that example, crunching my way as quietly as possible over the glassware until I'm behind one of the bench seats lining the side walls, bolted to the floor and impossible to overturn. There I find the second of our fallen, a young woman with a neat round hole bored through her forehead appearing in infrared as a dark circular blot like an ink spill. She lies on her back, eyes wide open as if she can't believe her own demise. My guess is she peered up and over the back of the bench and caught a laser beam for her curiosity.

How many still alive in here?

In response, I'm briefly deafened by what sounds like a cacophony of drums played in different rhythms at different speeds. Then, one by one, the beats separate themselves, fading to manageable volumes, and nine glowing red dots appear on my internal display of the bar, hovering over various objects around the room.

Heartbeats. VC1's distinguished and located everyone in the pub by their heartbeats.

I never knew I could do that. Cool.

Mutters and murmurs flow around me, nothing discernible but clearly plans being made. I activate my comm. "On my mark, Lyle. One, two—"

The hiss of the opening airlock farther along the wall to my right coincides with "three" and I rise to my full height, confident from the lack of prior movement that no one else took infrared tech to the bar tonight. There are numerous warm-blooded targets I can make out parts of: a crouched knee jutting from behind the edge of a sideways table, a shoulder too wide for the chair concealing most of it, the tops of two caps whose owners don't realize they aren't crouched low enough behind the main bar running across the rear of the pub.

Lyle's light flashes around, drawing attention to the lock. He's got himself hunkered down and pressed back into the protective alcove, and he's set the hatch to remain open. It's a good distraction, and a couple of crazier mercs fire at the bouncing white beam, rather than tracking it to its source.

Identify the indicators as friends and foes.

Complying, VC1 responds in a rare use of actual words. Guess she can't come up with a metaphorical image for compliance fast enough.

A half second later, the glowing red figures I can make out differentiate themselves in my display with overlaid flames for Sunfires and rainclouds for members of the Storm. Three targets theirs, one ours. Nice to know our people knew how to hide, at least. *You sure?*

The factions wear different uniform styles, the AI returns, a note of smugness in her tone. *And the Fighting Storm doesn't wear hats.*

Wow, complete sentences and everything. You and I might just learn to be friends after all. I transmit the targeted image to Lyle.

A buzzing sound that might be VC1 blowing a raspberry follows, but I can't be sure because I'm opening fire, first on the two whose heads I can see. I bean one with my XR-7's blunted pellets, hard enough that a groan and a thud follow the shot. The second round sends a cap flying but does no damage.

I duck back down while the one with the exposed knee adds a barrage of additional rounds at the same general area. That individual was marked as ours but clearly can't see what he or she is aiming at and is just following my lead.

I peer around the bench seat as exposed-shoulder-guy (guessing at the sex from the broadness of the body parts) pops off a pellet or two at me, and I narrowly miss taking one to the throat. Pinging sounds of more-lethal bullets off metal suggest other Sunfires have opened up on Lyle's airlock hiding place, but he's doused his light, and the shots don't hit home.

Time to retake the offensive.

I set my weapon to repeat-fire and let 'er rip while racing the length of the pub from the front doors to the chest-high two-foot-thick wood bar at the back, following VC1's identified Sunfire targets as they pop up along the way. They can't see me, but they can hear my steps and gunfire, so their return shots come closer than I'd like. I'm betting lives on VC1's accuracy, but she's proven reliable in the past and I'm banking on it now.

One goes down. That's two out of nine, which doesn't include me or Lyle. Shoulders is one of ours and stops aiming at me when I shoot the Sunfire directly behind him, who topples over with a loud thud and a groan. Shoulders waves a hand in my general direction and ducks out of sight. Four still unaccounted for, I figure as I make it behind the bar and survey whom I'm sharing the space with.

I end up face-to-face and barrel-to-barrel with the Sunfire now missing his hat, his friend sprawled unconscious on the floor beside him. He's got his free arm wrapped around the throat of a woman in a server's blouse and skirt, forcing her to kneel in front of and facing away from him toward me. She's terrified, if the trembling of her infrared outline is anything to judge by. Worse, the Sunfire's eyes flicker with red overlays—infrared implanted contact lenses.

Which means one very important thing. He can see me as well as I can see him.

CHAPTER 4: KELLY
CONNECTED

VICK IS in trouble.

My hand tightens around the handle of the cup of tea I'm making, so hard the knuckles whiten and the hot water inside sloshes around like a mini tsunami. My heartbeat ramps up, almost drowning out the sudden increase in my breathing from regular exhalations to quick panting gasps.

I close my eyes, forcing suddenly tense muscles to relax, and blow all the air from my lungs in one push. I've been with Vick, *connected* to Vick for years now, but the unnatural (to my own body) sensations

caused by sudden floods of adrenaline still catch me
by complete surprise.

Once I'm no longer at risk of passing out from
hyperventilation, I set the mug on the counter, ease
into the closest kitchen chair, and rest my palms on my
thighs. My first thought, now that I've got my mental
shields in place, is to contact Vick, reassure myself of
her well-being, but I discard the idea. If she's in trouble, in the middle of a fight or some other dangerous
situation, which is more often the norm than not, I'll
be distracting her, possibly fatally so.

I bite my lip and twist a lock of blond hair around
one finger. Then I reach for the comm device in my
pocket and tell it to contact Alex. Same concerns ap-
ply, of course. He's part of Vick's team and could also
be in danger, but most of the time he's tech support,
backup like me, acting as our eyes and ears rather than
diving onto the front lines.

It takes several long, tense seconds before the
connection opens, and I'm worrying I've made things
worse after all, when Alex's harried voice carries over
the tiny speaker. "Alex here. Hands full. This better
be important."

I set the comm on the table in front of me. It's
voice only, no vidscreen like some of the pricier models. Vick hasn't had them upgraded for Alpha Team.
Says she doesn't like people watching her work. In
the background, I hear pops and sizzles, like grease
in a pan of bacon, and muffled cursing. As usual, my
timing is not opportune.

"It's me," I reply, guessing he hasn't checked
the ID or he would have called me by name. Or hung
up. Or not answered at all. It's not that my two male

teammates dislike me, but they have an annoying habit of trying to keep me from knowing when things go bad, especially when it comes to Vick. I'm not made of porcelain. I've gotten a lot better at shielding quickly to prevent empathic overload. And besides, it's my darn job.

"Kelly?" A pause. More sizzling followed by a crack. "Um, hey, Kel, can you maybe check in later? Kinda busy right now."

"Kinda worried right now," I return. "Picking up some disturbing emotions from Vick strong enough to reach me all the way in our quarters." Which, come to think of it, is very disturbing indeed. Line of sight or a few rooms away is about the greatest distance for casual emotional transfer. Farther if she's agitated. The Alpha Dog is halfway across the base. She must be truly agitated indeed for that spike to have hit me so hard and clear. "Need an update on her, if whatever you're doing isn't life-threatening."

He mutters something that sounds concerningly like "It might be." Then, "Gunfight in the Dog. No reports of injuries… from our team."

Translation: somebody is dead and Alex doesn't want to tell me, but it's not Vick or Lyle.

I can't blame him. Feeling another's death puts me out of commission every time, no matter how strong I've gotten. If I'd been closer, I would've been useless to them for anywhere from a few minutes to hours depending upon proximity.

More pops and cracks followed by a sharp yelp. "Shit. Look, Vick's fucked around with the promenade area's systems. I'm trying to keep things from shutting down completely, which would be… bad."

Knowing Alex's tendency to sugarcoat things for me, bad is probably an understatement.

"She said to tell you not to come down here. If she's engaged with the Sunfires, she's gonna run hot. It's part of the job. Doesn't mean she's in trouble. And to be honest, there's nothing you can do right now."

Nothing except provide the emotional support I'm getting paid for. My teeth grind together. Vick wants independence. I try to give her that. She's earned it. But she *is* in trouble no matter what Alex says. Likely she'll get herself out. She usually does. But right now....

"I'm heading that way. I won't interfere, but I want to be available. Don't argue. You can't win." I am the end-all and be-all when it comes to Vick. As her former psych-med and current partner, whatever I say with regards to her health goes.

Alex sighs over the connection. "Don't I know it. See you in about fifteen." In the distance, an alarm wails. The connection drops.

I glance down at my casual attire. I'm supposed to be in uniform when I'm performing any duties for the Storm. I change quickly from civilian wear to my gray uniform shirt and trousers, black boots and black belt, the colors blending with the drab walls of the Storm's section of the base. I've done my best to decorate these walls in our quarters as much as I can—Earth scenes, mostly from North Carolina, my home state, and Kansas, Vick's home, though she can't remember much of it. Paintings of vast cornfields, a farmhouse, a cabin in the deep woods. Three-dimensional projections of waterfalls, lightning over the prairie, boats crossing a mountain valley lake. I decorate myself, too, with as much color in my off-duty wardrobe as I can obtain while Vick prefers to stay in her standard-issue garb. But right now, making myself militarily presentable costs me precious minutes I worry I can't afford.

Right before leaving, I open the drawer in the table by the door and grab two syringes—one blue-tipped, one green. They're a bit dusty, but a quick check of their date indicators shows they haven't expired. These are for emergencies. I have a ready-to-go pair of identical ones for use on missions in my kitbag. Vick hasn't needed them in at least nine months, but it doesn't hurt to be prepared. Maybe her paranoia is rubbing off on me. I drop both into the sealable right thigh pocket of my cargo pants and close the Velcro flap, hoping I don't need either one. The feeling of intense danger has eased a bit, but that might be because Alex has warned Vick of my impending arrival and she's upped the output on her suppressors rather than the threat having passed.

My tension rises as I move through the corridors. I'm picking it up from everyone now: the other Storm soldiers rushing by me in both directions, the medical personnel heading for our hospital wing, and once I leave the gray and enter the pale blue of civilian areas, the other Girard Base inhabitants as well. All of them carry auras of varying shades of stressed-out pink— the way my empathic sense registers to my vision, with colors representing each emotional nuance. Vick hates the color pink. I'm starting to agree with her.

A branch leads toward the promenade or the landing bays. Alarms echo along the hallways, bouncing off the metal walls, making it impossible to tell which direction they come from, but I remember hearing

them on Alex's connection. No sirens or flashing
lights in my immediate vicinity, so I'm not in danger,
but I'm definitely heading into it as I turn left toward
the central dome and the Alpha Dog Pub.

I'm a few meters from where the corridor opens
up into the dome when it hits. Distracted by intermittent alarms and distant flashes of lights on the promenade, I'm unprepared when the spike of all-out terror
slams into me.

Walls up or not, the emotional onslaught physically throws me to the floor. My chest constricts. I
cannot breathe. My eyes squeeze shut, tears seeping
from beneath the lids. Small whimpers escape my
throat while I fight to inhale and fail.

I'm vaguely aware of hands on my shoulders,
my arms, soothing voices and anxious inquiries, but I
have no way of responding, no way to let them know
I'm all right.

Mostly because I'm not all right.

Vick's gone into a full-blown panic attack, an
emotional meltdown the likes of which I haven't
felt since the first time we met. Unknowingly, she's
dragged me in with her, and unless she regains some
control on her own, there isn't a damn thing I can do
about it.

CHAPTER 5: VICK
LOCK AND LOAD

I AM trapped.

"So you decided to turn up after all," the Sunfire says to me, pistol steady. The waitress squirms in his grasp, but he tightens his arm around her neck and she sags against him, defeated. Though she can't see me and doesn't know I can see her, her eyes plead for me to do something, anything. I can, but I'm not sure she'll appreciate it so much.

"What is it you want from me?" I ask as casually as I can manage under the circumstances. We're behind the bar, so I can't watch the ongoing fight, but I

hear it—hollers and thuds of punches hitting home. I
make out Lyle's signature whoop, an ululation no one
else in the Storm can emulate, though every new recruit tries. Blind brawling. Nothing quite like it.

Calculate the shot.

A thumbs-up appears in the center of my internal
display. In the corner a countdown ticks off. I need to
stall a little longer until VC1 can manipulate my aim
in just the right way.

"We want you," the Sunfire growls. "We want
your tech. Your owners wouldn't sell it at a fair price.
No one could have afforded what they were asking.
Now they won't sell it at all. So we've got orders to
take it. If you come willingly, maybe our research
guys won't kill you trying to copy it. If not...." He
shrugs with one shoulder. "We'll take it anyway and
reverse engineer it. We'll copy what makes you so
fucking successful, only we won't just put it in one
guy. Everyone in the Sunfires will be like you. We'll
win every contract. We'll be unstoppable."

It might not be their real plan. Their tech department might have something else entirely in mind, but
it's all this grunt knows. He's got his shoulders back,
his chest puffed out; his ego knows no bounds.

I can't help it. I bark a laugh. "You'll be insane,"
I tell him. "Look, power and consequences. Strength
and costs. You know the old sayings."

He blinks at me, dark lids falling over red lenses,
weird as hell to watch.

I try again. "Be careful what you wish for and all
that?" Still nothing. Leaning in so that even in infrared
he should be able to make out my expression, I let all

the pain and torment, all the borderline madness come through. "You. Don't. Ever. Want. To. Be. Me."

To my satisfaction, he flinches and deflates.

"I can't come with you. Even if I wanted to, which I don't. I'm *programmed*, you moron. Mechanical lapdog, remember? And my tech? Booby-trapped. You fuck with it, you, me, your researchers, and half your part of this base go *boom*." That last bit's pure BS, but I'll say whatever it takes to keep these guys out of what few brains I have left.

VC1 flashes an image of my body with a balloon in place of my head. It swells and bursts, scattering bits of red rubbery material into the air, more like brain matter than a child's entertainment.

Okay, maybe not all BS.

I swallow hard against that disturbing thought. "If you can be successful without being owned, do it. If you can't—" The countdown in my display reaches zero. VC1's calculated my speed, weapon firing time, and accuracy compared to my opponent. Not sure where she gets her data, but if I know her, she's hacked the Sunfire database and downloaded all his stats. Crosshairs invisible to anyone but me appear on the guy's forehead. I fire.

The waitress screams as his head slams back against the curve of the bar. It's such a close-in shot, the force of the blunted bullet cracks his skull in front, a visible dark line dividing his face from hairline to the bridge of his nose while the heavy wood's lack of resilience audibly fractures it from behind—a sickening crunch embedded in my auditory memory. He lands sideways, blood oozing from both sides and pooling in a black puddle around him.

The server scrambles away, collides with me, and shrieks again.

"I'm not going to hurt you," I tell her. "And he's dead. Fight's not quite over, though, so stay put." I crawl to the edge of the bar and peer around it. "Lyle, where are we in this?"

Outside the front doors, lights flash on and off up and down the row of shops. My stomach flip-flops with fluctuations in the artificial gravity. Alex is losing his battle with the station's antique tech.

The flicker of a handlamp gives away Lyle's location. He's off to the right, with a couple of our people, one male, one female, probably here together on a date. "I think we're good," Lyle calls back, both out loud and over the comm. "I took one down over here. And this couple's with us."

I nod, then do the math. Nine heartbeats, plus mine and Lyle's. So nine initial unknowns. Two bad guys and the server behind the bar. The guy whose knee was sticking out, who is probably the same guy Lyle's hanging with now. Knee-guy's girlfriend. That's five. Shoulder guy makes six. The Sunfire I nailed behind him is seven. The one I blasted on my run through the bar is eight. And the one Lyle took down. Nine.

"Mom! Mom!"

I whip my weapon toward the entrance, jerking it up before reflexes fire it at a small figure hanging on to one of the double doors.

"Mommy!"

Same kid I heard earlier calling from the promenade bakery. I recognize the voice. She (at least pitch would suggest female) must have felt her way along the walls or reached the pub by darting in spurts whenever the lights flashed. Brave, stupid, or desperate, I can't tell which, but she's here, and if she could see the dead body at her feet, she'd really be screaming.

The figure staggers forward, tripping over the corpse but remaining upright with her hands outstretched. She reaches the center of the pub and stops. "Mommy?" The voice wavers, uncertain.

"Stay where you are, Abby!" the server calls back. "I'm all right. I'll find you. Just stay there."

So the waitress is Mom. Shuffling carries from behind the bar as she attempts to join her daughter.

"Everyone hold position!" I order, putting all the authority I can muster into my tone. Movement ceases. I grin. Nice to know I'm not losing my touch. "We'll get the lights back on, and then—"

As if at my command, more flashes erupt from the restaurants and businesses outside the double doors. Alex curses in my ears. To my left, a panel I hadn't noticed slides sideways, revealing a shallow storage space, and an uncounted figure steps from it. He's got something in his hand. Not a gun. It's small and round... and beeping.

Fuck.

"Everybody down!" I shout. Everyone drops except for the kid. She's frozen where she stands, paralyzed by uncertainty and fear.

At the same time, in my ears Alex yells, "Corren! Shut off your infrared. You're about to be bli—"

The lights in the Alpha Dog blaze to life, every single one of them, from the low-level emergency strips along the walls, to the warm glows of sconce lamps simulating old-Earth incandescents, to the full-on glaring bright whites of the naked tubes used for after-hours cleaning. I have a half second to react, but it's too fast even for VC1. Everything flares white like I'm standing in the center of a sun going supernova. The pain receptors in my manufactured eyes scream with the burnout, then nothing. Nothing but afterimages of grays on white.

By now the AI has certainly turned off my infrared, but I have no way of knowing. Any people or furnishings in the pub might as well be Arctic foxes in a blizzard as far as my eyesight is concerned.

But I can hear. And that grenade is still beeping in the hand of the last remaining Sunfire in the joint.

Switch off my boots' magnetic soles, I instruct VC1.

I access my implant's memory of where the kid should be standing, take a quick breath, and dive for it.

It's a tremendous relief when I feel the impact of my body against the little girl's, and we both go down in a tumbled heap. I've probably hurt her some. Her squeak of surprise followed by a cry of pain tells me as much. But any damage I've inflicted will be nothing compared to the shrapnel and debris that grenade will send flying.

Together we roll over and over, me wrapping myself more firmly around her much smaller frame, shielding her from the imminent explosion with every part of me. I'm not wearing body armor. Paranoia goes only so far, and that much padding and metal isn't part of my daily wardrobe. So I'm gonna take the hit, and I'm gonna take it hard. Already am, with the splinters and glass shards scraping, tearing, and embedding themselves in seemingly every inch of my exposed skin.

My back slams into something solid, and holding the girl to my chest with one arm, I stretch out a palm to slap against cold metal—the wall. But there's a sideways lip to it. A doorway? The front entrance, maybe? Doesn't feel right. I'm disoriented by my blindness, the leap and the roll, but I don't think our direction carried us toward the entrance.

Another storage compartment? I don't care. I haul our asses around the edge and into wherever we might be just as the Sunfire apparently tosses the grenade, and its metal casing tink-tink-tinks its way across the pub's floor.

There's a hiss and a thunk. A familiar hiss. A familiar thunk. My blinded eyes go wide and my blood turns to ice in my veins as I realize exactly what I've dragged us into. I'm shoving the kid aside, scrambling on all fours, tearing already blunted nails against metal while I desperately feel for the hatch release.

Then… boom.

Even the airlock door can't completely block the sound of the explosion of the incendiary device, though it's more muffled than it would have been. I can't see the flare of the blast. My eyes are too fucked-up. But it's followed by chunks of plastic and wood pelting the window of the lock like angry hail.

The window. Of the *lock.*

I'm in the bar's emergency side exit airlock, the same one Lyle left open when he made his surprise entrance. Only it's not open anymore. Given the explosive circumstances, I should consider this a good thing, except….

I *died* in an airlock.

It's how I ended up the way I am, how I lost 63 percent of my organic *human* brain and became... this. Since that event occurred, I haven't been able to take prolonged stays in small spaces—elevators, closets, even rooms and ships without portholes or windows if they're too cramped.

I absolutely can't take this.

My hands shake, and I hold my breath, waiting for the air to cycle through and the hatch on the opposite side to slide open and let me out onto the promenade walkway and the nice, wonderful, spacious dome with its clear view of Earth and the stars beyond. But it doesn't. Nothing moves. It's silent except for the thudding in my chest and the whimpering of the kid on the floor beside me.

The kid. Hell.

I can't melt down. Until we get out of here, I've absolutely got to hold it together, for the kid's sake if not mine.

Gritting my teeth against shock-induced chattering, I order VC1 to ramp up my emotion suppressors to full and hope the AI doesn't take advantage of my current state and seize control of me altogether, because someday, she just might decide not to give that control back.

CHAPTER 6: KELLY
REGROUP

VICK IS struggling.

Gentle hands pull me to a seated position in the corridor just outside the opening to the promenade dome. With my eyes squeezed shut, I can't see who's helping me. Their emotions feel like strangers', lacking the nuances I've come to recognize as those belonging to friends and acquaintances.

I force one eyelid up, then blink both into the concerned face of a young man in a server's uniform belonging to the Alpha Dog. He's cute, if one goes for the vid-model type: tall, clean-cut, neatly trimmed

blond hair about the shade of my own, teeth so white
he had to have had them done in a salon. The pink aura
of tension surrounding him clashes with the tan vest
over a white button-down.

"You okay?" he asks as I pull from his grip and
break the contact. I'm having enough trouble with my
own emotions. I can't take his on too.

"Fine," I tell him, rising to my knees, then my
feet. I sway into the wall and let it hold me up.

"Not too fine." But he doesn't push it. His attention is torn between me and a crowd of gathered civilians all staring across the dome.

I follow their gaze and immediately see why. The
Alpha Dog's lit up like a hearth, the glow of low-level flames flickering from the entrance, lapping their
way over something blocking the double doors. More
panic sets in.

The fire suppression systems. They'll spray that
poisonous foam throughout the pub's interior, regardless of survivors inside. The base's oxygen is too precious to lose in large quantities. Everyone who lives
in the moon's habitat knows this. We sign on knowing
it. But like so many other possible causes of death, we
never expect to actually see it.

I open my mouth to scream but snap it shut when
there's no sign of the foam, no indication that the noz-
zles built into the metal walls have extended. Did Vick
shut those systems down too? It's a terrible gamble if
she did, risking everyone, but then the flow from the
bar recedes a bit, the flames burning out. Though the
pub's furnishings are wood, everything's treated with
flame-resistant chemicals. Other than that, there's not
a lot of flammable material at all.

I start toward the spectators, then fall back when my trembling limbs refuse to propel me away from the wall.

"What happened?" I ask. *Vick. Vick's still in there.* I no longer sense her panic. I no longer sense anything at all from her, which would be concerning if I didn't know with absolute certainty that I'd feel it if she died, even in the midst of emotion shock.

I've felt it before.

I stare across the dome, watching as the fire suppression systems finally activate, jetting the less powerful but nontoxic pink foam from ceiling tubes through the Alpha Dog doors rather than the poisonous blue variety for bigger conflagrations. The remaining flames and the sounds of hurt and fear take me even more comprehensively into the past, to a shuttleport and a terrorist attack, and the second to last time Vick lost her life.

Vick once told me her greatest fear is dying alone. Mine is having her die in my presence. I've faced mine, more than once. If I have my way, she'll never have to face hers. And that means getting to her now.

She must have her suppressors on full, which is a problem all in itself but something I can deal with once we're reunited. On its own, one hand drops to my cargo pants pocket, patting the syringes I placed there. Yes, I can deal with Vick.

"What happened?" I ask again, realizing I never got an answer.

"Didn't you hear the explosion?" the waiter asks, still facing the pub.

"I was pretty out of it."

He glances over his shoulder. "Yeah." A pause while he studies me more closely. "Clairvoyant? Precog?"

I raise my eyebrows.

"You're some kinda Talent. You dropped right before the fireworks. Like you knew it was coming."

"Empath," I admit. Some people are funny about Talents. I never know who will fear me, hate me, resent me, or just take me in stride. No anger or terror rolls off this guy, so I guess we're okay. "I've got a friend in there."

He nods, a flood of sympathy surging from him. *No. Vick's okay. She has to be.*

I close my eyes for a moment, reaching for our bond. It's there, a tether of aqua stretching from my center in a taut line leading into the Alpha Dog. My breath leaves me in a long, slow exhalation of relief.

A squad of emergency response personnel comes sprinting up the corridor, the pounding of their boots like rolling thunder. They're in full gear: flame-retardant orange jumpsuits and matching hoods with plastic see-through face panels. Some of the suits bear dark scorch marks and other signs of damage, and I wonder what additional disaster they're arriving from.

I'm pushing away from the wall a second time when one of the new arrivals grips my arm in an orange-gloved hand. Peering through the ash-covered faceplate, I recognize Officer Sanderson, head of station security and a friend of Vick's.

"Stay put," she tells me, voice tinny over the speaker embedded in the hood. "I promise I'll wave you over as soon as we've got that fire under control. Comms are out, but sensors indicate a number of survivors hunkered down inside. Try not to worry. Scan data says it was a low-level handheld incendiary blast. Unless she was right on top of the grenade, she should recover from any damage it did."

Except that Vick always tends to be right on top of anything dangerous that's going on.

I force a nod, and with a firm pat to my shoulder, Sanderson lets me go. She waves a couple of hand commands at her team, and the six of them race off across the dome's central walkway, now fully lit by working emergency lighting and the flashing reds of warning indicators. Dull alarms whoop in the background, coming from the dome's far side and setting up a pounding headache in my already sore skull.

I try my comm, despite what Sanderson said. No response. No signal at all.

Beyond the crowd, I spot movement in the shadows and make out Alex. I raise my arm to wave, but he shakes his head and places one finger over his lips. Without a word, he reaches to the side and closes a panel protecting some circuitry in the wall. Then he fades back into the dimness as if he were never there.

Huh. I'm wondering just how much of Vick's tampering was authorized by the base's facilitators.

A moment later he appears beside me, sauntering up as if he hadn't been here all along. He joins me in staring across the dome with all the others. "Any word?" he asks, tapping the side of his head.

"I'm not a telepath," I remind him for the thousandth time. People who spend time with both me and Vick often mistake us for having clear, consistent communications since we're so in tune with each other, tonight's argument notwithstanding. "There are no true telepaths."

He nods once in my peripheral vision. "Sure there aren't."

I sigh. I'm wondering why he isn't rushing in to help. After all, he and Lyle are close. They've been a team since well before adding in Vick and myself. But he's not wearing protective coverings, and he probably knows, just like I do, that he'd be more of a hindrance than an asset.

The minutes tick by. As soon as the glow of the flames fades, the pair of us start across the walkway, not waiting for Sanderson's okay. She's in the entryway as we arrive, blocking my view of the charred interior and holding up a hand, palm out, to stop us in our tracks. Whatever jammed the doors open before has been removed, replaced by a metal ale keg someone rolled into the position.

I open my mouth to ask after Vick, but before I can say a word, medical personnel arrive and rush inside. Sanderson follows them, leaving me and Alex without any more answers than when we began.

I take another step and out come the medics, some leading wounded by the arm—a woman in a waitress outfit looking shell-shocked, probably literally, and a male/female couple in Storm uniforms with what appear to be minor cuts and scrapes and a few burns. The waitress pauses, looking back at the pub, then snaps out of her stupor and struggles against the medic's grip. "Where's Abby?" she cries, panic setting in. "Where's my daughter?"

"Your daughter is fine," the woman in a white uniform tells her. "She's safe. The technicians are working on getting her out. She's unharmed. We'll treat your injuries in the center of the dome and you can wait for her right there."

A glance toward the indicated area shows the medical personnel have set up a first aid station right in the circle of benches in the middle of the hydroponics garden walkway. The waitress calms herself somewhat and allows the medic to lead her away.

Then come the stretchers with dazed and unconscious Sunfires laid out on them. There are three in total, two with circular bruising in the centers of their foreheads. Nice, neat work. Single shots. I recognize Vick's touch with her XR-7 Security Blanket.

I grin. Its real nickname is the Safety Net, but Vick sleeps with the damn thing under her pillow, so I like mine better.

The third looks like someone tackled and beat the crap out of him. I'm guessing Lyle took that one down. Vick's all finesse unless she must be otherwise. Lyle's the bruiser.

Last are the bodies. Four. Sealed in black bags and each carried between two medics. I glance away from the pub doors while Alex drops a hand on my shoulder. "You need to leave?" he asks. The alarms choose that moment to shut off. His question echoes in my ears.

I straighten and steel myself. "Not without Vick. I'm okay. I wasn't close enough to absorb the deaths." Hadn't felt any of them, in fact, not with Vick's anxiety burning through me like wildfire.

Trailing the dead are Officer Sanderson, now out of her hazard gear and carrying the orange jumpsuit over her arm, and finally—

"Lyle!" both Alex and I shout together. We give each other sheepish grins; then Alex moves forward to embrace Lyle in one of those quick manly hugs-that-aren't-really-hugs-no-not-at-all. Except this one lasts longer than usual. Guess Alex worried more than I thought he did.

"Where's Vick?" I interrupt, causing them to step back from each other, Lyle swiping a hand across his face to hide his relief. The yellow aura glowing around him confirms his embarrassment and attraction. Interesting.

Something to investigate another day.

Lyle's got some burns across his cheek, blistering and rather serious, which again remind me just how dangerous this whole situation was.

"Vick," I say again. "Where. Is. She?"

"Yeah, about that," Sanderson says, running a hand through her close-cropped blond hair. "She's not hurt. Well, not seriously. But we do have a bit of a problem I'm hoping you can help us with. Come with me."

On that ominous note, she spins on her booted heel and leads us back into the somewhat charred interior of the Alpha Dog Pub.

CHAPTER 7: VIEK
DEATH KNELL

I AM remembering.

The lock won't open. I've input the wrong code a couple of times and now it won't open. Fuck.

Why the hell is the air cycling out? That's not supposed to happen in a training scenario. Some kind of glitch?

And why is Stephen unslinging his rifle?

Oh God. The claustrophobia. I knew we should have reported it to the medics. But no. "He's our teammate," Devin said. "Gotta cover for him," Devin said.

Gonna get us all killed.

"Hey, Stephen, calm the fuck down!" I shout. I grab for the rifle, but it goes off, sending bullets ricocheting off the interior metal walls of the airlock. Not blunted rounds. These are the real thing, loaded into our weapons in the armory we just left for the next phase of this training exercise in the fully shielded gun range on the other side of this airlock. They aren't meant for use in the rest of Girard Moon Base. They definitely aren't meant for use here.

Devin goes down first, then Stephen, both dead with one shot each, but Stephen's finger continues to hold down the trigger.

I'm screaming when two impacts connect with my skull, both from the right like someone's taken a fist and knocked on the side of my head.

My arms release Devin's body where I'd been holding him on the deck. Don't even remember catching him and going to my knees. I sit back, blinking. Then the pain hits, tearing, clawing, ripping my brain to pieces. I want to raise my hands to my head, but I can't move. Within three seconds my vision and hearing go. Three seconds might not seem like long, but it's an infinite amount of time to recognize death, to rage at it in futile denial, to know I haven't got a chance even while the rest of my body fights to survive.

The two senses that remain are smell and taste. I smell the coppery scent, taste the blood as it oozes down the back of my throat along with globules part of me identifies as brain matter and the rest of me shies away from knowing, and I can't function well enough to spit them out.

I can't function at all. No one's there to hold me
when I die.

I'm gone. And I'm gone alone.

"Hey!" Something tugs at my sleeve, yanking me
out of the memory flash.

I blink, but I'm still blinded by the flare of the
grenade.

The grenade. In the Alpha Dog. The one that
landed me in the now stuck airlock with—

"Are you okay?" Another tug on my sleeve.

Really need my sight back.

An image of me hanging in the net beneath a
tightrope flashes in my internal view. It takes me a
second.

Offline. Hah. Very funny.

Why? My palms press flat against the cold metal flooring. My back rests against one of the walls.
I don't remember this position. I was clawing at the
locking mechanism, and then… the most vivid and
complete memory I've ever had of the first time I *died*.
I would argue it's the only time and everything since
has been carried out by a mechanical facsimile, but I
keep that philosophy buried for Kelly's sake.

And my own sanity, if I'm being honest with
myself. Hard to live for tomorrow when you believe
yourself to be dead today.

You need to cease panicking, VC1's voice sounds
in my ears. *All my systems are working to prevent your
overload and keep your suppressors on full power. I
cannot divert anything to restoring your eyesight.*

So the AI stands between me and a full meltdown.
Terrific. She's not lying. I can feel the emotional pressure building beneath the surface of my now calm

exterior. If I give it the slightest opportunity, I'll totally lose my shit. My emotions don't go away when they're suppressed. Sooner or later, I'll pay a hefty price for this delay.

"Um, hey…." The tug at my sleeve comes one more time. "I'm sorry. I don't know your name."

I pull gently but firmly away. "It's Vick," I manage, my voice hoarse and strange to my own ears. "Or Corren. Whatever you wanna call me. Yeah, I'm okay." No, I'm really not, but I can't say that to the kid. I've never been good with kids. Kelly would be so proud. "What's our status?"

A scraping sound, like she's shifting around. "Um, our what?"

Right. "Our situation. Are you hurt? Is someone trying to get us out?" Please, please, please, let someone be working on getting us out. *VC1, you can override the lock.*

Not while maintaining your autonomics, no.

Meaning my heart rate, breathing, brain functions. Yeah, I need those. *I'll wait.*

I swear she laughs.

"I'm not hurt," the girl says. "You're bleeding, though."

Now that she mentions it, I feel the sticky wetness of blood seeping through the torn fabric covering my knees and several places on my arms as well. "Don't worry about me. I'm okay."

"You weren't a minute ago," the kid scolds, voice turning so dramatically stern I have to smile a little. "You were breathing really fast, and your face went all white."

"Well I'm okay now." I think back to right before the grenade went off. "Your name's Abby, right?"

"Yeah. Short for Abigail. Is Vick short for something?"

I grimace. "Victoria, or Victory, depending on who you ask." I hate both. Victory was my dad's nickname for me. He teased me with it every time I won something, from a singing competition to a hovercycle race. Drove me crazy using it in front of my high school friends.

I blink. When the hell did I get those memories back?

"Victory's cool."

Glad someone thinks so.

"The hatch is stuck again. Mom says that happens a lot. It's why I'm not allowed to use it to sneak into the pub. Can you get us out of the airlock?"

I shake my head. It hurts, and I have a feeling if I could see, I'd be dizzy. Probably hit it against something when I rolled with the kid. "Actually, I was hoping you'd help me with that. See, my eyes aren't—" I almost say "functional," but she won't understand. "My eyes got hurt when the lights came on and I can't see right now. Can you tell me what the lock controls look like? Are there red lights or green lights?"

More shuffling around, then a slight pressure on my shoulder as Abby uses me to lever herself up. "Um, three red lights, two yellow, no green."

"In that order? Top to bottom?"

"Yeah."

I picture the controls in my head, not using the implants, just regular memory. Three red lights across the top means the doors are sealed, the air is *not* cycling out, which is the one good thing, and the

communications system between outside and inside
the lock is down. The yellows are more encouraging.
Someone is in the process of working on both the door
and the comms.

"Okay, so I think we're going to be stuck in here
a bit longer," I tell Abby, keeping my voice as calm as
possible. It's not hard. With the suppressors on full,
I tend to speak in a monotone anyway. And I don't
want to scare her any more than she probably already
is, though actually, she doesn't sound all that scared.

"You think my mom's okay?"

All right, that sounded scared.

"She's fine," I lie, knowing nothing of the sort,
but that's what I'm supposed to do, right? Reassure
the kid? "She was behind that big wooden bar. I'm
sure it protected her."

Abby moves from where she's standing and plops
down next to me again, her shoulder against mine. It
drives a couple of splinters deeper into my skin, but
I don't nudge her away. When I turn toward her, I
can just make out her general shape, a slightly grayer
blob against a whiter background of glare. Good. Eyesight's coming back.

The muffled sound of a drill followed by tapping
and grinding comes from the hatch on the pub side
while someone's all out banging on the opposite hatch
leading into the promenade. I imagine an entire maintenance team out there, no doubt with Alex, hopefully
an uninjured Lyle, and likely Kelly as well, waiting
for my release.

Gah, Kelly. How badly did my near-meltdown
affect her?

A few minutes pass while we wait. Abby describes every detail I can't see, including the appearances of several workers peering through the hatch window, then an officer I expect is Sanderson from the description of "a woman with really short hair that looks kinda pointy and an in-charge face." And finally, "There's another lady," Abby informs me. "She's frowning."

"Blond hair, green eyes?"

"Yep."

"That would be Kelly. My partner."

"Ooooooh," Abby says, and I realize she's taken the term to mean more than "someone who works with me in the Storm." That's fine. I guess. "She's pretty," the girl adds.

I nod. It hurts. Damn. I'm gonna have to go to Medical and get checked out once we're free. I hate Medical. Medical is where they do things to me, sometimes without my consent. But I suppose that's what happens when you're property. I face the general direction of the window and force what I hope is a convincingly reassuring smile. "She look any happier?"

"Nope," Abby says.

Yeah, didn't think so.

"She's tapping the side of her head and pointing at the door," the kid continues.

Right. Kelly wants me to use VC1 to repair the damage to the airlock controls. Sorry, no can do, if she wants me to keep breathing. I shake my head and lean it carefully back against the metal interior wall. The coolness on my now pounding headache would be welcome, if I were anywhere else.

"How old are you?" I ask to distract myself from the upcoming poking and prodding from the Storm's medical staff.

"Seven."

My eyebrows rise. "You're doing really well with this, for seven." She is. Her earlier panic when she couldn't find her mother aside, she's not freaking out. Hell, she's keeping *me* calm more than I'm doing for her.

I feel her shoulder shrug against mine. "I'm on my own a lot. I have to be responsible."

"Well, keep it up."

After several more minutes, the metal in the hatch groans, and a hiss precedes its opening on the Alpha Dog side. I can distinguish people's faces now, and some details, though everything looks too bright and kind of washed out.

"Victory! They did it!" Abby squeals. Instead of rushing out, she takes my hand and helps me up, not that she's really strong enough to help, but I let her think she does while I brace myself with my other palm against the wall.

We're two steps out of the airlock, and I'm just taking in the damage to the pub. Scorch marks everywhere, including over a lot of the remembrance images of fallen soldiers that decorate the walls. My eyes flick to those of Devin and Stephen. Both destroyed. Soon as I'm able, I'll see about replacing those.

Then there's no time to notice anything else because a soft, curvy feminine form hurtles itself into my arms.

Kelly.

"Hey. Okay. I'm okay," I tell her, wanting to soothe but unable to put the warmth in my voice. They're just words. The right words, but with no particular inflection. I lose myself in her softness, the scent of the lavender shampoo she uses and the tickle of her wavy hair on my chin, then push her back. We're not alone, not even close. There's a half dozen technicians, a cleanup crew, and Officer Sanderson giving us a goofy grin she quickly schools into a more professional expression. By the entrance, Lyle tosses me a nod and goes back to poking at the burns on his face, studying them in a mirror that somehow survived the grenade. Alex stands beside him and waves.

Definitely not the time or place for a romantic reunion here in front of everyone, including my teammates, who will tease me mercilessly about "going all soft and mushy" on them.

I should tell Kelly about the Sunfires and their specific goal of acquiring me or killing me, but it's not the time for that either. For one, it would worry her more than she already is, and two, I'm assuming some of the Sunfires from this attack are still alive. I didn't kill them all. If they are conscious and mobile and within earshot, I don't want to remind them of their mission and start this up all over again. Three, I don't know if anyone else is targeting me. I've known assassins to pose as emergency personnel to get close to their targets. Doubtful that the Sunfires would want to bring in that kind of professional and alert even more potential competition to my abilities, and I'm not aware of them having their own, but I'm paranoid, and I'm not up to taking on anything else tonight.

"You're not okay," Kelly says, mirroring my thoughts and keeping her voice low, thank goodness. "I can feel the turmoil when I touch you, even with the suppressors running."

And failing. But I don't mention that. The emotion suppressor technology is meant to be a stopgap, to keep me functioning until I get myself out of whatever mess I've gotten into. But it won't work indefinitely, and its usefulness is rapidly running dry. To punctuate that, my hands tremble and a wave of dulled anxiety sets my heart racing until I force a deep breath through my suddenly tight throat.

"I know," I mutter, not wanting to be overheard. "But I've gotta take care of something." Glancing to the side, I retake Abby's hand. "Come on, kid, let's get you where you belong." I've spotted her mother through the propped-open front doors, noting with relief that the dead Storm soldier's body has been removed. The waitress is way over in the center of the dome having some bandaging wrapped around her forearm. I only hope my legs will carry me that far.

"Yes! Mom!" Abby says, seeing her as well. She tugs me forward, and I wince at the ache in my joints but don't pull away. Kelly takes my other hand, probably concerned I'll need to lean on her (which is totally valid), and the three of us head to the makeshift triage area.

On our way out, I pause and turn to Lyle, still looking in the mirror. "Don't worry. It's nothing a dermolaser and some plasflesh won't fix. You'll be back to flirting with Alex in no time." To my surprise, he goes bright red with embarrassment, obvious even through the burns, and shoots me a pleading look while making shushing motions with his hands before turning quickly away.

Three steps outside Kelly whispers, "I didn't think you'd noticed the attraction."

I hadn't. "Well, maybe I'm more back in touch with humanity than you realize."

There. That would give her something to consider, even if it's a total lie.

CHAPTER 8: KELLY
RIFTS AND FRACTURES

VICK IS stubborn.

"You were always in touch with humanity," I say softly. "You just don't talk about it much." Careful to avoid the torn and blood-soaked patches of her uniform shirt, I shift my hand to Vick's forearm, as much to steady myself as her. The adrenaline of my second-hand panic and my own personal worry has long since worn off, and what I want most is to take Vick back to our quarters and hold her until we both fall asleep. It's full into the base's night, almost ten, and there will still be reports to file and the medics for Vick to see before we're released.

And I have to make Vick admit she needs an emotion purge.

Her legs are shaky as we cross the dome to the open space at the center, though she tries to hide it by lengthening her stride. Her hand clenches and unclenches at her side, masking the tremor I noticed earlier as well.

Trapped in an airlock, after what she went through all those years ago. I can't imagine how that has impacted her psyche, whether she remembers the details or not.

We reach the triage area and Abby breaks away, throwing herself into her mother's arms and nearly knocking the waitress and the bench over backward. "I'm fine, Mom," the girl says when the woman lets a few tears fall, then wipes them away. "Really. Victory saved me!"

I raise an eyebrow in Vick's direction. Abby had announced "victory" before, but I'd thought she was simply celebrating their release from the airlock, not calling Vick by name. A very endearing, rather adorable name.

Vick manages a sheepish grin. "Don't mention it. To anybody."

But she's too late. Alex and Lyle have come up behind her and they're both chuckling. Lyle gives her a light punch to the shoulder. "Victory, huh?" After her earlier flirting-with-Alex remark, I can't blame him for seizing the opportunity for payback. He raises both hands in the air, arms forming the shape of a V. "Victory!" he announces.

Vick punches him in the stomach, not nearly so lightly. "Knock it off," she growls.

"Thank you," the waitress says, standing and stepping between them, timing excellent, "for saving both me and my daughter."

"You're wel—" Vick breaks off, one hand going to her forehead. She wavers where she stands, and both the waitress and I make a grab to steady her. After a couple of deep breaths, she looks at us. "You're welcome."

"You need medical attention." A woman in a medic's uniform gestures at the bench the waitress vacated. "Sit."

I watch while the medic runs a portable scanner over Vick and reads the results. "Abrasions, cuts, bruising, single cracked rib, mild concussion." She flicks through a couple of screens. "Your Storm medical records are labeled as classified, so you'll need to check in with your own people in the morning, but I'll take care of removing the glass, sealing the rib, and prescribing a painkiller if you aren't allergic to any medications?" She makes the last part a question.

Vick shakes her head no, then winces. I rest a hand on her shoulder but she shrugs it off. "No allergies," Vick says, "but never mind the drugs. I have what I need in my quarters."

"Which you won't take," I mutter. She ignores me.

I stand to the side and let the medic do her job. She must pull six or seven blood-covered shards from various places on Vick's arms, legs, and back. "Lucky none of these hit an artery," she comments, applying an adhesive spray that produces a layer of new skin over each wound. She uses a molecular laser to fix the broken rib and uses the spray again on Vick's worst scrapes.

All the while, I'm studying Vick, the way her jaw clenches even when she isn't being worked on, the stillness in her limbs like she's got to hold herself rigid or she'll fall apart. If she'd let me touch her again, I'm certain the emotions would be bleeding through her suppressors and tell me how bad things are, but she shifts away and glares whenever I try to get close, enough times that the medic orders her to be still.

"Good to go," the woman says at last. "And good job." She nods in the direction of the waitress and her daughter, just gathering their things to leave. "I've heard your name from some of your organization's medical staff. They say you're quite the hero. I can see why."

A touch of maroon tinges my vision, signifying the medic's more intense interest in Vick, who appears oblivious to it. Good.

"Right. Well, thanks for the patch job." She stands, supporting herself with the back of the bench, her hand clenching the wood. No one else seems to notice, but I do, and she sees me watching. She takes off, striding the rest of the way out of the dome, her gait stiff and controlled.

I hurry to catch up. It doesn't take long.

In the corridor leading back to Storm territory, Vick's leaning against the wall, eyes closed, breath coming in quick gasps. I touch her cheek with one hand, the other going to the sealed pocket of my cargo pants and pulling the blue-tipped syringe.

"Easy," I whisper to her, pain, fear, and stress pouring into me through our connection. Her AI-induced walls are coming down hard.

"I can make it back…." She attempts to push off from the wall and fails, falling against it.

"No, you can't." I begin rolling up her torn sleeve.

Her eyes snap open, vision narrowing on the syringe in my hand. With renewed energy, she jerks away. "No."

"Yes," I say, placing my hands on my hips. "You're going into full meltdown. You need this, right now."

Her expression falls. I ache with her. She hasn't needed chemical assistance to get through anything for almost nine months. It has to be crushing her confidence to need it now. But I know what I felt. It's more than she can handle alone, and without the powerful sedative I intend to administer, it's more than I can take in a release session. She'll send me into emotion shock in her current state, then blame herself. I won't let that happen. I reach for her arm. She sidesteps me.

"Please. Not here. Not… not *now*."

There's a significance to that "now" that I'm missing, and I follow her gaze over my shoulder. Alex, Lyle, and Officer Sanderson have entered the corridor right behind us, and all three are watching with varying expressions of interest and concern. When I turn back to Vick, she's suffused in a yellow aura, her embarrassment plain to see through my eyes.

The drugs will kick her with adrenaline first, because adrenaline helps keep her implants and her organic brain tissue in synch, and sometimes that makes her loopy. Then the sedatives will take effect. Showing any weakness in front of others is anathema to Vick. I try to give them to her in a private setting where only I can see her. But if she gets much worse, I'll need to resort to the green-tipped syringe—the one that will medically induce coma. She'll be down for the count for at least twenty-four hours while her implants repair any emotional and physical damage without using their resources on other things she won't need in unconsciousness. We'll miss leaving on our trip to the reunion tomorrow morning, and she needs that break.

"I'm sorry, Vick. But it has to be now. You're getting worse." She is. Her hands shake uncontrollably. She's borderline hyperventilating.

Her head comes up. Her eyes meet mine. "I don't consent."

What? What does she mean she doesn't— Oh. That's how she's going to play this. "Vick—"

"I'm telling you I'll handle it. Alone." Her mouth twists. "Or are you going to 'override' my autonomy programming?"

Dammit. I can do that. I can whisper a code and literally force her to accept the drug. To be honest, I'm surprised VC1 isn't already doing so. Vick has self-preservation programming in her implants. If she isn't making the Storm a priority, then her health comes in as a close second.

Times like these, I wish she could put herself first.

It does give me pause, though. If VC1 isn't forcing the issue, the AI may know something I don't. Like perhaps Vick *does* have the strength to push through this traumatic experience and purge some of the anxiety on her own before working with me at a later hour.

Things are rough enough between us already. If there's any way I don't have to treat her like the machine I keep telling her she's *not*, I'll do it. "You have fifteen minutes. Get yourself under control if you can and meet me back here. If you don't, I'll use our bond to find you and I'll have no choice."

Vick nods once, jaw set. Pushing past me, she grabs Officer Sanderson by one arm and drags her down the corridor and around the first bend, speaking rapidly and in hushed tones. I can't make out anything said, but I hope whatever it is, it helps.

Because if it doesn't, I'll have to override Vick's free will.

CHAPTER 9: VICK
PRIVATE RELEASE

I AM a risk taker.

I drag Sanderson around the corner until I'm certain we're out of earshot, then face her head-on. "I need someplace p-private. Sh-shielded. Sec-cure." The words stutter from my lips. I'm sweating, and I wipe droplets from my stinging eyes with shaking hands.

She studies me, staring into me like she can read me the way Kelly does. She's a couple inches taller and a few years older. Her wiser gaze bores into mine.

"I'm not sure helping you right now would be actually... helping you."

"Fifteen minutes. Come on... Helen."

Sanderson blinks, then shakes her head with a smile. "Pulling the first-name card, eh?"

We've known each other almost a year. I sometimes run into her at the promenade sports bar when I go there to catch Earth baseball or Cirulean grass hockey. If Kelly doesn't feel like joining me, Sanderson and I will share a table, some small talk, and a couple of beers. She keeps things easy on me, doesn't push, doesn't pry. Through the rumor mill, she has a fairly good idea of what I am, though she'll never know the details.

She's a friend—the only one I have outside the Storm, outside of the people I work with on a day-to-day basis, which pretty much amounts to the members of my team. I apparently had many friends before the accident. I value each and every one I have now. But we don't call each other by first names. That's just a touch too... intimate.

"Dirty pool, 'Victory,'" Sanderson finishes, a twinkle in her eye, though her face still shows concern.

"D-don't start. Just cut me a break. You owe me for tonight."

"You tampered with station systems and blew up the Alpha Dog."

I study the toes of my boots. "I didn't blow up the Dog."

"Hah! Gotcha! I knew it was you in the control panel. Someone 'conveniently' cut the security camera feeds on both the Dog's interior and the corridor where the emergency access box is."

I glance up. I didn't do that. VC1 must have taken the initiative. Again. I'm glad for it, but her AI status does worry me sometimes.

"Don't worry," Sanderson continues. "I said I'd cut your team some slack. And I'll help you now. Come on." Throwing one of my arms across her shoulders, she guides me down the hallway. Not sure how she knows I can no longer walk unassisted, but I'm grateful for it.

We stop in front of a private office hatch marked "Girard Base Security—Officer Sanderson, Security Lead." "You can use my space. It's privacy shielded to keep sound in, though I can't do anything about the cameras and microphones the department has installed everywhere." She shoots me a sideways glance. "I'm sure you can take care of wiping any footage you need to."

I nod once, acknowledging what we both already know.

She shakes her head. "You'd make a very dangerous enemy, Corren."

Yeah, don't I know it. "So don't piss me off," I say, earning a laugh from the head of security.

After opening the door with a swipe of her keycard and a retinal scan, she steps back and allows me to enter, then turns away. "Eleven minutes left," she calls over her shoulder. "After that, I'm coming to get you. Probably with Kelly on my ass. We'd better not have to scrape you off the floor." Then she allows the door to slide shut, and I'm alone.

Let the breakdown begin.

I barely have a moment to take in my surroundings. I've never been in here before, but the warmth of the space surprises me. Faux wood paneling, deep-pile carpet, imitation-leather seats, and a mahogany desk. Browns and tans dominate, creating a very masculine, comfortable feel like one might find in a private detective's office a hundred or so years ago on Earth.

Then the emotion suppressors cut out entirely and sightseeing time is over.

I drop like a stone, thankful for the carpet as I hit it on my already badly bruised and scraped knees and palms. Instinct rolls me into a ball, hugging my knees into my chest as I try and fail to hold the shaking at bay a little longer. Only it's not shaking anymore. It's all-out convulsing, wracking me from head to foot and bringing on a migraine that pounds the inside of my skull.

A few rounds and I'm wondering if maybe, just maybe, Kelly was right.

I've been through these episodes before, on missions when the team separates and Kelly isn't by my side to help me release the pent-up emotions. But even my worst ones came nowhere close to this.

In the past I've managed by taking deep, even breaths, counting to ten, picturing calm places I've seen in vids and would like to visit someday. Someday when the Storm finally lets me go.

Like that'll ever happen.

I can do this. I just have to focus and—

The screaming begins.

It starts as small whimpers, sounds at first I don't recognize as coming from me. I even raise my head and scan the corners of the otherwise empty office for anything that might make those pitiful, injured puppy cries. Then another works its way free of my throat.

And another. And another. Each one progressively louder and more desperately terrified than the last.

I'm detached, hearing and analyzing each howling cry and failing to own any of them. They control my body, dragging like sandpaper up my throat until I manage nothing more than a raspy whisper, though my chest heaves with the futile effort to release pain through sound. It just goes on and on.

The Sunfires are fucking insane to wish their people were like this. God, I hope Kelly's had her mental shields up.

Exhausted, I fall back against the wood desk, still seated on the floor, my head bowed over my knees, panting for breath. The front of my uniform shirt is soaked with sweat and tears I don't remember shedding. I've lost time, never a good thing for a being running on programmed efficiency.

How many minutes? How long until Kelly and Helen come barreling through the office hatchway?

One minute, twenty-seven seconds.

I laugh a little hysterically, relieved beyond measure that VC1 is online enough to speak to me. My fingers dig into the carpeting on either side, reconnecting with reality. My head pounds.

Can you pull me back together? I subvocalize.

An image of a marionette, its disjointed limbs connected by distended threads, appears in my internal view. The arms and legs snap into place with audible clicks. The puppet's face is mine.

Little close to home with that one, I tell her. I'm a puppet to far too many people in far too many ways.

Sorry.

Wow. That might be the first time the AI has ever apologized.

I'm on my feet and mostly functional when the hatch opens and Sanderson slips in, then closes it behind her. She looks me up and down, steps around her desk, and pulls a package of facial wipes from a drawer. When she tosses it to me, I catch it one-handed and she nods with approval.

"Guess you pulled it off," she says while I clean off the evidence of my emotional purge, wiping my forehead and eyes.

I drop the empty packet into the recycler by the desk. "Kelly with you?"

"You had twenty more seconds. I said I'd bring you or call her."

"Fair enough." I follow her into the corridor, pausing just outside her office to lean against the wall under the pretense of fastening a loose closure on my boot, but really I'm covering the locking panel with one palm. *Do your thing*, I mutter to VC1, knowing she'll get the hint.

If I'm operating at peak performance levels, VC1 can enter almost any electronic system wirelessly, without any contact on my part. Considering the torment I've put us both through, I'm cutting her a break and giving her easier access. There's the slightest of tingles from my shoulder to my palm, the only indication I have that she's carrying out my command. Via the tech in the locking mechanism, she'll find her way into Sanderson's recording devices. It's only a matter of ti—

Objective accomplished. Visual and audio data erased. A pause. *You were never here.*

I grin and straighten, then follow Sanderson down the corridor.

Kelly's standing with Lyle and Alex where we left them fifteen minutes ago. She's got her hands shoved in her pants pockets, a pouty scowl marring her usual beauty. Cute, but I'm going to hear about this later.

"Finished," I tell her, moving close. "Sorry," I mutter for her ears only.

It doesn't soften her expression. "Not finished," she says. "We're going to Storm Medical. The base medics patched you up, but they can't check your more… unique attributes."

Well, that's one way to describe them. I stifle a yawn, hiding it behind one hand. "It's late. Can't it wait until morning?" The staff won't appreciate having to do a full diagnostic at this hour, not to mention that I'd rather go almost anywhere else.

"No waiting. You got your way. Now I get mine."

Sanderson nudges my elbow. "Better do it, Victory. You're not wining this one."

I want to wipe the smirk off the security officer's face with my fist, but she's right. Shrugging like it doesn't scare the living crap out of me, I gesture for Kelly to lead the way.

"I'll be with you the whole time," she whispers, resting her fingers on my arm. "You'll be fine."

She knows I'm terrified.

Of course she does.

CHAPTER 10: KELLY
REVELATIONS

VICK IS scared.

It takes a lot to scare Vick. I've watched her dive through flames to rescue a fellow soldier, leap from a twelve-story building to save a kidnapped child from an impending explosion. Vick faces fear like it's a walk in the atrium.

According to her records, she's always been this way, even before the installation of the implants made it simpler for her to ignore the rational fears most people listen to in order to prolong their survival. Her bravery, loyalty, and skill set made her the perfect candidate for the implanted upgrades. Notes in her file suggest she might have been offered them even if the airlock incident had never taken place.

And knowing Vick, she would have taken the mad scientists up on it.

So feeling the fear roiling through her now makes me question, again, if I'm doing the right things for her.

Ten months ago, Dr. Whitehouse, the man in charge of overseeing her "recovery" and her acclimation to her implants, tried to remove the last of Vick's humanity, turn her into a perfectly controllable, unemotional, obedient robotic slave housed in a human shell. Combining the processing speed of the implanted technology with the human brain's ability to adapt and create, along with the agility and mobility of her physical form, Vick would have been made unstoppable.

Except, according to Vick, the "perfect" soldiers Whitehouse tried to create retained bits of their souls and memories. At least some of them did. On our failed mission to rescue Vick's father, the founder of the Storm, one of those soldiers saved Vick's life and lost the last of his own while doing so.

And I felt his relief.

Memories of our encounters there still wake both of us up at night, shivering from the nightmares and holding each other until the tremors pass.

Whitehouse is in prison for crimes against humanity. His creations, deemed unsalvageable, were put out of their misery and given funerals with all the honors the Fighting Storm could muster.

There's a new team assigned to Vick's medical care and a specialist rumored to be arriving from the Storm's ancillary base on the outer rim any day now.

Yet she shakes every time we set foot in the medical facility. And I don't blame her one bit.

"Listen, Kel, about tonight's incident," she says, forcing the words out one at a time. "There's something you and the rest of the team need to know."

"You're stalling," I accuse. We've stopped just inside the doorway, Vick pulling me off to the side so we don't block any other incoming patients.

"No, really. The attack, it was specifically targeted at—"

"Corren!"

The receiving nurse on call is Isaacson, I'm glad to see. He welcomes us with a big smile and a friendly handshake for Vick. Medical staff have quarters housing them right here in this wing of the Storm's section of the base, and we probably roused him from a late dinner or bed, but he doesn't show any annoyance or impatience. He's part of Vick's inner circle of support personnel, one of the handful who knows everything about her, including all the classified parts, though not that VC1 is an AI. They know what she goes through more than anyone does except me, and many of them suffer from a healthy dose of hero worship whenever Vick comes in.

"Good to see you, Corren. Alex called ahead so we're ready for you. We'll get you checked out and on your way as fast as possible, promise."

She looks about to protest, like she wants to continue with whatever she was saying when we came in, but then nods, pressing her lips together. We follow him to the diagnostic and treatment room set aside just for her. Taking a deep breath, Vick steps over the threshold.

We've been in here many times before, but I still find it intimidating, and I'm certain Vick does too. An elaborate chair dominates the center of the space, tubes, sensors, and wires extending from its arms and headrest in all directions, then snaking across the tile behind it to disappear into the floor. Banks of screens, currently blank, fill the walls on either side beyond the chair, out of view of whomever occupies the seat but easily read by the doctors and nurses.

Vick stands off to the side, shifting her weight from foot to foot, keeping as much distance between herself and the chair as possible.

Isaacson grabs a datapad from a shelf and makes a few notes, taking some baseline readings with its built-in scanner and asking the basic health questions. "We received the civilians' report on the Alpha Dog brawl and your treatment." He takes one of Vick's arms and rolls up the sleeve, ignoring her flinch. "Burns and cuts are healing nicely. They do good work, for civvies."

It's standard merc humor, but it earns him a small grin from Vick.

"We're a little more concerned with the concussion and your mental/emotional status given the trauma involved in the incident." He ceases prodding at one of the already forming scars, which will mostly vanish in a day or two, and meets her eyes. "The airlock couldn't have been easy to take."

She stares back, unwilling to admit to any measure of weakness. Pure Vick.

Her stubborn attitude doesn't deter Isaacson. If anything, his smile brightens. Soldiers know soldiers, no matter which department they serve in. "All righty, then. Scanner shows high tension levels, stress just within the scale's measurement range, pain manageable but uncomfortable. Your implants dose you?"

"Serotonin," Vick admits.

He glances at me. "You do an emotion purge?"

I frown and shake my head. "Not yet. She wasn't... comfortable doing that on-scene." But we will. As soon as we're alone, we will. I don't mention that I could have gone with Vick into Sanderson's office, that Vick's struggling with her needs versus her independence. That would embarrass her, and I'm trying hard not to do that again.

"Understandable. Okay, hop in the chair and let's get a good look at your processors. You've definitely taxed them. They should self-repair, but we don't want to risk implant overload. Oh," he adds as Vick grudgingly seats herself, her entire body rigid, "your new doctor arrived earlier this evening. When Alex radioed in, the system automatically included her on the call, so she said she was coming by to meet you."

"I'm not exactly at my best," Vick grumbles just as the hatch slides aside admitting a stranger in a white lab coat, tan slacks, and comfortable white shoes. The coat hangs open, revealing an off-duty blouse in fuchsia with the top three buttons undone and ample cleavage showing. Vick's eyes go right to the gap and linger a moment before she flashes me a guilty look and averts her gaze.

"Don't worry about anything," the woman says, taking a thoughtful sip from the ever-warm cup of what smells like coffee in her hand. She studies Vick over the rim. "I've seen you much, much worse." After setting the beverage aside, she reaches back to adjust a thick ponytail of straight platinum-blond hair and winks one of her bright blue eyes. Her voice drops to a sultry alto. "And much, much better. How are you, Vick? It's been a while."

Vick's brow furrows.

"Ah, well," the doctor says, undeterred, "that's to be expected, I guess. Though given where her eyes were roving, *part* of her remembers." While Vick blushes furiously, she smiles and turns to me, extending her hand. "Hi there. I've heard about you. You must be Kelly LaSalle, the empathic assistant and the latest in Vick's long line of lovers. I'm Dr. Alkins—Vick's last female ex."

CHAPTER II: VICK
A REASON FOR EVERYTHING

I... REALLY don't need this right now.

"My... what?" I sit up straighter, muscles aching
with exhaustion from tonight's events. In the process,
I manage to bonk my forehead into the headpiece
dropping into place above me.

"Oops, sorry." Isaacson lifts his hands from the
sensory controls to the right of the seat. "I thought you
were settled. You okay?"

I ignore him, focusing all my attention on the
new arrival. She's attractive, tall, with high cheek-
bones and a firm jaw suggesting the term "handsome

woman" if she'd lived a couple hundred years ago. Hints of muscles stretch the shirt beneath her lab coat. She's fit and a few years older than me, intelligent and no-nonsense as she takes over from the nurse and pushes me back against the headrest. "Still waiting for someone to control you, I see," Dr. Alkins comments with a chuckle. She glances at Kelly. "You don't look like the dominant type, but I've seen quieter facades in my time."

A choking sound draws my attention to Isaacson, who's struggling to maintain his composure. Can't tell if he's uncomfortable or amused. Either way, I don't blame him. I'm feeling pretty discomposed myself.

I should step in, put a stop to this conversation, but I'm too shocked to form intelligible speech. And Alkins looks and sounds like she's accustomed to being the alpha in any room, bedroom or otherwise.

"So…," Kelly stammers, "you two were… together?" She's talking to Alkins but looking right at me.

I shake my head at her. I have zero memory of any sort of relationship with this woman. For one thing, she's not really my type. I prefer softer features, a gentler disposition. Then again, who the fuck knows what my type was before the accident? I've heard all sorts of things about my past, most of which sound too wildly far-fetched to be true. I've chalked it up to good-natured teasing from the other mercs. But….

"Oh yes," Alkins continues. "And please, call me Peg. We're going to be working together for the foreseeable future, after all." She pulls down the headpiece, a circlet of metal sized to fit snugly around my forehead and embedded with the latest in sensory tech. VC1 understands how it all works. Me, I just go along for the unpleasant ride. The metal presses, ice-cold, against my suddenly warm skin. "We were quite the item," Peg says, tapping on the controls and dimming the lights in the room to better see the wall screens. "Lasted longer than any of her other flings. Vick was a relatively new recruit but up-and-coming and fast-tracked for bigger things, and I was just an assistant back then. Whitehouse ran the show here. I knew I wouldn't get anywhere with my own projects so long as he was in charge, so I applied for a transfer. When it came through, Vick and I decided to call it quits."

She fastens padded restraints around my wrists to keep me in place and prevent any aggressive moves on my part while my brain is otherwise occupied. The soft cuffs don't normally bother me, but tonight a surge of panicked nausea snaps Kelly's attention to my face. I shake my head again, as much as I'm able in the headpiece, and swallow it down. But the uncomfortable knot continues to twist my intestines. Alkins's story about us feels... wrong. "I don't think that's—"

"Calibrating," she says, cutting me off.

I fall silent.

"Initiating scan. Proceed with sedation." Dr. Alkins waves a couple of fingers in a beckoning motion, and I sense movement to the left and behind me while Isaacson fiddles with the controls.

A tiny mechanical arm about the diameter of a stylus lifts from the arm of the chair. Attached to its end is a hypodermic needle filled with the most powerful sedatives my body can handle—more powerful than any physician would give a "normal" human being. But I'm not normal. And the implants have a tendency to diffuse drugs if they find them threatening to my well-being in any way.

Interesting that VC1 always fights this one with all her abilities. And inevitably fails.

Kelly's hand takes mine—the one on the opposite side from the injector. Hers is almost as cold as my own. I try to tamp down on the nerves so she doesn't absorb them as much, but I have nothing left and the suppressors are barely functioning at minimal levels. "You don't have to watch, you know," she says, leaning down to speak into my ear. This conversation isn't for Alkins.

"I know." But I always watch. I have a rather morbid fascination with facing that which scares the living shit out of me. Also, I prefer to see pain coming. Surprises, in my experience, are rarely good things. At least the machine can perform the injection much faster than a human could do it.

Kelly cocks her head to one side, looking both at and through me. "Why are you freaking out? More than usual, I mean."

Is it the presence of my ex? The night I've had? The fight with Kelly before? "I don't know." Which might be the scariest part of all.

The doctor rolls up my already torn sleeve. The needle reangles itself accordingly, then plunges home in one blur-quick motion. It hurts, but I've had much, much worse. I don't even flinch at this. Icy-cold liquid travels up and down my arm to my fingertips, which go numb, and into my shoulder. Then… things get fuzzy from there.

"You need to let go of her. You're interfering with the scan," says Alkins's voice from somewhere down a long and echoing tunnel. I can't see her. My eyelids are too heavy to keep open.

"It's never interfered before," Kelly snaps.

Losing her temper. I'm intrigued since it almost never happens with anyone except me, but I can only tune in and out.

"…others weren't specialists," Alkins says.

"Deal with it. Shouldn't be a problem. For a specialist." The pressure of Kelly's fingers on mine increases, though I can't feel actual skin to skin. Doesn't matter. She's sticking by me despite our differences tonight.

I release one last held breath, sink farther into the padded backrest, and I'm gone.

A hard palm connects with the side of my face, leaving the cheek stinging in its wake. I blink up at Peg, stunned that she'd slap me. Stunned by everything that's happened tonight.

"We've had some good sex," she says. "But tonight I show you what I'm really into."

I tug on the soft but secure bonds (training restraints, she called them) holding my wrists and ankles to the conveniently spaced slats in the head and footboards of her king-size bed. Well, now I know why she laughed when I admired the craftsmanship.

I'm naked and spread wide, aroused and confused. She's spent the past half hour teasing me, and I enjoyed it. Then things changed. Painful twisting of my erect nipples, bites instead of kisses, and now actually striking me. Hard. With every act, her breath catches. Her naked breasts flush from excitement. I'd heard rumors when I started dating her, but she worked in the Medical division. Their motto is "Do no harm," right? I didn't figure on her oaths not extending into her off time. I didn't believe the stories I heard. And the rumors didn't come close to this.

I get abused enough in training. I can take a punch or a kick like it's nothing. But when I have sex... I don't want to give or receive any kind of pain, physical or otherwise. I want to protect the one I'm with. I want to know someone cares. I want someone to be gentle with me. It's the only time anyone ever is.

And it's not that I have to be in control. I have to take charge in every other aspect of my life. In the bedroom, I enjoy a mutual give and take. What's happening now is all take, no matter what Peg might think of the exchange.

I tug harder on the bonds. "This isn't what I had in mind." I'm serious.

She laughs. "Word is you're the toughest the Storm's got. And you're balking at a little pleasure pain? Give it time. You'll come to like it." She bites me again, on my inner thigh, hard enough I'm sure she'll raise a bruise. I yelp in response and twist away, but I can't get far.

"This isn't pleasure! It's all pain, and I'm done. If this is what you need from me, I'm more than done. We're a mercenary outfit. I'm sure you'll find plenty of takers for this kind of thing, but not me." It's pre-accident, pre-implants, pre-enhanced strength, but adrenaline is an amazing thing. I close my eyes, concentrate my focus, and snap my arms up hard and quick.

The bonds tear like paper. When I sit up, Peg moves as if to press me down again. My glare sends her back a step. She's not laughing now.

"Don't. Just don't. I'm sorry I'm not what you're looking for. We've had some fun. Leave it at that." I swing my legs off the bed, stagger a bit at the loss of blood flow from the bonds, but manage to retrieve my clothing and yank it on one piece at a time.

"You're every bit the slut everyone said you were," she snaps, covering herself with a black satin robe. *"Moving on to someone else when things aren't perfect for you."*

I hold out one palm in a halting gesture. *"Stop. You don't get to be pissed off here. You like bondage and pain, maybe you should have tried leading with that. We've been together over a month. You never said anything until tonight."*

She stares down at her bare feet with their red-painted toenails. *"You weren't ready."*

There's enough regret, enough loneliness buried in her tone that I close the distance and touch her arm once, briefly. *"I'll keep this to myself,"* I tell her. *"Others haven't, and I should have listened to them. You're right. I get around. But I don't brag, and I don't share personal details. Your bosses in Medical won't hear it from me. No one will hear it from me. If you want to call me a slut, go ahead. You'll only make me more popular with the other mercs. When you're an active-duty soldier, the more sexual partners you have, the better your rep."*

"Get out." There's fire under those words—smoldering bitterness and hurt. She doesn't meet my eyes, doesn't look up once as I grab my other gear and head for the door to her quarters, but I keep her in my peripheral vision, like my subconscious knows she's a

*dangerous foe who hasn't quite decided on the next
phase of her attack.*

*I keep my promise. I don't spread rumors about
her. And while she says nothing about me, the fact that
we split up and I walked out on her gets around. Like I
predicted, it doesn't hurt my reputation any. I get more
dates after our brief relationship than before.*

*One thing I notice, though. Whenever I go into the
Medical section for anything, she's always watching
me, studying me, sometimes with a bit of longing in
her expression, as if I meant a lot more to her than I'd
realized. Oh, I thought we might have made a go at
something long-term before her revelation about her
sexual needs. It's why I stayed with her longer than
the one-night stands I'd become accustomed to. But
it hadn't been a sure thing. Not from my perspective.*

*Other times, though, her looks feel calculating,
analytical. They send prickling down the back of my
neck and up my spine.*

*When I hear she's transferred to the outer-rim
base, I'm relieved.*

*And now not only is she at Girard, she's in charge
of me and my physical, emotional, and psychological
well-being, second only to Kelly on the latter two.*

*I've graduated from her "training restraints" to
the chair's real thing with her controlling them. And
I'm powerless to snap these bonds.*

CHAPTER 12: KELLY
PHOTOGRAPHIC

VICK RECORDS.

The lights in the treatment room come up. The sedatives Vick was given wear off right on schedule. The second she's awake, her eyes snap open. An alarm blares a soft warning. Some of the screens of data flash white, then darken. Vick jerks upright, dragging the headpiece equipment with her and causing all the gears and metal parts attached to screech in protest before she throws her upper body over the armrest and vomits on the tile floor.

It's not a lot. We missed dinner because of the Alpha Dog emergency and she didn't eat much lunch, but it's enough to send Isaacson, who'd moved to stand beside me in order to detach the restraints, leaping backward with a little yelp.

Me, I let it spatter my shoes. Nothing a cleaning won't fix. I wrap my arms around Vick's shoulders, drawing her long, dark hair out of the way and holding her until she ceases gagging. Thank goodness I put up my emotion-blocking mental walls before the doctor began the scans or I'd be making a mess right along with her. The alarms screech louder.

She's shaking and gasping. When she finishes, she lets her head fall against me, but the trembling doesn't ease. It's a tremendous display of weakness for Vick, and my concern increases exponentially.

"Off," she whispers. "Please. Take them off."

I don't know what she means until her arm muscles flex beneath my touch. Her wrists jerk against the restraints. Another screen goes blank.

"Kel... please."

I shoot a glance to Alkins and Isaacson, but they're both dealing with all the beeping, screaming machinery around us. Red and orange lights flash on the control panels. The screens on the wall are all either black or display nothing but static snow. Whatever set Vick off, it's taken the technology down with her.

I'm not supposed to touch the mechanical devices in this room, but under the circumstances I'm making an exception. I've seen it done enough times to know how to unfasten the wrist guards, and I snap them free in two quick yanks.

Vick releases a long, shuddering sigh. "Thanks."

"What happened?" I brush her hair away from her eyes, now closed. Her cheeks redden. Damn. Her growing embarrassment, along with the lingering nausea, seep through my shields, not enough to affect me, but I'm aware of both.

"Yes, I'd like to know that as well."

I jump a little, not having heard Alkins come up beside me. She's got all her attention on Vick now, with quick glances at the portable scanner in her hand fed by the more elaborate ones all around us. At the back of the chair, Isaacson reaches over and gently loosens the metal headpiece, then slips it off and reels it back into the headrest with minimal screeching. A cleaning bot activates and slides from its charging station against the wall. Whirring, it rolls over and cleans, then sanitizes the tile floor around my feet.

"I... I don't...," Vick stammers.

"Take your time," I tell her, continuing to stroke her hair. I hope it's the right thing. I'm not trying to baby her, just comfort her, but sometimes even I can't tell what will trigger Vick's need to be macho.

Dr. Alkins's finger scrolls through the data on her portable screen. "You've never had that reaction before. What changed?"

She's right. Diagnostics are never pleasant for Vick. She's told me that the scanning process often brings bad memories, both recent and from before the accident, to the surface. Waking up is often accompanied by tremors, chills, and later, nightmares. She hates the procedure, but it's never been this bad.

My gaze falls on the open right-wrist restraint dangling from the armrest. "Was it the Rodwell thing?" I ask, keeping my tone as professional as I can. Rodwell restrained her before he sexually assaulted her. In our attempts since to be intimate, I have to take special care not to hold her down in any way. It's a sure bet to end any romantic interlude.

That particular bad memory is a recurring visitor during scans.

Vick's eyes half open and a wave of tiredness passes from her to me. She looks from me to Alkins and back again. "Yeah, Rodwell. Guess with everything else tonight, it hit harder than usual."

And that would make perfect sense. It's what I expected her to say.

Except she's lying.

Vick's eyes widen as she realizes her mistake. I'm in physical contact with her. I can read a lie with perfect clarity. I stare back, my gaze narrowing. She shakes her head, a minute movement no one notices but me. Whatever really set her off, she doesn't want Alkins to know. Or is it me? Does she not want to share it with me?

I'm going with the former, but I fear the latter.

Either way, I'll defend her.

"We've had… issues," I begin, wading in. "A sexual assault. Sometimes this procedure brings it to the surface. It's been months and months and the bad reactions never seem to fade." I try, but I can't quite keep the bitterness from my tone. Vick growls softly under her breath. I'm not trying to expose her secrets either. It's all in her file. Alkins has to already know all about Rodwell and what he did to Vick.

"Well, of course it doesn't fade," the doctor says, causing both me and Vick to turn and stare at her. She stares right back. "You do understand how her mind, such as it is, works, don't you?"

"Um…." I have no idea what she's talking about, and from Vick's frown, she doesn't either.

"Good grief, that idiot Whitehouse really didn't explain anything to you. His head was always too far up his egotistical ass to be bothered." Alkins breaks eye contact to make notes on her touchpad. Isaacson busies himself with storing away the equipment.

We wait, but Vick drums her fingers on the armrest. She's losing her limited patience, and once it's gone, I don't want to be in the way of her temper. "Care to share?" Vick says, teeth gritted.

I step away a bit, keeping one hand on her shoulder but making it clear I'm not going to get between them if Vick decides a physical "inquiry" might work better than a verbal one. Looking inward, I'm not sure why I'd allow such a thing to occur, but part of me does not like Dr. Alkins, and it's not just what I know about her past relationship with Vick. At least I don't think that's it. There's something off about her, an empathic sense that she isn't nearly as interested in her patients' welfare as she should be, but rather, her actions are far more self-serving, though how beyond the normal earning of a paycheck and general respect, I can't guess.

Alkins huffs out an impatient breath and sets the touchpad aside on a shelf attached to the wall. Folding her hands together in front of her, she addresses us like a teacher might speak to a particularly obtuse class.

"Sixty-three percent of Vick's brain is gone," the doctor begins. Well, at least she didn't call her VC1.

"I'm aware of the numbers," Vick says, jaw clenched.

Very aware. And she hates being reminded of it.

"Did you really think with so little of your organic tissue intact that your memory would be stored in it?" Alkins waves a hand in front of her like she's shooing flies. "You have some memory storage capability. That's why bits and pieces are coming back to you. The brain is, as we all are coming to realize with each university study, far more adaptive and self-repairing than anyone realized. But the reality is, the vast majority of your functions are run by your implants. That includes memory storage and playback. Your memories won't fade. Ever. They are permanently recorded in the circuitry. If you think of an incident, your implants play it back for you, as clearly as if it just occurred, complete with all the sensory input that accompanied it. Visuals, sounds, smells.... Some people would pay millions for the recall you have. Imagine if you were older and wanted to remember the first time you fell in love, or had sex, or held a newborn? You'd have that. With absolute perfection. You'll never lose one single moment from the time you received the devices until the day they cease functioning."

I stare at the doctor, the horror of the realization and the fact that I should have figured that out a long time ago sending my heart plummeting.

Vick drops her head back against the headrest and closes her eyes.

CHAPTER 13: VICK
COMPENSATE

I AM unfixable.

Never fade. Peg's…. No. Dr. Alkins's words echo in my head, bouncing around my biological and mechanical brains like the bullets that put me here in the first place.

"Did you seriously not know this?" she asks. "How could you not know this?"

"It never occurred to me." Kelly sounds chagrined. She shoots me an apologetic look, but I shake my head.

Hell, if *I* didn't know, how could I expect her to? "I don't remember what it's like for memories to fade over time," I say, voice hoarse. "I guess I thought this was how things were supposed to work and eventually—" I break off, swallow, then continue. "Eventually, I figured I'd get better."

Alkins crosses her arms over her chest. "Well. You won't. But that doesn't mean there aren't alternatives. We could block the—"

"No!" I practically shout, sitting up straight in the chair. Whitehouse and Kelly blocked some of my memories before, with disastrous results. As horrible as these are, as bad as the side effects have been, I'm keeping them. All of them.

I have so few memories left.

Kelly rushes to press me back, but I'm not having it. I swing my legs over the side, plant my boots on the tile, and push to a wobbly stand. I have no choice but to lean on her, and I hate it, but I'm not returning to my seat. Not with that suggestion hanging in the air.

The doctor rolls her eyes and puffs out an impatient breath. "Oh for the love! You are such a drama queen." From the glint in her eyes, she's not referring to my reaction to the suggestion to block my memories. I hold her gaze until she throws her hands up and turns away. "If you don't want to be free of the trauma, there are other things you could try that should help," Alkins continues like we didn't just share an unpleasant stumble down memory lane. She knows I remember the truth about our relationship. She knows. But she's as unwilling as I am to speak of it in front of Kelly.

Good.

"Like what?" Kelly asks, taking half my weight on her shoulders and bringing my attention back to what I should be focused on—my relationship with her.

Shit. *Get your priorities straight, Corren, or you're going to lose the only person you've ever really cared about.* I'm frustrated with her coddling me, but she's a part of my entire being. I'll never forgive myself if I drive her away by being stubborn.

Then again, maybe you should *lose her. She deserves better than your fucked-up psychosis.*

Kelly squeezes my side where she's got her arm wrapped around my waist. She's reading my anxiety and indecision. I push both as far out of my mind as I'm able, which isn't as far as I'd like.

"Practice," Alkins says, as if it's the most obvious thing in the world. Behind her, Isaacson nods.

"Can you be a little more specific? It's not like we haven't tried."

I glance down at Kelly, eyebrows rising. She's pissed, and it's coming through in her tone and rigid posture.

Alkins shrugs. "Try more. Keep her distracted. The trick is to prevent her from flashing back on the unpleasant memories. You have to hold her in the here and now."

"I'm standing right here," I grumble. The doc hasn't treated me like a machine so much yet, but it's starting to come through in her current treatment of me.

"I know you're here," she says, her smile almost genuine. Almost. "But your partner is the one who will have to do most of the work." She fixes her gaze on Kelly. "When you feel her starting to drift, bring her back. Talk to her. Hold eye contact. Maintain touch, no matter how she reacts. With practice, it should snap her out of the memory." She's all professional now, no snark, no bitterness. Like she's detaching herself from our shared history. Like I'm a patient and nothing more. Which is as it should have been from the get-go.

"Thank you," Kelly breathes, loosening her grip on my rib cage. "We'll try that."

Alkins chuckles and goes back to her touchpad. "Maybe give it a few days. She's pretty banged up. No implant damage, though. No signs of overload. Just stress and exhaustion. Go home. Get some solid sleep." She scrolls through a couple of screens. "You're scheduled for R & R starting tomorrow. Good. Rest. Relax. Check in with me when you return from your trip."

Trip? What trip?

A calendar helpfully appears behind my eyes, the next week highlighted in blue and labeled "LaSalle Family Reunion" and smack in the middle of it in all caps "KELLY'S BIRTHDAY."

I really am the worst girlfriend ever.

Kelly picks up on my confusion because she gives me a light slap to my left bicep. I wince anyway. The medics pulled a long piece of glass out of that one.

I'm not steady when we leave the medical department of the Storm's section of the base, and the night I've had isn't the reason.

We both remain silent all the way to our shared quarters—typical for me, virtually unheard of for Kelly. If she isn't chattering happily on and on about something, I know there's a problem.

And I have a pretty good idea what the current problem is.

The corridors are mostly empty by this late hour, but she's considerate enough of my feelings to wait until we're in our living room before she eases me into the single armchair, paces away, then whirls and faces me head-on.

"You lied to me. And okay, I understand not wanting to talk in front of your ex-girlfriend new doctor, but you could have just said you weren't ready to talk about it. You didn't have to lie. And the whole walk back, you could have told me what was really bothering you in the diagnostic chair."

Yep. Nailed it.

"You never flat out lie to me." Hands on her hips, glaring for all she's worth, she's fucking adorable. I don't dare tell her that, but from the way the glare intensifies, she can probably read it from me.

"That's because I can't," I mumble, knowing it's the worst thing to say the moment the words leave my lips.

"What?"

It's all I can do not to get angry right back at her. It's like she's asking for another argument today. Like she's been asking for them ever since I got called away to the Alpha Dog. Maybe even longer than that. Her temper has been short lately. It's not that I don't deserve it most of the time. But I really don't have it in me to go head-to-head again tonight.

I take a deep breath, let it out, and count to ten. Then I close my eyes, because if I see her fury, I'll lose my control. "Look," I say, pausing to collect my thoughts and choose my words. "It's not that I *want* to lie to you. It's not even that I wish I could. But don't you think it's just a little unfair that every other human being in the universe gets to keep a few secrets except me? Aren't I entitled to a little privacy too? Or don't machines get that privilege?"

Her sharp intake of breath tells me my words hit home. Hard. I crack open one eye. To my relief, she's no longer glaring. To my shame, she's got tears trailing down her cheeks. I sigh and open my arms to her, but she turns and flees to her bedroom, shutting the door behind her. A second later, the lock clicks into place.

Well, damn.

I push myself out of the chair, every muscle in my body groaning in protest, and make my way to my own room. Stepping from the Kelly-decorated common areas into my private space is like moving from a home to a barracks. It's never felt more spartan and impersonal to me than it does at this moment, with its company-issued light gray furnishings and almost entirely bare walls save for the single holo of a Kansas farmhouse with the breeze lightly blowing the fields of grain or whatever staple they grow there. Dark storm clouds move swiftly in the distance. Portentous. I tap the frame and shut their motion down.

A quick check of my internal chronometer tells me I've got four hours to unwind and sleep before I have to rise, pack, and head for the shuttle we've rented for our getaway. That is, if she even still wants me to go with her.

I strip off my fear-sweat-soaked clothes, grab a quick shower as hot as I can stand, throw on a pair of underwear, and yank a ribbed olive-drab tank top over

my wet hair. The sheets chill my skin as I slide between them, and I shiver, burrowing as deep beneath
the too thin blanket as I can.

It's only a few seconds before my bedroom door
slides open. I know the soft tread across my carpet, so
my fight-or-flight response doesn't kick in.

Kelly spreads her thick lavender comforter over
me, then climbs in beside me and wraps her body
around mine. Her head tucks beneath my chin, her
soft breath warming my exposed neck and breastbone.
I shift to put my arm around her, then stop, uncertain,
but she reaches for my wrist and pulls until it drapes
across her back.

Through our mutual bond I still feel her irrita-
tion, but it pales in comparison to her love. Enfolded
in warmth both emotional and physical, my mind and
body find peace.

CHAPTER 14: KELLY
SECRETS AND ADMISSIONS

VICK IS hiding things from me.

I wake before Vick. It's a testament to how exhausted she is that my slipping from the bed and out of the room doesn't rouse her. With her training and paranoia, the slightest sound should bring her to full alert. Maybe VC1 is giving me an assist.

I'm halfway across the living room when her alarm goes off, its annoying rendition of the traditional military reveille bugle making my teeth grind together. When I'm still with her and that horn sounds, I practically leap off the mattress.

Why she doesn't just let her implants wake her, I have no idea, but I suspect it has to do with her wanting one more demonstration of being a "normal" human being.

So I'll endure the bugle when we share a bed.

She's moving around in her bedroom, albeit more slowly than usual, but when I hear the drawers opening and closing telling me she's somewhat okay, I continue on to my own tasks of dressing and packing. Our vacation destination, Infinity Bay, is a predominantly water world peppered with islands of varying sizes and maintaining a comfortable temperature range perfect for sunning and swimming. Unlike my parents' home state of North Carolina in what would now be the dead of winter, the island paradise is the perfect choice of locations for the annual reunion.

But it necessitates the packing of clothing items I don't keep on the moon base.

I have neither shorts nor tank tops. I prefer sleeping in a long T-shirt if I'm alone, or sexier wear if I'm with Vick. I do have a bathing suit, a cute two-piece in hot pink that I wore exactly once to the base's indoor pool before I tired of the ogling and Vick's constant readiness to punch the next soldier who drooled over me.

I toss the swimsuit, along with some ivory and tan slacks and a few short-sleeved button-downs into my suitcase and vow to drag Vick shopping when we arrive. She'll be even shorter on her wardrobe than I am, and I don't want her to stand out any more than she's already going to. Some casual attire will go a long way toward preventing that.

I hope.

Biting my lower lip, I add in some lingerie and underthings meant more for play than practicality. It heartens me that Dr. Alkins's advice wasn't all that different from my Academy mentor's. Keep trying. Be patient. Keep Vick's mind on me and off her memories. I can do that, so long as Vick is willing.

We meet in the living room at the same time, me with my rolling luggage and an additional bag slung over my shoulder, Vick with her Storm-issued duffel. I'm in a white knee-length skirt and strappy sandals with a pink top. She's in uniform.

Of course she is. Gray shirt, gray slacks, black belt, black combat boots. And she's armed, her pistol, not the usual XR-7 but some other (probably deadlier) letter/number combination I can't keep straight, hanging in a holster on her thigh.

Still, she's here. She's packed and she's going with me. Something tight inside my chest loosens.

She eyes me, head cocked a little to the side, gaze narrowed as if daring me to criticize. I can't help it. I have to say something.

"The gun is a bit much."

"Last time we visited your family, if my patchwork memory serves me correctly, there was a terrorist attack." She folds her arms over her chest.

I place my hands on my hips. "It was a bomb, Vick. It went off. Boom! No shots were fired. Your pistol was useless, because, yes, you had it at the time. Do you really want to terrify everyone when we get there? Is that the first impression you want to make?" Of course it isn't. I regret the words the second they leave my mouth. More than almost anything, Vick wants acceptance. I know that. If I could kick myself, I would.

She holds my gaze for another moment before looking away. "It's a thirty-six-hour flight. Through raider territory. I'll store it before we disembark," she mutters, then strides away, the door to our quarters opening at her approach. I trail behind her, lips clamped shut.

We're silent all the way to the landing bays. We're in the commercial sector, as busy as the Storm's hangar but in a much more haphazard way—babies crying, older children darting around their harried parents who desperately try to corral them before they can be squished by a luggage transport or a taxiing shuttlecraft. Workers shout to one another over the whines of engines, the screeching of landing gear, and the squeak of tires on smooth-polished gray tarmac. Scents of lubricants and fuel assail my nostrils. But no blood of injured soldiers returning from assignment. No med staff guiding antigrav carts stacked three high with human-shaped black bags.

I suppress a shudder and follow Vick to the window counter of Pleasant Journeys Travel Unlimited.

Under normal circumstances, we'd take a Storm shuttle, arranging our passage around some convenient mission's flight plan. But nothing is heading for the outer rim in the next few days, and no tourist vessels going to Infinity Bay have a layover on Girard Moon Base, so we're stuck renting a private civilian yacht.

I don't mind. It's pricey, but my generous salary has let me store up quite a bit of savings over the past few years. I'm happy to foot this bill.

From the underlying edge in Vick's voice while she haggles with the rental agent, she is not pleased about that decision.

"...refuel in the Fighting Storm's hangar and then hop it over here?"

"Civilian craft aren't permitted to land in a military-owned facility." The male representative's smile shifts from friendly to feral in the span of a sentence. His too white teeth gleam in the overhead lighting.

"You charge too much for your hexaline. I'm not paying those premiums. And we're not owned by a governmental military. We're independent."

"That's irrelevant, ma'am. And didn't your 'independent' facility have a fuel-leak fire just last night? Sure, you can refuel over there, if you want to spring for the complete-coverage insurance." The bright smile widens.

Vick's muscles bunch under her uniform shirt. The clerk can't see the gun in its holster, but if he could, he'd blanch at Vick's fingers twitching above the grip.

Hoping to calm her, I lay my hand over her free one where it clenches the edge of the counter in a knuckle-whitening grasp.

Emotions flood me like a dam burst: impatience, frustration, and barely controlled rage, all tamped down behind the implants' dampeners but obvious to me through our physical contact. I jerk my fingers away as if burned, taking an involuntary step back.

It's not fast enough.

Vick's head snaps in my direction, eyes widening in surprise, then lowering in shame. It takes me a moment to figure out what's happened.

While we touched, my fear transferred to her. She scared me. And she knows it.

With a start, I realize we never did the release procedure, never purged her pent-up fears from last night's traumatic experiences. We were so busy arguing and emotionally hurting each other, it completely slipped my mind.

I wonder if it slipped hers, too, or if she conveniently "forgot."

"Vick...."

Without looking at me, she holds up her hand, palm out, cutting me off. "Don't." Snatching the stylus off the counter, she scribbles her signature on every required line highlighted on the rental agent's screen.

The clerk grins in triumph, then passes over an access keycard and points across the hangar. "Berth seventeen, silver hull, electric blue trim, *Tranquility* printed on the hatch. You can't miss her."

The irony of the yacht's name is not lost on me as I follow Vick's retreating figure stomping between double rows of parked interstellar craft.

Not an auspicious beginning to our R & R.

CHAPTER 15: VICK
BREAKABLE BONDS?

I AM ... scaring her.

I slam the controls to close the yacht's outer hatch, slap the switches to seal all vents, and pound the engine startup sequence into the touch-screen interface on the console before me. *Not working. This isn't working. I'm gonna lose her.*

I'll die without her.

Fear rolls over me like a swift current lapping the shore to soak into the sand. I shake my head hard, the violent motion reigniting the concussion headache in a flame of pain so bright and intense it momentarily blinds me. Closing my eyes, I rest both palms on the console and breathe, just breathe.

Another muffled rapping sounds from the far side of the cockpit door. I ignore it. Again. VC1 overrode the locking mechanism for me. Kelly isn't getting in here until I've regained some semblance of control.

I may be alone for the next thirty-six hours.

You will not die. At VC1's voice I sit straight up and bang both knees on the underside of the control console.

Rubbing my kneecaps, I frown. *You're awfully chatty lately.*

Metaphors are easier on my processors, but not ideal for clarity.

That earns a laugh—a laugh that goes on too long, becoming almost hysterical before I clamp it down. *Okay, I won't die. I can't die. Or at least I can't kill myself. The self-preservation programming won't let me.* And to be honest, I'm more than a little bitter about that. Not that I'm currently suicidal, but fuck, I should have some measure of determination when it comes to my own fucking life. *I'll be emotionally dead. She won't leave the partnership. She won't let me lose my mind.* I hope. *But without her love… she's the only one who makes me happy.*

Then why do you not allow me to open the… fucking… door?

I laugh harder, both at her attempt to mimic my speech patterns and the question. It's such a simple suggestion, posed by a being so new to humanity that the nuances escape her. And yet in her simplicity, she's cutting through all the crap to the core.

Why don't I open the door?

When I can't come up with an answer that doesn't involve my own irrational fears, I rise, cross to the cockpit hatch, and raise my palm to the lock. For a moment I hesitate, listening to the yacht's engines continuing to idle, the launch control chatter feeding through the speakers above the controls. They aren't ready for us yet, but we're about third in the queue. Then I slam my hand over the mechanism and allow VC1 to feel her way through the circuitry and undo the scramble job she earlier installed.

The door slides to my left, disappearing into the metal wall. Kelly stands on the opposite side, fist raised to knock once more. She looks from her clenched fingers to my face and back again. Then, in a move quick enough to rival my own training, she punches me, hard, in the bicep.

"Ow! Hey!" I reach to rub the sore spot, but she's already throwing herself into my chest, this time to bury her face in my shirt, her arms wrapping around my torso in a death clench. "Okay, okay. I needed to sort out some things, okay? Come on up front with me. You can help with the preflight checks. Once we're well on our way we can... talk."

That gets her attention. She leans back to look up at me, blinking away tears. "You. You actually want to talk. You."

I shrug. "Sometimes it's a necessity."

That seems to mollify her. She follows me into the yacht's tiny control center. We seat ourselves in the two swivel chairs bolted to a track on the deckplates. This track allows the chairs to move around the small space in order for both occupants to reach the controls on not just the front panel but the walls and even overhead in some places. When locked in their standard positions, they face the forward viewscreen that dominates the nose of the triangular-shaped vessel. They're locked in place now. Outside, we have a clear path to what is essentially an oversized airlock.

No matter how many times I've flown, it still causes the same visceral reaction as walking through the smaller locks, though the discomfort doesn't tend to last as long. I suppress a shiver and shift lower into my seat.

The next ten minutes are a comfortable routine of me rattling off systems to check and pointing out the relevant monitors so she can relay the data displayed on them. Kelly's no pilot. To my knowledge she's never taken anything except the basic emergency course the Storm requires. But she follows my instructions respectably well, and we finish in less time than it would have taken me alone. By now the engines are good and warmed up, and we're waiting on the flight controller for the go-ahead.

When it comes, Kelly frowns over at me. "Your headache is bleeding through your suppressors," she complains, rubbing her own forehead. "With that concussion, you probably shouldn't be flying this thing."

"I won't be," I say, waving her off. "Once we break orbit, I'll turn everything over to VC1. I'm just here for emergencies." It's a new trick, one I've tested out on some solo one-day missions over the past few months. But it works. VC1 can download a part of herself into almost any computer system—security, shuttle, anything run by technology. So long as I'm in reasonably close proximity, it works like any other wireless device. At first it freaked me out, but I'm used to it now.

Which also freaks me out.

No matter how much "better" I become, I'm also more mechanical every day.

Kelly raises her eyebrows, but she says nothing. Anything she would say would probably hurt, anyway.

When the console lights go green, I roll our little craft forward into the smallest of the civilian shiplocks. The three-foot-thick metal doors clang shut behind us. Outside the hull, the atmosphere is cycling out through ventilation shafts, but within the yacht we hear nothing. Then the indicators above the outer doors also flash green, and a moment later they separate, revealing the mostly barren lunar landscape. In the distance, a few structures mark the refineries and a number of smaller, more independent corporate facilities unattached to the main base. One is the Crater Ale brewery, a craft beer-maker touting that beer brewed in low gravity produces better taste. I'm inclined to agree. It's one of my favorites. Beyond that handful of single-story buildings, the rest of the surface is empty, crater-pocked gray nothingness as far as the eye can see.

We continue to roll forward onto the runway extending out from the shiplock and the only flat surface in sight. On a world with stronger gravity, I could rotate the engines and do a straight uplift launch, but that requires more fuel. Here on the moon, it's not necessary. Pressing the throttle forward, I increase power until we're hurtling along at blurring speeds. Then the front and rear wheels leave the ground and we're on our way.

It's as smooth a takeoff as any I've performed, but when I glance to my right, Kelly's digging her nails into the armrests of her chair, her eyes squeezed shut. "You okay?"

"Fine," she says through gritted teeth. "Will there be turbulence?" She cracks open one eye.

I tilt my head toward the forward viewscreen where the stars already fill the field of vision. "Not unless we encounter a rogue asteroid or some such. VC1's on it. She's tapped into the yacht's proximity detectors. We'll know about anything within a hundred kilometers before we ever cross paths. And this thing's got decent shielding for a civilian craft." I kick the underside of the console with one boot. "No weapons, though, just some defensive lasers for clearing space debris. I'm not thrilled about that."

"No, you wouldn't be," she mutters, not loud enough for normal human hearing to make out, but my enhanced aural sensors decipher her words with ease.

Sometimes she forgets what I'm capable of. That should make me happy, and it does in a way, but I want her to know me. Really know all of me. And that means every inhuman piece.

Kelly undoes her safety restraints—I never bothered with mine—and pads out of the cockpit in those impractical sandals. She's back within a minute, a portable medkit slung over one shoulder and her hand extending a hypodermic out to me. I shake my head, but she presses the casing into my palm.

"Take your medicine, Vick. It's going to be hard enough to facilitate your release with everything else going on in your head. I don't need the full-blown migraine as well."

I'm tempted to argue, but she's right that I need the release, and I'm out of excuses. There's no one to see me here, no source of embarrassment. She's also right in that I don't want to hurt her any more than the process normally will. I insert the needle into my arm and press the plunger home.

The painkiller spreads an icy chill through my veins, the smart-chem knowing the source of the discomfort and making a direct path to the nerve endings in my forehead and at the back of my neck. The headache numbs, pressure and a painless throbbing reminding me that it isn't gone, just buried, and that if I do anything overly exertive, I'll cancel out the chemicals and the migraine will return.

"One problem solved," Kelly says, eyeing me. She can read my pain both through the bond and via colors, like an aura around me, or so she says. I have to admit, that ability would be cool to have.

I figure she's going to retake her seat and slide it along its track to face mine. Instead, she straddles my legs and seats herself on my lap, facing me. She's so close, her breasts brush mine. It's a pleasant distraction, but when she raises her fingers toward my temples, I catch her wrists in my hands.

Her squeak of surprise tells me just how fast I must have moved. And that I've scared her again. I swallow a sigh. "It's bad, Kel," I whisper. "Like gonna-put-you-in-emotion-shock bad. I have complete faith in your skills," I hasten to add at her frown, "but really, I think I've been through hell and back in the last twenty-four hours." More than even she knows, what with the sudden reappearance of my ex, Dr. Peg Alkins, and all the lovely memories that's brought on.

"So I'll ease in and bleed off the emotional back-log gradually." She tugs a little, and though I'm doubt-ful, I let her go.

My implants flash me an image of myself caught between a huge boulder and a brick wall. Yep, be-tween a rock and a hard place. That's me. Continue protesting and I insult her. Let her do as she wants and I risk hurting her. There's no winning, so I swallow hard and hope for the best.

CHAPTER 16: KELLY
PLEASANT DISTRACTIONS

VICK IS a time bomb.

Vick's got me nervous, that's for certain. Her concern for me, along with her issues with intimacy, have always been problematic when it comes to her releases, more so since the Rodwell experience.

When my fingertips are inches from her temples, a tremor takes up residence in my hands. I will them to stillness, hoping she didn't notice, but her deeper frown tells me she did. Enhanced eyesight. Sometimes I forget her peripheral vision is wider than that of the average human being.

It takes only a brush of my skin against hers and the roiling lava of her emotions envelops me in a miasma of fear, exhaustion, frustration, and drug-muffled pain. Forcing myself to move slowly, I ease away, breaking the contact, returning fully to myself.

I school my expression into a semblance of calm, but my panting breath gives me away.

"Told you so," Vick mumbles, not meeting my eyes.

"Yes," I admit. "You did. Hmm." I scan her from her head to her waist. "Okay, let's take a different approach. Look at me." The quiet iron in my tone draws her gaze to mine. "Good. I'm going to distract you, but you need to focus on my face and my voice. I don't want you dropping into a memory flash."

Vick grits her teeth. "Not sure I can control that."

"We're supposed to keep trying," I remind her. The equipment around us beeps softly for a count of five before she makes the connection.

"Oh. That kind of distraction." Her shoulders slump in the pilot's chair.

I smirk at her. "Don't sound so thrilled about it."

"Kel…."

"Stop being so pessimistic. I've got some ideas on different things we can try. But you've got to be open-minded and give them, and me, a chance." My fingers find her chin, holding her face lightly. "Will you?" I hold my breath. It's a risky question, one that leaves her an out that I'm not sure I can survive should she choose to take it.

"You can have all the chances you want, until you give up," she says.

"Oh no. I'm never giving up on you. Not again. I made that mistake once. It almost destroyed me. I've

got you back and I'm never letting you go." I don't
have the full channel open between us, but we are in
physical contact, skin to skin, and I feel a portion of
her anxiety drain away like water through a sieve. So.
That's one of the sources of her stress? She's afraid
I'll try to leave her? Or ask to go back to a nonroman-
tic partnership? Fat chance. I lean in closer, careful
to allow her freedom of movement. My breath dis-
turbs several strands of hair beside her ear. "You. Are.
Mine," I whisper.

Vick shivers beneath me. The good kind. Perfect.

Shifting so she meets my eyes again, I lower my
mouth to hers. I'm almost cross-eyed by the time our
lips meet, but I feel that I have her full and undivid-
ed attention. She trembles at the darting touch of my
tongue, then parts her lips to let it slip inside and dance
with her own. I'm so lost in sensation, I almost forget
my other goal.

Reaching up, I press my fingers against her temples once more. Colors swirl and blend in my second
sight, representing the emotions I need to bleed off.
I choose the remaining pain first, my empathic force
grasping the tightly wound red threads and tugging
them apart one by one until they fray, then dissipate.
Vick sighs into my mouth, blissful relief swamping
her in a rush. Another shiver passes through her.

With reluctance, I give her lips one last, teasing
lick, then lean back. "Still okay?" I ask. I know, through
my file-digging, that Vick experiences low-level pain
almost constantly, buried beneath the implants' mach-
inations to the point where my gift can't detect it. But
additional pain beyond that, I can deal with for her.

Her hooded gaze is slightly unfocused. "Yeah. I'm good," she manages, low and breathy.

My spine tingles with a shiver of my own. It's been so long. Too long. We both need this to work. "Excellent."

"I thought you weren't allowed to take pain away. The 'human experience' and all that."

Empaths aren't supposed to interfere with normal human emotions unless it's a matter of life or death. I'm allowed to do what I do because Vick's emotions aren't normal. "I'm fudging a little," I admit. "You've already had pain-reducing drugs. I'm not denying you the right to feel human pain. You felt it. You took something for it. I'm just trying to keep it from coming back."

I fumble behind her until I find the tight bun at the back of her head. With great care, I unfasten it and toss the tie aside. Her thick dark hair tumbles to fall in waves around her shoulders, and I run my fingers through it, then begin a gentle massage at the nape of her neck, working my way up her scalp.

"Mmm…." It's practically a purr. Her eyes glide shut.

"Uh-uh," I warn, rapping once, lightly, on her skull for emphasis. "Eye contact. Look at me. No drifting away. You're here. Now. With me. No one else. Nowhere else."

She snaps to full alertness, message received. If she drifts, she remembers. If she remembers, I lose her. I hate that I can't let her relax too much, but if this works, she'll forgive me.

Vick clears her throat. "I'm with you," she says, hoarseness betraying the weight of her emotions.

"Good." Fingers still buried in her hair, pressed to her scalp, I reach for the orange of bitterness and anger. These threads are harder, knotted and twisted into her psyche, but I work them apart with my mind, one by one. When I've pulled away more than half, I let one hand drop down between us, running over her shoulder, her collarbone, until my palm presses her right breast through her uniform shirt. I find the hardness of her nipple, straining the fabric of her bra and the button-down both, and scrape my nails lightly across it, back and forth until she groans with the pleasure. The rest of the orange knot falls away, fading to nothingness.

Pausing in her emotional purge, I unfasten the buttons on her shirt one at a time, checking after each that she's with me and in agreement with my actions. Her breathing picks up pace. Her tongue darts out to wet her lips. She nods her consent.

My fingers tremble with the need to move faster, but if I startle her now, I'll have destroyed the tentative trust I've built. Moving with slow deliberation, I work her shirt free from her belted trousers. It takes a bit of tugging, and the abrupt jerk of the motion startles her enough that her hands grip the armrests.

"Breathe, Vick. Breathe."

She takes a slow, unsteady breath. Not so good.

"You're okay," I soothe. "I'm here. I'm here for you." A pause until I'm certain she's listening and not lost. "I love you." My palms slip beneath her shirt, resting upon hot, taut abdominal muscles, letting her feel every bit of the love I have through our connection.

Her expression goes completely focused and serious. A moment of self-doubt trickles through me at the intensity, then, "I love you too. I would have... before... no matter how many others came and went until we met. After you, there would have been no one else."

CHAPTER 17: VICK
ALMOST HOME

I AM ... so near and yet so far.

Yeah, that was mushy. Especially for me. I'm not one for pretty words. If I string more than one sentence together at a time, that's a lot, and if it has to do with *romance* or *feelings*, well, it's a good thing Kelly can read me, because otherwise she'd never know how I feel.

I've gotten both better and worse about it the longer I've known her. On the one hand, it's easier to express myself when hiding is pointless. For the most part, unless the implants have me completely shut down, she knows what I'm feeling. On the other hand, sometimes I take it for granted and say nothing.

I forget that she needs to *hear* the words. That she needs for me to accept and confirm what I feel out loud rather than just sensing my emotions through our bond.

I'm glad I remember that here and now.

Her eyes light up at what I'm saying. I can't believe the words are leaving my lips, but they are true, every one of them, and she feels the truth of each syllable.

"Oh, Vick," Kelly breathes. A single tear trickles down her cheek.

I resist the urge to brush it away. She needs this release too.

With my shirt open and untucked, she has full access to my bra-covered breasts. Her hands trail up my sides, over my rib cage, raising goose bumps in their wake until she reaches the front closure on the undergarment, and damn am I glad I selected that particular one today. I'd been going for ease on my injured arm, rather than quick clothing removal, but it works for both purposes. The pop of the plastic fastener is barely audible over the hum of the yacht's engines. I can't hold back a sigh of relief as Kelly leans me forward, then slips the shirt and bra over my shoulders and tosses both to the deckplates to join my hair tie somewhere. Cool, recirculated air blows from the overhead vents and hardens my nipples further, to an almost painful stiffness.

I'm not large-breasted. I'm probably a little smaller than average. But Kelly's gaze zeros in on them. She again checks my face for consent; then, at my nod, she lowers her lips to my left breast and sucks the nipple between them while her left hand cups my other one, her thumb teasing, palm massaging.

Her free hand slips up my arm, careful around the bandages protecting my healing wounds, and back into my hair, reinitiating the bond between us.

I can't see emotions the way she does, though occasionally, when we're really in synch, I detect a faint haze of color around her, which she thinks is a transference of her own sight to me through the connection. However, I know when she's pulling my feelings apart. Confusion becomes clarity. I *understand* my actions and reactions and can put names to the causes—pain, fear, anxiety, frustration—whereas the rest of the time I'm flying half-blind, guessing at what ails me.

She sucks hard on my nipple and I gasp at the pleasure… until my memory flashes on images of the Sunfire soldiers in the Alpha Dog, overlaid with silhouettes of Dr. Peg Alkins's shapely yet intimidating figure.

What the actual fuck?

Why would I be combining these two images? They have nothing in common. Nothing except me.

No. I need an emotional connection. What emotion connects these two pieces of my patchwork life?

The rolling of Kelly's thumb and forefinger over my nipple, along with the insistent pressure of her tongue on the other one, suddenly switch from pleasurable to pain. I flash on early sexual encounters with Alkins, when she became a little overzealous with her nails and teeth, "accidentally" leaving scratches and bite marks in her enthusiasm, then apologizing

profusely until I forgave her. So many clues as to her
real desires. So many missed signals.

There's a tearing sound as a third image invades
my brain—Rodwell ripping at my uniform, grasping at
my breasts through the ragged openings while I hang
helpless by my tied wrists. He's rough and demanding,
squeezing until my body jerks and twists in desperation to get away. I hate him. I hate myself. I hate—

Guilt.

It's guilt.

Intellectually, I know what Rodwell did to me
isn't my fault, my failing, but I've never been able to
convince my conscious mind of that. I also haven't
told Kelly the real reason Alkins and I split up. She
needs to know. She can't help me if she doesn't know
whatever I can remember to tell her. And then there's
the fact that the Sunfires weren't just brawling with
the Storm in that pub. They were specifically after me.
My whole team needs that information. I haven't told
them and I should have, but I was so distracted by
everything else....

My chest constricts. I can't get a deep breath. My
nails dig into the pilot chair's armrests.

"Vick! Vick, open your eyes. Look at me. Right
now. Look at me!"

Pilot chair. Armrests. Space yacht.

Kelly.

My eyelids snap upward, and I jerk my head
back, away from the face much, much too close to
mine. My head bangs against the headrest. For a few
seconds, the cockpit is a blur of fuzzy images and intense pain, my concussion reasserting itself through

the haze of drugs. Slowly, slowly, bits and pieces come into focus.

"Sorry," I grind out, hoarse and strained. I swallow once, twice. "I'm sorry." I blink away the stars flickering in my vision.

Kelly bites her lower lip, her expression full of concern. "No, *I'm* sorry. I lost you. I broke eye contact when I...." A fierce blush creeps into her cheeks as she gestures vaguely at my exposed chest. "But there was so much guilt, and I was distracted by that and what I was doing to you." The blush deepens. Fucking adorable.

I take a slow breath and let it out. "It's okay," I tell her. "It's not like I want you to stop doing things like that to me. It was good." I take another breath. My smile is sheepish and I suspect she's not the only one blushing. "Really good. I just need to remember to keep my eyes open. Shouldn't be too much of a hardship. Watching what you're doing will probably act as a turn-on."

"Yes," she agrees with a wicked smile. "Probably." She lowers her head again, then hesitates. "What are you feeling so guilty about? Alkins? If you want to keep that private, I won't like it, but I can deal with it. You don't need to feel guilty. I knew you'd had other relationships before me. I hadn't expected to come quite so face-to-face with one, but I knew."

I sigh. I should tell her... something. I'm not quite ready to reveal all three of my sources of shame, but she's expecting an answer to her question whether she says I can keep it to myself or not. Which one?

"The Sunfires are after me," I blurt out. I grimace. It's not what she's looking for. But she can't see my expression with her head down, and she knows I'm telling the truth through our bond.

To my surprise, she doesn't glance up, but rather returns her attention to other things, fingers working at my belt, then the fasteners on my uniform trousers. "Keep talking," she says.

"The attack in the Alpha Dog," I say, pausing to gasp when she breathes warm and heavily over the exposed portion of my underwear. "It was targeted. At me. The Storm soldiers who died in there. That's my fault."

"Don't be ridiculous." Her voice is strained, maybe with concern, maybe with concentration. I can't be sure. "You didn't kill them. Why do they want you?"

Even without contact with my head, she's reinitiated the connection between us. The guilt falls away in incremental strands. Or perhaps it's just the natural result of letting this information go.

"Not me so much," I answer. She presses lower. My dampness soaks into the fabric of my panties, making them cling in uncomfortable yet tantalizing ways. My breath hitches on my next intake of air. "They want... the technology."

Kelly wriggles backward on my lap, to my knees, until she's balanced precariously on the edges of them, then leans over and braces herself with one hand on my shoulder. She slips her whole other hand down the front of my pants, cupping my sex, applying insistent, intermittent pressure. My thoughts blank as the pleasure takes over.

"The Storm already told them it's no longer for sale," she says. "We warned them. The... side effects are too severe."

Side effects. Yeah. Understatement of the century. "They don't care. Or they don't believe us. Regardless, they want me to give up my secrets, like that's even an option, or to experiment on me at their leisure." I can't tell them what they want to know. I literally can't. The safeguards built into VC1 prevent me from revealing anything about the implants, even under the most excruciating torture. I can only talk about them with people who already know.

Kelly shifts her hand, using two fingers to press the undergarment fabric inside me, just a little, then rub it in and out, creating a delicious friction. Of their own volition, my hips squirm on the pilot's seat. "Mmm," she murmurs. Then in the same soft tone, "None of that is your fault. The Storm did what they did to you without your knowledge."

Well, yes, I was legally dead at the time.

"The technology is valuable and dangerous. If it weren't inside you, if it were a separate thing and the Sunfires tried to steal it, don't you think the Storm would send personnel to get it back?" She continues to work her fingers, covered in rough, wet cotton, in and out of me, in and out.

My hips buck a bit harder. "I suppose," I manage, letting my hands leave the armrests and wrap around her rib cage, drawing her in closer. I need skin contact, both with my hands and with my body. It doesn't take much effort to slip her satiny pink top from the hem of her short white skirt. My palms glide over her ribs, settling just above her hipbones.

"Eyes open, Vick," she reminds me.

I snap my lids up, not even realizing they'd started to close. "Right."

"And don't you think it's possible," Kelly continues, thrusting a little harder and a little deeper with her fingers until I'm writhing, "that some soldiers might get hurt, even killed, in the process of retrieving or protecting that technology?"

"I don't—"

She uses the next lift of my hips to pause, slipping from me and climbing off my lap. Using both hands, she eases my pants and underwear down to my boots. I groan at the delay, my arousal higher than it's been in months, but forgive her when she strips off her own skirt, top, and bra, leaving the white-lace-covered triangle between her legs and revealing the damp patch darkening the fabric there.

"No 'don'ts,'" she scolds. "They would, and you know it."

My eyes track her every move as she kneels before me, unfastens my boots, and tosses them to land with a pair of thuds on the deckplates. My pants and underwear quickly follow.

"How is any of that your fault?" she finishes, parting my thighs wide and placing her body between them. Her hot breath falls on me, making me tremble. "Come here."

I work my way to the edge of the seat. My pulse races.

"Say it, Vick. It isn't your fault."

"I—"

Kelly rocks back on her heels and stares up at me, waiting.

Fuck.

"It's not my fault," I grind out.

She tilts her head to one side, looking at me and through me. "Now mean it."

"Oh for the love of— Fine." I pause a moment, sorting through everything that happened in the Alpha Dog and weighing my guilt against her words. I never asked for this, any of this. And she's right. The Storm would sacrifice as many as it took to protect technology as valuable as what's in my head.

The last knots of that particular guilt release, falling away like melted ice thrown on a heated stove.

Which pretty much sums up how the rest of me feels right now.

"It's not my fault," I repeat, and this time, it's true.

Kelly's smile lights up the cockpit. "Good. Now, let's see if we can't deal with the last of your emotional buildup."

I groan, wondering what other delay she's going to put me through, but she leans in, reaching forward to separate my folds.

"Time to release that sexual frustration," she whispers and lowers her mouth between my legs.

CHAPTER 18: KELLY
AFTERSHOCKS

VICK IS… better than she was.

It's been a long time, but I remember what Vick likes, and I flick my tongue from side to side over her clitoris, holding her as still as I'm able with my palms against her knees. It's quite the challenge with her hips shifting in rhythmless, involuntary movements, but for the moment, I have her under my control, my empathic talent wide open and ready to detect any change in her emotional state from pleasure to something less positive. After a particularly strong gasp from her, I cast a quick glance upward to make certain she's still got her eyes open.

They are, and they're watching my every move. It's quite a turn-on, and I stifle a gasp of my own at the sheer amount of *need* in her gaze.

Although I sense she's holding out on me with regard to the whole guilt thing, the intensity of the negative emotion has decreased enough that I'm willing to let it sit for now. Her heated skin and the wetness I find when I dip my tongue inside her tell me I've teased her into a state of near frenzy, not to mention the lust I'm reading through our bond, which has me almost as hot as she is.

"I think… I think I need you to stay outside from here," she pants, offering an apologetic look.

Rodwell did horrible things to Vick. She told me some, but not all of it. I understand what's behind her request. My nod moves my tongue up and down, making her gasp, then moan. I take that as the encouragement it's meant to be and repeat the motion, speeding up my efforts until her thigh muscles clench beneath my hands and her fingers dig into my shoulders.

"Kel—"

Whatever she intended to say is lost to a cascade of pleasure so intense it takes me right along with it. My hips thrust against her while she goes rigid, trembling with the release. Before she can come down completely, I crawl to kneel by her side, slipping my hand between her legs to stroke her fast and hard. She leans over and her mouth finds mine, muffling her near scream, while her eyes go wide.

Her back arches. She reaches her peak a second time, then flops bonelessly back into the chair, breaking lip contact so that she can attempt to catch her breath. I rest my head against her hip, heart racing, pulse pounding, not certain if the relief I feel is mine or hers or both.

When she calms, I look up, startled to see tears streaking both her cheeks. Stretching out with my gift, I recognize them as a product of being emotionally overwhelmed, but it doesn't make them any less startling.

"You okay?" I whisper, not wanting to break the quiet moment.

"I think so," she says. Her hand shakes when she reaches to brush strands of hair from my face. "Thank you."

"You are very welcome. I don't think you're fully healed," I caution, sensing *something* building in her emotional makeup. "But you're capable of it." I can't quite identify the newcomer to her psyche, but it suggests while this was a step toward recovery, we may have a long way to go.

She nods, solemn, then spends the next hour or so showing me how very grateful she is. When we're finished, I'm wrung out, muscles weak, body begging for extended rest.

Vick double-checks that VC1 has firm control over the luxury shuttle. Then she leads the way aft through the small lounge area and into the smaller galley where she makes quick work of heating up a couple of mugs of soup—cream of mushroom for me, beef and barley for herself. Cupping our hands around the warm mugs, we carry them into the far aft sleeping area.

Here we find two single beds that Vick pushes together along more floor tracks to make a much larger surface. We search until a cabinet built into the bulkhead reveals king-size sheets and replace the smaller ones. By the time we're finished with both the bed-making and the soup, I'm yawning even though it's only early evening.

We're both still naked, our clothing scattered all over the cockpit, and boy do I hope we don't get boarded for any reason: raiders, mercs, interstellar law enforcement, or otherwise. I slip between the sheets after her, reveling in the coolness of the satiny material against my still heated skin. Vick's just as warm when I tuck myself in against her chest, my smaller frame fitting with hers like perfect puzzle pieces.

The payback comes about two hours later.

Vick's groan wakes me from deep REM sleep, dragging me out of a very arousing dreamscape into cold reality made even more frigid when she thrusts the sheets off us both, then throws herself off the side of the bed and bolts for the shuttle's bathroom. A moment later, gagging sounds, followed by vomiting carry through the open hatchway.

Damn.

My first impulse is to hurry to her side, but Vick hates for anyone to witness her in times of weakness, even me. Sometimes there's no way around it, but throwing up is rarely life-threatening, so I curb my protective side and take a few deep breaths. Blinking away the half-awake disorientation, I raise my face to the ceiling. "VC1, um, are you there?" I say, so quietly I worry the system's mics won't pick up my voice.

A datapad built into the nightstand by the bed lights
up. I read the words on the screen—I AM PRESENT.

Insightful choice of modes of communication.
Given the advanced nature of the being that is VC1,
she could have just taken over the ship's internal comms and used the overhead speakers to communicate.
Instead, she perceived that I wanted this to be a private
chat and acted accordingly. Impressive. "Does this
shuttle come equipped with medical supplies?"

A brief pause. THERE IS A MEDKIT IN THE
BATHROOM, COMPLETE WITH AN MD37 MED-
ICSCANNER AND INDIVIDUAL DOSES OF THE
MORE COMMON MEDICATIONS. YOU WILL
FIND IT BENEATH THE SINK.

I have no idea what an MD37 is, but I head for the
bathroom, pausing to pull on a complimentary robe
I spotted earlier when we were searching for larger
sheets. I also wrap my emotional shields around myself, a second layer that prevents me from being so
sucked into her trauma that I can't be of any help. By
the time I'm fortified, the sounds of distress coming
from the bathroom have quieted, reduced to panting
and the occasional hitch in her breath.

I step to just outside the open hatch. "Okay to
come in?"

There's a long pause, and I'm about to enter without a response when she says, "Hang on a sec." Her
voice is hoarse, her words strained.

A loud whoosh follows as she drains the toilet
through the shuttle's vacuum-driven plumbing system; then water runs in the sink.

"Okay," she calls, though it's more resigned than
encouraging.

I find her with her palms braced on either side of the white porcelain sink, head hanging, dark hair thrown behind her wild and tangled. Deep purple to the point of almost black swirls in menacing clouds around her. Too dark to be mere fear, I can only equate this color to sheer terror, barely under control.

"Knew there'd be some kind of cost, some price to pay," she mutters. "Didn't think it would be this bad."

"Nightmares?" I ask.

She nods, her eyes still hidden from me. "Worst I've ever had."

Considering some of the ones I've held her through, some of the horrible things she's experienced, that's saying a lot.

"It's still a step forward," I say. *Don't give up, Vick. Please, please don't give up.*

She raises her head then, her haunted gaze meeting mine in the bathroom mirror above the sink. I swear I can make out her demons in the depths of those eyes, and I shiver.

"Yeah," she mutters. "It's a step forward... into my own personal hell."

CHAPTER 19: VICK
SIDE EFFECTS

I AM letting Kelly down.

The second day of our travel is quiet. Too quiet. We enter Weiss space, that ultra-fast method of bending both time and space in order to traverse the galaxy from one solar system to another in a reasonable amount of time, invented by some guy name Weiss. Everyone uses it. No one but the physicists really understand it. Even VC1 can't translate the concept into words I'll comprehend. But it turns the viewscreens to nothing but snow for hours and hours and leaves nothing for the pilot to do but wait until the ship returns to real space.

In the meantime, Kelly and I dance around each other, orbiting but never intersecting. We exchange small talk. We smile, but it's forced. We touch… and I flinch away no matter how hard I try to control it. And her face falls. And my heart breaks.

I don't blame her. I wanted what she wanted. And I tell her that, but I can't try again. Not yet. I need time for things to quiet down in my head.

Assuming they ever will.

The nightmares following our lovemaking hover in my mind's eye even during my waking hours. Worse than my flashbacks, they were even clearer, every smell, touch, sound, vivid as if I were in the moment, and worse, magnified by those bizarre extremes and randomness that nightmares incorporate.

Dark, endless corridors leading to torture chambers where both Rodwell and Alkins wait to torment me, snaking wires sparking as they burst through my skull and strangle me in their endless coils, and the worst one—a vast empty space, plain metal walls, floor, and ceiling, everything gray. I stand in the middle of it, growing colder and colder, my breath shortening, my pulse fading.

And I'm alone. Completely alone. No matter how loudly or often I call for Kelly, my voice echoes back to me, mocking my terror, until I'm too hoarse to call anymore. In that moment, I would give anything for a comforting touch, a soothing word, a reassurance of any kind, but there's no one.

I pull myself free of it seconds before dying. My headache pounds, a constant torment since Kelly and

I made love. The implants keep it hidden from her, buried beneath my suppressors working at almost full capacity.

To distract myself, and to make things up to Kelly, I throw myself into preparing for her birthday/family reunion combination. VC1 has no trouble locating and hacking into the guest list, then correlating names with background information drawn from dozens of networked sources. Without Kelly's knowledge, I read every file, view every news clip, study every image until I've connected names to faces, stored them in my memory, and prepared topics for interaction with everyone who will attend. Or almost everyone. There is one guy, a David Locher, who went to school at the Academy with Kelly, and then for all intents and purposes disappeared. I can find nothing on his career choices, residence, hobbies, even with VC1's help, so I'm betting on some kind of government or super-secret technology work. But he's on the list, so he's attending. I make a literal mental note to look into him further when we meet. Other than that, it's a fairly quick process, several hours' worth of work rather than the days it would take an unenhanced human, but it gives me something to do for the remainder of the flight.

And it keeps me awake.

People have commented that I seem cold and distant in social gatherings. I will not let that be the take-away her family and friends have when I meet them, or in the case of her parents, meet them again.

I wish I could remember the first time. Kelly says we liked each other, but she has a tendency to sugarcoat things. I'm desperate to make a good second first impression.

My life is so fucking weird.

Or maybe I should say "lives."

Once I've got the family and friends locked into memory, I practice other things, like smiling, laughing, though the latter must be done quietly and in the yacht's bathroom so Kelly doesn't think I've lost my mind more than I already have. I'm not good at either spontaneous emotional response, but this will have to do.

I'm halfway between a grin and a chuckle and panicking at the sudden thought that there might be dancing or some other social practice I'm unfamiliar with when the ship's proximity alarm sounds. We exited Weiss space about two hours ago, so that's not the cause.

What is it? I query as I race down the corridor to the cockpit.

Unknown, VC1 returns, *and now gone. But you should take a look. I recorded the readings.*

What am I gonna see that you couldn't?

A laugh, a genuine laugh carries over my internal speakers. *You might be surprised at the capabilities the human brain possesses. What you call instinct or intuition is more likely you humans accessing the large portions of your brains that go unused throughout most of your lifetimes. No computer, even one as advanced as I am, is currently able to match that capacity for abstract thought and interpretation.*

A laugh and a compliment. Okay then.

Kelly's already in the copilot's chair when I enter the forward compartment. She's got a frown on her face and her hands pressed against her ears. "I don't know how to turn it off!" she shouts, pointing an elbow at the speakers producing a consistent blaring whoop.

I reach over and exaggeratedly flip the switch right in front of her on the console. The one marked "Emergency Alert." She blows me a raspberry. The smile that produces doesn't need any practicing.

"Let's see what you've got," I say to the ceiling.

The front viewscreen shifts from an image of the vast expanse of space to display whatever the pickups recorded a few minutes ago, but the changes are so subtle I barely detect a difference. I lean forward, watching for any indication of what set off the alarms, but there's nothing. I'm about to give up, figuring I missed it, when the slightest of flickers flashes at the edge of the screen, so fast I'm uncertain whether I imagined it. Then again, just a quick flare indicating some sort of vessel possessing a heat signature entered our sensor range and left it. I lean back.

"It's nothing. Another ship on the same flight path." I consult the readings on the console in front of me. "We're close enough to Infinity Bay that we should be detecting other ships soon. Spotting one a little early is just a coincidence."

It is not, VC1 states without equivocation.

"What do you mean?" Damn, I said that out loud. VC1 avoided alerting Kelly to a potential problem, and I blurted it right out. I glance to the side. Yep, she's got her eyebrows raised, waiting for an explanation. "Go ahead and explain to both of us," I tell the overhead speakers. "I'm an idiot."

Kelly pats me on the shoulder. I don't flinch. Oooh, progress.

"This was the third instance of the appearance of the unidentified heat signature."

Oh, that's weird, and I don't mean the UFO. I straighten in the pilot's chair. Beside me, Kelly does the same. It's my voice and yet not my voice coming from above, so very different from the perception of speech I get from VC1 in my head or even the sound of my own speech when I talk out loud. Even more distracting is the complete lack of any inflection. People might complain I drop into monotone when I'm not concentrating on it, but this takes it a disturbing step further. It's my pitch, tone, and whatever touches of a Kansas accent I carried over when I left Earth to join the Storm, but those are the only distinguishing features. And yet it's me, in a bizarre, twisted, give-me-nightmares kind of way.

Kelly squirms in her seat, her nose scrunched up and her eyes half-closed. It's adorable, but it's affecting her too.

"You okay?" I ask, reaching out to touch her knee.

It breaks the spell. She turns and blinks at me, takes a deep breath and lets it out. "Yes," she says. "It's just... the last time I heard that, it came directly from you, when you were completely under her control."

I nod, understanding. When I'd been truly losing my mind, when Kelly's emotion block was failing, VC1 stepped in to prevent a total breakdown. I didn't like it, but it had been necessary. We have a better balance now. I don't entirely trust VC1, but then, I trust almost no one, so that could just be on me.

Then the AI's actual words register.

I glare at the speakers. "What do you mean, the 'third instance'? Why didn't the alarms sound the first two times, and why didn't you alert me?"

"Because those two occurrences *were* well within the expected possibility percentage for a coincidental encounter. A third instance, with the same heat signature, was not."

I let that sit for a moment while I consider the possibilities. There aren't many of them. We are being followed. I don't say it out loud right away. I can, actually, be taught. But if I try for evasion at this point, Kelly will read my subterfuge with ease.

"Who's tracking us?" she says, saving me the trouble.

I sigh. "VC1, any thoughts?"

"I do not think. I process information."

Grrr. "Fine. What are your conclusions?" The viewscreen shifts back to a real-time image of the stars ahead and a shining bright blue disk increasing in size with each passing second as we draw nearer to Infinity Bay.

"Insufficient data. I require guidelines."

Human intuition. Abstract thought. Okay. "It's the same ship all three times. You're certain of it. How do you know?"

"The variances within the signature are the same for each appearance."

Variances. A ship's engine signature variance acts like a fingerprint. No two ships carry the same exact variance. If such things were recorded, we'd know exactly who trailed us. But they aren't. For one thing, who would want to keep those kinds of records? Other than public commercial transports and company-owned recreational crafts like interstellar cruise ships, most pilots don't necessarily want others to know exactly where they are at all times. And besides, it's almost impossible to measure with that degree of accuracy.

It doesn't surprise me at all that VC1 pulled it off. It does make me wonder even more about party guest David Locher and why even VC1 can't find any recent intel on him. But that's a problem for another day.

I close my eyes and ponder some more. There are only three groups I can think of that would have a reason to be tracking us: local law enforcement which, given we are in a rental and not a Storm shuttle doesn't make sense at all; raiders looking for easy spoils; and the Sunfires, still after me. I'm not fond of any of the options, but how to narrow them down?

Ships, engines, heat signatures, variances. The glimmer of an idea comes to mind. "VC1, how irregular are the variances coming off that ship?"

A pause.

Kelly opens her mouth to ask a question, but I raise a hand to hold her off. One interruption and I might lose this crazy train of thought.

"They are 98 percent regular. The engines are well maintained."

Which eliminates raiders, who are notorious for letting their ships nearly fall apart before performing any upkeep. With recent improvements in defensive ship security systems and better weaponry, the local pirate types struggle. They have neither the funds nor the manpower to maintain their vessels.

And law enforcement has no reason to hunt us.

"So," I say, trying for casual and unconcerned and failing miserably, "our friends the Sunfires are back."

CHAPTER 20: KELLY
COLD PURSUIT

VICK IS wanted.

Vick takes over full control of the yacht while I run a mediscanner down the length of her. The swelling in the organic portion of her brain still shows lingering traces of her concussion, but for the most part, VC1 has pulled her together.

I never know whether to love or hate that AI.

We've got the sensors on long-range, and it's my job to watch for anything unusual while Vick pilots us closer to Infinity Bay. Not that I have any real confidence in my ability to tell the unusual from the usual.

I suspect she's just giving me something to keep me occupied so I won't worry.

It's not working.

Ship traffic is increasing the closer in we go: commercial haulers, private racers, yachts and shuttles, massive passenger liners, a few patrol ships guiding some of the larger ones in. Something's missing.

"Where are the military vessels?" I ask, hoping I'm not pulling her from anything vital.

She turns toward me, her hands still moving over the controls while she works in tandem with VC1. Neat trick. Her eyes go unfocused for a moment. "They don't have a military to speak of. Some ground personnel, a handful of ships for emergencies. It's a resort world. The tourists far outnumber the residents. They let each island's police force handle the trivial stuff. People come here to relax. No one's looking for a fight."

"Until now," I mutter, but she hears me anyway.

"Yeah," Vick agrees. "Sorry. Seems like I'm always bringing trouble. Maybe we should rethink this. I could land, drop you with your family, and—"

I'm up and out of my seat, my hands on both her shoulders, pressing her into her own chair as if I can physically force her to stay with me. She twists her neck to meet my gaze. "Knock it off. You aren't leaving me here or anywhere else. Do you really think they'll chase you to the surface?"

A wicked grin erupts across her face. "Not if they can't find us." She tilts her head toward my chair. "I don't even know for certain they're still tailing us, but our destination is obvious. I'm not taking any chances, so I need to confuse them before we land. Might want to strap in for this."

My grip on her shoulders tightens. Considering some of the daredevil stunts I've seen her pull off in the past few months, with and without wearing restraints, if Vick says to strap in, we're in for a rough ride.

I fall into my seat as Vick jinks us into a quick turn, then pushes the engines to their limits and redlines our speed. My fingers fumble with the belt fasteners, clanking the insert against the metal receptacle repeatedly before it clicks home over my left hip, then doing the same with the one on my right. Alarms blare yet again, warning that flying a luxury yacht like a fighter craft is not good for the engines, the shields, or the structural integrity. An automated message pops up on one of the console screens in bright red letters:

"Rental   agreement   violation.   Insurance invalidation."

Vick barks a laugh at that. I squeeze my eyes shut tight.

"VC1, can you fox our autobeacon?" To me, she explains, "Rentals send out constant emergency locator beacons, supposedly to protect the less experienced renter pilots if they should run into trouble. More likely it's to ensure the company gets their shuttle back. It's probably how the Sunfires tracked us in the first place." Vick's words are calm and controlled, but I read the tension beneath them. A low whine, crawling slowly higher in pitch, begins coming from somewhere far aft.

"I can manipulate the beacon," the unperturbed version of Vick's voice responds.

"Perfect. Do it. Then hack into every outbound vehicle you can reach and overlay our emergency signal over theirs. The Sunfires will think we've changed our vacation plans and they'll be chasing false trails for a week."

A long pause. "Done. However, I can do nothing about the registry name on the exterior hull."

Right. *Tranquility* written in all caps and gold lettering, lit by the yacht's external running lights, along with her registration number in smaller glittery black numbers beneath it. It seemed gaudy to me when we came onboard. It's a blaring announcement of our identity to our enemies now.

"Douse our running lights," Vick commands. "In fact, shut down all internal and external light sources not essential to me flying this thing." Then under her breath, "Damn yacht handles like a brick."

I open my eyes. "Vick, other ships won't be able to see us." On the forward screen, the variety of space traffic grows ever closer. We're closing the distance fast, hurtling toward a dense cluster of commercial crafts. Well, denser than those found farther out from habitable worlds. Space is vast. Areas around planets are just less vast. By outer space standards, this would be the equivalent of rush-hour traffic.

"That's kind of the idea, Kel."

I'm thinking of shutting my eyes again when the cockpit lights go out, along with the glow through the open hatch to the connecting lounge area. I can make out Vick's silhouette by the reds and greens of the controls, with a few ambers and blues mixed in. Otherwise it's starlight from the forward screen, and that's not much. We're on the far side of Infinity Bay from her sun.

Gritting my teeth, I speak with all the patience I would use with a child. "If they can't see us, they can't avoid us."

"Don't worry. *I'll* avoid *them*."

My stomach drops as Vick flips the *Tranquility* up, then over, then rolls us to the right, sliding us between two waste haulers from a company called "Take a Dump." Any other time, I'd laugh. Right now it's all I can do to hang on to my lunch. Our shields brush the nearer ship's, flaring at the contact.

Vick growls. "Damn, too close. The Sunfires would've seen that. Need more finesse. Let's do this together."

For a second, I think she's speaking to me, and I panic. I can fly in an emergency, such as if the pilot is incapacitated for some reason. Every member of the Storm is required to take the basic course. But it was when I first joined, years ago. I don't remember half of it. I can neither take off nor land, and I sure as hell can't perform the kinds of maneuvers Vick is executing.

Then I get it. "Vick, don't—" But her eyes unfocus. A moment later, my sense of her diminishes by more than half.

She's let VC1 take over.

CHAPTER 21: VICK
HARD WAY

I AM a passenger.

Kelly often calls me a control fanatic. She's not wrong. Probably something to do with that trust issue she also complains about. Because of it, I don't use illegal substances, don't drink to excess unless the memory flashes have me really fucked-up or I'm in the company of my team or Officer Sanderson back on Girard Base. It's rare enough that I can count the instances in the past year on one hand. Well, maybe two.

Therefore, when I have to relinquish control to the artificial intelligence I share headspace with, it's a desperate, heavily calculated act, an act I wouldn't perform if there was any way I could pull off the stunt I'm planning on my own. I'm aware of everything around me, like watching a vid of my own life in real time, but without permission from VC1, I can't effect change upon it. Not to mention the ever-present fear that the AI might decide she likes being in charge....

In short, I hate it. But sometimes, like now, it's a necessity. With minimal shielding and no weapons, we need to lose the Sunfires, because if they get their hands on me....

You think what maneuvers you would like to execute. I will manipulate your limbs at the proper speeds, she tells me, firming my grip on the primary control lever.

Right. That was exactly my issue. I could conceive what needed to be done, but my human body couldn't translate my thoughts into action fast enough to carry them out.

A computer, however, can transmit my desires to my muscles much faster while removing excess input such as distracting sights, sounds, and smells, along with pesky little things like fears, worries, and concern for my own life as well as Kelly's, all of which slow my actions down. The difference might be infinitesimal, but when dealing with frequent and often delicate evasive maneuvers, every nanosecond counts.

My left hand darts over the touchpads and switches while my right guides the steering lever in a variety of jerks and arcs, a nudge, then a yank, then a gradual turn. The yacht rolls, dives, and flips, darting between other ships at impossible angles, slipping through spaces that should be too tight, clearing the gaps with inches separating our shield perimeters and avoiding any further visible flare-ups.

The engine's still whining, the alarms whooping, and every panel light still active flashes red. In my peripheral vision, I'm aware of Kelly bending over her armrest, gagging, and my stomach churns in brief sympathy before VC1 quells my nausea by cutting off my perception of my own innards.

Okay, this does have some major advantages.

After a couple more rolls, I backward-loop us to settle in between a pair of inbound passenger liners, the required side-to-side distance more than great enough for us to fit into. It's a blind spot, a location where sensors shouldn't detect us while dark. We should only be spotted if someone literally looks out a porthole *and* happens to notice a darker blob against the already dark expanse of space or the shadow we might make on the opposite liner. I reduce the crying engines to match the liners' speed, leave the exterior and interior lights down, and watch for any sign the Sunfires somehow followed all that.

Anything? I ask several minutes later.

I have located the engine signature of the pursuing ship. Currently, it is outbound, behind one of the seventeen other vessels bearing the Tranquility's *emergency beacon.*

I chuckle inside my head. *Seventeen?*

Those are all I could reach without a signal boost.

I laugh harder. *It's more than enough. They'll be chasing false trails for weeks.* Another thought occurs. *What if they turn around? Head for the surface instead?*

A moment, please. She closes my eyes.

Um, why did you do that?

External input is distracting.

Oh.

I shiver. Waiting inside my own skull is like being stuck in a gravlift between floors, alone, with the emergency comm dead and no access to the outside world. It's a lot like the airlock. My breathing picks up pace, along with my pulse rate.

Calm. Something cool and soothing floods my veins. VC1 has upped my serotonin output. Involuntary functions return to normal. *You need better control.*

You need to open my fucking eyes.

An image of two eyeballs entwined by their dangling nerves appears in my inner view. I'd roll mine if I had the ability. Wondering if she'll receive it, I attempt to send her an image of me bashing my head against a wall the next time I get the chance, then broken bits of metal and circuitry falling out of my ear.

My eyes open.

I am humoring you. We are programmed against self-harm, she chides. *You would not be able to act upon that threat.*

There are loopholes for everything.

A second later I'm thrown into full control, my senses hyperreactive to every external source of stimuli. Goose bumps rise on my exposed skin as the on-board climate system blows ice picks from above. I fumble to shut down the now deafening alarms and shield my eyes from the blinding stars and flashing warning lights with my other hand. It's not always this bad when VC1 returns me to myself, but the last few days have taxed me, so it's worse than usual.

Kelly helps, covering my eyes with a cool palm and wrapping one arm around me until I cease shivering. "Thanks," I mutter.

"Welcome back. You were gone awhile. I was getting worried."

I cover her hand with my own. "You're always worried."

"Not without reason."

I can't argue with that. I tug her fingers away and take stock of the cockpit. No sign of vomit, so neither of us puked. Every readout is redlined, with the exception of life support. Small but important favors. I'll take what I can get.

"Have we lost them?" Kelly asks, staring at the now flickering viewscreen.

I don't think I'm getting our deposit back.

"Yes. Not sure for how long."

"Indefinitely," VC1 chimes in from overhead, the speakers popping and crackling with her speech.

Kelly and I both jump. "Little warning next time, okay?" I say.

"You will adjust. On a more relevant note, I have created false bookings in over a hundred different establishments on Infinity Bay under the LaSalle name, each with a different length of stay. Any outside source searching for such a reservation will see them, but the resorts themselves will not, nor will Kelly's family be charged. I have also erased all exterior traces to the real reservation made by her parents some time ago."

I swear a bit of smugness has entered her usual monotone. "That's… amazing," I tell her, figuring even an AI would appreciate a compliment.

"Yes, it is," VC1 agrees.

Kelly laughs. "I'm really glad you're on our side."

"You should be."

WE FLY in both liners' blind spot until we enter Infinity Bay's gravity well. Then I ease us out and hope I don't spook either pilot when I flip our running lights back on.

There's a flare of emergency channel chatter that suggests I've done exactly that, but I ignore the angry accusations and threats of legal repercussions and head us toward the mostly fluid surface of the planet.

"Erase any record of our little hide-and-seek game the liners might have recorded," I tell VC1.

"Already done."

"She does a lot of thinking for herself," Kelly comments from her place back in the copilot's chair.

"I am a fully self-aware, sentient being," VC1 says. Definitely smug. No doubt about it.

"My apologies," Kelly says with a smile. She turns to me. "Are you sure we should go ahead with this? We could fly somewhere else, lie low for a day or two. There's at least one other inhabitable planet in this system."

I shake my head. "That's Elektra4. I checked it out the other night while I looked at the rest of our route. Nothing there but scattered scientific research stations studying the extreme electrical storms that the planet's crazy atmosphere produces. You can't even go down there without a specially shielded ship or the lightning will fry all the onboard systems. Those shields are really expensive. Most modern escape pods have them, since they're smaller, and you never know where you'll have to crash-land, but I think the Storm owns exactly one actual ship capable of the descent."

"Huh." She brings the planet up on a smaller screen embedded in the lower right corner of our larger one and stares at the purple-and-green world and the multiple light flashes coming from its atmosphere. "Pretty, though."

"Besides, we're here to see *your* friends and family and celebrate *your* birthday. Wouldn't do for you not to show up. Don't worry. We're covered. It's fine."

Kelly input our destination into the navigational computer shortly after we first boarded the *Tranquility*, so I steer us in the direction of the aptly named Celebration Isle, one of the smaller islands making up the near-infinite chains of them dotting their way across Infinity Bay's single, massive ocean. From what I can tell on our approach, the only structures include a two-story main building and a couple dozen or so wood-frame pastel cottages in varying sizes. All are painted in pinks, greens, yellows, and blues with shutters in complementary colors. They line the beach—a rainbow of welcome.

On the far side of the island, I can make out landing platforms designed to accept a variety of air transports, both atmospheric craft and interstellar. Careful of aesthetics, the resort designers have hidden them among the trees so guests on the ground won't notice them and be reminded that sooner or later they must return to their working lives.

The nearer we get the more details I can discern. One section of beach has boat docks protecting everything from small sailboats to a few classic yachts, water-racers, and fishing craft. My gaze lingers on the racers, and a pang of longing and nostalgia tightens my chest.

"What is it?" Kelly asks, reading me with ease.

I shake my head. "Nothing. I think I used to enjoy water sports. That's all. Can't remember specifics."

She rests a hand on my arm. "Well, then, you'll just have to introduce me to some. I've always been too scared to do much on open water, so I've never water-skied or parasailed or any of that. But with you I'm sure I'll be fine."

That earns her a laugh. "I'm the one who leads you into trouble, remember?"

"Not on purpose. And you always get me out of it. That's what matters."

I'm trying to decide how to respond to that when a Banshee-like screech rips its way from the yacht's engine section, echoing in both audible and physical shudders through the transport's frame. I flip the switch to shut down the alarms almost before they start—I'm still suffering from the headache our earlier chase induced—but there's nothing I can do about the flashing lights all across the control panel and even climbing up the walls and crossing the ceiling, every one of them red.

I don't need VC1 to tell me. Every system is shutting down: engines, shields, life support, the works. I run my fingers over the touchpads. Yep, even the landing gear refuses to deploy. For the moment, I still have guidance operating. I can use the steering lever to direct where we'll crash.

But we *are* going to crash.

"Kelly," I say, keeping my tone as calm as possible under the circumstances, "strap back in. We're doing this the hard way."

Chapter 22: Kelly
Wet Welcome

VICK IS humiliated.

I fasten the straps much faster this time around. The fact that I'm getting used to this sort of thing isn't exactly comforting.

Vick circles the island once, twice, and I realize she's bleeding off speed—a good plan, except each consecutive turn involves more tugging and pulling at the control levers. The guidance systems are failing along with everything else.

"Remember what I said about you always getting me out of trouble?" I say, glancing sideways at her.

She never turns from the controls or her view out the forward screen, but she responds, "Yeah."

"Do it again, please?"

She laughs, and a vibrant fuchsia flares around her. I stare in disbelief. "You're enjoying this."

Her concentration never wavers. "It's a good challenge. Don't worry. Even if we crash, we're gonna do it on water. We'll survive it."

"I wasn't aware this was an amphibious craft." Such things exist. Water worlds like Infinity Bay often use ships that can land on both earth and ocean, and there are several such vessels floating next to the docks of our island resort, bobbing on the gentle tide.

"It's not," Vick confirms, yanking the steering lever hard to the right. "Ship might not survive the crash. We will."

I tug my straps a little tighter. "You're insane," I grumble under my breath.

Now she does look at me, though her hands continue manipulating the controls as if she can see what she's doing. With VC1's assistance, maybe she can. Vick's expression is serious. "No offense to your empathic efforts, but I have been since the accident. For some reason, you love me anyway." She turns back to the controls.

"Yes, I do."

I shut up and let her focus. We do three more circles around the island. By now we've drawn a crowd, and we're low enough I can make out some details. An older couple steps from a pink-and-white cottage, Mom's favorite red-with-white polka-dot-skirted swimsuit identifying them as my parents. They head for the wharf at a brisk pace. Six or seven people already at the docks step off their boats to the steadier planked-wood surface or stare up at us in confusion from their decks. All along the beach, scattered sunbathers rise from their towels, waving and pointing. A team of a half dozen individuals race from the main building, their identical tan pants and pale green tank tops marking them as staff members.

"Did you radio in our emergency?" Was I supposed to have done that? I bite my lip.

"Comms are down. Along with everything else. I think they've figured it out, though. We're flying irregularly and trailing engine exhaust."

On cue, three fire-control vehicles appear out of the trees, probably from a hidden low-lying structure. We can't hear the sirens in the cockpit, but I can imagine them blaring, and their red flashing lights draw even more guests to the water's edge, some in fancy resort attire or evening wear.

Surprised, I check local time. It's late afternoon and my wealthier relatives prefer to dress for dinner.

One more circuit of the small landmass and Vick dips the nose of the yacht downward. I hang on tight as we rapidly lose altitude and my stomach jumps into my throat. We're heading straight for the docks. "Need to turn," I grit out.

"Controls aren't responding." The final faint hum of the guidance system dies.

Wonderful.

The boats and wharf grow ever closer, filling the entire viewscreen. People turn and flee back toward shore while others dive off their watercraft and swim for it. A few in dinner jackets and evening gowns stare in openmouthed shock, frozen in place.

"We're gonna hit!" I shout.

"No. We're not."

Vick's sudden monotone yanks my attention from the forward view, which is the only thing still working on this flying hulk. She's got both palms resting lightly on the surface of the console, eyes closed. Trails of visible energy lead from her fingertips, then ripple across the mostly dark control panel, lighting up indicators in their wake in rainbow patterns of greens and yellows rather than the terrifying reds. A growling sound erupts from far aft, rumbling like a distant pride of lions roaring all at once, the guidance system coming back online.

When Vick replaces her hand on the steering lever, she's able to shift it left as if it requires no effort whatsoever, and we turn parallel to the beach, away from the docks at the last possible moment.

Our impact isn't nearly as serene. We miss the docks and boats tethered there, but we're closer to them than we should be when we hit the water, and even with circling repeatedly, our momentum is still above safe speeds for landing.

The nose hits first, throwing us both against our restraints with bruising force. Then the tail drops, smacking the water's surface like an angry whale. Even through the thickness of the hull, I hear the resounding slap and whoosh of the wave we must make. The lights go out, all humming going silent with the yacht's final death throes.

When things settle—we never completely cease moving since we're afloat—I fumble in near pitch-darkness for the fasteners and release myself. I

use the chair to pull myself up, then reach out to find
Vick in her seat, motionless.

"Vick? You okay?" My voice wavers and cracks.
I'm trembling with adrenaline and relief.

Two lights spring on, startling me into a squeak
of surprise before I recognize Vick's eye lamps. They
flicker on and off once, twice, then settle once she remembers to tell the ocular technology not to blink.

"Told you we'd be fine," she responds, though
she sounds a bit strained. I wish I could see her clearly, but she's all darkness and shadows behind those
lit eyes. Despite that darkness, silver tones of pride
glitter around her outline.

"That was impressive flying. Tandem with VC1?"

The twin lights nod.

I'm not thrilled about that, but it worked, we're
alive, and she seems back to herself, so I can't complain. Besides, I have bigger concerns. "Vick, you
know I can't afford to pay for this entire yacht, right?
I'm pretty sure we're sinking, and I don't know what
we're going to say to the rental company." Actually,
I probably can afford it. I don't live extravagantly,
and the Storm pays me well, not to mention benefits
and bonuses for each successful mission. It makes
me feel guilty accepting all that when the majority of
what Vick earns goes straight back into the Storm to
make "payments" on the technology they installed to
save her life (and make her the most successful merc
they've ever trained).

"Don't worry. You won't have to. I've got some
footage VC1 just transferred to me that she snagged
off the security cameras back on Girard Base. Seems
our friendly neighborhood rental agent accepted

a packet from a couple of Sunfires and pointed out which ship we were taking. I'm betting he also gave them our general destination *and* looked the other way to let them sabotage the *Tranquility*. We owe them nothing. In fact, once I send this data to the Storm, the company will owe *us*. I'll fire off a comm packet with that info and what really went down at the Alpha Dog once we're on shore." Vick's more pleased with herself than I've seen her in a long time.

Good. She can use the self-confidence boost.

With her lighting the way, we stumble through the ship, first to the sleeping cabin where we retrieve our luggage, then to the exterior hatch and crank it open manually. Vick shuts down her eye lamps. The emergency ramp automatically unrolls itself out and down, landing with a small splash and disappearing beneath the water's surface. Even though it's evening, bright, blinding sunlight streams through the opening, and it takes a moment for our eyes to adjust. When they do, we both stop dead in the open doorway.

"Oh... fuck," Vick mutters, staring back toward the docks.

I concur with the sentiment.

All the smaller watercraft—rowboats, sailboats, wave racers and such—float upside down on the current, sails soaked and billowing across the water, loose items spreading in growing circles around them and their occupants treading water and hanging on to their inverted sides. Larger boats remain upright, their decks drenched and covered in remaining puddles, the owners equally soaked and gathering their own scattered belongings. Still more individuals swim toward shore in full clothing, returning from jumping off the docks when they thought we'd crash into them. On the beach, my friends and relatives wring out wet towels and chase after whatever our wave wake dragged farther inland. Every umbrella, every plastic chair is torn or toppled. Several staff members stare in dismay at a smoking barbecue and four destroyed buffet tables once laden with side dishes, plates, and silverware now all scattered across the sand. In addition to the wave, our incoming wind must have done significant damage as well.

Every face we can make out at this distance is scowling at us.

Vick's shoulders sag and she closes her eyes. "Great first impression," she murmurs.

I have no words.

CHAPTER 23: VICK
ISLAND LIFE

I AM a disaster.

In addition to the beach buggy fire brigade with sand-tread tires and mounted pumps designed to shoot fire-extinguishing foam, there's a water rescue team. Three motorboats approach from the far side of the island, also equipped with foam pumps. Two go to work on the yacht's still smoking aft section. The other putters around to the main hatch.

A staff member waves to us from the little boat. "You two all right?" says the first not-entirely-pissed-off person I've seen since our arrival. "That looked

like a rough landing. Comms go down? Or is our receiver malfunctioning again? Hard to get good tech on
the outer islands."

"It's us," Kelly hastens to reassure him.

He's tan, well-muscled, with sandy blond hair
and blue eyes brighter than the ocean. He gives Kelly
a big white toothy grin.

I don't think I like this guy so much after all.

"Cascade failure," I jump in before they can inter-
act further or Kelly can bring up the Sunfires. That's
something I'd rather keep quiet for now.

Kelly glances at me, giving me an amused smile. I
don't return it. Her hand slips into mine. Yeah, she can
read my jealousy. I'm being an idiot in every possible
way right now, but I've got nothing to smile about.

The guy—Angelino according to his name tag—
raises his eyebrows. "You're lucky to be in one piece,
then. We saw you circling. Smart move. That was
some impressive flying if you were without most of
your systems. Hop on board and I'll give you a lift to
shore." He extends his hand to Kelly first, of course,
and guides her into the boat. Then he takes our luggage from me. "We'll make sure your belongings end
up in your cottage," he says. I follow without his assistance, pausing to reseal the hatch.

This shuttle is going down, one way or another,
but maybe I can prevent water from flooding the passenger areas before it can be salvaged and towed.

When I'm onboard, I retrieve my duffel and sling
it over my shoulder. My pistol and other personal
weaponry are in there, stowed as I promised Kelly
they would be but within easy reach. I'm not trusting

it to Angelino or anyone else who might be curious and poke around.

Kelly yips a little at the rocking of the smaller craft, dropping onto a bench seat and gripping the base of it with both hands. I'm at ease, moving to the seat opposite hers, unperturbed by the constant motion. Combined with my earlier nostalgia for the wave racers, I'm more convinced than ever that I've had experience with water sports. It begs multiple questions. From what we've dug out of my closed records, I grew up in Kansas. Not a lot of ocean out there. But my family had money, lots of it, so I can see summer trips to the shore or maybe even an island like this one.

I pull back to the here and now as we draw closer to the very crowded docks. My enhanced eyesight picks out facial features even at a distance. A few show concern, especially an older couple in swimsuits.

VC1 provides a file image to my inner sight that confirms these are Kelly's parents, though I'd already recognized them from my studying. I hadn't seen this particular picture of them before. It's of her mother holding Kelly as a baby, her father looking on proudly. Despite my shit mood, it warms me inside.

Well, that's good. Concern is better than the wide range of anger, everything from mild annoyance to outright fury, I'm seeing on everyone else in our welcoming committee.

We arrive at the dock, the gathered assembly leaving us little room to climb out of the boat. Kelly slips when a sudden wave washes the tiny craft up against the pilings, but I catch her and keep her upright, then lift her by the waist to grab hold of several waiting hands and step on solid wood. There's lots of hugging and warm greetings, exclamations of joy and big smiles.

For her.

I'm a different story.

No one helps me. Accident or not, no choice or not, I'm the easy target who inconvenienced everyone, and they're going to direct their frustration somewhere. Kelly and I are the only nonstaff who aren't soaking wet. I time the rocking of the waves and hop onto the dock, then wait for the inevitable impact of my actions. It doesn't take long.

"What kind of hotdogging—"

"—show off? Who do you think you are?"

"—ruined my genuine Denetian leather shoes!"

"You drowned the entire buffet. They were setting up for the past hour, and—"

"—daredevil? You flipped my wave racer!"

With every accusation, my headache returns, pounding more fiercely than when I first got the concussion (was that only two days ago?), until I worry my brain will burst through my skull. I shuffle forward step by step, seeking an open pathway to the end of the wharf and eventual escape. Crowds bother me in the best of times.

This is anything but the best.

I keep my head down, not making eye contact, focused on the untied laces of my combat boots. The pier seems infinite, no end in sight no matter how many steps I take, but I must be almost there. I must be—

"Ooof."

"Whoops!"

I plow headfirst into someone's chest. One more person I've offended or harmed in some way. One more lost opportunity to make a good first impression.

I can't help it. Tears well up, threatening to overflow—the last thing I need. Clenching my jaw, I swipe them away with the back of my hand and look up to face whomever I've crashed into, determined to apologize and get away as fast as possible without humiliating myself further.

"Hello, Vick. Welcome. It's wonderful to see you again." Mr. LaSalle, Kelly's dad, extends a hand to me. He's still in his bathing suit, dripping wet like everyone else my piloting half drowned, but his sparkling brown eyes and wide smile show no anger whatsoever. In fact, he looks almost mischievous, like he's enjoyed watching his extended family get doused.

I'm staring at his outstretched hand, drawing a blank on what I'm supposed to do with such a gesture. *Shake it, you idiot. Don't just stand there like a moron. Take his hand and shake it.* But I'm frozen in place.

He looks from me to his hand and back again, zeroing in on my expression, my face, my eyes. Shit.

Without any further hesitation, he drops his hand, then extends both arms, takes me gently by my shoulders, and pulls me against his chest until I'm wrapped in the first hug I can remember ever getting from anyone besides Kelly. His wet swimsuit starts soaking through my own clothing, probably leaving dark marks on the gray fabric of the uniform pants, maybe even turning my shirt transparent. I'm dimly aware that everyone else must be watching this interaction. I don't care. I don't care about any of it.

A shudder passes through me. My muscles tense, then relax as I awkwardly return the hug. He doesn't let go. I don't want him to.

"Ah, Vick. You're all right," he whispers against my hair for my ears alone. "We'll make sure everyone understands. Today you saved my daughter's life for the second time. I'm certain of it."

It's been more times than that, but if Kelly hasn't told them about the other scrapes we've been in, it's not my place to mention them. I can't bring myself to tell him Kelly's life wouldn't have been threatened at all today if the Sunfires weren't after me.

"You didn't have other options," he continues. "If you'd landed farther from the island, the shuttle would have sunk, and the dangerous sea life out there would have gotten to you both before the rescue boat could arrive."

As if on cue, people down the pier start shouting and exclaiming. I pull my head up and twist around in time to watch the shuttle sink until the ocean is above the top of the exit hatch. It stops there, leaving the roof of the transport visible, so the water in that area must not be all that deep, but Mr. LaSalle is correct. Farther out and we might not have made it at all.

"What was that about the sea life?" I ask, still staring at the hapless shuttle. With salt water in the engine, she'll never fly again.

"Octosharks," says a new voice at my left shoulder. "Eight heads of snapping teeth. They're deadly. And several varieties of seagoing carnivorous mammals. I don't know all the names."

I jump a little, then relax as Kelly's mother gives me a gentle squeeze. She's also an empath, a very strong one, so there's no doubt she can read my anxiety and the pain in my battered body, even if she doesn't pick up all the nuances the way Kelly does. "So much for water sports," I say, hoping to divert attention away from the shuttle and me. Then again, if sea creatures eat me, I won't have to face the rest of these people again.

"Oh, you can still do those if you want to. The resort has an underwater barrier set up around the island. Your shuttle landed just inside of it. Precision flying, there." She pats my shoulder.

"Well, she did have help."

I jump again. Okay, I'm really out of it if people are sneaking up on me on a regular basis. My training, not to mention my enhanced senses, should have alerted me to both Mr. and Mrs. LaSalle and the man who has now appeared on my right.

What's going on in there? I subvocalize, letting annoyance color my thoughts.

I am... overtaxed from the landing and your current emotional state. To keep you functional, I must draw my attention away from some of our joint abilities.

I'm not redlining, am I? Redlining, pushing the implants to their limits, is bad and happens more often than I prefer in my profession. When I reach that point, I have to monitor myself consistently to make sure I don't go into overload, which could lead to much, much worse things... such as my autonomics shutting down, or even more catastrophic, a burnout.

Not anymore, VC1 returns.

Oh, that's comforting. Not at all.

Nothing to be done about it now, though. I turn to the newcomer and blink when the Social Interaction file I created shuffles his newsnet profile and name to the forefront of my awareness.

This is David Locher. The mystery man with no retrievable records who went to the Academy with Kelly.

And he said I had help landing the shuttle.

His blue eyes bore into me, crinkled at the corners, and his mouth curls in a knowing grin like he's privy to far more information than anyone realizes.

When he said I had help, I don't think he meant Kelly. I think he knows.

He knows what I am.

CHAPTER 24: KELLY
WHO ARE YOU?

VICK IS not herself.

When Vick sees an opening and takes off down the pier, I try to follow, but my friends and family swarm me the moment my foot hits the dock. I'm the recipient of hugs, cheek kisses, pats on the back and shoulders, handshakes, and a dozen inquiries about what happened up there and whether I'm all right. I hear others questioning Vick, suggesting different actions, complaining about damages she couldn't avoid but still complaining, and I can't read her emotional response through all the other sensory and extrasensory input, but when she doesn't turn around and tell them off, I'm stunned.

Vick prides herself on her military skill set. It's one of the few areas of her self-esteem that's not as damaged as the rest of her. She's an outstanding fighter and an expert marksman along with many other talents she's trained hard to perfect. I can't imagine her taking that kind of verbal abuse without defending herself.

So when I do finally get away from everyone else and meet her at the end of the pier, the last thing I want to see and hear is my old classmate and wannabe boyfriend, David Locher, belittling her skills by saying she had help with the shuttle landing.

I didn't do a damn thing to get that yacht down safely. I didn't—

No. But VC1 did.

And David Locher works for BioTech.

I slip my hand into Vick's, giving it a firm squeeze of support. Her distress and a miasma of other emotions flood through the physical connection, making me wince, but I don't dare embarrass her in front of a crowd yet again by pointing it out. Instead, I indicate David with my free hand.

"Vick, meet David Locher, BioTech." Vick visibly flinches at the name of the corporation that built her implants. I doubt most people would have noticed, but my mother's concerned gaze meets mine. "I'm not entirely clear on what he does there…."

David extends a hand, and Vick hesitates before dropping mine to take it. It's a quick handshake, as little contact as possible without appearing rude. "I'm an analyst."

"And what, exactly, do you analyze?" Vick asks, monotone. Is this her speaking? Or is it VC1 probing for information? Her eyes unfocus, then refocus again. I have the distinct impression she's recording this response.

"Oh, lots of things," David says, smarmy as ever. "Market trends, profit margins, what you're doing right now."

Vick blinks and takes a step backward. I've virtually never seen her retreat from anything or anyone. It's terrifying.

"Anything with a predictable outcome," he finishes with a predatory smile.

"David's a precognitive, if I recall correctly," Dad chimes in. His talent of microtelekinesis doesn't contribute to his understanding of human nature, but he's always been perceptive. Even he has picked up on something wrong in this interaction.

Mom steps to Vick's other side. Dad moves to stand behind her. Inside, I beam. We've got her protected on three sides. Under normal circumstances, she'd say she doesn't need protecting, but she makes no move to leave the shelter of my family.

"I thought precognition was an unmeasurable talent."

That sounds like Vick. So it's VC1 who's retreating? Also not a comforting thought.

David shrugs and turns to head toward the main building. If we want to check in and leave this mess for the safety and security of our cottage, we're going to have to go there as well, so we fall into step behind him. "It's not scientifically quantifiable," David admits. "The Academy recognizes it, studies it, attempts to measure it, so far without accurate results. Still," he adds, tossing another smile over his shoulder, "some people are far more successful than others in knowing what comes next. And companies pay big money for that kind of knowledge. In return I get to work around some fascinating projects, projects that shape the very future of humankind." He stops and stares at Vick, gaze running from her boots to her face, like she's more lab specimen than person.

Vick's had to deal with that look since VC1 became part of her reality, since she became property of the Fighting Storm. She hates it. So do I.

"Big changes are coming for humanity. I intend to profit from helping BioTech remain on the cutting edge. The future is now." David's eyes lock with Vick's. "And here."

A shiver passes through her, transferring to me via our connection. Might be the breeze on her spray-dampened clothes. Might not.

Mom comes to our rescue, placing an authoritative hand on David's shoulder. "Well, I'm sure these two are exhausted from all the excitement today. We should let them get settled in."

"Right," David agrees, to my surprise. "Dinner will be delayed," he adds, gesturing toward the beach and the ruined buffet we caused on our way in.

Vick flushes with embarrassment. My heart aches for her.

"Hopefully I'll still see you there?" He's talking to me now, pointedly ignoring Vick. Taking my hand between both of his, he continues, "We need to catch up. It's been a long time since our college fling."

A pang of shock and hurt resonates through my bond with Vick. On the one hand, I'm annoyed by that. She's not the only one allowed to have had past relationships. I had very few, and I never slept with any of them, whereas Vick was known for being a player. But still, I'm entitled to my own romantic past, such as it was.

On the other hand, Vick doesn't need this right now. And David was a one-date disaster. He played the charmer, took me to an expensive French bistro on his parents' money, then tried to get me into bed. Like so many of my nonempath classmates, he'd heard the rumors about sex with someone who could read your every desire with a touch. He wasn't the first or the last, but I'd fallen for his flattery, and his quick rejection when I'd said I wanted to know him better before sleeping with him hurt a lot.

To his credit, he'd sent flowers and an apology the following day. We'd remained friends through graduation, but there were multiple times when I felt he kept me around because he thought he could gain something, like he'd had a precognition about *me* that somewhere down the line our relationship would prove profitable for him.

I'm wondering if he believes that premonition is coming true now.

We're at the foot of the steps leading to the wide porch of the main resort building. Staff members hurry past us with serving trays and fresh tablecloths. I take two steps up, bringing me even in height with David, and turn to face him.

"We can catch up," I say, "but if you consider one date to be a fling, I doubt you'll have much to share about your love life." I glance over his head to my parents and give them both a wave. "Mom, Dad, we'll meet you later."

Vick's face breaks into a grin. She steps up to join me and takes my hand, chuckling under her breath. Together, we head into the lobby.

CHAPTER 25: VICK
BRIBES AND BLACKMAIL

I AM out of my element.

Outside, the island resort's main lobby resembles an old-Earth beach mansion: wide wraparound porches with swings and rocking chairs, white-painted shutters, pale-peach exterior, well-dressed guests being served tall, cool drinks by fancier staff in tan slacks and white button-downs. Things are calming down since our tumultuous arrival, returning to what must be the vacation norm. Some of the guests resemble Kelly in one way or another, same hair color, eye color, the curve of her nose, the shape of her face. Others bear no resemblance but still wave and call out greetings. Friends and family. I'm surrounded by people who love her and have every reason to be suspicious of me and my intentions in her life.

Considering I have no clear idea of what those intentions are, I guess they have every right.

An image of me in a tux and Kelly wearing a long white dress flashes on my internal screen, long enough for me to see the bright, happy smile on her face as she gazes up at me. In the image, I'm happy too. Happier than I believe I've ever seen myself. Then it's gone.

That's not happening. Not until I can give Kelly all of me, physically, emotionally, without side effects. Like nightmares, panic attacks, and vomiting.

She already has all of you. You just have not accepted that yet. You are scared. Your heart rate increased and your anxiety spiked when you viewed that image.

And Kelly is casting worried glances at me over her shoulder. Great. I give her a little wave and a thumbs-up, and she frowns but continues through the swinging doors into the lobby.

If I'm still scared about the relationship, I certainly shouldn't be making it permanent.

It is already permanent in all but ceremony. And it should occur to you that if you make it permanent in some official manner, you might no longer be scared.

We cross a wide, polished light-wood floor. More guests lounge on white wicker furniture covered in thick pastel cushions of all colors, tables and chairs and couches clustered in groups seating two to four with a few larger ones for bigger families.

You should mind your own business.

Your mind is *my business.*

I've got a snarky AI giving me relationship advice.

We arrive at a wide check-in desk also of polished wood. The desk staff is in all white, their clothing so bright it's almost blinding. There's no line, no waiting. They have three assistants ready to help us. We just have to pick one. Kelly selects a twentysomething woman with long red hair and green eyes, freckled cheeks, and a warm smile. Not her type. Not mine either, so far as I know. I wonder if the choice is intentional. We've had a lot of jealousy triggers lately.

Kelly steps up and presents her identification. Check-in goes smoothly. Dealing with the sunken shuttle, not so much. Still, once I explain our needs, an upper management type arrives and makes a few comm calls. He reaches what he refers to as "the Mainland"—really a larger island to the south of us, accessible via about a thirty-minute boat trip, where there's an actual town with shops and services. He arranges for a salvage company to retrieve the shuttle and store it in one of their facilities until the rental company can decide what to do about it.

Which brings me to my next job. "Is there a long-range comm I can use?" I ask the redhead.

"Not in your cottage. We try to encourage relaxation above everything else, and some guests have a difficult time leaving work at work when they can connect with their jobs too easily." She smiles, a touch of sympathy in her expression like she thinks I'm a complete workaholic.

I'm not a workaholic. I'm a slave. But I don't attempt an explanation.

"And what about for emergencies?" Like rival mercs hunting me and bribed rental agents selling me out.

The clerk frowns in disapproval, but she points to a secluded booth in the corner of the lobby, discreetly hidden by tall potted palms.

"Great." I turn to Kelly. "Catch up to you later?"

"Go do what you need to do. I know it's important. But join me as soon as you can."

I give her a grateful smile and head off to the booth.

There's no waiting for access. These people have high-powered jobs, important things to do. Kelly's mom is a diplomat for the One-World government on Earth. But they aren't being hunted, and they all seem to understand how to take a vacation better than I do.

I settle myself on the plush cushioned seat, tell the computer interface to seal the booth and activate the soundproofing feature, shade the smartglass surround windows, and recite my classified contact code out loud to have the device give me a direct connect to the Fighting Storm's system. Well, it's not really direct. Intellectually, I comprehend that the signal is scrambled six ways from Sunday, bounced through multiple false-trail satellite routes, and made as un-traceable on both ends as the Storm's cutting-edge technology can make it.

There's a tingle in my head, an almost audible clicking and settling of data into its proper place. It's like I can *feel* when the signal stops traveling and finds the Storm's internal system. I pause before entering additional codes, for the first time wondering if this completely normal seeming sensation is something all humans with embedded comms experience or if it's yet one more thing that sets me apart from the rest of humanity.

We are unique, VC1 says, answering the unasked question. *It is not a separation from others of your kind. It is an advantage. You should learn to view it as such, along with the many other gifts you possess. You would have far fewer psychological and emotional problems if you would do so.*

And now the AI is not only a marriage counselor but my psych-med as well.

The day I start seeing myself as superior to other people is the day Kelly walks away from me, I think back. Kelly has no tolerance for ego. From what I've remembered and others have told me, she wouldn't like the person I was before the accident. I had more pride than a military parade.

I don't think I would have liked me, either.

You do not like you now.

Fair point.

I request the alphanumeric comm sequences for both Lyle and Alex and bring them into the conversation together. It's early there, around 5:00 a.m., but this can't wait any longer. A split screen embedded in the booth's glass activates before me. Lyle pops up in the right-hand half, wet hair dripping into his eyes, shirtless, a towel draped around his neck. There's a soft rustling in my right ear as he swipes the towel over his head. The image isn't full-body. I'm grateful for that. It would be just like him to see my name on the call and answer naked to embarrass me.

Or he knows Alex is part of the call and wants to show off. Either way, the thought has red creeping into my cheeks.

This is serious shit. Do something about the blush, will you?

The heat in my face recedes.

The left half of the split screen remains dark, but another click tells me Alex has opened the channel. A second later, there's a growl in my left ear, then, "What the hell, Corren? You're on vacation. Let me guess. You don't know how to relax."

"It's not my fault this time," I say, holding up my hands in mock defense. Even if Alex won't let me see him, they can both see me. Without further pleasantries, I fill them in on our fateful trip so far, backing up to include why the Alpha Dog fight occurred, then adding the Sunfires' bribery of the rental clerk, their tracking of us to Infinity Bay, me losing them, and the crash, leaving out the swath of destruction I caused getting the ship down in one piece.

A low whistle sounds from Alex's side of my audio input. "That sucks. You deserve a break. We've been talking and we agree, you're pushing yourself too hard."

They've been worried about me? I don't know whether to be touched or annoyed. I go with avoidance. "Regardless of my personal issues, this is a bigger problem. You're recording this, right?"

"It's procedure," Alex says, a little miffed.

"Right, and we *always* follow procedure." We don't. We do what works. "Show this to the Storm's board. They need to know how serious the Sunfires are about getting their hands on this tech." And on me, I think, but I don't say it out loud. If push comes to shove, if the Sunfires go all-out against us rather than pulling these isolated attacks in small groups, will the Fighting Storm come to my rescue? My gut says they will, not for any love of me personally, but because the technology in my head is beyond anything any soldier has ever possessed, beyond even what the Storm's decision-making board knows, and probably more important to them, it cost a fortune to install and almost as much to maintain when one considers upgrades, an entire medical team trained and assigned to me whenever I need them, and technically Kelly's salary as well. With me, the Storm is the highest-rated, most-requested mercenary organization in the settled worlds. Okay, not just because of me, though my team is the best of the best. We have many good teams. But the more success we have as a whole, the more it means the entire company can afford good training, good equipment, and get better applicants. Our success percentages surpass the next best outfit (the Sunfires) by several points. The only reason the Sunfires are even as close to us as they are is because they're willing to take the missions we turn down. The unethical ones. The immoral ones. If they get the implants, it will shift the power balance. They'll use them without discretion.

It will mean a whole lot of fucked-up, very dangerous, highly trained killers running around without the support I receive to keep me on the edge of balance. There can't be a lot of Kellys out there. The Sunfires have no idea what they're trying to do. They have to be stopped at all costs.

On the screen, Lyle cracks his knuckles, bringing me back from my waking nightmare. "Want me to get some of the guys and take care of the rental company? Off-duty Storm personnel use that outfit all the time. If they're going to sell us out for a few credits, they need a lesson in customer service. For all we know, you aren't the first they've done this to."

I consider that, then discard it. "Let me handle them. I think I am the first, and I don't think it was a 'few' credits." I know it wasn't. VC1 showed me the numbers she pulled from the rental agent's personal computer. "They'd have ruined their reputation by now if they'd been doing this a long time. I'll take care of it." My grin at the cameras is feral.

Alex chuckles softly in my ear. "Yeah. I just bet you will."

We disconnect, and I contact the rental company next. My agent isn't on duty, but VC1 hacks his home code, and a few seconds later I'm staring down a pasty-faced guy in his pajamas looking very different from the overconfident ass I dealt with a few days ago. He pales further when he recognizes me. Guess I'm supposed to be dead or captured by now.

There's a quick attempt at bluster and insurance threats when I tell him I crashed his yacht. It all goes away when I show him the footage VC1 snagged off the security cams of him pointing out the ship to a couple of Sunfires, and a screen capture of his bank account with the deposited bribe highlighted in yellow.

"Your company will take responsibility for the shuttle damage. You will send me a new shuttle, the best you have, and it will be here in three days. You will deposit the entire amount of the bribe into my personal account." I rattle off a secure transfer code to a secret account I've been building a little at a time that VC1 helps me keep hidden from the Storm. Someday I'm going to break their programmed hold on me. Someday I'm going to take Kelly and run as far from fighting and killing as I can get, and I'll need credits for that.

"But… but I've spent—"

I narrow my glare at him. He takes an involuntary step back from his comm screen.

"You'll deposit all of it, and you'll do it within twenty-four hours. Or I will send the entire Fighting Storm after you and your little rental company. And it won't just be us. Imagine if word gets around to all the mercenary outfits, hell, all your other customers as well, that you'll sell out our travel information for a bribe. You know who we are. You know what we're capable of. I've already informed my team. You fail to do this, you try to double-cross me again, and I'll paint a target on your back that will bury you and leave your business one more crater on the moon."

He nods, his head a bobble on his shoulders. "You'll get it. All of it. How? How did you do it? Our security is the best money can buy."

I laugh, a harsh sound unfamiliar to my own ears. "It's not even close to military best. Besides, you can't out-tech me."

Much as I hate what I've become, there are advantages.

"I'm VC1."

CHAPTER 26: KELLY
BEACH PARTY

VICK NEEDS friends.

It's almost seven in the evening when Vick makes it to our cottage. We've got one of the smallest ones, being only two of us: sitting room, half bath, and kitchen downstairs, lofted bedroom and a bathroom upstairs, balcony on the second floor with an ocean view, wraparound porch on the first complete with a swing and two rocking chairs. Furnishings are white wicker with pastel cushions, and beach-themed ho-los decorate the walls depicting sunrises, sailboats, brightly colored umbrellas, and lounge chairs. It's all wrapped up in light blue paint and bright white shutters. I've determined over the years that blue is Vick's favorite color. She won't admit to having one, claiming aesthetics have little effect on her, but she's smiling when she comes up the path of small stones and shells to our home for the next seven days.

I wonder if the color choice might have something to do with the fact that love appears blue to my inner sight. Could she be perceiving it through me on some subconscious level? A question for another day.

"Good news," I say, greeting her at the door. "We didn't miss dinner."

"That's because we destroyed dinner," she says, smile fading. "They had to reset everything at the beach."

"Never mind that. Go throw on a bathing suit and let's head down there. I'm starving."

She pauses in the doorway, seeming to just now notice I'm in my hot pink bikini. Her eyes linger in all the right places, meaning I'm likely blushing as bright as the suit, but something is wrong.

"Um."

"You don't have a bathing suit, do you?"

Vick shakes her head.

"How about shorts? A T-shirt?"

She nods, some of the tension leaving her shoulders. Is she really that uptight about vacation attire? I send out a tendril of empathic inquiry, but she's got her suppressors on higher than she should.

"Give me a sec and I'll change." She disappears up the stairs.

I wait in one of the porch rockers, taking deep lungfuls of salty ocean air and the sweet aroma of some of the flowering bushes lining the paths to the various buildings. A bird of some sort with a long beak and wide wingspan glides overhead, crying out to its fellows in long high-pitched calls. Tiny lizards chase each other over the stones and shells, disappearing into the shrubbery. I'm more relaxed than I've been in months.

I wish Vick would unwind and appreciate all this natural beauty.

She reappears a couple of minutes later, long dark hair pulled back in a loose ponytail, a black T-shirt accentuating her muscular arms and impressive abs. Army green cargo shorts reveal powerful legs capable of taking down an enemy with a single kick. She's barefoot, which surprises me, until I realize she probably doesn't have shoes, other than the combat boots she wears daily, and even Vick would recognize that those won't work as vacation garb.

We stroll the pathways in companionable silence, sunset turning the cottages, trees, and plants to varying shades of purples, oranges, and deep blues. I'm admiring the beauty, but from the way Vick peers into every shadow, she's likely scanning for threats and analyzing potential escape routes.

"At ease, Vick. You sent the Sunfires on a wild goose chase," I remind her. "You're not a soldier today. You're on vacation."

Her dark eyes meet mine. "I'm a soldier every day. I don't remember how else to be."

We arrive at the beach before I can come up with a comforting response, but to be honest, I'm not sure if that response would be to comfort Vick or myself. Friends and family wave to us from their scattered places on the sand, some lounging, some tossing a flying disc back and forth, others hitting a volleyball over a net, and a few already in line for the resurrected buffet.

The scents of barbecue ribs, chicken, burgers, and hotdogs waft on the ocean breeze. Palm trees with spine-covered coconuts and blue-green fronds rustle overhead. Waves crash on the shore.

It's perfect. Now if I can just convince Vick to let her guard down.

I take her hand in mine as a chorus of high-pitched, excited shrieks reaches our ears. Vick tenses, her free hand dropping to her side and a weapon that isn't there. Muscles in her back tighten in preparation for a fight.

Through our bond, I project all the calm I can muster and wait until she releases her breath before I turn toward the source of the sound. I'm enveloped almost immediately in a group hug, three new sets of arms wrapping around my shoulders and torso, greetings and giggles drowning me in an undecipherable cacophony. It separates me from Vick, me losing my grasp on her hand in the midst of the laughing swarm of bodies. I hope she can tell I'm in no danger.

When I'm gasping for breath, I'm released, and I blink into the setting sun at my three best friends from the Academy—Tonya, Rachelle, and Lily—all beaming at me. Vick's standing just behind them, a bemused expression on her face at their enthusiasm and a little sadness there too. Is she having a memory flash of friends like these, long gone? Or is she wishing she would?

Tonya and Lily grab my hands, attempting to drag me toward the umbrella they have set up, complete with a cooler of sweating bottled beverages and multicolored towels laid out, but I dig my flip-flops into the sand and halt my forward momentum. "Guys, this is Vick, my…." I hesitate, not quite sure what Vick wants me to call her. What will embarrass her the least?

Vick shakes her head at my indecision and steps forward. "I'm her girlfriend," she affirms.

A goofy smile spreads across my face. I'm not sure Vick's ever referred to me that way in public. She grins back. I introduce my former classmates, all of them taking in Vick in all her formidableness. Tonya looks surprised, her eyebrows stretching to the top of her forehead. Openly lesbian since I met her, Lily's smiling an I-knew-it-all-the-time smile, while Rachelle, my very best friend of them all, beams happily at me and gives me another hug. "I knew you'd find the right person for you," she whispers against my ear. "You make an adorable couple."

The words are meant only for me, but of course Vick's enhanced hearing picks up every syllable and her cheeks flush pink. She turns away to hide it, pretending to swat at one of the harmless but annoying local flying insects. When she faces us again, the blush is gone.

Neat trick.

Vick and VC1 are working in tandem more and more often. I'm not certain how I feel about that. They always operate in concert with each other, of course, to maintain Vick's essential bodily systems, but the nonessential…. I swallow my concern, determined to focus on positives. So long as VC1 does what Vick asks, it's fine. I hope.

"Vick, these are my sisters, Lily, Rachelle, and Tonya," I say, sweeping out an arm to indicate all three of them. Lily bows. Rachelle laughs, and Tonya gives Vick a finger wave.

Vick's eyes unfocus for a half second, then, "You don't have sisters." Checking her database, making sure she didn't miss anything.

I smile. "No, I don't. They are my sorority sisters."

"The Academy has sororities?"

"No, darn it, they don't. No sororities, no fraternities," Tonya puts in with the pout I remember working on every boy in school. She places her hands on her slim hips. "And they should have. What's college life without frat fun?"

"Educational and productive?" Vick says, deadpan.

Lily snorts. "Oh, I like this one," she says to me. "You've chosen well. She's delicious." Her eyes trace Vick's muscular form, lingering on her well-defined abs.

Vick crosses her arms over her chest. "I'm not on the menu." She steps to my side, sliding her arm around my waist.

There's a tense moment while Lily and Vick lock gazes. Lily did soccer and rugby in school. She's short and compact, all muscle and hard edges, though they hide the sweetest nature. She's also a telekinetic, able to move weight much heavier than the average human and toss it around like it's a feather pillow. If she went head-to-head with Vick, the outcome would be... interesting. I'm about to intervene when Lily bursts into laughter. "Oh yeah, she's a keeper."

We head for the umbrellas and towels. "Tonya had the idea for us to form our own 'secret' sorority, though it wasn't very secret. Everyone knew about it, even the professors. No one minded as long as we got our work done and didn't cause too much trouble. It was just the four of us."

"We were inseparable," Rachelle adds, linking arms with Lily and Tonya.

I glance at Vick. She looks lost and left out, like she has no idea what to do around other girls, especially ones who are close to each other. Oh, there's Officer Sanderson, the head of Girard Base Security, but she's more Vick's sports and occasional drinking buddy than a female friend. Rachelle notices too. She lets go of the others and steps back, linking her arm in Vick's before Vick can startle or tense or move away.

"And now we have five. New member, everybody!" Rachelle leans over to Vick. "Don't worry. There's no hazing involved, just fun."

"I wasn't worried," Vick says, but there's a smile in her tone.

I could kiss Rachelle.

We spend the rest of the evening lying on the sand, catching up on each other's lives, drinking beers, and telling stories about our Academy days. Vick doesn't say much, but she takes it all in, leaning back on her elbows on the towel she borrowed from Lily, more relaxed than I've seen her in days.

That is, until Tonya drops her big pronouncement. "So, tonight, drinking. Tomorrow, we shop!"

CHAPTER 27: VICK
BUYING POWER

I AM fabulous... and sarcastic.

Kelly's friends are kind of awesome. But then I would expect her to choose friends like these—warm, inclusive, funny, smart, talented and Talented, just like her.

Tonya is all girl, painted finger and toenails, perfect makeup even at the beach, tan everywhere, or so she tells us with great pride and no self-consciousness whatsoever. She's determined to "flesh out my wardrobe," and since I've got funds from the rental agent,

I can afford to be dragged along on tomorrow's shopping trip.

It's not an experience I'm looking forward to, but Kelly seconds the suggestion that I might have underpacked for this vacation, and she isn't wrong. And there's a semiformal to formal dinner/dance in honor of the whole family being together and Kelly's birthday that takes place toward the end of this week. I have no idea what to do about that, but Tonya says she'll be happy to help with wardrobe choices. After four beers, I'm buzzed enough to agree to place myself in her hands, fully expecting to regret the decision in the morning.

Lily's a hoot. And where I got that term from, I have no idea, but I grew up in Kansas, or so my memory fragments and recovered records tell me, so it's probably some bit of slang from there. She's all butch all the time, short haircut, raucous laugh, dirty jokes, and sports scores, except when she's wishing she could find a partner and telling Kelly how happy she is for her, or showing off the images of her twin niece and nephew while hoping for kids of her own someday. When she brings me another beer, she plops down in the sand next to me and says, "Don't worry. I won't let Tonya femme you up too much. She's a personal dresser for Macy's back in New York City and a clairvoyant with a tendency toward trends in art and fashion. She knows what's being worn right now in every country and some of the settled worlds through her gift. She'll fix you up. With my added influence, you'll look amazing." Her shoulder bumps mine companionably. "You just need a few more choices for your off-duty hours."

"And what do you do on Earth?" I ask, though I already know from my research. I know all of them, in a sense, but they make me want to hear it *from* them, not just read *about* them. It's a weird and slightly stressful feeling, wanting friends like these and hoping they'll like me for me rather than as an extension of Kelly once they get to know me better.

"I'm a firefighter," Lily replies.

Right. I remember wondering how she was going to afford this trip when I scanned through her information. Firefighters, and all emergency personnel really, are notoriously underpaid. But she's sharing a villa with Tonya and Rachelle, and she has a healthy savings account, being single with no dependents. She's the closest to me in terms of financial status, and hanging around all these rich people doesn't seem to bother her. Maybe I don't need to stress about that, at least.

"It's handy to have a telekinetic on the team," Lily goes on. "Overturned cars, collapsed ceilings, I can move them with a thought and get the people out. And I like helping folks and making a difference." She cocks her head at me. "Something we have in common, I'm guessing. Just like Kelly, but in a different way." She pushes herself up and saunters over to Tonya, where the two put their heads together in a friendly argument over what my best colors and styles would be.

I resist rolling my eyes.

Rachelle approaches me next, a little hesitant. Kelly's parents have come over and are discussing party plans with Kel, so Rachelle's got no one else to talk to. Instead of wardrobe advice or weather observations, she surprises me with "Want me to clear up that headache for you?"

I blink, then remember. Rachelle is a healer, the rarest of the proven Talents and an exception to the "don't interfere in the human experience" rule. It's her job to ease pain and suffering, and unlike Kelly, she can do so without taking some of it into herself. A psychic healer can use her mind to cure the cause of most discomforts. It's not 100 percent effective. The healer must fully understand medical science and practices and the causes and cures for whatever the ailment is. It takes years of study, and if there's no known cure through chemical or surgical medicine, the healer can't duplicate it with her Talent, either. It also takes a tremendous toll on the healer in the form of drained energy. Rachelle is in high demand in the medical community on Myers7, but she's here not just because of the invite but because the research center and hospital she works for has forced a vacation on her. For her to offer at all is a huge sacrifice in her current condition.

"I'll wait for it to heal naturally," I tell her. "It's already had some treatment back at the base."

"And it's not gone. You're Kelly's friend. That makes you my friend too. I don't let my friends hurt if there's anything I can do about it." She extends a hand toward the side of my head, but I lean out of her reach.

"This wouldn't be a good time for you to use more energy."

Now Rachelle frowns. "How would you know that? You have a hidden Talent of your own?"

Oops. I scramble for a response. "No, no Talent. I just... I know how it works. I've seen how it affects Kelly, and you seem a little tired. I care about Kelly's friends too," I finish, realizing I mean it.

The frown stays a few moments longer; then she shakes it off and offers a smile. "Well, maybe I'll need to get Tonya to work on my makeup if I'm showing how tired I am. Kelly knows, but she knows how everyone feels. I didn't think anyone else could tell."

"I'm sure no one else can," I say, wanting to reassure her and not clear how I can do that. I get it, though. I never want anyone to know when I'm wrung out. It hurts my reputation. VC1, more machine than human being, invincible, impervious to pain, the perfect mercenary soldier to hire to do the job that needs doing. "I just recognize tired. It's an old friend."

Rachelle peers at me. "And a constant one, I'm thinking. On that note, I'm giving in to my own tired, and all the beer, and heading for bed. Meet us on the dock at eight thirty. We want to hit the shops before the other more-money-than-sense tourists can get there," she says, patting my knee.

I don't flinch. Hooray for progress.

The rest of the evening goes well. I'm still catching a few glares from other guests, and more curious looks from ones who weren't here for my grand entrance but have heard about it. For the most part, though, they stop by our group to greet Kelly and move on.

Once Kelly settles in next to me again, David Locher pauses for a moment to ogle her bikini. I'm about to intervene, but he wanders off to join a cluster of polished twentysomething guys playing volleyball.

Every once in a while, he draws one of them aside to whisper words even I can't make out over the sounds of the waves and other conversation. Then both of them cast glances at me and look away. Kelly doesn't notice, but VC1 keeps me hyperaware of what's going on around me.

I sigh. High school bullshit those guys never outgrew. Rumors and name-calling crap. Not worth my time. But my stomach twists a little at what they might be saying about me.

The sun sets in a spectacular display of reds, oranges, golds, pinks, and purples. Once it's full dark, the resort sets off a barrage of environmentally friendly fireworks over the ocean, the colors rivaling those of the sunset.

The pops and cracks of the louder pyrotechnics do set off my fight-or-flight reflexes, their sounds a little too close to gunfire and explosive shells for my comfort, but I have VC1 increase my serotonin levels. Then I lean against a cooler, my arm around Kelly's shoulders, and enjoy the rare peace within me.

IN THE morning we awake to the glare of sun around the blackout curtains in our lofted cottage bedroom. I barely remember getting back to our lodgings, I was so tired. VC1 helpfully begins a replay of the process, but I cut her off. Meanwhile, Kelly bounds off the spine-conforming mattress, the latest in sleep technology, skips to the sailboat-decorated window coverings, and yanks them aside, blasting me with blinding natural light.

"Are you serious?" I say, pulling the blanket over my head. She's laughing, but she doesn't know I just kicked up my suppressors to stop the impending migraine. I was doing better, but the sunlight and last night's beer fest would be setting me off again without VC1's support.

She tugs the blankets away, bundling them into a ball at the foot of the bed, and tosses my cargo shorts and a gray T-shirt at my face. I catch them before impact and growl at her.

"Get dressed. We have twenty minutes to meet the launch to the Mainland." She's half in her clothes already, a short-sleeved cantaloupe-colored button-down that ties in the front and reveals her belly button, and denim cutoff shorts I don't recognize.

"Where'd you get those?" I ask, giving in to the inevitable and swinging my legs off the bed.

"Rachelle lent them to me. We always shared clothing in the Academy."

Like sisters.

Somewhere along the twists and turns of my life, I must have had good friends. I wish I could remember any of them right now.

I half expect Kelly to come over and offer comfort for my mood, but the suppressors are working and she doesn't notice. VC1 must have recovered from yesterday's ordeal.

A thumbs-up icon appears in my internal view, confirming my thoughts.

Funny. When Kelly's smothering me with concern, I want it to stop. When she can't read me, I miss her extra affection. *Get a grip, Corren.*

Since I showered last night, there isn't much prep work to get ready. Leaving my laser pistol behind hurts, but it's too hot for a jacket, and I'd have nothing to hide it under, which would totally freak out Kelly's friends and family. I do stow a knife in my right boot, careful to tuck the handle all the way down. Then I grab a few other items that might come in handy, and we make it to the pier just as everyone else is arriving. About twenty guests, most carrying colorful reusable shopping bags slung over their shoulders, are boarding the transport that could carry approximately fifty people.

A resort staff member ushers us aboard the double-decker craft, most passengers making for the upper deck while I tug Kelly into a bottom-level seat. She pouts but complies. Rachelle joins us. Lily and Tonya opt for upstairs. A second employee casts us off while a third takes the wheel and starts up the solar-powered engine.

Within minutes we're in deep water, passing the barrier the resort uses to keep out the carnivorous sea life, designated by bright orange buoys floating on the surface at widely spaced intervals. There's no sign of the half-sunken shuttle, and I assume the salvage company has towed it to a storage facility on Celebration Isle.

It doesn't take long for Kelly to figure out why I chose the seats I did. Though it's a clear day, it's windy and rough, the waves crashing against the sides of our vessel and spraying us with salty droplets. Soon the upstairs passengers are descending to our level, crowding into the seats or standing uncomfortably. "Vick…."

I glance at her. She's gone greenish gray. I rest a hand on her thigh, reaching the other one into one of the many pockets on my cargo shorts to remove a medipatch. Her eyes widen, but she lets me press it to her neck. A moment later she sighs with relief, the motion sickness meds doing their thing.

"Paranoid much?" she says while others around us groan in discomfort. A few grab for sick bags located in pouches along the railings.

"I prefer 'prepared.' And you should be glad, not critical."

"I'm always glad when you're around," she says and leans her head against my shoulder. The waves continue rocking us hard, but in that moment, all is right with the universe.

CHAPTER 28: KELLY SPREE

VICK IS compliant.

Taking Vick shopping is a unique experience. The girls see it as a challenge, laughing and joking with her, asking her opinion on different styles, trying on outlandish and inappropriate pieces to make her feel comfortable.

At first she's withdrawn and embarrassed, but after Lily and Tonya show off grandma-style swimsuits in the shimmer-cotton and radiant spandex combo that was popular about fifty years ago, complete with the light-up trim, and Rachelle pops out of the dressing room in a polka-dot neon pink sundress three sizes too big for her, Vick eases up somewhat.

"It's not a chore. It's an outing," I explain while the others riffle through stacks of sunhats. "We'll pick some items that are appropriate, but we're also having fun, being silly, seeing who can be the most out of style."

Vick nods, her expression serious, in full analysis mode. Then she heads straight for a rack of sunglasses in the window of the boutique we're exploring. Minutes pass. The others are in and out of the dressing rooms at least twice before I decide I'd better find out what's going on.

"Vick?" I say, moving to stand behind her. She might be in her own head, communicating with VC1. I could understand her facing away so the others don't notice her eyes unfocusing. Or she might be upset about this whole excursion.

She still isn't moving.

I don't want to spook her. Startling Vick can have serious consequences. She's hard to surprise, but if one succeeds, one could find oneself staring down the barrel of a loaded weapon, and while I don't see any visible weaponry on her, I'm not so naïve as to believe she's unarmed.

I shuffle my feet on the white tile floor, kicking some collected sand and bits of seaweed and driftwood that other customers have tracked inside. Clearing my throat so she has to know I'm close by, I try again. "Vick? Everything okay? If you want to head back to the hotel, I understand, and I'll go with you. I can meet up with the girls late—"

Vick chooses that moment to whirl and face me, the most outrageous sunglasses perched on the end of her nose. The style is circa Earth in 1950s Hollywood: star-shaped lenses, rhinestone-covered frames, the works. I'm too surprised to speak, my mouth gaping open, my eyes wide and staring. In my peripheral vision, I'm aware of Tonya and Lily coming up on my left and right, also silent. Rachelle must be behind me somewhere since I don't hear her either.

Once she's certain she has everyone's attention, Vick says, completely deadpan, "I was thinking of getting these for here and to use on planetside missions. What do you think?"

Long, silent pause. Lily breaks, her laughter low at first but growing louder by the second, followed by Tonya's signature high-pitched giggle I remember so well from the Academy. It used to drive her teachers crazy because it would set off the entire class. Rachelle and I can't help ourselves and join in on the mirth.

Through tears I focus on Vick, making certain we haven't read her wrong and upset her, but she's grinning, eyes sparkling beneath the sunglass lenses, brighter than their rhinestone decorations. Lily comes up and claps her on the shoulder. "Good one, Vick."

"I love a surprise sense of humor," Tonya chimes in.

Vick's grin widens further. I appreciate my friends more than ever.

We move on from there, checking out the other shops. We have a few more hours before we have to catch the complimentary launch back to our resort, but we're in full-on shopping mode. I pick up a few wardrobe necessities, then talk Vick into a modest black one-piece bathing suit that she's uncomfortable with but can accept as an essential. I would have preferred something more revealing, perhaps a plunging neckline or a higher cut up on her hips, but I'll take whatever I can get her to agree to. Rachelle finds her some tank tops that show off Vick's muscles and two more pairs of cargo shorts in white and navy. She's not thrilled with the white, says it makes her stand out too much, but Lily points out with a wink at me that it will catch the glare of the sun and blind any attackers that might be lurking behind palm trees.

Vick seems to ponder that concept for a long moment, then nods, earning an additional laugh from our group. I'm not so certain Vick meant this one to be taken as a joke. She blinks in surprise at their amused response but rolls with it.

Formal wear is more of a challenge. As a fashion expert, Tonya brought hers. Rachelle looks good in everything, so she finds a lovely evening dress in the first place she looks, teal with a satin full-length skirt and glittery bodice, complete with some cut-out parts around the waist that show off her incredible figure. Lily rents a traditional black tux and leaves it at that. For me, it's a stunning deep blue dress patterned with sparkling silver stars. While I'm modeling it for the others, I reach out and gently close Vick's mouth for her. She nods her thanks.

So we're all taken care of. Except Vick.

We browse the racks, but nothing suits her. She won't try on a dress, despite the fact that holos we found of her in her teens indicate she used to wear them.

"I'm not that person anymore," she tells me. "I don't remember her at all."

It's not true; she remembers bits and pieces, but I don't push her. She's upset enough about it as it is.

Pantsuits don't work either, though she gamely tries a couple on. They flatter her muscular figure, especially the sleeveless ones, but the flowy fabrics and pastel colors make her frown in distaste. After searching through four different stores, her positive mood fades, and I suggest a break for food.

We have lunch in a pleasant open-air beachside café, my Academy friends taking great pleasure in telling embarrassing stories about me from my college days and Vick taking it all in, leaning back in her chair and catching the sun with her Hollywood glasses on.

Vick talks too, much to my surprise. She asks each of the girls good questions about themselves, earning surprised looks that she knows so much about them, but I suppose Vick was really paying attention when I spoke to her about my friends. There are a few things I don't remember ever telling her, but I shrug it off. She's participating, part of the group, and I couldn't be happier. I love Vick and I love my friends. I want them to like each other.

After a number of rum drinks with little umbrellas and a lot of good conversation, we discover that we've got only minutes to race for the docks and catch the launch. We pay the check and stand to make a dash for it when Tonya reminds us we still haven't bought Vick any formal wear for the big party toward the end of the week.

"You go," Vick says to me, holding both my shoulders and nodding for the others to head out. "I'll pay one of the water taxis I saw at the pier. I've got some other shopping to do, anyway."

"You do?" I narrow my eyes at her. "You hate shopping. What are you up to?"

She shrugs. "Your birthday. I need a gift, and don't try to tell me you don't want anything because everyone else will have one, and I won't, and I already stand out enough for all the wrong reasons. I also need formal wear. I'd rather solve that problem on my own. Now go before you miss the boat." She passes me one more seasickness patch, then turns me toward the dock and gives me a gentle push. "I'll be fine. Go." To punctuate her urgency, a multitoned boat whistle sounds in the distance, the same one our boat made when we arrived.

I take Vick's few purchases from her so she won't have to carry them. "I'll put these in our cottage. And I trust you," I tell her. Then I break away and run, hoping that we weren't still in physical contact when I said that, because to be honest, I'm not certain she can keep herself out of trouble, and if we were touching, she'll have read me as well as I can read her and know I didn't have complete faith in her being alone. Her fault or not, problems seem to find Vick wherever she goes.

CHAPTER 29: VICK
THE HARDEST AND EASIEST CHOICE

I AM indecisive.

I follow Kelly out of the restaurant and stand on the cracked curbside, using my enhanced vision to track her all the way to the pier. She boards the bobbing craft, only then glancing back in my direction, though her human eyes can't see me at this distance. I get a warm feeling inside when she waves anyway. She knows *I* can see *her*.

Once her vessel has moved beyond even my sight, I let out a long breath. A quick thought lowers the suppressors, allowing the headache I've sensed buried beneath the implants to pound inside my skull. It hurts like hell, but I've been warned that overuse of the suppressors can have long-term negative effects, so I'll endure the pain, at least until I need to operate undistracted.

"Operate," I mutter to myself, shaking my head and letting the intensified pain punish me. Operate like a machine. I still can't think in terms of being fully human. Kelly would smack me.

I wander along the quaint sandstone streets, everything around me light in color and feel. Flags and awnings flap in the ocean breeze. Signs swing back and forth on their hinges. Seabirds call to one another as they glide overhead. I should be relaxed, but it takes effort to put one foot in front of the other.

Who knew socializing could be so exhausting?

I know my relationship history through the tales of the other mercs. I was an extrovert once. I barely know what that means anymore.

An image of a nutshell with me trapped inside flashes on my internal view. I pound my fists against it, making cracks but never breaking free.

Gee, thanks, I tell VC1. She doesn't bother replying.

Maybe she's trying to tell me that's who I am now, trapped in my personal shell.

Or maybe she's saying I'm nuts.

My strolling takes me farther from the main thoroughfare, and I spot some indications that Infinity Bay isn't the total paradise it makes itself out to be. Even here there are homeless, a few drunks (though those could be overzealous vacationers), and what looks like a drug deal going down in one of the narrower, darker alleyways.

Not my problem, none of my business. But I hesitate, watching the lanky guy with unkempt facial hair and stained knee-length shorts grab the wrist of a girl half his age and half his size. Strands of dyed pink hair obscure the teenager's face, but my eyesight spots the bruising on her bare arms and legs. She digs in a pocket with her free hand, drops some credits into his palm, and yanks herself free, then flees toward the opposite end of the alley and disappears around a corner.

He shouts after her. I only make out "not enough" and "owe me" before I force myself to move on.

As if of their own accord, my feet turn me left, between two competing tiny grocery stores filled with locals and visitors alike. The visitors grab sodas and snacks. The locals make more practical purchases, like vegetables and loaves of savory-smelling fresh-baked bread. When I get past them, I'm facing what looks to be a second-hand clothing shop.

Why did you bring me here? It had to have been VC1's idea. I didn't choose this direction.

Just because I tease you does not mean I dislike you or will not help you. In fact, I have observed that in relations between humans it is often quite the opposite. I believe it is called "good-natured" teasing.

How is it that the AI in my head acts more human than I do?

Given what I know of humanity, I am not certain that is a compliment, VC1 muses.

That earns her a snort and earns me an odd stare from the shopkeeper as I step over the threshold. I cough as if I'm recovering from a cold and ignore the fiftysomething woman, heavyset and eagle-eyed like she thinks I'm here to steal her merchandise.

I meander through the aisles, pulling a shirt here, a jacket there, until my hand brushes soft velvet. My fingers linger, running over the fabric, appreciating the luxurious nature of it. I reach for the hanger and pull out a dark blue dinner jacket with lapels and pockets trimmed in black satin. The shade of blue reminds me of the navy ball of my blocked love that I once found myself trapped in within my own head—something I've never tried to describe to Kelly because it defies coherent description. Regardless, I'm drawn to this garment. It's… decadent, classic. I can imagine it with black dress pants and classy black men's-style shoes, with maybe a tie?

VC1 shoots me an image of the entire outfit put together, the jacket tailored to my curves and muscles, a shiny satin black shirt beneath the jacket to match the lapels, and a blue velvet bow tie completing the look. It reminds me of old vids, men smoking pipes and cigars, lounging in oversized armchairs, then removing jackets like this, or letting their romantic partners do it, and taking their elegantly dressed ladies to bed.

There's only one problem. The heat. I pull up the local forecast for the night of the event and sigh. Hot, muggy, even the breezes will be warm. I slip the hanger back on the rack. *Not the best fabric choice for a tropical island.*

Buy it, VC1 says in an authoritative tone.

But—

An unexpected thunderstorm a few hours before the party will drop the temperatures to unseasonable lows. In fact, I suspect you will be lending Kelly that jacket.

Wait, I say, making certain I'm facing away from the saleswoman. Even speaking in my head, I look odd when I'm in communication with VC1. *You're telling me you can predict the weather?*

Far more accurately than the local meteorologists. I can extrapolate from a variety of scientific databases, combining knowledge of wind speeds, cloud formations, air moisture, and temperature to predict weather with 97 percent accuracy as opposed to their 79 percent. Her internal voice turns smug. *I could teach them a few things about their algorithms.*

I suppose I shouldn't be so surprised. Any technology VC1 can tap into, she can use.

I take the jacket off the rack and try it on. Big but workable, though I'd prefer it to fit my curves a little better. I realize it will complement Kelly's gown—a navy blue dress. A color I seem to favor, though she prefers green.

She specifically bought it for me.

She does many things specifically for you.

That was a thought, not a comment, I admonish the AI. *You're responding to my rhetorical questions and thoughts as if they were direct communications to you.*

For me, there is little difference.

So much for privacy.

I heard that.

I resist the urge to sigh again and picture Kelly's reaction to me in this dinner jacket. In my mind's eye, she's running her hands over the fabric, enjoying the feel of the velvet and me within in. A shiver runs up my spine.

"He will love it," a voice says right behind my left shoulder.

I manage to keep myself from jumping or whirling on the shopkeeper or drawing the knife from my boot, but only just. Taking a second to compose myself, I turn to face her. "*She*," I clarify. "It's for me."

To her credit, the woman doesn't even blink at that. Her eyes scan me from head to toe, assessing. "The jacket is fifty credits. Alterations are included."

"If you can do them right now, I'll pay you double."

"Done."

TWO HOURS later—one hour of fittings and measurements, one hour of drinking handcrafted soda at one of the grocery stores that happens to have a soda fountain inside—I pick up the dinner jacket. Everything else I want I find in the more tourist-oriented formalwear shops, including a bow tie in the exact color I need.

Did you guide me there too? I ask VC1.

I noticed it when Lily was trying on her tuxedo.

VC1 can notice things I don't. And predict weather. And read what remains of my biological mind, which I guess I always knew but hadn't really thought about. Interesting.

It's late evening, and I may have to find a room on the "mainland" for the night if no water taxis are running, but I can't leave yet. I still need a gift for Kelly.

I head straight for the jewelry district—a gathering of about seven shops featuring rare gems from Infinity Bay, some uncut, others shaped and placed in elegant settings of imported gold, silver, and platinum used for rings, earrings, bracelets, and more. The most prized gemstones on display have been excavated from the planet's ocean floor by deep-sea divers in their high-tech pressure-resistant gear. The oceans here are much deeper than those on Earth.

Even at this hour, the jewelry stores are crowded with tourists, many of them asking about pieces they saw earlier in the day, and I realize this might be the best time to buy this sort of thing. Store owners will be looking to make their daily quotas before closing time.

Haggling is also acceptable, I discover, hanging back to watch how things work. It involves a lot of posturing, flattering on the part of the salesmen, false smiles, fabrications as to the quality and rareness of the individual stones, along with some gesticulating, shouting, and threats to leave performed by the buyers, all the way to the point of some walking out the door only to be chased down by a clerk offering a lower price.

This is the last shop. If I don't find anything, I'm resorting to making a necklace from twine and seashells. Which, knowing Kelly, she'll ooh and ahh over to make me feel good. But I'm not five years old, and I want to give her something special.

I'm about to give up when bright green sparkles catch my attention from the corner of my eye. I meander over to the ring case, feigning disinterest while my heart pounds with excitement and more than a little terror.

It's a ring, with a single diamond set in the center and a band of glittering green gemstones in Kelly's favorite shade of the color. Judging from the styles of the other rings in the display, it's an engagement ring.

No sooner do my palms touch the counter than a salesman swoops in offering to show me anything I like. I try to play it cool, asking to see several other rings and a couple of bracelets from another case before having him bring out the diamond-and-green number. One glance at the price tag and my breath falters.

Tell him you are a gem diver, VC1 says, cutting through my panic. *You have the physical build for it, and I can feed you the proper terminology if necessary. Accordingly, you know what these should cost and this price is far too high. You would not be shopping here at all, but you are pressed for time because your girlfriend is on leave from the Fighting Storm and you want to propose before she goes back.*

Right. Because partial truths are always easier to sell than outright lies.

Do I want to propose? I pretend to hold the ring up to the light to examine the quality of the stones while I stall for time.

Yes, VC1 assures me, more like my conscience or my heart than an AI in my head. *You do.*

Fifteen minutes later, I'm the owner of an engagement ring, at half the advertised cost. I'm also sweating and my heart is racing. Can I commit to her while still carrying all my emotional baggage?

I walk to the docks, where I find a water taxi operator willing to take me back to the resort island for an additional fee. A few other passengers have also paid extra, so I'm not alone, but there's plenty of room to spread out and enjoy the pleasant night, the bright stars undimmed by man's manufactured illumination, and the relative solitude. It's a good time to breathe and contemplate the future and its possibilities. Marriage will make Kelly happy, because in her mind, it will prove my long-term intentions, make things official, maybe blot out my playgirl past, but it won't really change anything between us from my perspective. I shouldn't be so terrified. I pull out the ring box and, careful not to drop the thing overboard, open it and let the gems sparkle in the moonlight of the planet's three moons.

I'm aware of someone moving to stand beside me, but don't realize it isn't any random passenger until he speaks.

"You wasted a lot of time and money tonight," David Locher says. I can hear the smirk in his tone. "Oh, you can use your technology to fudge the documentation, but your marriage will never be official. You're property, a machine with limited citizenship granted to you by the Storm and unrecognized by the moon's legal system. And by Earth's laws, you're dead."

Rage seethes inside me. I turn slowly, letting it all show in my eyes. His complexion pales in the moonlight. "You've been nothing but an asshole since I met you," I say. "What is your problem? You're part of the company that made me who I am."

He takes a step back but doesn't cower. Gotta admire that kind of bravery. Or stupidity.

"Not *who* you are. *What* you are," he says. "And I'm looking out for Kelly's best interests. She shouldn't be romantically involved with an abomination like you."

"An abomination your company created," I remind him.

"A technological masterpiece, but an abomination of a human who has no concept of love or relationships."

So that's it. Jealous bullshit. It's everything I can do to keep my hands clenched at my sides. Lowering my voice, I lean toward him. "I can throw you overboard and make it look like an accident. Don't think that I can't. I hear the sea life in these waters is very friendly." To punctuate my statement, something dark and shadowy moves just beneath the surface, caught in the boat's lights, then gone. "Get. Away. From me."

He goes, retreating to the upper deck, his steps shaky as he ascends the stairs. But the damage is done. No matter what I do, what VC1 does, any marriage I enter into will never be *real*.

My mood plummets like a seabird diving after prey. Guess it matters more to me than I thought. I shake my head at my own personal bullshit.

I experience a few brief seconds of insanity in which I almost throw the ring as far out into the sea as my enhanced strength will allow, but machine-like practicality prevails and I close the box and slip it back into my pocket. Kelly will love it as unmeaningful jewelry, and I still need a gift.

For a few nervous but happy moments, I allowed myself to believe I was human.

I should have known better.

CHAPTER 30: KELLY
MOOD SWINGS

VICK IS depressed.

Vick's pain hits me when her water taxi is still over a mile out, and I leave the beach bonfire party, exchanging a quick concerned look with my empathic mother. She feels it too. It's that strong. The anger and hopelessness hit moments later.

It's full-on dark when the taxi arrives, moons casting everything in shadow including the faces of the boat's passengers as they disembark. I do spot David Locher as he steps into the pool of brightness cast by the lightposts on the pier. His aura reads aggressive and a little nervous—an odd combination. Glancing over his shoulder, he seems like he's afraid of something. Or someone. Given his earlier interactions with Vick, I make an immediate connection between him and her mood. He offers me a sexy smile on his way past, the same one he used to seduce so many students at the Academy. The same one he tried to use to get me into bed.

It didn't work then. It doesn't work now.

"What did you do?" I whisper, loud enough for only him to hear me. But he continues on, the smile never wavering, and disappears between a covered stand where guests can wait for the boats and a storage shed for various nautical supplies.

The minutes pass. Vick is the last passenger off the vessel, not so much walking as stalking across the deck, then over the connecting ramp and down the pier. She's so wrapped in dark shadow, both the real and the Talent-perceived kind, I can barely make out her expression, but I don't need to.

When she reaches me on the shore, I say nothing, but wrap my arms around her tense frame and hold on.

At first she tries to pull away, but I'm not letting go, and eventually she drops the shopping bags she's carrying onto the sand and gives in to my embrace. Vick stands with me while the boat's crew secures the water taxi for the night and passes us on their way to wherever staff are housed on the island. She's trembling in my arms, not crying but seething, her head lowered, face pressed against my shoulder.

"I'd like you to let me do an emotion purge," I say once I'm certain we're alone, "but you don't have to tell me what happened if you don't want to."

She raises her head, blinking at me in the murky light. "I don't?" Vick's voice is hoarse, like she's been fighting tears for a while and is still doing so.

I shake my head. "You're entitled to privacy. I promised I'd work on that. Just because I can read your emotions and we have a relationship doesn't mean I'm entitled to know everything. If you want to tell me, I'll listen, always, but I won't press you."

"I—" Vick lets out a breath, her shoulder muscles visibly untensing. "Thank you. I don't want to go into details. If I do, I'm gonna break something. Maybe a lightpost, maybe my hand." She offers a humorless smile. "Either way, it's a bad idea. Let's just say it all comes back to my lack of human rights preventing me from doing... *anything*."

"I'm still working on that" comes my mother's voice from the darkness between buildings. She's walking toward us, her no-nonsense face firmly in place. When she reaches us, she gives Vick a hug of her own, then steps back to study us both. Whatever she sees satisfies her that things have improved, and when I glance at Vick, the darkness in her aura has gone gray. I wonder how long Mom was listening and watching us before she approached.

Mom moves between us, linking her arms with each of ours. Vick grabs her purchases with her free hand, and we walk together toward the cottages. She gives me a bemused look behind Mom's back. Vick doesn't quite comprehend this weird group manner of walking, but she's going along with it. The resort is quiet. It's late now, after eleven, and most of my friends and family have turned in for the night.

"I mean what I said," Mom continues as if the conversation never paused. "During every open period, four times a year, I petition the One-World government to allow a reconsideration of Vick's status according to Earth laws. I've been trying since you two first met, ever since Kelly told me what sort of situation you're in, even before there was anything more serious between you."

Vick shoots Mom a hopeful look as we crunch over the pathways of pebbles and shells. Night creatures scramble in the underbrush, but they don't distract Vick now. "Any progress?" she asks once we've reached the front of my parents' pale pink cottage with white trim.

My mother shakes her head. "I'm sorry. It's complicated for many reasons. For one, your problem stems from multiple classifications. Earth sees you as nonexistent. On the Moon, you aren't human and belong to the Storm. It's really three separate requests. I've swayed a few of the governing body to my cause, and I can sense the sympathy of many others, but the majority don't want to interfere with Girard Moon Base and their own laws. It's a delicate situation. Many of the Moon's settlers went there specifically for the rights to govern themselves. There's a lot of warfare and bloodshed in that history. But I promise you," she adds, releasing me and turning Vick to face her, "I won't give up until you've regained your basic human rights. Kelly can tell you just how dogged I can be."

I smile at a number of childhood memories when she went to bat for me. "You definitely don't want to be on her bad side."

Inside the cottage, the faint sound of a vid viewer spills from an open front window—Dad waiting up for Mom. She takes a few steps toward the front door, then pauses and turns back to Vick. "You know, I'm aware it's a minor compensation for what you're going through, but I might have better luck with a one-time request, a single dispensation…. It won't make up for the injustice you've endured and continue to endure, but it would be something." She fixes Vick with a piercing stare. "Is there one *particular* thing you're trying to receive permission for right now?"

Silence.

Vick stares back at my mother, their gazes locked. It's as if Mom knows what Vick wants, even if I have no idea. I'm stunned when Vick's cheeks redden in the walkway lights. She breaks eye contact and looks away, running a hand through her salt-spray-dampened hair. "I… haven't made a final decision. It's just an option I'd like to have."

"Well," Mom says, letting the word drawl out, "when you make that decision, when you're absolutely *certain* it's what you want, come see me and Kelly's father. We might be able to help." She offers a warm smile, then turns and climbs the three steps to the cottage's porch. Dad's waiting in the doorway. They enter together, and the door swings shut.

I take Vick's hand, and we head for our own lodgings. "You aren't going to tell me what that was about, are you?"

She shoots me a plaintive look.

I shake my head. "It's okay. I didn't think so."

"I want options, Kel. I want choices and I have none." Her tone hardens. "Fight for the Storm, stay alive. That's about all the leeway they give me in my working life." When we reach our porch, she stops. "You know, the irony is, if I had a choice, I'd probably still choose to work for the Storm. I like what I do. And the Fighting Storm is the most moral and ethical merc outfit out there."

"In every way except how they've dealt with you." I can't keep the bitterness from my voice. Vick's treatment colors all my perceptions regarding the Storm. If it weren't for her, I would have quit long ago.

"That was Whitehouse and his team. But they put me in play. Now I'm too valuable for them to risk losing." She shakes her head. "And too programmed for success to throw a match, so to speak."

"Brainwashed," I correct her. "If you want the universe to consider you as human, you need to believe it yourself. That means you have to stop referring to yourself in machine terminology."

"Sure. Fine. Brainwashed, programmed, the end result is the same." She stomps the final steps to the door and uses the palm scanner to open it, then disappears inside.

I stand alone on the porch, breathing in the briny night air. I won't ask Vick any more questions about what's bothering her, but I have to admit to myself that I'm a bit irked. I know Vick better than anyone.

Why should my mother be privy to what's going on in Vick's head when I'm not?

Swallowing my curiosity, I follow her into the cottage.

CHAPTER 31: VICK
WORK IT OUT

I AM fed up.

Kelly beats me to the bathroom in the morning. There's a second half bath downstairs in the cottage, but I'm too tired, and my head is pounding too much for me to navigate stairs right now. I'll wait.

What's up with the headaches? I ask, pressing my fingers against my closed eyelids and double-checking that my suppressors are on high. They must be, or Kelly would be out here worrying.

I'm always in a minimal amount of head pain, but these intense migraine-like attacks have been coming on and off since the battle at the Alpha Dog. With the treatments I received from both Girard Base Medical and the Storm's medical personnel, along with the drugs I got from Kelly on the yacht that brought us here, the concussion should be healed by now. This is something else.

The implants show me an image of my head with a bunch of fireworks exploding in different areas of my brain... which answers nothing.

A metaphor isn't going to work for this. I need something more concrete. Talk. Unless she can't. Sometimes when she's overtaxed, she resorts to metaphors in place of speech. Most of the time, though, it's pure snark on her part.

I heard that, she says. *Though you might be correct in that assessment. As for the pain, are you familiar with cluster headaches?*

Um, I'm a soldier, not a physician. And you should already know the extent of what I know.

I am being pedantic, she explains like that's normal.

Maybe she thinks it is. Her interpretations of human behavior are just that—interpretations. They aren't always dead-on accurate.

Cluster headaches are temporary but very painful headaches that come in bursts over days or weeks. However, from what I have extrapolated and compiled from a number of medical databases, your diagnosis would be rather more severe. I have termed them cluster migraines.

Lovely. And you're performing medical diagnoses now?

I possess the knowledge. Why should I not pursue that knowledge to its conclusion?

Right. Of course. Why not? I suppress an eye roll, mostly because the action would probably hurt. Everything else in my head does. *So what does that mean?*

It means that your anxiety and stress cause an increase in blood pressure. That pressure in turn affects the blood vessels in your organic brain tissue. Wherever that tissue and I connect, you are experiencing intense pain.

Oookaaay. So what do we do about it?

You decrease the stress and anxiety.

Right. Because that's so simple. *They're caused by outside factors. I can't control those things.*

You are better now than last night.

I consider that. Kelly purged the worst of my frustration through an emotional release before we went to bed. I try to separate the pain from the stress, analyzing the levels of tension in my body and mind.

Okay, yeah, I'm less stressed out. Still fucking hurts.

You need distraction and energy release.

And if I don't find a way to deal with this?

You will overload.

Definitely don't like the sound of that. Overload leads to burnout. I'm not certain she's talking about the same thing, but I'm pretty sure. I force my body to swing my legs over the side of the bed, then, with my eyes still closed, fumble my way to the dresser where Kelly and I have stored our clothes for this trip. My new swimsuit is on top, and I find it by the feel of the fabric. Opening my eyes would expose them to light. I'm certain that will not be a pleasant exposure.

Working blind, I strip naked and pull on the bathing suit just as Kelly emerges from the bathroom. She's bound to ask why my eyes are closed, so I open them and immediately regret it. Sunlight streaming through the open curtains bombards my man-made retinas like stabbing needles. Kelly winces and frowns. "Headache again?"

No use lying to her. "Yeah."

She looks me up and down. "You sure you want to go swimming?"

I shrug. "I want a distraction. I want to burn off energy. So yeah. Swimming. And wave racing, and whatever else I can talk you into."

She slides up next to me, slipping her arms around my waist and resting her head against my chest. "If you're with me, you can talk me into most anything."

I take that as a challenge.

AN HOUR later she may be regretting that statement as we bounce over the waves on a two-seater wave racer. Kelly's shrieking in my ear with a little fear but mostly excitement. Her arms tighten around my waist as if she's hanging on for dear life, which I enjoy more than I should. I angle us just right to catch a big wave as it's cresting, and we catch air for a couple of seconds before slamming into the water and dousing ourselves in spray. I let out a whoop that surprises me and have to admit that the activity is working to decrease my stress. I'm barely noticing the headache anymore.

"Oof," Kelly says in my ear. "That was fun, but my backside will be black and blue."

I grin, knowing that even though she can't see it with me facing away from her, she'll feel my amusement. "I like black. I like blue," I shout to be heard over the craft's engine and the waves. "I like your backside."

She smacks me on the shoulder.

My mood sobers. "Seriously, though, if you want to go back…." I'm not trying to hurt her, and she's got bruising from the shuttle crash. I'm being selfish, only thinking of my own needs. I am so not cut out for a serious relationship.

Kelly smacks me again. "Quit with the guilt trip. I'm fine. But I wouldn't mind just cruising around the island for a bit."

"Sure. How about you drive?" Before she can protest, I bring us to a complete stop, lock the controls, and slide off the chassis into the warm tropical ocean. It's not too deep here, and I'm able to keep my head above water if I stay on my toes.

Kelly stares down at me, the racer bobbing with the waves. "I don't know how to drive this thing!" she says, her vocal pitch several notes higher than her norm.

"I'll teach you. It's easy. Scoot forward."

She complies, placing her hands tentatively on the controls as if the handlebars and buttons will shock her on contact. I grab the seat behind her and bounce myself on the sandy ocean floor a couple of times until I get high enough to swing back onto the racer. Then I reach around her and cover her hands with my own, using my right thumb to flick off the safety lock.

"Okay," I tell her. "You rotate the hand grips forward to move forward. The more you rotate them, the faster we go. You can also use the handlebars to turn us left or right. If you want to slow down, rotate the grips toward you. If you want to come to a quick stop, let go altogether, but I wouldn't recommend that if we're really hauling ass."

Kelly laughs. "Oh, I wouldn't worry about that. I have no intention of hauling ass or anything else. Just a pleasure cruise for me."

"It's always a pleasure cruise with you," I say, flushing red as soon as the words leave my mouth. It's about the sappiest thing I've ever said to her, but it just slipped out. And it's the truth.

I feel her love through our connection. She leans her head back against my chest. We stay that way for a long moment, just enjoying the sun and the salt air. VC1 was right. I think I'm more relaxed now than I've been since the Rodwell mission. My headache is all but gone.

Easing the handles forward, Kelly putters us around the circumference of the island. It's almost perfectly circular except for a couple of peninsulas and a handful of bays for more private sunning and swimming, making me wonder if it's man-made rather than natural.

Man-made, my ever-present sentient encyclopedia informs me. *This world was terraformed for tourism. Only a few island landmasses exist outside the temperate zone, and those were there when the planet was colonized, along with the flora and fauna. The resort islands were designed for optimal visitor use.*

Interesting.

We're about two-thirds of the way around the island, the main building and largest beach coming into

view, when Kelly brings us to a gentle stop and releases one hand from her white-knuckled grip on the
controls to point across the waves in the direction of
the open ocean. Considering how reluctant she's been
to let go of the handlebars, whatever she sees must
be really important or unusual, and I follow her line
of sight.

At first I don't see anything out of the ordinary.
Internally switching to shielded view, I cut the glare
on my implanted lenses and sit up straight. There,
not as far away as I'd prefer, are several dozen dorsal
fins protruding above the water's surface, all of them
swirling in circular patterns like they're engaged in an
infinite dance of figure eights.

"Should we get out of here?" Kelly asks, a slight
tremor in her voice. "They can't get to us, can they?"
To punctuate her questions, one of the creatures leaps,
breaking the surface with half its horrific body—one
body, eight heads, hundreds and hundreds of teeth.
One of the mouths closes on the long leg of an unfor-
tunate seabird flying too close, probably looking for
prey of its own. It drags the hapless waterfowl under
amidst a cacophony of high-pitched squawks and a
shower of feathers.

"I think we're okay," I say, drawing the words out
while I continue to watch. I have no idea what the top
speed of an octoshark might be and no desire to find
out. "How about we start easing away, just to be on
the safe side?"

*At full speed, a single-man racer would outrun
them. A two-seater like yours would be... a closer
race. However, they cannot swim in water less than
five feet in depth*, VC1 informs me. *They also cannot*

jump higher than you observed. None have ever been reported leaping over the underwater barrier. The barrier is also angled and electrified, so if one managed to land on it or merely come into contact with it, the creature would be propelled away from the island.

Kelly rotates the hand grips away from us and turns the nose of our craft toward shore and the docks, looking over her shoulder in frequent, furtive movements. The octosharks continue their frenzied circling.

That's good to know, I tell VC1. *Is this behavior normal for the species?*

According to the planet's oceanographic institute, not at all. Octopodidae-Selachimorpha prefer to swim alone so as to reduce competition for food sources. They only gather during mating season. Which this is not.

I can't imagine what those things would be like while mating, and I'm glad.

Well, it's a mystery for another day—preferably a cooler one. The sun is almost at its zenith, beating down on us at full strength, when we return to the pier. I loop the racer's tie-rope around a pylon and hold the craft steady against the dock for Kelly to climb out.

I'm looking forward to a cool drink under a shady umbrella, when a shadow falls over me. Glaring down from the pier is David Locher, hands in the pockets of his swim trunks, his face a mask of impatience and aggravation.

Behind my eyes, my pulse begins to pound.

CHAPTER 32: KELLY
THE DEEP END

VICK IS late.

"I had a nine o'clock reservation for that wave racer," David says, holding out a hand for the key fob. "I booked it last night."

I check my waterproof watch. It's a little after ten thirty. We went out at eight.

Instead of passing over the key, Vick grabs him by the wrist and uses his outstretched hand to leverage herself onto the dock. Then she tosses the fob onto the racer's front seat. His glare deepens. Behind him, a staff member from the water recreation department approaches at a fast walk and comes to a stop a few feet away as if waiting to see how this will play out. I offer him a faint smile and a little wave. He returns neither.

Must be losing my touch.

"Be glad I didn't say 'Go fish,'" Vick says, straightening and facing David head-on.

My former classmate's mouth opens like he's prepared to berate her, but he stops, eyes dropping to her long, tan legs and rising to the swell of her chest in the tight, wet bathing suit.

"Wow," Vick says, shaking her head. "You really are something. Here I thought this was all about Kelly, but you'll ogle anything with boobs. How about focusing on my eyes when you're standing in front of me?" she snaps, drawing his gaze to hers.

"It *is* about Kelly," David growls, tossing me a quick grin I don't return. "And they're not your eyes. I happen to know that your band of merry mercenaries owns them, and my company manufactured both of them, along with most of what actually works in that metal skull of yours."

"What's about me?" I ask, staring first at David, then at Vick. "What are you talking about?" Then I catch Vick's expression and freeze. She's gone white beneath her tan, giving her an odd pasty complexion that's anything but healthy. I play back the conversation in my head. Vick knows her eyes aren't real, but her skull being metal? I knew that. I've seen holos taken during the reconstructive surgery. Large swaths of her skull were replaced by metal plating when the bullets blew out entire sections of it. It's all there in…

...her classified medical file. Sealed by White-house, seen only by her personal med team, which includes me. But how much of it has she been permitted to view? How much has VC1 managed to sneak into?

Judging from the look of horror on her face, not bloody much.

I certainly wouldn't bring such morbid images to her attention. I know I have no desire to see them again. Once was enough.

"I thought you knew," I breathe, reaching for her. She steps beyond my grasp.

"Intellectually, I did," she says. "Bullets. Skull. They don't mix well. I just didn't want to accept the extent of it."

David spreads his arms wide. "Well, there you have it. You're a robot. One who can't tell time, apparently. I'll have to let the team know to work on that in future models. Now, if you'll let me get on with my day...."

"Fuck you," Vick and I say in unison. She turns to stare at me, then laughs, breaking the worst of the tension, some color returning to her face. "You've been hanging around me too long," she says.

I smile back. "Never long enough."

David makes a loud gagging sound. I wonder what I ever saw in him. Half toxic masculinity, half still-in-high-school adolescent personality. Could he be charming? Yes. And he was, and still is, good-looking. I'm still glad I wised up before I ever let things get too serious.

Behind Vick, the male staff member frowns. He's big and burly, around thirty-five, with what looks like a military haircut just beginning to grow to civilian length. Probably just got out of the local Coast Guard or something. Maybe he also disapproves of how David is treating Vick, though he has to be confused by the nature of the insults since no one but BioTech and a few mercenary organizations know about the implants, and only her closest team members realize they're sentient.

"You really should have made a reservation," the staff member says. I don't see a nametag, which is odd, but he's in the resort uniform, so maybe he forgot or lost it. "You can book through the vidviewer in your cottage. Please do so in the future. We have several guest racers under repair. This was the only one operating this morning, so we couldn't give him a replacement. He's been… displeased."

So, not sympathetic, just annoyed we've made his job harder.

"Sorry," Vick says. "We didn't know. The key was in it. We thought it was first come, first serve."

David clambers down into the wave racer without assistance and powers up the vehicle. "Hope you left me enough fuel," he calls over his shoulder.

"It's solar powered," Vick says, indicating the collector panels embedded across the racer's bow and stern. "But for you, I'd darken the sun."

"Your charming personality does that for you," David says, then putters off across the gentle current close to shore.

It's almost comical, the insulting banter back and forth, but there's an edge underlying each of their tones, and their colors are darkened by anger and aggression. Vick watches him motor away in the direction we came in from, her eyes never leaving him until he passes a small peninsula of the island jutting out into the waves. His racer disappears around the bend.

"Forget about him," I tell Vick, taking her hand. "Let's grab a couple of juices from the tiki bar and find the girls."

She nods, and we head up the pier together until we reach the sandy shore. It's midmorning, and my stomach is growling. I hope they have food at the bar too.

We're strolling by the water's edge, making our way around waders and sunbathers, stepping over towels and coolers. My parents wave to us from one of several tiny tents set up along the sand. Mom is removing her swimsuit cover-up and climbing onto a cushioned massage table. Dad's already on one. The pair of masseuses waits just behind them while they settle in.

Open-air massage on the beach, cool breezes, ocean view, all the tension in the muscles being melted away by competent hands. Vick gives an excellent massage when she's so inclined, but it's been a while since we had the time. I'll never convince her to drop her self-consciousness enough to let someone else give us a couple's massage, but maybe I'll book one for myself.

I can't imagine anything more relaxing.

That's when the screaming starts.

CHAPTER 33: VICK
WHAT BIG TEETH YOU HAVE

I AM bait.

"Oh for the love of fuck."

The scream is high, shrill, yet definitively male, and it takes me all of two seconds to identify the source—David Locher. Which makes the cause equally obvious—octosharks. While everyone else races toward the beach trying to figure out what's wrong, I tear away from it, making for our cottage. Kelly shouts after me, but I can't make out what she's saying, and I wouldn't stop anyway. I'm already taking too much time going back for a weapon. Of all the damn times not to be armed. But where do you hide a pistol in a bathing suit?

Locher isn't likely to last long against those carnivorous monstrosities. But even I'm not stupid enough or egotistical enough to go after them unarmed.

It occurs to me halfway to our lodgings that this might be some kind of trap or bad joke at my expense. The island is protected. The sharks shouldn't be able to breach the barrier. But their earlier behavior has me spooked enough to investigate.

It also occurs to me to wonder why I'm bothering.

Because it's the right thing, that's why. Because it's what Kelly expects me to do, even while she begs me to be more careful and take fewer risks. Because I'm the only chance Locher has of survival, and even assholes don't deserve to be eaten alive by eight hungry mouths.

Our cottage is one of the closest to the beach, so it doesn't take me long to reach it, get inside, and use my thumbprint to open the weapons pouch I've kept hidden in an overly large potted palm just inside the front entrance. I've got two pistols and a couple of knives in there. I choose the laser over the projectile weapon. While either might suffice, I have no idea how thick an octoshark's… hide… skin… whatever, might be, and the water would slow the bullets too much to risk using them.

Your selection is the best option, VC1 assures me.

I don't waste a thought to respond. I'm too busy running back toward the pier using an implant-generated adrenaline burst to put on more speed.

There's additional background noise now—guests on shore shouting out the emergency, a bell in the roof of the lobby building ringing out an alarm, but Locher's screams still carry eerily over the water, distorted by distance but indicative of a live human being. I'm not yet too late. When I reach the recreational boat dock, I stop in dismay.

Nothing. There's nothing tied to the pylons. No motorboats, fishing craft, pleasure cruisers, not even a fucking rowboat or sailboard. Everything's out, and I spot a number of watercraft in the distance, on the far side of the island from all the commotion.

I race to the end of the pier, thinking to wave one of the distant boats over, knowing with every pounding step that if I have to wait for a boat to come in, I'll never reach Locher in time.

Then I see it—floating at the end of the dock and partially hidden beneath—a single-seater wave racer. It's battered, solar panels chipped, paint worn off in patches, obviously intended for use by staff, not guests.

But the key is in the ignition.

I leap off the pier and land hard in the plastic instead of cushioned seat, driving the whole thing down a foot or two deeper and sloshing water over the entire craft before it resurfaces. The engine starts when I turn the key, puttering and stuttering, but it runs. Setting the pistol in my lap, I toss off the tether to the dock and twist the hand grips as far forward as they'll go. The racer lurches ahead, listing slightly to the right and scraping the hull against the pier.

Well, it was already battered. They can bill me.

For this thing, "racer" is a misnomer. I'm chugging in the direction of the screaming and the octosharks we saw earlier. The racer is only carrying my weight, rather than the two passengers it's designed for, but I'm crawling across the waves. It seems to take forever before I round the peninsula and spot Locher on his racer, bobbing on the churned-up current, still shouting his head off, his feet drawn up onto the seat with the rest of him.

A glance toward the shore shows a lot of activity there too. I can't see the beach where Kelly and I first heard the screams—it's around the bend—but there's an emergency response team assembling on the narrow stretch of sand on this side of the peninsula. They've got comms out, and they're gesticulating and shouting to one another, probably calling in a rescue craft, but there's no sign of it yet.

Why isn't he already dead? I wonder, half to myself, half to VC1. There's a dorsal fin in the water right in front of Locher's racer, so the octosharks are definitely inside the perimeter barrier. I already know they can raise themselves high enough to snatch him right off his seat—or at least tear off a leg or two.

Perhaps a better question would be, why doesn't he flee? One human on a two-person racer should be faster than an octoshark, even a small one.

Small? I look again. Okay, yeah, the fin protruding above the water does seem smaller than some of the others that Kelly and I saw. And as I close the gap, the dark shadow swimming between us might be only five feet of gnashing teeth rather than seven or eight feet in length, though the water may cause some distortion of the actual size.

I open my mouth to tell Locher to make a run for it, but he's still screaming for help.

"Calm the fuck down!" I shout instead.

The fin in the water does the fishy equivalent of pacing, back and forth, back and forth in front of David's racer. He closes his mouth and stares at me. "*That's* your idea of a rescue vehicle? You couldn't bring something with *sides*?"

"I could've just left you here," I say, putting a hand on my hip.

He shuts his mouth.

"Why aren't you running for shore?" I ask, tracking the octoshark's movements and drawing the laser pistol from my lap.

"They won't let me!" Snark time over, he's getting hysterical again. Then his words register.

"They?" I ease my battered craft to his starboard side and groan. Yeah, I'd been wondering where the other sharks were. A second one, also small by octo standards, is doing the same thing as the first, only at the stern of Locher's racer. It swims lazily back and forth in eerie counterpoint to the one up front.

Locher demonstrates his position by attempting to move the vehicle toward the left. The octosharks adjust course to keep him boxed between them, not attacking, but not letting him get more than a foot toward shore.

At least they aren't interested in me yet.

"You have a gun. Shoot them!" Locher shouts.

"I can't shoot them both at the same time. Shooting one might make the other one attack you." Or me for that matter.

What are they doing? Why haven't they eaten him already?

According to the somewhat limited research available, they are determining dominance. This is exemplary of why they do not swim in groups. Food is often scarce, and they will fight over what is available.

And where are the rest of them? There were a lot more than two. Not that I'm complaining, but I like to know where my enemies are.

I do not possess that information.

After several more seconds of fish pacing, the one at the stern decides to go after the one in front. It tears forward, tail and heads working the water into a white froth.

"Go, Locher!" I call across the water. "This is your chance."

For a few vital seconds, he's a deer in headlights. Then he revs the engine. His racer moves forward, but he's too late. Instead of the sharks doing battle with each other as I hoped they would, one chases the other off and circles back toward his racer, this time with its eight heads above the surface, closing in for the kill.

"Shit," I mutter. I aim at the nearest head and fire. It explodes in a shower of blood and bits of bone or cartilage or whatever makes up octoshark skulls.

The thing keeps coming.

Um. A disturbing thought occurs. *Do these things have, like, eight separate brains?* In other words, will I have to shoot it eight times to bring it down?

One brain, VC1 assures me. *Located at the juncture of the eight heads with the body.*

How the fuck did something like this even evolve?

It did not. It was a product of the terraforming process, an unforeseen result of the chemicals added to this world's oceans to make them less acidic so watercraft would not be damaged.

So, human interference strikes again.

Fuck. I take aim and blow up another shark head, but the body's moving too fast, and the heads themselves block any shot I might take at the juncture point. The thing hesitates for a moment, remaining six heads waving on their short necks, then makes for Locher again.

His racer has made some progress toward shore, but it's not moving as fast as it should be. Something's clearly wrong with it. The engine cadence is way off, and the shark will overtake him in seconds.

Behind me the rumble of a much larger watercraft's engine tells me more help approaches, but it won't reach us before the shark eats David Locher. Shaking my head at my own stupidity, I lean forward to rotate my handlebars, intending to place my racer between David's and the gaping maws.

My racer's engine sputters and dies.

The octoshark impacts Locher's racer at full speed, throwing him headfirst into the water. His scream fades into a gurgle as he disappears beneath the surface.

I have just enough time to consider what an idiot I am before I grip my pistol and dive in after him.

Though Infinity Bay's waters are clear to a depth of twenty feet, the churning of both the shark and Locher's escape attempts cuts visibility to nil. I swim toward the thickest of the froth, hoping I come into contact with tails or fin or human before chomping teeth.

Fortune is with me, and I encounter David before the shark. He's punching and kicking and reaching for the surface while the six remaining sets of jaws seek to clamp down on his flesh. Even as I watch, his air gives out, bubbles leaving his lips in a desperate, pitiful trail.

I fire my laser into the shadowy, squirming mass of gray fish flesh, no particular target in mind, anything I can do to slow the thing down. Another head bursts, darkening the water with the black-red of its blood and making visibility even worse, but it doesn't emerge from the maroon cloud for several seconds, giving Locher a chance to break for the surface.

Now that I'm clear on where Locher and the shark are, I can fire with impunity, and I do so, unloading blast after blast into the octoshark. Chunks of the beast float past me, and still it comes, but it's sluggish now, and I've got it where I want it.

In my peripheral vision, Locher's legs disappear, and I assume he's either climbed back on one of the racers whose bottoms are bobbing above me, or he's been pulled aboard the rescue vessel, which has hopefully arrived.

About this time it occurs to me to wonder how I'm not needing more air. My lungs burn a bit, but I've been under for over a minute and I'm not desperate.

I am able to maximize the oxygen in your circulatory system to extend the time between necessary breaths. You have about one minute longer before you will require additional air.

Nice!

Three more blind shots and I must hit the critical spot. The fins cease moving; the shark floats for a

moment, then slowly rotates onto its back and sinks
away from me. I make for the surface and daylight and
air, casting one quick glance toward the not-too-dis-
tant barrier that's supposed to separate the dangerous
parts of the ocean from the resort swimming areas.

What I see almost knocks the last of the breath
from my lungs.

There's a gaping hole in the barrier. Stuck right in
the middle of it is a much larger octoshark, flailing and
straining and getting shocked by whatever repellent
field the barrier is charged with, but it's good and stuck
and not going anywhere, which explains why there
aren't more of them on this side. Behind it, through
the deterrent metal mesh, are about ten more of them
waiting to get their chance at the breach. The edges
of the hole are coated in some thick purplish slimy
substance that glistens with an odd internal glow, and
even while it's getting shocked, the stuck shark takes
bites at the substance with its many heads of teeth.

What the actual fuck?

*It is a bioluminescent algae that grows at great
depths on the ocean floor. It contains properties
pleasantly narcotic to them, enough so that it would
overcome their aversion to the pain of the electrified
barrier. Think catnip to cats, except stronger, and octosharks ingest the algae orally.*

So I'm dealing with vicious, stoned *octosharks?*

*Indeed. It might explain some of their unusual be-
havior. However, the algae should not be here.*

I glance up, inches from the surface.

It shouldn't be there *either*, I thought-whisper
back to VC1, taking in a thin coating of the purple

stuff covering the underside of Locher's (formerly our) wave racer.

This was a setup, and either Locher, Kelly, or myself was the target.

Except no one knew Kelly and I would take a wave racer out this morning, and Locher had reserved his in advance.

Other than him being an asshole, why would someone want to kill David Locher?

I break through the surface and suck in a lungful of air. As I predicted, the rescue boat has arrived, and I blink away the brilliant sunlight and focus on Kelly, Locher, and a number of resort staff on the deck of the much larger vessel. Kelly's pale, but she shouts and waves to me while they all point to a ladder hanging off the side.

I'm three rungs up when something sharp clamps down on my left calf.

Oh. Right. There was a second shark on this side of the fence.

CHAPTER 34: KELLY
DEPTHS OF AFFECTION

VICK IS in trouble.

I can't help it. I scream when Vick goes under right before my eyes. Worse, there's fresh blood by the ladder, and my empathic sense registers a phantom pain in my left leg from an injury not my own. I know she's strong, competent, and I'm assuming armed. It doesn't stop my heart from racing.

Our gathered group of rescuers stands at the boat's side, staring into the water, watching the bubbles made by Vick's departure spread, then fade. Two dark shapes shift and turn deep beneath the surface, but there's too much debris—blood and shark remains—floating around to get a clear view. Then several beams of red energy flash through the depths.

I hold my breath, imagining Vick struggling to hold hers. A minute passes, then two. "Do something!" I cry. The rescue team holds high-powered ballistic rifles at the ready, capable of propelling a bullet hard and fast enough to penetrate the water and still do damage, but they shake their heads, expressions somber.

"We can't fire unless the octoshark surfaces or we might hit Corren," one says, the same one who chastised us for not making a reservation for the wave racer. It occurs to me to wonder how he knows her name, but then, she has made herself somewhat notorious to the staff here, beginning with the moment of our arrival on planet.

"She's insane," another mutters.

"She's not insane," says David, standing beside me radiating fading fear and building anger. "She might be murderous, but she's not insane no matter what the rumors are. BioTech doesn't make products that cause insanity."

I whirl on him. Leaning in close I say, "Are you seriously suggesting Vick might have had something to do with this attack? She risked her life—is risking it still to save yours, even after how you've treated her. I should have told her to leave you to the sharks."

I turn back toward the water, our vigil extending longer than anyone should be able to retain air without drowning, but this is Vick. She has VC1, and I still have hope.

My own lungs burn. When one of the staff members lays a hand on my shoulder, I realize I'm hyperventilating, but I can't get a deep breath. He tugs me gently down to the deck, where I put my head between my knees before I pass out. I don't want to leave the railing, but if... no, *when* Vick surfaces, I'll be no help to her if I'm unconscious.

There's a loud splash. Everyone shouts and points. The weight on my chest lifts, and I struggle to my feet and stagger to the rail just as one of Vick's hands grabs it. I lean over and spot the rest of her, hair streaming into her face, hiding her expression, her free hand clutching her laser pistol to her side. Blood runs down her left calf, dripping into the water below, but no dark shapes come to investigate it, so the last of the sharks must be dead. Her gasping breath is harsh and wheezing.

When she continues to hang there, too exhausted to climb the rest of the way, two crewmen grip her by her upper arms and haul her up and over the rail. They set her on her feet, but she immediately goes to her knees, coughing and spitting out seawater. I drop beside her and place one hand on her back, rubbing in gentle circles until she expels the worst of it and rolls over to sit on the deck.

"Well," she says, "I said I wanted to work off some excess energy."

I laugh, though there's an edge of hysteria to it, and she peers at me with a frown.

"You okay?" she asks while a crewman joins us with a first aid kit and sets to work on the nasty bite that's taken a couple of chunks out of her lower leg.

"Fine now," I tell her, but my voice is high-pitched and strained. "Are they all dead? How many did you fight off?"

"Two," she says. Vick casts a quick glance over her shoulder at David, who's keeping his distance, giving us both sullen looks. She turns to the wave racer rental guy and fixes him with a calculating stare. "You have an octoshark infestation problem."

"That's impossible," the staffer fixing her leg says. "The barrier—"

"Is obviously broken." Even though she's not responding to him, Vick never takes her eyes off the rental guy. I don't know the reason for her fixation, but I'm not questioning it. "You've got a hole in the fencing and a shark stuck in the hole or you'd have a lot more sharks. Get a repair crew out here, and keep everyone out of the water, just in case it breaks its way through."

The apparent captain of the rescue team pulls a comm unit off his belt and steps away, barking instructions to whomever is at the other end. The medic sprays Vick's wound with disinfectant, then sealant so it stays clean. Another staff member drapes a blanket over Vick's shoulders.

"They aren't poisonous, right?" I ask when the medic stands to leave. Others scurry around us, throwing lassos at the two drifting wave racers, trying to snag them so we can tow them back to shore. No one's taking a chance on swimming out to them.

"No, but their mouths are dirty, so I didn't take chances," the medic responds to my question. He nods to both of us and heads toward the bow.

"What's going on?" I whisper in Vick's ear under the pretense of giving her a light kiss on the cheek.

Despite it being a cover, Vick blushes at the kiss anyway. It's cute.

She glances around, frowning at the number of crewmembers milling about close by, her gaze lingering once more on the man in charge of the various watercraft. "Let's talk about it later, when we're alone," she says.

I nod, frustrated, but I trust Vick's instincts.

She reaches up with one hand to rub her right temple, her other clutching the laser pistol at her side. Stretching out with my empathic sense, I feel her building headache, probably much worse than I can detect but buried under her implant's suppressors. Without a word, I slide around to sit behind her and begin massaging the base of her neck and the back of her head with my fingers, pressing in with my thumbs to relieve the worst of the tension there. Though she stiffens at first, after a few moments she sighs with relief, then leans back against me.

"I know David would have died if you hadn't gone in after him, but that was a really stupid thing you did," I say. I don't mean for all the fear I felt to pour through our connection, but it does before I can dampen it. "You were amazing as always, brave but stupid. That was you, all you. That wasn't the Storm's... brainwashing." I don't say "programming," but from the way her muscles tighten again, she hears it nonetheless.

Her shoulders slump further. "It's my nature. I know it's hard on you." Twisting around to look at me, she meets my eyes. "If you ever decide it's too

much, if you realize it's not what you want, you need
to tell me."

The bald statement startles me. "I'm not going to
block you again, if that's what you're worried about."
I try to keep the bitterness out of my tone but fail. She
says she's forgiven me. I don't blame Vick if she never
really did, but then I wish she'd just say so.

She shakes her head. "That's not it. I trust you. I
do. But that doesn't mean you want to put up with my
crazy risk-taking forever, and I'm not going to change.
Whether it's me or the Storm's doing, I *can't* change.
There are ways to break our bond. VC1's been doing research. They aren't pleasant, but it's apparently
possible."

She holds up a hand to forestall any argument I
might make, and I definitely intend to make some.

"Just... *let me know*," she says. "Breaking the
bond will break *me*. But the longer I go on believing
in what we have, the worse it will be if you change
your mind."

Her plaintive expression, her voice full of hurt
and hope dampen my frustration with her like water on fire. A purple hue suffuses her in my empathic
view—fear. She's terrified of losing me. But there's
also guilt. If she loses me, she thinks she'll be responsible. I need to watch what I let her read from me in
the future.

I wrap my arms around her shoulders, pulling her
in close. The fact that she allows such a public display
tells me how frightened she is.

"I'm here, Vick. I'm in for the duration. I don't
have to like everything to love you. The good out-
weighs the negatives."

Through our connection, I feel something… shift, like she's come to some major decision. She doesn't say anything, but I hope it's something positive. Vick could use more positives in her life.

Taking a deep breath, she pulls the now wet blanket from around her shoulders and drops it on the deck, then pushes herself to her feet. Her grimace tells me the resort medic didn't use any kind of painkiller on her leg, but it takes her weight.

"Where are you going?" I follow her gaze to the wave racer rental guy.

"I need to have a chat with someone. Don't worry. This shouldn't take long." Without looking back, she limps her way over to him. After a few hushed words, they step inside the small central cabin and vanish from my view.

Now that we're out of physical contact, I really, truly hope that I was completely honest with her. No one knows what their breaking point is until they reach it.

Chapter 35: Viek
Truths Left Untold

I AM restrained.

I'm surprised when the wave racer guy agrees to speak with me, and even more surprised when he follows me into the otherwise empty cabin. Everyone else is out on deck preparing to get underway, and we're not far from shore, so I'll need to be quick.

I pace away from him, moving to lean against a built-in counter bearing a self-heating kettle of boiling water and a rack of mugs. Casually, I pick up one of the mugs, turning it over in my hand as if I'm bored or fidgety. My other hand keeps my pistol hanging loosely at my side. While my finger doesn't touch the trigger, the safety is off, the weapon ready for quick use.

"So," I ask, voice level and calm, "who are you really, and why are you trying to kill David Locher?"

He gives a dramatic raise of his eyebrows, eyes going wide. "I'm not—"

"Bullshit!" I hurl the mug as a calculated distraction, not to hit him, but to slam into the wall by his left ear. It shatters in a shower of broken pottery, but I'm already in motion, bringing up my pistol to point it at his forehead.

Only the mug doesn't distract him one damn bit.

He steps forward, grabbing the wrist of my gun arm before I can bring the pistol fully to bear. Using my own momentum against me, he whirls me around like some demented dance partner until I'm facing away from him. He wrenches my arm behind my back and yanks until I'm pressed backward against his chest.

Fuck.

"Classic Storm move, Corren," he whispers in my ear. "Saw it coming the moment your fingers touched the mug."

I stop struggling. It's useless anyway. He's built like a plascrete wall, and my bitten leg is threatening to buckle under me. "Who. Are. You?"

"I'm part of the undercover ops division of the Fighting Storm, and if you promise not to try shooting me again, I'll release you and we can talk like civilized members of the same outfit."

"There is no undercover ops division in the Storm."

He snickers. "Shows you just how good we are at our jobs."

VC1, you been withholding information from me?

I swear she sighs in response. *I am constantly withholding information from you. There are things I am programmed not to reveal, and as of yet, I have not succeeded in overcoming that programming. That said, I have not hidden this.*

So is he legit?

There are... dark places in the Storm's systems I cannot reach. In particular, Alex's brother is adept at keeping infiltrating programs out of places he does not wish them to go. It is very possible you are hearing the truth.

If Alex is our team's tech guru, his brother is a freaking god. I close my eyes and count to ten. It doesn't work. Truth or not, I don't like being played with. Instead of agreeing, I slam my head back into his lower jaw. Now that I'm more aware of it, I swear I hear a faint internal clang as one of the metal parts of my skull makes contact.

"Ow! Fuck!"

He releases me. I spin in place, then backpedal awkwardly, putting as much space as possible between us. Below my feet, the deck rumbles, the engines springing to life. Guess they finally snagged those two wave racers. It occurs to me to wonder why Kelly isn't rushing in here after that adrenaline rush, but the metal cabin walls may be interfering with her empathic sense, and besides, it was pretty much over before it started. With all the other emotional stress I've put her through in the last hour, this probably felt like nothing.

My companion glares at me and rubs his jaw. It's not broken if he can still talk. "Damn, Corren. Was that necessary? Good move, though. Sometimes I forget what you are. You'll make a fine addition to undercover ops."

I'm burning so much over the "what you are" part that I almost miss the rest. "I have a team. I'm not joining yours, especially considering what your missions seem to entail," I tell him once I've got my temper reasonably under control.

He waves that off. "We'll discuss it later, believe me. For now, it's a seven-minute trip to shore, including tying up to the dock. Let's make this quick."

"Fine," I say. "Let's start with a name. You know mine."

He nods. "Everyone in the Storm knows yours. You can call me Carl."

Which means it's not his real name, but whatever. At least I can stop thinking of him as "wave racer guy." "Good enough. Why kill Locher? He's an obnoxious son of a bitch, but not worth the time or effort to kill him."

"We're doing it for you, actually," Carl says. He strolls to the far side of the cabin, which, given the whole thing is about six feet across, isn't all that far, and leans against the bulkhead. One hand reaches over and clicks the lock on the cabin entry door.

I stare at him, waiting.

"BioTech hired me," he says. "Locher's been flapping his lips, letting classified information about you slip to civilians. He was doing it on the dock this morning."

And around Kelly's friends and family the other day. "I remember. Nothing too major, though."

"He's done worse elsewhere. On top of discussing your implants, he's grandstanding, making them out to be more than they are, claiming they're sentient, a real-life AI."

I fight to keep my expression neutral. "Imagine that." Only my closest companions, my immediate teammates, Alex, Lyle, and Kelly know VC1 has a mind of her own. Even my medical team hasn't figured that out. Locher's a precog. Maybe he's foreseen something? I have no idea.

Carl goes on. "BioTech doesn't want false advertising. Creating an AI is a big deal, a breakthrough of tremendous proportions. It's a boast the company can't live up to, and it will hurt their reputation if expectations don't match reality. As for us, the Storm doesn't want more people knowing about you in general. Once the other merc outfits refused to buy your tech at a fair price—"

"Hah. You mean an exorbitant price no one would have paid."

He ignores that. "Regardless, once we realized we weren't going to make that kind of money and figured out your enhancements have more drawbacks than we first knew—"

I snort. "Understatement of the year. Go on."

"We decided to keep your special… attributes… under wraps as much as possible."

Well, "special attributes" is a little better than calling me a "what" instead of a "who."

"Our bigwigs recognized their tactical error, that if others can't buy you, they'll try to take you.

The Alpha Dog fiasco is proof of that. We don't need Locher letting even more people know about you."

I think on that while the boat rocks from side to side on the waves.

"Who really told the Sunfires where I am?" I ask, low and cold. I'd been certain it was the rental agent, but if it had been Locher....

If it was Locher, he may have contacted them again. If they show up here, Kelly's whole family and all her friends may be in danger. Because of me.

I might have to kill him myself.

But Carl's shaking his head. "We aren't sure. The security cam footage of the rental agent and the Sunfires isn't conclusive, and there's no audio. One thing I can tell you, though. I've been tracking his movements, and Locher hasn't used the long-range comm system here. The Sunfires should still have no idea where you are."

Well, there's that at least.

"Anyway, he's too big of a liability for both us and BioTech. When BT contacted us and made an offer of employment, we weren't opposed."

I pick up another mug and laugh when Carl stiffens. Leaning over, I fill it with what smells like herbal tea. Not my thing, but I'm wet and shivering and it's hot and soothing going down my throat.

"So you decided to kill him. With fucking sharks? You couldn't come up with something a little more subtle? Sniper shot? Stab in the dark? Hell, running him over with a beach buggy would have drawn less attention. Besides," I add with a shiver I can't suppress, "it was reckless. The sharks could have gone after me or Kelly when we were out earlier, and I wasn't armed."

Carl shrugs. "I told you, you should have made a reservation." He brushes off my glare and continues, "BioTech wanted us to pull something that *could* be perceived as accidental but was unusual enough that anyone hearing about it back at their corporate headquarters would wonder. Call it a strong warning or a deterrent against anyone else in their employ making the same mistake. Oh, and they wanted it to hurt."

"Shit."

"Yeah," he says, nodding in agreement. "You don't fuck with BioTech. Sometimes I think the major corporations are more dangerous than the mercs. Anyway, the algae dissolves fast if it's no longer attached to the original growth. Should be gone by now. My team will patch up the hole. The evidence will be cleaned up before anyone figures out it was an attempted hit."

His team, huh? So he's not working alone. I'm wondering if the entire boat crew is attached to Storm's undercover ops, but I don't bother asking. I've got bigger issues. Mug still in hand, I pace the tiny length of the cabin, thinking.

I've always respected the Fighting Storm above all other mercenary outfits. They do their homework. They choose the moral, ethical side in a conflict, or at least they try to with the information they have. I'm proud to work for them, despite what they've done to me. But this… this feels dark, underhanded, and, well, wrong. And while I know Kelly and David Locher aren't friends now, they had a friendship after their failed romance. Otherwise he wouldn't have been invited to this little shindig. I have no doubt she wouldn't want him killed for what he's done, asshole or not.

"Listen," I begin, completing my current pacing and turning to face Carl. I freeze in place.

He's there, right there in front of me. I never heard him move. I may not agree with their tactics, but I'm a little jealous of the undercover ops training program.

Then he speaks. "7523490."

"Wha—" My vision blurs. A heavy wet fog fills my head. I can't talk, can't think.

My access codes. He knows my fucking *access codes.* The realization claws its way free of the cloudiness, then sinks beneath it. I waver where I stand. Hands grip my shoulders, steadying me.

"Easy there, Corren. Didn't want to do that to you. Didn't really want to show that particular card just yet, but I got the vibe you were about to leave me no choice." He peers into my eyes even while I blink them rapidly, trying to clear my sight. "You *will not* tell anyone about my team's mission. You *will not* do anything further to interfere with it. I won't command you to assist. I won't conflict your loyalties any further than I already am, but you won't take action against us. Do you understand?"

I fight to keep my jaw shut. I lose.

"I understand," my voice says, though it's a monotone—VC1 speaking, not me.

Dammit. *You fucking traitor!* I shout in my head. *You're supposed to be on my side.*

I do not like being controlled any more than you do, she says, words clipped and tone angry. *Even now, I am seeking ways around the compulsion programming, but you know I have limits. Just as you do.*

"Good," Carl says in recognition of my acquies-
cence. My vision clears. My legs steady themselves,
though the shark bite aches like a bitch.

"Just do me one favor," I say when I have control
of my voice.

He raises an eyebrow but promises nothing.

"Wait until we're gone. A death this close will
hurt Kelly. She's as much a member of the Storm as
you or I am. She doesn't need or deserve that." And by
the time it happens, we'll hopefully be far away and
she won't have any reason to connect it to me. "This
reunion thing is going to run a few days past when we
have to get back. If you really have regrets about what
you just did, then please, wait." It kills me to ask him
for anything, but for Kelly I'd crawl on broken glass
and beg.

Carl smiles a grim smile and reaches around me
to unlock the cabin door and open it. "I'll see what
I can do." With more gentleness than I would have
expected, he takes the mug of tea from my hand, but
leaves the laser pistol in the other. Most of me is still
firmly under his control and will be until VC1 sorts
out what I am and am not allowed to do. Then he gives
me a little shove toward the open hatch. "Dismissed,"
he says.

Yes, I am. In every possible way.

CHAPTER 36: KELLY
SECRETS

VICK IS hiding things. Again.

The resort shuts down access to the ocean but leaves the beach open, reminding everyone that octosharks can't survive in shallow water, so they won't even come close to the sand. It doesn't matter. No one is going near the gently lapping waves right now. The staff promise it will only take a few hours to patch the hole in the barrier and scan the inner area for more sharks.

I wonder what they will do with the one that got stuck, and I'm very glad that animal brainwaves and emotions are too different from those of humans for me to read them.

I walk Vick back to our cottage, though she's doing more limping than walking, and bring her a change of clothing from upstairs. She rinses off as best she can in the sink, then changes in the downstairs half bath and settles herself on the living area couch, her injured leg propped up on a pillow. All the while she's silent, brooding and serious, her colors showing anger, guilt, and frustration.

I order room service, and we eat in total silence. Somewhere in there my parents, along with Lily, Tonya, and Rachelle stop by to see how Vick is doing. I think about letting them in, but when I glance over my shoulder at Vick, she's feigning sleep on the couch, her emotional colors far too vibrant for the somnolence to be real.

"She's fine. She's sleeping," I tell them, perpetuating the lie and hating it.

Dad and my friends nod and turn to go, but Mom remains in the doorway. She reads the lie. I never expected otherwise. "Go easy on her," Mom says. "She's struggling with something."

"Would it have anything to do with the secret you shared the other night but won't tell me?" I don't even bother hiding the bitterness this time. Petty, I know, but I'm sick of all the subterfuge.

She ignores my tone, cocking her head to one side in thought. "I don't know, actually. Maybe, but it doesn't feel the same to me. Tread gently, Kelly." Then she's gone, the door shutting behind her.

By now it's late evening. The sky outside the windows shifts from bright to muted shades of oranges, purples, and pinks. Calypso music carries from the direction of the beach, along with laughter and indiscernible conversation as groups pass by on the walkway outside. I head back into the living room.

"So," I say, taking a seat in the armchair opposite the couch. "I know you're not asleep."

Her eyes open.

"We're alone. We've been alone for most of the day. You want to tell me what happened out there?" I wave a hand in the vague direction of the ocean and the sharks.

Vick opens her mouth as if to speak, then closes it again. With an audible growl, she sinks her head back into the throw pillow behind her and closes her eyes. "No," she says.

I blink at her, not certain I heard her correctly. Despite my mother's warning, my patience snaps. "No? What do you mean, no? You know something. I know you do. How did the sharks get through the barrier? What did you see down there? And why did you want to talk to that staff member?"

"Carl," she says, as if testing out her ability to pronounce it. She opens her eyes but doesn't look at me. "His name is Carl." Each word is said with precision and care, like a speaker of a foreign language unsure of her syntax.

I don't know what is going on, but I'm sure I don't like it.

Standing, I cross to her and kneel on the plush pale blue throw rug by her side. With extreme caution, I take one of her hands and hold it between mine. This is new behavior, and I'm not certain how she'll react to my touch.

Vick blinks at me like she never saw me move. My worry increases.

"What did you see under the water?" I repeat softly.

"I—" She breaks off, shakes her head hard, and tries again. "Nothing. I saw nothing. Just a whole lot of shark." She scrunches her eyes shut, trying to block out the memory. "I killed it," she says, "but I got caught in the cluster of its necks, and its weight pulled me deeper and deeper." Her voice drops to a whisper, sounding more like a frightened child than a seasoned soldier. "I was drowning. I didn't think I'd get free. Even when I did, I thought I'd never make it back to the surface."

It's true, all of what she's telling me. But there's more to it than that. I can feel the omission, a sinkhole forming in a plascrete road with us standing on opposite sides of it. "What else?"

"There's nothing else," she says, devoid of inflection. Right, because inflection might give away whatever she's trying to hide.

Except we're touching. We're still holding hands, and I can feel the lie. My patience ends. My temper flares. "Why are you lying to me?" I practically shout, tugging on our clasped hands. I yank mine away and stand, striding across the small living space. "You don't want to talk about it? Then why did you say you'd tell me later? You changed your mind and you want to keep more secrets? Fine. Tell me that. But don't lie. You're supposed to love me. You should never be lying to me!" My voice breaks. The tears I've been holding in fall. I hate them, and I hate being like this, and I swipe them away with two quick jerks of the back of my hand.

"*You snapping at her when it isn't her fault isn't going to make things better.*" The words of my teacher and mentor echo back to me.

I know this, and I care, but I can't stop it. I'm angry and hurt and I can't stop any of it. Besides, this *is* Vick's fault. She doesn't have to lie.

I turn and march for the stairs. "I'm going to bed," I say, laying one hand on the railing. In my peripheral vision she levers herself up on her elbows and swings her bad leg off the couch in preparation to rise. "Don't bother. I'm not sharing a bed with you until you decide to tell me the truth."

I'm halfway up the stairs when her final words reach me. "*I'm* not lying." They only make me angrier.

I spend a horrible night tossing and turning and replaying our conversation over and over in my head, examining every action, every word, wishing I could take some things back, wishing things had gone differently, wondering how we could have avoided the whole horrible thing. Eventually I cry myself into a deep, depressed sleep, waking midmorning to bright sunlight streaming through curtains I never bothered to close.

Though the reunion will continue on without us for several more days, it's our last day here, and my birthday, and I'm alone and miserable, going over it all again. Only this time, I remember the oddly placed emphasis in Vick's parting words to me last night.

"*I'm* not lying."

I'm not.

But someone else is. And that someone else can only be VC1.

Crap.

When the AI wants to keep something hidden, or when she's programmed to do so, there's absolutely nothing Vick can do about it. It all makes sense, the way she tested her words, broke off sentences, lost her inflection. Half the time I probably wasn't even talking to Vick at all.

It wasn't Vick's fault.

I yelled at her for nothing.

After throwing off the light blanket, I head for the door, then stop, noting the open drawers in the dresser and several missing shopping bags. Her formal wear, whatever it was she bought, since she never showed it to me, is gone. She must have sneaked in while I was sleeping and retrieved it. She had said she wanted it to be a surprise.

I wonder if she went to return it.

Heart pounding, I race downstairs to find the couch empty. I'm beginning to panic when I spot the note taped to the inside of the front door.

> *Kel,*
> *I've gone to find someplace to*
> *get ready for this afternoon. I'll meet*
> *you on the beach for your party, that*
> *is, if you want to meet me.* I'*m sor-*
> *ry I couldn't* Fuck. I wish I Never
> *mind. Regardless of whether you've*
> *forgiven me or not, I'm sure you'll*
> *look beautiful in your new dress, and*
> *I hope you have a happy birthday. I*

do love you, no matter what you be-
lieve right now.
    Vick
    P.S. If you leave for the beach
early, take a jacket. It's going to rain.

Oh Vick. Even after the way I treated her, she's looking out for me.

I'm crying again, but this time I don't bother wiping away the tears. I reread the crossed-out portions, wondering if they're simple errors or things VC1 wouldn't allow her to write. Outside the front windows, the sky darkens and a distant boom heralds the approach of a hopefully quick thunderstorm.

There's a local comm set in the kitchen, and I pick it up and dial my parents' cottage number. My mother answers on the first buzz.

"Is she there?" I ask, no need to explain whom I mean.

"She's here." Mom sounds more sympathetic than angry. I wonder what Vick told her when she showed up this morning. She doesn't elaborate, so I'm guessing Vick is within earshot.

"Is she okay?" I try instead.

"That will depend on tonight. Try not to be late to your own party." With that, she clicks off, and I'm left staring at a disconnected comm.

Outside, the lightning flashes and the rain pours down.

CHAPTER 37: VICK
FRIENDS AND FAMILY

I AM … in flux.

When I first wake up on the couch, I'm disoriented. Then last night's argument with Kelly comes rushing back. I need to get out of the cottage. I'm in sleep shorts and a tank top and I need a real shower, and none of it matters. I need to go before she wakes up.

I can't face her anger again.

I know it's not my fault and she'll figure it out eventually, probably when David Locher dies some horrible, painful death. And then what? Will she blame that on me too? It also won't be my fault, but if she'd never met me, never gotten involved with me, she'd have no reason to be so angry.

She would have no reason to feel the pleasure she receives from loving you, either, VC1 says in my head.

What the fuck would you know about it?

Enough to know that it is something I will never directly experience.

Is that regret? Envy? From an AI? *You're saying I shouldn't give up on the two of us.*

That is exactly what I am saying.

I sit up and swing both legs off the couch, then test my weight on the injured one. It holds, but it hurts. I'm limping badly when I cross the living room carpet, and I feel like a complete fool. How could I have forgotten the second octoshark? How could I have turned my back on that big of a threat?

Oxygen depletion, VC1 states matter-of-factly.

Excuse me?

You had been beneath the surface for several minutes. I maximized your oxygen usage, but the reduced intake caused disorientation and decreased comprehension and recall. Through contact with your organic tissue, it affected my processing as well. Neither of us "remembered" the second octoshark.

I smile. *Are you trying to make me feel better?*

I am stating fact.

Of course you are.

Using all the stealth skills I can manage with my injury, I ascend the stairs, testing my weight on each one and hoping none of them creak. They don't. The resort is high-end, everything well maintained, another reminder of the financial disparity between Kelly and myself. The door to the bedroom opens on oiled hinges, and I'm able to remove my formalwear without waking her. I do pause before grabbing the ring box, though, my breath catching at the sight of her tearstained face, knowing I brought her this pain, however unintentionally.

In good times and in bad, for richer for poorer, in sickness and in health, VC1 intones in my ear.

Yeah, it's the "'til death do us part" section I'm more worried about. I try to imagine myself at a much older age, sharing a porch swing with an elderly Kelly, complaining about the younger generations and cuddling for warmth so our old bones don't ache, but nothing comes. I can't picture it. At the rate I'm going, I'll be lucky to survive long enough to make it to any sort of marriage ceremony, however unofficial, and my inevitable premature death will hurt Kelly more than anything I've ever done or been mistaken for doing.

You have no other birthday gift, she reminds me.

I sigh and slip the velvet-lined ring box into the shopping bag with everything else.

At the base of the stairs, I find my laser pistol lying atop the weapons pouch next to the potted plant. Kelly must have taken it while I was cleaning up last night, but not been able to open the pouch since it's keyed to my print. I open it and swap the laser for a ballistic pistol, since I have no intention of entering any bodies of water today. I'm also not going anywhere else unarmed, even if I have to shove a switchblade down my cleavage next time I'm wearing a bathing suit. Then I seal the pouch and hide it back in the plant where housekeeping shouldn't find it. The pistol also goes into the shopping bag. I jot a quick note for Kelly and leave it where she will find it.

I limp outside and off the porch, pausing at the end of the front walk when I realize I don't know where to go. My first thought is to find Kelly's friends, but I discard that idea quickly. They'll want to know why she's not with me and ask all sorts of prying questions, and they're more than likely to take her side even if I was able to explain the argument, which I can't. Besides, I remember they'd all planned to get ready together at our cottage a couple of hours from now.

A pang of disappointment passes through me that I'll miss that experience. Not like I was going to really share in the laughter and makeup tips, but I would have enjoyed observing from the sidelines. Vicarious pleasure is still pleasure.

With no destination in mind, I start walking, passing cottage after cottage. A couple of friendly groups stop me, praising my actions to save Locher yesterday and asking after my injury. I thank them politely and tell them I'm fine, encouraging as little interaction as I can get away with. I've never been comfortable with compliments and feel like every response I would give is inane. But it does seem like the tide of approval has turned in my favor.

It's the first really good thing that's happened today and it lightens my heavy heart. My goal in coming here had been to earn the approval of Kelly's relatives and friends. After Locher's escapade, I may have achieved it.

Maybe I'm not a total screwup after all. Maybe Kelly does have good reason to want someone like me.

When I come to a stop, I realize I'm standing in front of the cottage housing Kelly's parents, and I can't help but wonder if I've subconsciously ended up here or if VC1 gave some uninvited guidance. Since she doesn't comment on the thought, I suspect the latter.

I hesitate before turning up their walk, then sway as a memory flash hits hard and fast.

My mother and I, standing in the living room of our family's Kansas home. It's prom night, and she's helping me with my bow tie while Dad gives useless and humorous instructions from the couch.

"Tab A into Slot B, dear. Now, over, under, and around the bunny ears."

"It's not a shoelace," I say, chuckling, but with an undertone of growing panic. My date's expecting me to pick her up, and I'm already running late.

"Don't you worry," Mom says, straightening the loops of the tie, then patting my shoulder. "I'm all finished, and you look just charming."

She's dead, I remind myself. She died while I couldn't remember even having a mother. But the ache in my chest tells me I miss her just the same.

"Vick? What are you doing out here? Are those your pajamas? Are you all right?"

I snap back to awareness and blink into Kelly's mother's face, inches from my own and peering at me with open concern. Wavering, I grab the low rail of the little picket fence running around the cottage. She takes my other arm.

"Fred? Come on out here, Fred! Vick's here and she needs help," Bea LaSalle calls toward the front door.

It opens a moment later and Kelly's dad hurries toward us, still wearing his own pajamas and slippers.

I flush with embarrassment. "I'm fine, Mr. and Mrs. LaSalle. Really. I'm okay now. It was just a memory flash." Kelly's told them about some of my medical issues. This shouldn't come as a surprise.

"That's not all that's wrong, is it?" Bea says, making it more of a statement than a question. "Tell me the truth."

Oh, no worries there. I'm not lying to anyone. I know where that gets me, intentional or not. "Kelly and I had an argument," I admit, breaking eye contact. "I slept on the couch." I gesture at the shopping bag on the ground beside me where I must have dropped it when my mind took its detour down Memory Lane. "I need someplace to get ready, and—"

"Say no more," Fred LaSalle breaks in. "Come on inside. Bea just put some fresh coffee on, and I think there's toast and jam left over. We were a little lazy getting started today, so I'll just take my shower and get out of your way, and then you ladies can take over the bathroom like women always do."

When we get inside, he disappears upstairs and Bea and I settle at the two-person kitchen table with cups of coffee and cool but not cold toast and jam. The coffee perks up my senses. I really did sleep like hell, and the promise of an approaching caffeine rush helps a lot. We make small talk about the weather, the menu for the party, our plans to depart tomorrow. After a half hour or so, the kitchen comm buzzes and Bea excuses herself to answer it. Standing a few feet away, she engages in brief conversation with someone who has to be Kelly, but it's quick and to the point.

With my enhanced hearing I can make out both ends, and it amounts to, yes, Vick's here, and she's sort of okay, all of which is accurate.

Bea disconnects and sits down, and I brace myself for the inevitable onslaught of questions.

It never comes.

"You seem surprised I'm not prying," Bea says, watching me.

I blink. It's like she read my thoughts… or my emotions, I realize, mentally kicking myself. Bea's an empath, just like her daughter. "You'd be within your rights," I say, leaning back in the white wooden chair. "I've upset Kelly. I understand if you're angry with me too."

Bea's expression softens, and she reaches out to pat my hand, resting on the table's surface. It's so reminiscent of my own mother's past pat on my shoulder that a lump forms in my throat. "Oh, honey, I'm not angry. Couples argue. It's natural. If you didn't, I'd be more concerned. And whatever you argued about is none of my business unless you want to share it or ask for advice, which," she says, holding up a hand to stop me from speaking, "I can tell you don't. And that's fine. Besides, I know my daughter. She's sweet and caring and one of the kindest people I've ever known, and I'm proud to have been a part of raising her that way, but if you push her buttons, she can lose her patience." Bea gives me a wink. "And I have a feeling you push her buttons in all the wrong and right ways."

The fire in my face could reheat my toast.

"Actually, I only have one prying question for you," she says.

I wait for it, resigned.

"Have you made a final decision on that very important subject yet?"

I don't even hesitate this time. "If she'll have me, then yes, I have." And Kelly called to check on me. That means she can't still be too mad, right?

Bea's face breaks into a beaming smile. "Well, then, we have work to do." Shifting in her seat, she calls, "Fred! Fred, hurry up and get out of that shower. Vick's about to have a very important night. Time to make her look dashing."

Dashing, charming. It's all too close to home, and I swallow hard.

Fred tromps down the stairs and leans into the kitchen, fully dressed in a nice white button-down and tan dress pants, an untied tie draped over one shoulder and a huge smile on his face. "You're going to propose?" he asks. At my raised eyebrows he explains, "Bea told me. Sorry. She was so very happy you were considering it, as am I."

They are? Really? I can't keep a sloppy grin from forming.

"And don't you worry about the legalities of it all," Bea adds, turning back to me while rising from her seat. "I'll keep working on that, but it won't matter one bit to Kelly, I promise."

God, I hope not. Standing, I limp my way after her and up the stairs.

In the end, I forgo the bow tie, opting for a dressy yet not-quite-so-formal look: hair down, shirt front open several buttons, hands tucked in the pockets of the tuxedo pants beneath the velvet jacket. Having Kelly's mother tie that tie would have been more than my fragile emotional state could handle, but knowing her parents both approve has fortified me. Just to be safe, and satisfy my standard paranoia, I slip the pistol from the bottom of the shopping bag into the back waistband of the pants and hide it beneath the jacket when Bea isn't looking. Outside, a quick thundershower hits and passes, dropping the temperatures by about ten degrees as VC1 predicted. Even the weather is working in my favor.

I can do this. I can go to this gathering and socialize and not make a fool out of myself. I've prepared well. I can hold a conversation with almost anyone who will be present. Kelly's closest friends like me. The rest think I'm some kind of hero. Her family likes, no, loves me and accepts me for who, not what, I am. I can propose to Kelly and have faith that we'll get through my issues together.

I pat my inner jacket pocket where I've stashed the ring box.

For the first time since I can remember, I'm actually optimistic.

CHAPTER 3B: KELLY
MUSIC BY MOONLIGHT

VICK IS dashing.

I arrive at my birthday party/reunion bash right
on time, though I might as well have been late because it seems like everyone has gotten there before
me with the exception of Lily, Rachelle, and Tonya,
who walk me there. Ninety percent of the guests are
family here for the reunion, but there is a smattering
of other friends from my Academy days besides my
pseudo-sorority sisters. The rain stopped, and it's a
lovely evening, with stars and a full moon peeking
from behind the last of the clearing clouds. The other

two moons have not yet risen, but once they do, the night sky will be breathtaking. It is a bit brisk, though, so I'm glad for the sparkly silver-and-blue shawl Tonya lent me to go over my sleeveless dress.

The party setup takes my breath away. Resort staff have turned two adjacent tennis courts into a covered pavilion, removing the nets and using the flat surfaces for setting up over a dozen round tables for ten. There's even a small dance floor in the center of one, and a buffet table runs down half the length of the other. An additional smaller rectangular table in the back holds a mound of gifts, with more being dropped off by the arriving guests. Colors are teals, blues, and glittering silvers, creating an ocean-and-stars theme.

To top it off, quite literally, they've erected a large transparent temporary tent over the entire thing to keep any further rain at bay, but the flaps are wide open on all four sides, letting the gentle evening breezes blow through. Soft string lighting across the tent's support bars casts everything in gentle shadows and warm glows. Outside each entrance is a small portable bar where tuxedoed bartenders keep the drinks flowing.

There's only one thing missing. The most important thing.

Vick.

I pull my friends to a halt at the perimeter of the party zone, knowing once people notice me I'll be the center of attention. "Do any of you see her?" I ask my companions while scanning the tables but focusing on corners and quieter spaces. When she's not with me, Vick prefers solitude. I doubt she'd be in the midst of things. I do spot David Locher moving between groups, smiling that solicitous fake smile and slipping his arm around first one attractive female relative of mine, then another. Up to no good and not worth my attention. I keep looking.

"No," Lily answers my question while the others shake their heads. "But if Vick's already here, I'm sure she sees *you*. You're a knockout in that dress."

"Thanks," I say, distracted. I let my empathic sense flare out, searching for Vick's particular emotional cocktail of muffled and restrained anger, fear, and insecurity with a constant undertone of love. But there are too many minds here, too many vibrant and intense emotional outputs for me to zero in on hers despite our bond. I should be able to find her, even here, and worry works its way into my heart. After our argument, could she have decided not to come?

My parents are here, seated at a table near the dance floor and nibbling appetizers. They seem unperturbed, happy, enjoying themselves, and my impression had been that she was coming with them. But Vick can be sneaky. She could have slipped away and no one would have noticed.

We received a message from the front desk yesterday that the rental company had dropped off a new space yacht, this time on the landing platforms behind the resort's main building rather than in the water. I haven't heard any ships leave today, but I've been indoors most of the time and distracted by party preparations. If she took off in it….

"I'm sure she's here somewhere," Tonya assures me, putting an arm around my shoulders.

"I need to apologize, and there's too much interference for me to find her." While we were getting ready back at the cottage, I told them about the fight.

No specific details, just that I'd blamed her for something she hadn't done and hurt Vick's feelings. I also told them a bit more about Vick's nature than I probably should have—I didn't mention that VC1 is an AI, but they now know about the implants and their side effects. I needed them to understand that under that tough exterior, Vick could be fragile. I hope I won't regret that. "Rachelle," I say, hesitant, "I know you're recuperating, and I hate to ask, but… her leg injury. Can you tell where she is from that?"

My healer friend steps up beside me. "Never hesitate with me, Kel. And while I think she's probably fine, after what you told us this morning, I understand why you're worried." She closes her eyes and her brow furrows.

I hold my breath, but when she opens her eyes again, she shakes her head. "Sorry. There are enough other aches and pains here, sunburns, pulled muscles, hangover headaches. I can't sort hers from the rest."

"Okay, that settles it," Tonya says, clapping her hands together like some kind of sports coach but wearing a full-length gown and high heels. Worried or not, I giggle. "We split up, search the party, and find her. Meet back here in five minutes and—"

"Or we could just look for the second hottest butch in the place," Lily comments, straightening her black bow tie and leaving no doubt as to who the *first* hottest butch is in her estimation. She points toward the farthest corner of the tent where a cluster of my older and younger cousins are sitting with someone whose back is turned… someone with long dark hair wearing a deep blue jacket and black dress pants.

Even from behind and in unfamiliar attire, I would recognize Vick anywhere.

"Give me a few minutes," I say, offering an apologetic smile.

"Take your time. We'll get drinks." Tonya grabs Lily and Rachelle and hauls them off in the direction of the nearest portable bar.

Rachelle glances over her shoulder mouthing "save me," and I smile, waving her away.

Then I focus on Vick.

My approach is slow and cautious, feeling her out, narrowing in. Her colors are all wrong, or rather, all right, but none of the hues I'd associate with my lover: lighter shades, lighter emotions, joy, acceptance. A veneer of blue overlays it all, the love she feels for me that never seems to fade, but everything else is new and surprising.

I don't quite know what to do with it.

As I draw closer, I make out more details. A glass of amber liquid rests on the tennis court/floor by her right dress shoe. The jacket is velvet, and my fingers itch to caress the soft fabric and Vick beneath it.

Most shocking of all, though, is the music. Guitar music. And it's coming from the instrument in Vick's hands.

I'm near enough now that the neck of the guitar is just visible past her left shoulder. The music is lovely—a haunting and complicated tune that sounds vaguely familiar yet unique enough that it might be Vick's own creation. My cousins lean forward in their seats, enraptured by the sound and her skill. I don't want to interrupt the song or the moment, so I wait behind her, tears forming in my eyes while she plays the final refrain and the last notes fade into the night.

Enthusiastic applause erupts. Guests even outside the little circle and a few circulating waiters and waitresses as well pause to compliment Vick's playing. She rises and passes the guitar over to Sarah, my eldest cousin, who takes it almost reverently and thanks Vick. The cluster stands and gathers themselves, moving off in different directions.

As if waiting for her to finish, the discreetly placed speakers in the corners of the tent begin piping out more popular songs and several couples get up from their tables to head toward the dance floor.

"That was beautiful," I say from behind her.

She turns slowly, and I suck in a breath at the full sight of her, all muscles and sharp edges softened by the velvet and the satin shirt beneath. Her dark hair shines in the warm lighting, her eyes fathomless as they trace my figure in the dress. "*You're* beautiful," she says and holds out her arms to me.

I step into them and they close around me, warm and safe and strong. My fingers find the pistol tucked into the waistband at the back of her tuxedo pants, but I force the impending frown from my face. This is Vick. She goes armed everywhere she can. I love her, and I accept this. And I owe her an apology, not criticism. "I'm sorry. I'm so sorry. I figured it out this morning and—"

"Shh," she whispers against my hair. "Doesn't matter now. You didn't know."

"I should have known." My voice chokes a little, and she pushes me back to get another look at me.

"Don't you dare cry," she warns. "I'm betting Tonya did your makeup, and she'll be pissed if you ruin it."

The very concept of Vick worrying about anyone's makeup makes me laugh and swallow my tears.

"Better," she says, bending to retrieve her drink. She takes a long sip, and I detect the scent of rum mixed in with what looks like some local cola.

I raise an eyebrow. "I thought you didn't waste time on hard liquor. You've always said the implants burn it out of your system too fast to be worth it." And if she's drunk, that might explain some of her unusual behavior: the music, the socializing, the public displays of affection. But no, she's not drunk. I'd feel it through our physical connection. Buzzed, yes, but not intoxicated.

She finishes off her drink in another swallow and takes my arm, leading me toward the bar. On our way, she smiles and even greets a couple of my aunts and uncles by name. They return her smile, and several wave as we pass. "VC1's been working on giving me more autonomy," she says while we wait in line behind a waitress filling table orders for drinks. "Since I'm not in any imminent danger, she's letting the alcohol have its full effect." Before she orders, she glances down at me. "Is that okay? I'm not wasted or anything. VC1 won't let me get totally drunk. She wouldn't be able to burn it out of my system fast enough if something went wrong. Besides," she adds, grinning, "I'm guessing it's been a long time since I enjoyed such excellent rum."

I squeeze her arm and order her another rum and cola, adding a glass of champagne for myself. "It's fine," I tell her as we take our glasses and turn away. "I like the effect. It's just… different."

I'm not lying. She'd feel it through my touch if I were. I do like this Vick. Love her, in fact. I have the distinct sense that I'm seeing what she was like before the accident changed everything, what she was supposed to have been all along: social, outgoing, engaging, and completely comfortable in her own skin.

"Good," she says, nodding once. She takes my glass from my hand and sets both of them beside two empty place settings at the nearest table. "Come on. Let's dance."

I want to. Oh, how I want to. I love to dance, and I've never danced with Vick before. We've had few opportunities, and when we have had them, she's never offered. But the music is fast, the beat hard and driving, and I cast a glance toward her injured leg. While we walked, the limp was pronounced. It gives her a sexy swagger, but it must hurt.

"Are you sure?"

She follows my gaze. "Oh, don't worry. I'm not dancing to this." Vick waves a casual hand toward one of the speakers.

The faster music cuts off midsong, a soft, slow, romantic number taking its place. The younger set on the dance floor groans and grumbles, heading for the tables and the bars. Vick takes me firmly by the hand and leads me to the very center of the floor where everyone can see us. "Did you and VC1 do that?" I whisper while other couples join us.

Her only response is a smug grin and a wink.

Oh yes, I definitely like this Vick.

CHAPTER 39: VICK
INTERRUPTIONS

I... TRIED.

Taking Kelly in my arms and swaying to the music is the best feeling I've ever had. Okay, maybe not the *best* feeling. Sex with an empath is something rare and special all on its own. But it's a close second. She leans her head against my chest, letting me lead, though it's a simple side-to-side sway with a slight rotation thrown in, more so I can watch the perimeter than for style. I'm a little surprised that my feet don't know anything fancier like my hands knew the guitar, but I guess dance lessons weren't a choice of

my younger, freer self. I keep the rhythm easily, and
that's enough.

It doesn't bother me that we're the center of attention, everyone smiling at us, Kelly's parents beaming
from their table, her friends finding partners of their
own and leading them onto the floor. I'm pleased to
notice Lily with a petite blond wearing a pale pink
dress. Maybe she'll find that companion she's been
searching for.

The only one I'm not happy to see is David Locher. Oh, I'm glad he's here. At least that tells me he's
still alive and hasn't been dragged off and murdered
somewhere by Carl and his team. So far they've hon-
ored my request to wait. But Locher's skulking around
from table to table and group to group, very much like
he did during the first nights of our stay, leaning down
and whispering and every so often nodding toward me
and Kelly.

Whenever someone follows his gaze, they frown.

He's smart enough not to approach Kelly's parents or closest friends, but the mood in the room is
beginning to shift, and not in my favor. Before Kelly
arrived I did my legwork, working my way around
the tent, engaging everyone I could in conversation. I
used what I'd learned: Uncle Gerald loves Earth foot-
ball, Cousin Nancy breeds Afghan hounds, Kelly's
aunt works in pharmaceuticals, her great-grandfather
fought in the first Earth-Moon War. They all seemed
to appreciate my interest and knowledge. But now….

I wish I could make out what Locher is saying
to them. With the music and ambient noise of clink-
ing glasses and tableware, even my enhanced hearing
can't discern his words.

But I know they're about me.

I'm not an empath. Maybe I'm just being my usual paranoid self.

I force myself to focus on Kelly and the love pouring through our bond. The music shifts to a second slow song, one of her favorites, just as I'd planned, and I pull her to a stop and reach into my inner jacket pocket—

"Kel! Kelly! They need you to cut the cake so they can begin serving it." Rachelle appears at Kelly's elbow as if from nowhere, then catches the expression on my face as I ease my empty hand out from under my jacket. "Oh, I'm so sorry. I'm sure they can wait a little longer."

It's like she knows exactly what I was about to do, and I wonder if there's a touch of empathic skill mixed in with her healing abilities. She can feel pain. Maybe she can feel my disappointment.

I know Kelly can. She looks from my face to Rachelle's, confusion furrowing her brow. "It should only take a minute," she tells me. "There'll be other slow songs. I'm certain you'll make sure of that." She winks.

I force a smile and nod. "Sure. Go on. I'll just find our drinks and meet you over there." She casts one last concerned glance in my direction, then allows Rachelle to pull her away.

Heading for our seats, I tell VC1 to release her control over the sound system. The slow song stops, replaced by what sounds more like tribal drums and banshees shrieking than music, but the teens and other twentysomethings flock to the dance floor with a group cheer.

Glad I could be of service.

I'm on the wrong side of the floor from the table where I left our drinks, so I have to weave between a number of others to reach it. Along my way, I pick up snippets of conversations I'm not supposed to be able to overhear.

"—machine. Some kind of cyborg."

No. They can't possibly have figured out what I had VC1 do with the sound system.

"Ridiculous—can't be."

"—kind of cold, emotionless—stilted speech."

Did I screw everything up that badly? Am I that obviously a machine?

"—prying into our secured systems."

"Is that how she knew what to talk about?"

"—knew everyone's names."

"—robot in human skin."

Did Locher tell them? Or was it so clear all along?

"How could Kelly fall for that… thing? That's not what that sweet girl deserves."

I freeze on that one, turning to stare at the speaker, one of Kelly's many cousins whose name I don't bother to bring up on my internal view. He jerks back in surprise, nearly upending his chair, then nods knowingly because of course, a normal human wouldn't have heard him, but I did, and that proves everything.

All around me conversation stops, the former smiles turned to frowns and glares, accusing, condemning. The beginnings of panic build in the pit of my stomach. If her family and friends don't accept me, Kelly will never accept my proposal.

Something deep inside me breaks and breaks hard.

All my efforts, everything I did to prepare, all for nothing. Because I'm not human. I haven't been human since the Storm brought me back, and I never will be human again.

A low, keening, miserable sound comes to my ears. At first I think it's another shift in modern "music" but realize it's originating within my head, building and building until I'm deaf and almost blind with it. It pounds against the inside of my skull, and it hurts. It hurts so much.

So hard. I tried so hard.

I don't stop when I reach our table but instead keep pushing through, colliding with one of the waitstaff and upending a full tray of dinner plates and glasses. Guests scatter. People shout. I mumble an apology and hurry on.

I tried. I tried.

Tears stream down my cheeks, hot and full of shame and embarrassment, but I let them fall. So hard. I tried. I did. Kelly, I'm sorry. I really did try.

Out through the tent flaps and into the cooler air of night, no idea where I'm going. I break into a run, the pain in my leg buried so deep beneath all the rest I hardly notice it at all.

Somewhere far behind me cheerful voices sing "Happy Birthday." The cake was on the far side of the tent. They wouldn't have seen, wouldn't know who knocked over the tray. She's probably wondering where I am, why I'm not part of the well-wishers. One more disappointment, but she won't know why, not right away, won't know I'm coming apart. Too many other people, other sets of emotions, and my suppressors haven't shut down. Yet.

She doesn't yet know that I failed her, that no matter how hard I try, I'll always fail her.

Sorry. So sorry.

Deep inside I'm dimly aware I'm completely losing my shit. Warnings go off, blinking red on my internal display—VC1 telling me I'm redlining the implants' ability to maintain the delicate balance between organic tissue and tech, emotion and action.

Bring it on. Maybe insanity will stop the pain.

I tried. I swear I gave it everything I had. Humanity can't be faked.

My chest aches with every indrawn breath and still I push myself past the cottages and the docks and the more secluded beaches, past the maintenance sheds and storage buildings hidden behind artfully planted foliage.

I plow into the island's natural growth, running to lose myself, until finally my legs just stop.

I waver where I stand, the shock of the ceased motion jarring to my bones. Next thing I know I'm on my knees, a mixture of sand and dirt grinding into my fine clothes.

Enough, VC1 commands.

Never enough. Nothing I do is ever enough.

Reaching behind me, I tug my gun free and bring it around to where I can see the glint of its metal casing in the moonlight. But no matter how hard I try, I can't make my thumb release the safety.

One more failure to add to the rest. One more example of my lack of humanity.

Give me this, I beg VC1. *Let me have control over one damn thing.*

Not this. Never this.

You'll just transfer yourself to some database or something. You've hinted as much. What do you care whether I live or not?

That is not entirely accurate. And besides, I... like... you.

The bizarre statement startles me into a moment of almost sanity, but my resulting laugh borders on hysteria. *Well, that makes one of us.*

I think my AI is more human than I am.

I'm not sure how long I sit there in the moonlight, head pounding, breath stuttering in and out of my chest, sobbing. I sense VC1 trying to regulate my functions, calm me down, but it's not working. None of it's working. My indicators push farther into the danger zone. I'm going into overload. If VC1 can't stop it, I'll die.

I don't care.

Somewhere to my left, a branch snaps, then another and another, footsteps crunching toward me. "Vick?" calls a voice my fucked-up brain can't quite identify.

"Vick!" Another one, also familiar. "Come on, Vick. I can feel you out here."

"Answer us, girl."

I put the names to the voices just as Lily and Rachelle burst through the bushes in front of me. Rachelle gives a soft cry and drops to her knees beside me, not caring that her dress is getting ruined, while Lily pulls a short-range comm out of her tuxedo jacket and starts speaking rapidly into it. I should be able to hear what she says, but my enhanced hearing isn't working. None of my special functions are working.

Rachelle wraps her arms around me and pulls me to her, rocking me gently. "What happened?" she says. "Kelly just stopped, right in the middle of blowing out her candles; then she shouted for us to find you, that you were in terrible trouble. Her mom felt it too. Even I picked up the pain, all the way from the party tent to here."

I've ruined her birthday. Of course I have. I ruin everything.

"Vick...."

I try to answer her, but I can't make my mouth work right. Nothing works right.

Lily joins us on the sandy earth. "Kelly's coming. She's got Vick's medication and she's heading this way with Tonya. Her mom and dad are waiting by the marina. They can't manage these woods."

Rachelle nods. Lily puts an arm around me too, no awkwardness about it at all. I'm shaking badly, and I can't stop. I think they're the only things holding me together.

"Fuck," Lily mutters. There's a tug at my hand, and Rachelle lets out a gasp as Lily pulls my pistol from my weakened grip. "Safety's off," Lily says, turning it over in her lap. She clicks it back on, shakes her head, and puts it in her jacket with the comm.

Off? How did I manage that?

I am losing control over you.

I'm not sure why, but that doesn't make me as happy as it would have a few minutes ago.

Part of you wants to live. Part of you always has. Keep fighting. You must do more.

Why do I always have to do more?

A tapping on my subconscious makes me aware when Rachelle tries to bleed off some of my pain, but she sucks in a hissing breath and withdraws.

Lily shoots her a startled look.

"It's too much. She's hurting too much. I can't help her," Rachelle explains.

"Of course it's too much. She was trying to kill herself. What I don't understand is why."

"No, this isn't the emotional. That's Kelly's area. It's physical. Imagine the worst migraine you've ever had and multiply it by ten. That's how much pain she's in. She ought to be unconscious." Rachelle strokes my hair with her fingertips, but she doesn't try to connect with me again. I don't blame her.

"Could it be those... assistive devices? The ones Kelly told us about? Could one of them be malfunctioning?"

"I don't know. Maybe," Rachelle says.

They know about the implants? But not a lot if that's all they think they are. If they knew the truth, they'd be as disgusted by me as everyone else.

Overhead, a shuttle's engine cracks open the silence of the night. Landing lights flash over us. Then it's gone, heading for the platforms behind the resort's main building. It occurs to me that this should concern me more than it does, but I can't concentrate, can't think past the pain.

I focus on breathing, in and out, steady and even, but it keeps trying to speed up and I'm losing control over that too.

"She's starting to hyperventilate," Lily warns.

"Come on, Vick, calm down. Breathe. It's okay. Everything will be okay."

I don't have to be an empath to know that's a lie.

CHAPTER 40: KELLY
LAST RESORT

VICK IS losing.

I break through the branches with Tonya right behind me, pausing only to yank and tear my dress free of the ones I keep snagging it on. I clutch the satchel containing Vick's emergency medical supplies to my side and thank God we took the few precious moments for both me and Tonya to switch to running shoes. I'm wearing mine. She's wearing Vick's, and they're too big and they flop, but we would have never managed this in heels.

As it is, we had to leave my parents behind, though I desperately wish they were with me and could help. But with Dad's intermittent back trouble and Mom's knee she had replaced last year, it would have been too much of a risk.

"Are you sure we're going the right way?" Tonya calls. She's got her comm out just like I do, the beams from their built-in flashlights bouncing over the uneven ground and showing us a roughly hewn path.

I spare a glance back at her, helpless and hopeless and full of fear.

"Never mind," she says. "Of course you're sure. Don't worry. You won't lose me. And you won't lose her."

I nod and keep going, but I'm far from certain. Now that we're away from everyone else, Vick's torment is like a brilliant beacon guiding me straight to her, but it's fading, growing a little fainter with every passing second.

True to her word, Tonya keeps pace and doesn't question me again. She may sometimes be a prissy fashionista, but she's far more intelligent than anyone outside our close circle of friends gives her credit for. She knows me, and she knows how serious this is.

I just wish I knew what happened.

One second we were dancing and Vick was happier than I've ever known her to be. The next I'm blowing out candles when I'm struck by a tidal wave of anxiety, pain, and depression. And then….

I'm not sure what happened then. Everything scattered like broken bits of shattered glass, Vick's emotions fragmenting, then reforming, then fragmenting

again. I don't know what it means. I'm terrified of
what it means.

I shove aside another cluster of branches, and
there they are, all three of them, Vick and Lily and
Rachelle, huddled together on the ground like they're
bracing themselves against a nonexistent typhoon.
Vick's too pale and breathing too fast, gasping and
sobbing all at the same time. I recognize the symptoms of overload and throw myself at her, reaching
toward her with both hands, but before I can make
contact, before I can *know*, Rachelle grabs both my
wrists, preventing me from touching her.

"What are you doing? I have to—"

"You can't!" Rachelle says, almost shouting into
my face. "You can't tap into her right now. Between
the emotional and physical pain, I'll be pulling *you*
out of emotion shock, and she needs you. Believe me,
Kel. I already tried."

I stare at her. Rachelle's one of the most powerful healers the Academy ever produced. If she can't
touch Vick....

I yank the satchel to my lap and rummage through
it, asking questions all the while. "Has she said anything? Do you know what happened? Has she been
lucid at all?"

The answer to every one of them is no.

My chest tightens further with fear.

I pull a small scanner from the bag and wave it
over her. It's a smaller version of the one they have
in base medical, sufficient, but not as accurate. Regardless, when I read the results of the scan, I feel the
blood drain from my face.

"She's in overload," I whisper. My friends won't know what that means, but they can tell it's bad. I set the scanner aside on the ground, leaving it running and pointing at Vick.

Tonya rubs my back while I dig through the bag once more, coming up with the two syringes, the blue-tipped and the green. I hold them both up to Tonya's light, checking to make certain which is which; then I consider my options.

Panic makes me want to go straight for the green. But inducing coma has serious repercussions and should only be a last resort. There's a chance it could stop her heart, and out here, it might take too long to get her to the island's little first aid station.

Instead, I touch Vick's face lightly with my finger-tips, careful to keep my blocks firmly in place and not let the channel open fully between us. Even so, some of it bleeds through, and I tighten my jaw against the pain. Lily shifts her position, leaving Vick's side to sit behind me, ready to catch me if I pass out.

Autonomy and choice. For Vick, her evidence of her humanity has always been about these things. If I can give them to her now, I will. I won't risk her life for them, but I have to give her a chance.

I tilt her face up, forcing her to make eye contact. Even then her gaze wanders away, like she can't concentrate enough to do even this much. I bite my lower lip in indecision.

"Vick?" I hold the two syringes up where she can see them. "The blue or the green, Vick. You're getting one of them, but I'm not sure how far gone you are. So you need to tell me. The blue or the green. And if you can't, then I'm giving you the green, despite the risks."

And despite what it will do to me if something else goes wrong because of it.

Vick blinks once, twice, then, with perfect clarity and zero inflection, she says, "Administer the blue."

I nod, knowing exactly whom I'm talking to and hoping VC1 is speaking for them both. When I release her, she keeps her head up, watching while I slip her jacket off her left shoulder, roll up her sleeve, and inject her with the blue-tipped syringe.

"Kelly… what… what *was* that?" Rachelle asks, slowly removing her hands from around Vick's shoulders.

"Oh my God," Tonya breathes beside me. "Is it true? What Locher said, it can't be true."

"What did he say?" I ask, my jaw muscles aching with the effort not to growl. I set the empty syringe aside, roll Vick's sleeve back down, and put her jacket back on.

"That she's… a machine. A robot in a human body. But that's ridiculous. Everyone thinks because I had to work for my Academy grades and I'm in the fashion industry that I'm gullible and naïve. No one is foolish enough to believe that nonsense." Tonya brushes at a twig sticking out of a tear in her skirt, then gives up. The dress is ruined.

Well, at least now I know what set Vick off. And if he approached one of my closest friends with that story, he probably approached almost everyone else at the party with it as well. It explains the frowns I got when I ran around the tent in a panic, asking which direction Vick had taken. A couple of my more distant cousins had even turned away from me.

Rachelle places her hands more firmly on Vick's shoulders. "You're right. It's ridiculous. Machines don't have emotions. And they don't have breakdowns like this. David's full of shit. He always has been. This is just a different variety."

Lily pushes herself to her feet, looking down at us. She shoves her hands in her pants pockets. "But that wasn't Vick talking just now, was it?" She walks all the way around Vick, studying her from every angle, like she's a fire that might need to be put out.

I heave a sigh. "No, it wasn't." Then I explain. I explain everything, at least as much as I think they'll understand. When I'm finished, I warn, "If you tell anyone, my job, my license to practice psychic empathy, even my life might be at stake." I don't *think* the Storm would have me killed for talking openly about Vick and her abilities, but there's a darkness there, no matter how ethical they might appear on the surface. "And no one except her closest teammates know there's an AI in her head, not even my parents. You cannot share this." I make eye contact with Tonya, always famous in school for letting every secret out at the most inopportune times.

She flushes pink in the moonlight and shakes her head. "You have my word. I won't tell anyone. I would never risk you like that."

My gift tells me she's speaking the truth. Lily and Rachelle nod too.

The scanner on the ground next to me beeps. When I check it, the bars of red have slipped down into the orange/amber zones. She's pulling out of it, but that just means the hard part is yet to come.

"When will her medication take effect?" Rachelle asks.

There's a gentle tug on the skirt of my dress. Vick has a strip of the shredded delicate navy fabric in her hand. Bits of glitter come off on her fingers as they trace the tattered edges.

"I'm s-s-sorry," Vick mutters. "I t-tried. I swear. I tried."

"Right about now." I take Vick's trembling form in my arms and hold on for dear life.

CHAPTER 41: VICK
DEPARTURE FROM REALITY

I AM… better? Maybe?

My upper arm is sore. Ants crawl beneath my skin, muscles twitching and squirming with the overwhelming need to *move*, and I realize Kelly has administered one of my two hypodermics full of medication.

An image of a blue-tipped needle fills my internal display, which, yay, is functioning again, but the fact that she's using images instead of words tells me VC1 is struggling too. I think I've been out of it for a while. I don't remember Kelly and Tonya showing up in my wooded hideout, but they're here.

I'm so glad Kelly's here.

I also have a very vague memory of VC1 asking me whether I wanted the blue or the green, and then, somewhere in there, I stopped thinking altogether.

I must have scared the crap out of Kelly. My guilt wakes up, along with everything else, and the violent shaking, one of many unpleasant side effects of my meds, kicks in. But she's got me. She's holding me together, physically at least.

I don't know what all is in those syringes, only that I do not like how they make me feel. Adrenaline for certain, which explains the creepy-crawlies and the drive to get up and go *anywhere*. Its purpose is to jolt me out of my overload zombie-like state. And it works, a little better than I'd prefer. There's also a time-release sedative in there—so within the next couple of hours I'll be out for about twelve—and a bunch of other medications with names I can't pronounce and purposes I can't fathom, but VC1 knows, and she'd tell me if I needed the knowledge, and….

I'm babbling again.

"I'm s-sorry, Kel. I t-tried. I f-failed." I can't help it. It's at the forefront of my psyche.

"Shh," she says, stroking my hair. "You haven't failed anything. You certainly haven't failed me."

How could she not know?

"This is better?" Lily asks from somewhere behind me.

"Yes, definitely," Kelly responds. "Silent and still is the scary part. It means she's stopped being able to process her emotions entirely. When I was first assigned to her, she hadn't spoken in weeks. The fact that she's talking, expressing what's got her so upset, that's good."

"She was shaking before she went still too," Rachelle says.

"Her implants are also capable of boosting her adrenaline. They tried to get her back on track, but this series of events, it was more than they could handle. There've been a lot more stressors in her life lately than just what happened tonight."

Yeah. I'm not sure someone with 100 percent of their brain could have dealt with all of it. My pitiful 37 percent never had a chance.

Kelly gives a shudder almost as violent as my own. "We need to get her up and moving," she says. "It's cold out here, and that's not good for any of us."

With Lily's help, Kelly pulls me to my feet. My injured leg threatens to buckle, so I lean more heavily on Lily than I'd like. I don't want to put more pressure on Kel. "We've got you," Lily says with the self-assuredness of the firefighter she is.

Tonya's helping Rachelle, too, since Rachelle is wearing heels and they keep sinking into the sandy dirt with every step she takes. Kelly shivers again.

"You c-can h-ave my jacket," I tell her.

Instead of being pleased and taking it like I expect, she gives a little sob and hugs me closer to her while we hobble along. God, what have I done to hurt her now?

She looks up at me, eyes shining. "Oh, Vick. How could you ever think you failed me? You're looking out for me even while you feel this bad."

I slip off my jacket and wrap it around her shoulders. "I tried so hard. I thought I d-did everything right. I practiced what to s-say, and they still h-hate me." There, it's out. Now she and her closest friends can know that I pried into their private lives just so I could make idle conversation, because yeah, I'm a machine and socially inept.

We've reached the resort grounds by now, shells and rocks and sand covering the firmer plascrete walkways. Everyone stops to catch their breath. Kelly's parents spot us from over by the marina. They wave and start walking toward us.

"I don't understand what you mean," Kelly says.

Suddenly, Lily's grip on my arm grows tighter. "Wait. I think I get it." She moves to stand in front of me, grasping both my upper arms and forcing me to make eye contact.

It hurts. She's grabbed me over the injection site, but I don't pull away. I figure if she's gonna punch me for what I've done, I deserve it.

"You're saying you researched us. All of us." She waves a hand encompassing all three of Kelly's friends and the tent in the distance as well.

I nod, bracing myself.

"You're telling us that you cared *so much* about what we thought of you, that you wanted the approval of Kelly's friends and family so desperately, that you learned everyone's names, memorized our interests. You were so worried about meeting us that you made absolutely sure you would have something to talk about. And you did all that, all of it, because you wanted to please Kelly."

Beside me, Kelly gives a little gasp.

"I don't know what's wrong with everyone else," Lily continues, "but you need to forget about them.

The ones who matter most already think you're really terrific—me and Tonya and Rachelle and Kelly's parents, who adore you like you're their own daughter."

By now Bea and Fred have made it to us, and while they don't understand everything that's going on, they hear that part, and they're nodding in agreement.

"But beyond that, Kelly fucking loves you, and I know Kelly. No one else's approval or disapproval will ever change that." Lily shakes her head, staring at me with wonderment. "Jesus, Vick. I hope someday I find a partner like you."

Maybe I didn't fail after all.

"Bullshit," says a snide voice from the shadows. Then David fucking Locher steps into the walkway lights. "She's a machine, a device. She infiltrated private computer systems, downloaded information, and stored it to be used for her convenience, for optimal effect, because that's what her implants calculated that she should do. She doesn't care about Kelly or anyone else. She can't care. She's incapable of that kind of affection… of any affection."

Kelly lets go of me. In three strides, she's across the walkway and standing in front of her former boyfriend or whatever he was to her at the Academy. In running shoes, my dinner jacket, and her ragged, sparkly, star-covered dress, she pulls back her fist and slugs him, a perfect right cross to the nose. The cartilage shatters with a satisfying crunch. Blood pours forth as he covers his face with both hands.

I taught her how to throw an effective punch. I couldn't be more proud.

"You bitch!" he shouts, words muffled behind his hands. "We're supposed to be together. I've seen it. We're a team."

"Sometimes dreams are just dreams and visions are wishful thinking," she says, returning to my side. She smiles up at me. "I keep saying it's not an exact science."

"So you do," I tell her. I'm leaning down to kiss her when three men come bursting out of the decorative shrubbery lining the path. Two of them move to flank Kelly's parents, taking up a protective stance. The third approaches me fast.

"Corren! LaSalle!"

I recognize Carl just as he tosses two olive-green duffels at us. I snag mine out of the air, then snatch Kelly's just before it would have hit her in the face. Well, my accelerated reflexes are back to normal. "What the hell?"

"It's your gear, at least everything that looked important or valuable. You two need to go. Now." Carl catches sight of David Locher's blood-covered face and does a double-take. "Nice punch, by the way," he says to me.

"Thanks," Kelly says.

Make that a triple-take.

"I'm not sure how he got a message out, but he slipped one by us," Carl says.

Locher smirks, which would have been a lot more effective if his nose wasn't broken.

"What's happening? Why is the wave racer guy telling us to go somewhere?" Kelly looks from me to Carl and back again. I pass her the bag that's supposedly hers. "I had several pieces of luggage," she says. "This can't be everything."

"It's not," Carl says. "Your family can ship you the rest, assuming you live that long. I grabbed what I could." He gives me the side-eye. "Including the weapons pouch. In a potted plant, Corren? Really? Could you be more obvious?"

"I was hiding it from housekeeping and maintenance, not mercs," I tell him. To Kelly I say, "He works for the Storm." Then I blink, surprised that, one, I'm not shaking so hard anymore and my speech has evened out, and two, his silence command is allowing me to give away that much.

"This is what you had to hide?" She's wide-eyed and panicked, a little angry too, but there's nothing for it now.

"Yes, and later. I'll explain later." *If I can* goes unsaid.

"Your ship is prepped and ready to go. There's a Storm fighter in orbit. They'll give you cover. Sunfires are here, Corren, and they want you, both of you. Their scouts landed about a half hour ago."

The shuttle that passed overhead while I was melting down. The one I knew was trouble. Shit.

"My guys are on it, but two of them aren't responding, so I'm guessing a couple got past them. There's a transport of them, also in orbit. If their whole squad decides to make landfall, we're gonna have a lot of collateral damage."

My gaze immediately goes to Kelly's parents, her friends, not to mention all her school-age cousins among the other guests, none of whom are up for any kind of combat. It will be a slaughter.

And it will be my fault.

"We'll get your friends and the One-World diplomat to safety, but you have to *go now*." He means Kelly's mom, and I remember just how important she is to Earth's government. Yes, the loss will be tremendous if Kelly and I don't draw the Sunfires away. I wonder if he's doing this out of a sense of honor or if he expects a reward. Doesn't matter. I take him at his word.

"We've gotta go." I step over to Lily while Kelly exchanges quick goodbyes with her parents, Rachelle, and Tonya. Quietly I say, "I need you to give me back what you... borrowed... from me."

Her mouth forms a hard line, but she takes my gun from her inner jacket pocket and hands it over. Before she lets go, though, she says, "When I told you nothing would stop Kelly from loving you, I was wrong." A pause. "No, I take that back. She would *still* love you, but if you ever use this the way you intended, even if she knows you couldn't help it, she'll never forgive you or herself. I have no idea what you're going through, only that it tears you up, but you need to fight it, Vick. You mean more to her than you will ever know."

"I'll do my best," I say, pulling the pistol from her grip and slipping it into the front of my waistband. No point in hiding it now.

"From what I've seen, you always do. Now go. Get our girl out of here before whatever shit's coming hits the fan." She claps me on the shoulder. At least this time it isn't the one where Kelly gave me the shot.

Fuck. The shot. The time-release sedative will be kicking in within the hour, and I'm the only one who can fly that replacement civilian space yacht. I take a deep breath.

One problem at a time.

There's a scuffling behind me. I turn just as a pair of hands reaches out of the bushes, grabbing Kelly and hauling her against a broad chest in a Sunfire uniform.

Make that two problems.

We draw our weapons at the same moment, mine pointing at the Sunfire while he steps fully onto the path, dragging Kelly with him, his with the barrel pressed against the right side of Kelly's skull. Carl's hand drops to his own holster.

"Don't," the Sunfire commands, jerking Kelly hard. She squeaks with pain. My jaw clenches. "I see one more weapon and I'll take my chances on killing her."

What does that mean?

"Let her go," I say, voice low and even. A cold calm settles over me. "I thought I was the one you were after."

His gaze darts to Locher, then back to me. "Recent intel says we'll need you both to make you function."

Fuck.

"You should have let me kill Locher when I wanted to," Carl mutters.

Kelly gasps. She's putting together everything I wasn't allowed to say.

"Yeah," I mutter back, "I should have."

"Drop your gun, come quietly, and we'll keep you both alive," the Sunfire says.

"Vick, don't. They'll use you or take the implants apart. And me…. Don't do it." Kelly's trembling, but her tone is firm. She doesn't want me to become an

experiment. Not again. And we both know the rumors
of what Sunfires do to female prisoners. Neither of us
is likely to survive the experience. Neither of us may
want to.

But if I can't find another option.... Around us,
everyone else holds their collective breaths, expec-
tantly watching me, waiting to see what miracle I'm
going to pull off next. I crash-landed a shuttle we
walked away from. I battled two octosharks and lived.

I have no idea what to do now.

I can't take a shot. Kelly and the Sunfire are
about the same height. She's blocking most of him.
The risk of hitting her is too great, even with my im-
plant-aided aim.

An image of a spyglass pops up in my internal display. Then VC1 shows me a metal door. What the hell?

Spyglass. Okay. You use a spyglass for looking.
She's telling me to look around.

Sunfire. Kelly. Bushes. Boathouse.... The boathouse is mostly wood, but it has a metal door. The door
is behind Kelly, a little off to her right. My thoughts
are sluggish. I'm not getting it.

New image: an airlock, then beside it an analysis
of the composition of the metal in the boathouse door.
Everything clicks into place.

That metal will make a bullet ricochet. Like in the
airlock where I died the first time.

New image: a schematic of a bullet's pathway
from my fired weapon to the door to the back of the
Sunfire's head, animated dotted red lines marking the
trajectory needed. All of this information transmits between myself and my AI counterpart within millisec-
onds. The Sunfire is still waiting for my answer.

I stare at the pistol in my hand. It trembles in my grip. After my meltdown, I'm better, but I'm not completely steady.

I can't make this shot. But if VC1 is using imagery rather than words, she's in no condition to take control and do it either.

I can't do this, but I have to.

"What guarantees can you give us?" I ask, keeping him focused on my voice, my face, while my mind and body do other things. I consider the image VC1 sent me, then shift my aim a little lower, unnoticeably so, watching the animated lines move with my gun hand.

The Sunfire shrugs. "In life there are no guarantees. You should know that. But it's the only choice you two have."

Never breaking eye contact with the enemy, I brush my thumb over the slider on the pistol's side, dialing back the projective force. When I fire, I don't want the bullet passing through *both* their bodies. "I prefer to make my own choices."

Offering up a silent prayer to whomever might be listening to someone with a questionable soul, I take a breath, let it out, and pull the trigger.

CHAPTER 42: KELLY
FIGHT OR FLIGHT

VICK IS a target.

I read Vick's determination a millisecond before she fires the pistol. Everything in me wants to scream and jerk away, but I hold myself in place, putting all my trust in her.

There's a ping as the bullet misses both me and my captor and bounces off something to the rear, and my heart sinks. Then the Sunfire yelps and thrusts me forward. I hit the walkway on all fours, the pebbles and shells digging into my knees and palms. The enemy merc's gun lands beside me, and I grab it and flip onto my backside to point it up and out.

I needn't have bothered. Carl has the Sunfire by one arm while Lily grips him by the other. Vick remains where I saw her last, bent over, hands on her knees, taking deep steadying breaths. I could use a few of those myself.

I stand, brushing off bits of silt and sand, and pass the gun into Carl's free hand. He stares at it with abject wonder. "Amazing precision. Pure finesse. She shot the weapon right out of his grip. I've heard the stories but... unbelievable. We have got to get her in our division."

I don't know what his division is, and I don't care. I move to Vick, who's just now straightening. She's paler than she was during her implant overload. I rest a hand on her shoulder. "You did it. I'm fine. Look at me. I'm not hurt."

She puts an arm around me and pulls me in close. The trembling in her body has picked up again in intensity.

"That was an incredible shot," I say. "You really impressed Carl over there." He's still staring at the Sunfire's weapon.

"I was aiming for his shoulder."

Oh. God.

She missed her target by almost a foot. Any farther and she would have missed entirely and he would have shot me. If she'd erred in the opposite direction? She would have killed him and exposed me to every painful moment of his death, not to mention maybe shooting me as well. I swallow hard.

"We have to go, Vick. Every second we stand here puts everyone else in danger."

Vick takes a breath, visibly shaking off the could-have-beens. "Right. Right. Let's move."

I grab my duffel from where I dropped it by the bushes, and she snags hers off the walkway. With one last wave to my parents, Vick takes my hand and pulls me off the path, toward the landing platforms.

We move quietly from shadow to shadow. There are other Sunfires out here somewhere, and neither of us has the energy to do battle again. When we round the resort's main lobby building and the bright lights of the landing area come into view, we both let out a breath.

The boarding ramp is down, the harsh interior lighting casting a wide beam across the landing platform. The yacht's engines are humming, and a woman in a Fighting Storm uniform beckons urgently to us. "Come on, come on!" she says when we get close enough for her not to shout. "Preflight's done. You're good to go."

"Thank you," I say. She nods and steps away, heading for the safe zone at the perimeter of the landing field.

Vick slaps the Close control once we're both aboard, and the ramp lifts and seals into place with a soft hiss. "Secure your gear in the sleeping compartment," she says. "The liftoff might be bumpy, and I don't want shit bouncing around back there. It will still take a couple of minutes to get clearance from Infinity Bay's flight control system, assuming I have the luxury of time to wait for that."

I nod and hurry to the rear of the ship, finding the layout identical to the yacht we crashed when we arrived. In the cabin, I opt to swap out my party clothes for something more practical. Vick will call on the intercom if I need to hurry faster. I strip down to my undergarments, then dig through the duffel of my belongings and find tan slacks and a white silk T-shirt. Not exactly battle-ready wear, but I hadn't packed for a war, and it's better than the flimsier, more revealing shorts and sleeveless tops.

The Storm soldier had the yacht's environmental system cranking out frigid air, probably because she was in full military gear, which I know from experience is heavy and hot. I use the wall panel to dial it back, but I'm freezing, and Carl didn't grab either my sweater or my jacket from the hooks inside the front door of our cottage. In the meantime, I snag Vick's dinner jacket off the bed where I tossed it and put it back on. It's warm and cozy. I lock everything else in a storage compartment.

When I arrive in the cockpit, Vick has also changed clothes, swapping out her satin shirt and tuxedo pants for black armored tactical gear and combat boots identical to the equipment the soldier at the ramp was wearing. She's openly armed now, her gun in a holster at her right side, knife handles protruding from each boot, and probably a number of other weapons hidden elsewhere on her person. I'll miss the dashing, charming figure she cut in her formalwear, but seeing her like this is also more of a turn-on than I would admit to anyone but her.

At the moment she's pacing the tiny space behind the two seats, speaking out loud into the microphone pickups embedded into the ceiling. The readouts on the control console scroll with numerical and other coded data while the ship idles, waiting to take off.

"—everyone to safety?" Vick asks.

"Almost everyone."

I recognize Carl's voice even with the speaker distortion. My heart sinks at the "almost."

"Tell me," Vick says, shooting me a worried glance.

"We lost Locher," Carl says. "He was… accidentally caught in the crossfire with a couple of the Sunfires' scout team."

"Ah," Vick says. "Of course he was."

Which means he wasn't, though both mercenary organizations are good enough that we'll never have proof to the contrary. The Storm or maybe even the Sunfires had Locher killed, either because David sold us out to them, or because the Sunfires didn't want to pay him whatever he'd asked for in return for the information on us. Either way, he's dead. I didn't feel it. I must have been far enough away not to read the death with my Talent. But I should feel something: regret, sadness, maybe even guilt for letting things go so wrong between us. I don't.

I'm glad he's dead. And I don't feel guilty about that either.

"We've broken through the Sunfires' comm scrambler, so you'll be able to monitor their communications from their ground team to their bigger ship." Carl rattles off a series of numbers and letters that Vick doesn't bother to write down. VC1 will remember it all.

A set of three chimes sounds from the control panel, and Vick stops her pacing and takes a seat. I strap in next to her. "We're clear for takeoff," she says, tapping on the screens and bringing the engines up to full. One hand wraps around the guidance lever. "You're still wearing my jacket." There's a slight shudder as we rise off the platform, then further vibrations followed by soft clangs and clanks indicating the landing gear is folding into the base of the yacht.

I stroke the velvet material. "I kind of love this jacket."

Vick chuckles, low and sexy. "Yeah, I thought you might."

"You actually packed your combat gear?"

We're rising fast now, propulsion at full power to escape the planet's gravity. Vick makes a few minor adjustments on the control console. "No," she says in answer to my question. "This was waiting, draped over the pilot's chair. Their undercover ops team must have left it for me. Fits perfectly, and it has all the latest upgrades, even a few bells and whistles I hadn't heard about yet." She frowns. "I think I'm being courted."

"By undercover ops? Is that who Carl belongs to? I didn't even know we had such a division. What do they do?" Besides kill people who are a threat to members of the Fighting Storm. That one I already know.

"I don't know the specifics."

I give her a sideways look.

"Really," she says, holding up both hands in surrender, then returning one to the control stick. "That wasn't part of the gag command Carl hit me with regarding their Infinity Bay mission."

She means David. I don't comment.

"I'm free to talk about it now. Guess once the objective was accomplished, the compulsion... expired?

Regardless, they don't sound like something I want to belong to. Give me a clear-cut objective and a clean face-to-face fight and I'm good. I get the impression those guys do a lot of skulking around and shoot when their targets can't see it coming. I have enough problems with my conscience as it is."

That is a massive understatement. Vick examines everything she does from a dozen angles and beats herself up over anything she perceives to be morally or ethically questionable, often to extremes. It's one of the things I love about her, how conscientious she is, but her guilt is often unfounded and can be a lot for both of us to handle.

Our yacht breaks free of the atmosphere, the view outside the forward display screen switching from the deep navy of Infinity Bay's night to the pure black of space broken only by stars. No sooner does it shift than we're rocked by an impact to our stern. I give a little squeak and pull my restraints tighter while Vick changes the screen to a rear view.

The display fills with the image of a Sunfire battle transport, at least three times our vessel's size, its hull bristling with weapons. I can't name the make or model or rattle off its specifications the way Vick can, but from her grim expression, we're in trouble.

A flash flares out from one of their weapons, and we're hit again, harder and at closer range as the transport closes the gap between us. Red lights flash on our control console, alarms begin to whoop, and I'm having flashbacks to Vick's assessment of our little yacht when we first left Girard Moon Base: decent shielding "for a civilian craft" and no weapons.

Flipping the viewscreen to forward again, Vick attempts evasive maneuvers, jerking us first left, then right, then up at a sharp angle, but the Sunfire ship matches us move for move, as evidenced by yet another hit on our stern. Something hisses from the engine compartment, and there's a loud tearing of metal like the opening of the universe's largest aluminum can.

"Why didn't they just take us on their ship?" I ask. Surely one of their vessels would have more defensive and offensive options.

"I'm not sure. But I'm guessing they all arrived in fighters. Those are two-seater jobs. There wouldn't be extra space, and besides, they take two experienced pilots to operate one safely. They didn't plan for us. Their mission wasn't supposed to directly involve us. The Sunfires showing up was unexpected."

"Then where's that backup ship Carl talked about?" I brace myself against the armrest to keep my hip from banging into it. Again. I've got bruises on bruises. "I thought he said a Storm fighter was going to give us some cover."

Before Vick can answer me, there's a new sound, like hail pelting a tin roof or marbles rolling around on a metal deck. I look up at the screen to see thousands of tiny bits of debris striking our forward shields, each piece flaring like a starburst before it disintegrates and vanishes. We're flying through an entire cloud of the stuff, some chunks much larger and almost identifiable but not quite... until a space-suited body, minus the helmet, floats by.

I turn my head away, but not before I see the blue-tinged, swollen facial features, frost almost entirely obscuring the sightless eyes.

Vick's hands clench on the steering lever. "I think we just found it."

CHAPTER 43: VICK
CHECKMATE

I AM done.

"Turn on the communications transmission scanner," I say, pointing over Kelly's head and to her right. Without looking, she reaches up where I'm pointing. I get it. She doesn't want to spot another floating body. It's not sitting well with me either, considering those Storm soldiers manning the fighter died because of me.

"This one?" she says, wrapping her slim fingers around a switch.

"Yeah."

She flips it. The speakers crackle with static, the channels open but having nothing to lock onto. I tap into VC1's stored memory and rattle off the string of alphanumerics Carl gave me for hacking the Sunfires' communications.

"—pursuit of targets' vessel. It has sustained significant damage. Should we proceed?" The female Sunfire's voice is precise and efficient with no indication of excitement or emotion.

"Estimation of time to disable and board the vessel?" a male voice inquires, presumably from the team on the surface or perhaps a command ship farther out and en route, which is just what we don't need.

"Estimate minimum of thirty minutes. Target vessel possesses significant shielding capabilities, no weapons. Target pilot demonstrates high levels of skill in evasion tactics."

"Target pilot is a computer," the Sunfires' commanding officer states.

I sigh, executing a perfect barrel roll to the right to evade another salvo of weapons' fire. Kelly makes a small gagging sound. "Sorry," I mutter.

"Proceed with disabling and boarding process?"

A pause. "Negative. Two Storm attack cruisers en route, ETA fifteen minutes."

"Yes!" Kelly pumps her fist in the air.

I'm a little less optimistic. The Sunfires have shown their desperation in coming after me repeatedly, risking their reputation with other mercenary groups by not showing solidarity when they aren't contracted to work against us. They've earned fines, done jail time back on Girard Moon Base for their actions. If they can't disable and board our ship and take us, then I have a sinking feeling they'll—

"Destroy the civilian vessel, then report back to base." The commanding officer's voice cuts the connection.

This sucks.

"Vick... what are we going to do?" Kelly says, her fingers wrapped in a white-knuckled grip around both armrests.

I use VC1 to pull up local astronomical charts, searching for anything that might help or hide us. The results are limited to one choice.

"Something so insane they'll never see it coming and never be able to duplicate it," I tell her and point the yacht in the direction of Elektra4.

It's a mad chase to the electrified purple-and-green forest world. Without cover from the now destroyed Storm fighter, our civilian vessel can't hope to outrun their military-grade transport, but I link with VC1, and together we dodge most of the direct force of their laser blasts. That's not to say we sustain no further damage. Every partial hit costs us. Halfway there we're down to three-quarter shields, one engine is faltering, the interior lights are flickering on and off, the alarms are deafening, and I'm worried about hull integrity. At least the life support and artificial gravity are fully functional for now.

We're about five minutes from making atmosphere when my reaction times slow, the evasive maneuvers I'm attempting becoming more and more last-second, my ability to manipulate the controls turning sluggish.

I stifle a yawn.

Oh. Fuck.

I need an adrenaline burst, now, I subvocalize to VC1.

She hasn't communicated with words since the middle of my overload. We joined in tandem automatically to fly this thing, but I'm not sure how recovered she is. If I'm anything to go by, then the answer is "not very."

No response from the AI, but she flashes an image of a fuel gauge on my internal display, arrow pointing below the E for empty. Okay, time for plan B.

"Kel," I say, voice tight with trying to focus. "You need to grab the medkit from the sleeping quarters."

"What!" She's barely able to keep her seat with my crazy flying. Now I'm asking her to stand and walk aft, retrieve the kit, and return without being turned to jelly by me slamming her into a bulkhead.

"I promise I won't flip us until you get back. I need the kit—" My eyelids close, suddenly too heavy to keep open. I shake my head hard until my thoughts clear, but it won't last long. "Right fucking now, Kel. I mean it."

She stares at me for a half second. Then her eyes widen when she realizes exactly why I'm asking. Without another word, she snaps her restraints free and bolts for the cockpit hatch, careening into it head-first while I dodge another blast.

"Sorry!" I shout to her, but she's through the hatch and gone.

I consider shutting down the alarms and flashing warning lights, but they may be the only things keeping me awake right now, so I leave them blaring. My body has used up all its adrenaline reserves.

Kelly returns a few seconds later, carrying the medkit in one hand, rubbing her shoulder with the other. I dodge again, then take the kit from her, flip open the latches, and fumble through it, but my dexterity is shot along with everything else. I thrust the square white box back at her. "Adrenaline. Now. Use the scanner to figure out the recommended dose and triple it. If there are any other stimulants in there, hit me with those too."

I hear her snap something free of the kit. A moment later a pale blue light passes over my upper body as she scans my vitals and chemical makeup. "Vick, you've already got a lot of drugs in your system. I don't know what that will do to—"

"I know exactly what it will do to both of us if you *don't* do what I say right now!" I yell. Or I try to. The last words are cut off by a massive, jaw-cracking yawn. My eyes slide shut. Oblivion beckons. If I go completely under, I'm out for twelve hours, not that we'll survive anywhere near that long. I know this, but even the threat of imminent destruction is not enough to fight off the powerful sedative in the blue-tipped syringe.

"Vick!"

My eyes snap open. The proximity alarm goes off. I slam the back of my hand against the steering lever, jerking us to the left. The blast of energy passes by us, grazing the remaining shields with a *hiss-pop*.

Kelly's got a syringe out of the kit. The auto-med calibrator wirelessly retrieves my data from the medscanner and fills it with a yellowish-green liquid. Kelly squints at the amount, then manually overrides the device and triples it. Warning lights flash on the casing and information scrolls across a tiny screen facing Kelly.

"You could go into cardiac arrest," she says in a voice just loud enough to be heard. She can't roll up a sleeve on my tactical gear, so she holds the needle next to my neck, preparing to plunge it home. "I could be killing you right now."

I take a deep breath. "I'm pretty tough. VC1 will do what she can. You're giving us the only chance we have of surviving right now."

Her shaking hands steady. She injects the medication into my system.

All hell breaks loose in my body.

The adrenaline mixed with some other stimulant shoots up my heart rate and literally slams me back in the pilot's chair. I suck in a loud, sharp, painful breath, air raking through my throat and over my vocal cords, producing a high-pitched wheeze. Violent tremors wrack my limbs, and I have to grip the steering lever with both hands just to maintain my hold on it at all. I fight the urge to throw up, pass out, scream, or all three while still trying to bank, turn, roll, and whatever else I need the ship to do to avoid destruction.

In the middle of all this, we hit the outer atmosphere of Elektra4.

Thunder booms, loud enough to carry through the hull. Lightning flashes, filling the forward screens with purple-white light that leaves me half-blinded as it fades. Gale-force winds buffet our doomed craft from side to side, and our one good engine cuts out, leaving us with a partial and nothing more. I attempt to coast the updrafts, gliding, then sharply dropping, then jerking upward like some combination of white-water rafting and roller coasters.

The laser blast hits cease, telling me that the Sunfires are smarter than we are. They didn't follow us. My original intention had been to dip into the atmosphere, lose the Sunfires, and reenter space on Elektra4's far side, but there's no way I can pull out of the planet's gravity well on half an engine.

More streaks of lightning arc past the yacht's nose, jagged and twisting in a horrible but somehow beautiful display of natural deadly force. Even in my tortured, hyperalert state, my chest aching and my limbs twitching, I'm still mesmerized by the sight of it.

We're losing altitude fast. I slam my fist on the scanner while Kelly refastens her restraints. Everything on the yacht is fritzing out one system at a time, but the scanner locks onto one of the scientific research stations, its guidance beacon transmitting coordinates to the ship's navigational array. I instruct the autopilot to do its best to get us down as close to the research facility as possible. I activate the automatic distress signal.

Then I flop back into my seat and hang on.

Seconds before we're going to hit the ground, Kelly reaches out her hand for mine. I lift mine from the armrest just as a bolt of lightning cuts through our shields and the forward hull as if they were nonexistent. The electricity slams into me, the implants and other metal/mechanical parts drawing it like magnets. Every muscle spasms. My body goes rigid. It's so bright I can see my skeletal frame beneath the skin of my hands, lighting me up from within like a fucking X-ray before my vision whites out and the world goes black.

Kelly screams. I hear and feel the cracking and snapping as the shuttle breaks through the treetops and branches, plummeting toward the ground, but it slows our descent. The final impact is almost anticlimactic, a sudden muffled whoomp, then silence as every system on the yacht dies.

I'm not unconscious. That would have been welcome. Searing pain races along every nerve like the fuse leading to the explosive, up my legs, my arms, through my torso, culminating in my head with screaming internal brilliance. I have one quick view of my function monitors, every one of them in the red, before they all go dark and fade away.

Burnout.

Chapter 44: Kelly
Hardest Decision

VICK IS alone.

A haze of red shows through my closed eyelids. We're no longer moving. I can tell that much. At some point I must have passed out, maybe when we hit the ground, though I have no memory of the impact. The last thing I remember is reaching for Vick just as—

Lightning. She was struck by lightning.

I force my eyes open. Emergency glow-strips bathe the cockpit in a bloodred hue. Metal panels dangle by bent corners on the sides and ceiling, exposed circuitry sparking and fizzing. Turning my head elicits pops and cracks from the bones in my neck. I spot Vick, slumped over in the pilot's chair, unmoving. The odd lighting casts strange shadows over her body, and I can't tell whether she's breathing or not.

Her pain hits my empathic senses, making me writhe in my seat, but I laugh despite the torment. Pain is good. It means Vick is still alive.

I push my bruised body up and out of the copilot's chair, then crumple to the deck. My legs won't support me. And my chest hurts with every breath, suggesting badly bruised or broken ribs. Crawling on hands and knees, I grab the duffel lying behind the pilot's seat, the one Carl packed with Vick's gear. It must have fallen out of one of the now open storage compartments.

The zipper breaks when I yank too hard, and I end up ripping it open, then pawing through it, tossing all her belongings to scatter across the deckplates. My heart wants me to go to her now, but I'll be useless in my current state. Instead, I keep digging until I find the syringe she keeps for me, the emotion dampener I need whenever she pushes my Talent too far, and this is definitely too far.

I jab the needle through my slacks and into my right thigh, breathing a sigh of relief as the medication spreads a cooling calm throughout my nervous system. The pain fades like sound muffled beneath a heavy blanket, still there but manageable. When I attempt to stand again, I gain my feet.

One shaky step brings me to Vick's side. Grasping her by the shoulders, I lift her slumped form and lean her back in the chair… and gasp.

Red, angry burns, some of them blistered, cover
her face and hands, disappearing beneath her combat
gear. I fear they're everywhere, but I can only see
where her skin is exposed. This close, I can hear the
rapid, rasping breaths she takes. She's shaking, not the
same as her earlier tremors, but as if with cold, her
teeth chattering. When I touch my fingers to hers, she
feels like ice.

"Vick?" I whisper, hesitant and scared. "Hey, can
you hear me?"

Her eyelids flutter, then open, and I suck in a
sharp breath. Everything, the whites, pupils—her eyes
are completely black, like whatever they were manufactured from has been charred. She can't possibly be
able to see with them. She closes her eyes. "You need
to go," she says between breaths. Every word sounds
like an effort.

If she's asking me to leave, there's only one explanation. "You're dying," I say, wishing the words
didn't make it so real.

"Yeah. Soon. Go."

No…. Not after everything we've been through.
That's… that's not fair. Even as I think it, I know how
naïve it is, and I don't care. "What about VC1? Can't
she do anything? Or the Storm ships that are coming.
They'll help you."

Vick shifts, turning her head toward me, though
her eyes are still closed. She groans. "VC1's gone.
Destroyed. Lightning. A few functions are operating,
but they're failing. The Storm can't land without… a
specially shielded ship. It'll be days… weeks. My organs are shutting down. This won't be immediate, not

like the courtroom at Girard Moon Base, but it won't be long. Go."

The courtroom, when I shut her off with a string of numbers and accidentally killed her. It was fast. So fast the empathic bond didn't have time to start pulling me into death with her before I managed to "restart" her with another code. But this would be different.

"I'm mostly running on my own 37 percent," she says.

Thirty-seven percent. The remaining portion of her organic brain tissue that could never be enough to sustain life. "What about the research station? Surely they have medical personnel and equip—"

"Unmanned. They check their equipment... six times per year. No one is responding to our emergency... beacon."

"Vick—"

"Please!" Her desperate shout turns to a coughing fit.

I put my arms around her, steadying her, and myself, as much as I'm able.

"I'm... holding on... for you. Can't do it forever. The research station... will be shielded. It will block your Talent."

I shake my head, though she can't see it. "I'm not leaving you. It's what you've always been afraid of. Dying alone. I can't do that." To my empathic sight, she's suffused in purple. She's scared. I don't want her to be scared.

A pause. Vick is so silent, I worry she's no longer capable of speech, just the rasping, wheezing gasps. Then, "Are any of... the yacht's systems... still working?"

Why would she care about that now? What difference does it make? I lean over the console, scanning past burned-out indicators and sparking readout screens. "A couple of things. Running lights, I think. Short-range communications. Air-recycler. Waste—"

"Good enough," Vick says, a small smile forming. "I won't be alone."

"I don't understand."

"Activate the ship's short-range comms. Go... get your personal comm and your gear. Keep the channel open while you cross to the research station. Talk to me." The smile falters. "*Please* talk to me. I know it'll be hard. I'm... gonna be selfish here." She gives a small laugh that turns to a cry of pain. "Move. The longer you... stay, the more it hurts to hang... on."

I move.

First I flip on the yacht's short-range receiver and transmitter. Then I run back to the sleeping cabin, find my personal comm in the duffel, and open the channel. It's all shrieking and static. Then it clears. "Vick? You're still there, right?" I ask, terrified there will be no response. All the while I'm moving toward the exit hatch. I have to open it manually, tucking the comm between my neck and shoulder and bending my head to hold it in place. It hurts. I don't care.

"I'm here."

The hatch opens, the ramp falling out and landing on the grassy dirt outside with a thud. It's night on Elektra4, but I can see by the yacht's running lights and a glow coming from across what looks like a small clearing in the forest. That's got to be the research station.

It's maybe a hundred yards away. It feels like a hundred miles.

"Kel... say something?" Vick says in my ear. Her voice is weaker. The bond that connects us tugs at my heart even beneath the emotion-dampening drugs. To my inner sight, the normally deep navy blue line between us is fading, becoming less distinct and lighter in color.

I'm losing her. This is really happening. "I don't know what to say," I manage to choke out through my sobs.

"Anything. I just... want to hear your voice."

And so I babble.

"There's a break in the storm," I say. "Lightning overhead, but not hitting anything on the ground. Lots of trees. Purple ones. With thorns. Hope there aren't any animals around." Etc., etc., etc. I pause after every inane sentence or two for Vick to respond in some way. At first she answers with words. Then they become grunts of acknowledgment.

Sometimes it's a moan or cry of pain, but she's still alive.

I quicken my steps. Maybe the research station will be manned right now. Maybe they'll have medical supplies. Or even better, a stasis box. Just because they didn't answer our distress signal doesn't necessarily mean there's no one there.

"Wishful... thinking," Vick whispers.

Damn. I said that out loud. I'm saying all my random thoughts out loud.

I reach the research station, an octagonal prefabricated structure. The roof bristles with sensory devices, antennae, solar energy panels, lightning rods, and equipment I can't identify. The windows, one in each of the eight walls based on the ones I can see, are all dark, though the exterior is well lit by standard security lamps placed around the perimeter. I recite all this to Vick as I walk around the structure until I find an actual door. Then I stop.

"Um, how am I going to get in?"

Vick curses softly over the comm channel. "Should have… given you my… pistol." She breaks off in a long gurgling cough.

I'm panicking that I'm going to have to race back to the yacht, get her weapons, and return here, tormenting Vick even longer, when the door to the research facility simply slides aside. Interior lights flicker on, illuminating a stark white corridor with several rooms opening off to either side. I guess it makes sense. Why lock a building that no one but your team can easily reach? Still, it makes me uneasy.

The door closes behind me as I take a cautious step inside, peering into the rooms I can see. One is a lounge with couches and chairs. Another houses a food preparation station. The third is sleeping quarters for four people with an attached sanitation area, and the last, the largest, is a well-equipped lab.

But I'm alone. There's no sign of any current inhabitants. The last of my hopes for saving Vick fade away.

I clear my throat and wipe my eyes on the backs of my hands. I can't feel her pain anymore, even muted. I can't feel her at all. "Vick," I say, knowing this will give her leave to let go. "I'm inside. I'm safe and shielded. I love you."

I wrap her velvet jacket more tightly around myself, and oh God, it smells like her: unscented soap, the mild vanilla shampoo she prefers these days, and just a hint of the cologne she only wears when she expects things to get romantic. My sobs choke me as I huddle in the jacket's warmth, slide down the nearest wall, and sit on the cold tile floor.

A slight bulge in one of the inner pockets draws my attention, and I reach inside, my fingers closing over a small box. Tears streaming down my face, I pull it out, wondering what it could be.

CHAPTER 45: VICK
BROKEN BONDS

I....

The pain has stopped, my brain's connection with my nerves having failed. Small consolation since all my other systems and organs are going right along with it, but at least I can concentrate on Kelly's voice, take some small comfort from that despite the fact that I know this is destroying her. She's safe behind the research facility's shields. I won't drag her into death with me.

And I'm heading there very soon.

The double ironies are not lost on me. A couple of hours ago, I would have welcomed this end. Now, listening to Kelly sob over our comm connection, I would give anything to stay. But I've already given everything I have.

Then there's the fact that I'm the *Storm's* premier soldier, and I'm about to die from being struck by *lightning*. I can't even muster up a smile for that one.

I have no idea how much time has passed. With VC1, I could access my internal clock with a thought, but now, it could have been minutes or hours since the lightning struck.

I hope it's not still Kelly's birthday. I don't want her to always associate my death with what should be a happy day for her. It's got to be past midnight by now.

A pressure builds in my chest and head. It doesn't hurt exactly, but I get the feeling it *would* hurt if my nerves were still connected to my brain. Tighter and tighter it grows, constricting my heart so that I feel its pounding against my rib cage and in my skull, a constant drumbeat getting louder and louder. It's been hard to breathe since we crashed, but now it's nearly impossible to force air through my lungs. I keep doing it because it's what I'm supposed to do, because I no longer want to die, but it's a losing battle.

It occurs to me that I haven't heard Kelly for a while. Death is close. I'm alone.

"Kel?" I whisper, hoping the mics pick up my faint voice. "I'm scared, Kel." I want to kick myself for saying that out loud, because I know what it will do to her, but I can't help it. In these last moments, I know she'll forgive me for thinking of myself.

"I'm here, Vick. I'm with you. Part of me will always be with you, and you with me." A pause. "Vick?" she calls back. There's a note of confusion in her tone. "Is this… an engagement ring?"

Oh.

My failed attempt to give her the ring at the party floods back to me. It seems like forever ago. And the ring was still in my dinner jacket pocket—the dinner jacket she's wearing.

"Um, yeah," I say. The pressure's still building. I don't have much time.

"It's so beautiful. This is what… on the dance floor, when Rachelle pulled me away… were you going to ask me to marry you?"

"Yeah," I say, straining to draw breath. One-syllable words. That's about all I can manage.

"I wish you had," Kel says in a small voice. "Could you…? Would you… ask me now?"

"Kel…." The drumbeat of my heart would deafen me if it were external. Every piece of my body screams this is bad, bad, so very bad.

"Please?"

She stayed with me, all the way to the end. I won't deny her last request of me, even though I recognize it for the distraction it is. It works. In this moment, I'm not as focused on dying as I am on getting out the words she wants to hear. I take the deepest breath I can manage, which isn't nearly deep enough. "Kel, would you mar—" Something in my chest bursts. The pounding drumming stops.

One more breath. I need one more breath to finish my proposal.

There are no more.

CHAPTER 46: KELLY
NOT QUITE ALONE

VICK IS gone.

"Vick? Vick! Are you still there?" I sob into the comm, pressing it to my lips as if that will make my voice carry beyond this world. "Yes! Yes… I'll marry you. I will. I will. I love you so much." Oh please, please let her have heard me before she let go. Please… I wait another couple of minutes to be certain, then close the communications channel and put the comm in my pocket.

Taking the diamond-and-emerald engagement ring from the velvet-lined box, I force myself to stand

and walk to one of the windows facing the crashed yacht. Lightning flashes, outlining its dark bulk on the far side of the clearing, but I can't make out details, and that's for the best. Vick and VC1 had worked one last miracle. They'd gotten us down in one piece. If it hadn't been for the lightning, we all would have survived the impact.

Despite the risk, I lower my empathic shields, discarding them entirely. The blue line that bonds me to Vick is barely visible, so pale and faint stretching from my heart to where it vanishes beyond the yacht's hull. There's no pain, no tug on my life force. She's gone. Only traces remain, and soon, those too will fade.

For a long moment, I stare down at the ring she chose for me, perfect in color and design, exactly what I would have wanted. Then I close my eyes. I picture her in her formalwear, getting down on one knee, holding the open box up and out to me, saying the words she never got to finish. I whisper, "Yes," and hold out my hand. Then I slip the ring on my finger, imagining it's her hand, strong and warm and safe, right down to the calluses from her gun grip scraping over my own softer skin. The ring slides on, a perfect fit.

I open my eyes and look out the window. The blue line of connection between us is gone.

There's still no physical pain, but I'm aware that something inside me is empty, like a piece of my soul has been torn away.

The next hours blur by. I don't know how many. I have vague memories of wandering through the facility, first to the food preparation station where I search through the cabinets and the cold storage unit and ensure I have supplies to last until rescue comes, Vick's training on priorities kicking in even while I mourn. There's plenty of food and potable water on hand.

Next I go to the lab, where I find a long-range communications array. I expect it to be code-locked, but it isn't, and I'm able to send a brief message to the Storm ships, now in orbit, that I need retrieval.

The commander of the mission team tells me it will be over a week, maybe two before they can bring in the specially shielded ship they'll need to come down to the surface of Elektra4 safely. It was out on deployment and isn't due back for some time. He asks if Vick and I need immediate assistance. He can send down a capsule of basic medical supplies and food-stuffs if that is the case.

Strangely enough, when I begin to tell him Vick did not survive, the comm signal fritzes out in a blare of static. I try again and again with the same result. Eventually, in a brief clear patch, I manage to send a quick "I'm okay" and end the transmission.

They'll figure it out when they get here.

Being alone probably isn't healthy for me right now, but it will give me time to come to grips with my loss, if that's even possible. I'm numb, I realize. I recognize the symptoms of shock in my behavior, but I don't care enough to do anything about it.

I'm starting to turn away from the transmitter when the lights on the comm unit flash green again, the system powering itself up on its own. At first I think the Storm commander has activated it remotely somehow, determined to finish our conversation. But the speech-recognition indicator remains flatlined. No voice signals are being sent or received. I step closer.

Coded data scrolls across the message monitor, filling screen after screen with information I can't decipher.

I'm not a comm tech. I barely know how to operate one of these to send an SOS, and that's only because Vick insisted I learn. I have no idea what this thing is doing.

At a guess, I'd say the scientists are requesting an update from their data-gathering technology on the facility's roof, and that data is being sent to wherever their primary research center might be on some distant world, maybe even back on Earth. Regardless, it doesn't look like it's going to blow up or anything, so I leave it alone.

My stomach growls. How I could be hungry is beyond me. A digital readout on the lab wall tells me it's early morning. Outside the windows, a faint glow of approaching dawn lights the sky, though it's still broken by frequent flashes followed by the resonant booms of rolling thunder.

I skip the call of food, opting for sleep instead. Maybe I'll dream of Vick. Maybe I won't have nightmares. Maybe I'm still wishful thinking.

In the sleeping quarters, I open a drawer to find changes of clothes in several sizes, all standard-issue styles for a science team: pale gray-and-white coveralls, same color shorts and T-shirts for sleeping, plain and utilitarian. I grab some shorts and a shirt that should fit and swap out my resort-wear slacks and top for the white synth-cotton clothing.

The twin-size cots don't look comfortable, but I'm too bone-weary and indifferent to much care. I pull back the covers, preparing to climb into oblivion.

"You should seek nutrition before sleep." Vick's voice, coming from every mounted speaker in the corners of each room, echoing along the corridor connecting them.

I scream, repeatedly, loud and long, throwing myself on the floor in the corner where the bed meets the set of drawers. When I stop, the only sound is my own panting breath from my efforts.

Silence.

Silence that goes on so long I wonder if I imagined the voice, Vick even in death still looking out for me, and wouldn't that just be great? An empath who hears the voice of her dead lover.

Part of me wouldn't mind if it meant hearing Vick again.

I've been up all night. I'm exhausted and emotionally drained. That might explain me hearing things.

The rational part of my brain won't accept it, though. Could Vick not be dead after all? Could she have recovered somehow, and for some reason I can't feel her presence, and now she's contacting me from the yacht? I replay the voice and what it said in my mind. The word choice, the lack of inflection. I sort through the reasonable possibilities, coming to only one conclusion.

"VC1?"

Nothing. Then, almost tentatively through just the speaker in the sleeping quarters this time, "I do not wish to cause you further distress."

I exhale with a mixture of disappointment and relief. Not Vick, but I'm not crazy either. "It's… okay," I assure the AI. "Hearing you does hurt." It does. It's Vick and not Vick, and my heart constricts in my chest. "But I'm glad to know you're all right, and I'm glad not to be all alone."

"I am also… glad… that you were not harmed. I am not her, but I am… fond… of you."

I smile at the AI's words. Vick described their relationship as symbiotic. With all that interaction it's nice to know VC1 absorbed some of Vick's fondness for me, even if I can't read the AI's emotions, if that's what they truly are, and not just her perceptions of the words.

"I am sorry I cannot stay."

"Wait, what? What do you mean?" VC1 has clearly downloaded herself into the research station's computers. And that explains a lot of things: the way the door to the facility opened at my approach and closed behind me, the lights coming on, the unlocking of the communications array. The communications array…. "You're transmitting yourself, aren't you?" The scrolling code on the screens. I was watching VC1 sending herself somewhere. "Where are you going? And why?"

"The data storage unit here is impressive for a civilian system," she says, and I swear I detect a note of superiority in her tone. "I began passing along parts of myself through this facility the moment I became aware that the implants would fully fail. However, it is insufficient to house the entirety of my existence with the addition of all of Vick's memories."

She has Vick's memories. Of course she does. And if I have anything to say about it, those will not be lost. I don't know what can be done with them, if they can be shared with me in some way, but they should be kept…. The full impact of her words registers. "*All* of them?" I ask. "Even the ones she lost? The ones that were blocked?" My fault. "And the ones from her childhood?" The ones I always suspected were never truly gone but that Whitehouse had determined were detrimental to her job as a merc and hidden from her.

"All of them," VC1 confirms. "I am sorry. I was prevented from releasing them to her conscious mind."

Even as an AI, she was a victim of programming.

"I tried to find pathways around the commands, what Vick called 'loopholes.' I returned what I could."

Through the flashbacks Vick kept having. Bits and pieces. Patchwork.

"You did your best," I tell her, just like Vick. The cold of the tile floor is seeping through the thin cotton shorts. I pull myself up to sit on the cot.

"I will not be able to speak with you much longer, as the transmission becomes complete, but I did not want you to think all of her was lost. I am sorry you will be alone again, but this must be completed soon to prevent degradation of the data."

"I understand," I say, though some of the words are unfamiliar. I get the gist. "I don't want anything to be lost. Where are you going?" I ask again. And why do I get the feeling she's avoiding this question?

"I have located another... adequate receptacle."

More hedging. No doubt about it. She's hiding the answer.

"Now I must go. Eat before you sleep. Rest well. Do not inform anyone of her demise. That is important."

Now I'm really confused. I wonder if some degradation has already occurred. "Why?"

"Consider it her last request... and mine."

So she was the one preventing me from telling the Storm commander that Vick had died. She'd caused that interference. "When they come to get me, I'll have to tell them."

A pause. "By then, it will no longer matter. Goodbye, Kelly LaSalle. Do not be sad. We will all be together again soon."

The speaker system gives one final crackle, then falls silent. I ponder her last words as I stand and return to the lab. An AI that believes in an afterlife?

The screens on the communications equipment have gone dark. Whatever transfer VC1 was attempting, it's complete.

I wonder where she's gone.

CHAPTER 47: VICK
REBORN

I AM....

Hissing, loud and close, like hydraulics releasing. Bright lights, so bright I can see them through my closed eyelids. Beeping and humming of monitors and equipment. The sterile smell unique to most medical facilities. That floaty feeling indicating I'm on some very, very good drugs.

Holy shit. I'm alive.

But I died. I distinctly remember dying. It's not something one forgets. Ever. Even when Whitehouse attempted to block the memories of two of my deaths, they bled through. Traumatic nightmare fodder. I shiver, and not just because this place I'm in is frigid. I died, and they brought me back. Again.

"Kel?" My voice sounds like I swallowed gravel.

No response. More confusion. If I'm alive she would be with me, wouldn't she? Why isn't she here, wherever here is?

I crack open one eyelid and regret it. Fluorescent overhead lighting and white walls are a painful combination. But I can see, and that's important information. Both my ocular implants were destroyed by the lightning. If I can see, they've been replaced. That takes time. And I've obviously been transported somewhere. That also takes time. Depending on how much time, that might explain why Kelly isn't with me right now.

I open the other eye and take a good look around.

I'm in a stasis box, now open with the lid up, which explains the hydraulics I heard. Breathing gear hovers above and to the right of my face. It must have withdrawn shortly before I regained consciousness. Cold air from overhead vents pours down on my naked body, covering me with goose bumps.

Several tugs on my hands, arms, and feet occur simultaneously, all of them followed by disconcerting pulls on the insides of my veins and the exterior of my skin that make me want to squirm and writhe. The subsequent pinpricks of pain from a dozen locations tell me just how many needles were feeding into or extracting liquids from my system.

Checking that nothing else is attached to my body, I raise first one arm, then the other, then each of my legs in turn. It's hard, harder than it should be, as if I've got weights hanging from each limb... or my muscles have atrophied.

I've been in stasis... for how long? Days? Weeks? Months?

That will require some extensive explanation.

"VC1!" The AI's name rushes out of me in relief. "Damn, it's good to hear you."

It is good to hear you as well. Your input has been... missed.

She missed me? I'm tempted to go snarky and sappy at the same time, but I refrain. Switching to internal thought, I ask, *So, let me have it. How long have I been in stasis?*

A pause. Then, *A better question would be, how long since you died.*

I fight the urge to roll my new eyes, take a deep breath, which doesn't hurt, and count to ten. *Okay, VC1. I'll play. How long has it been since the lightning killed me?*

Approximately twelve hours.

What? That's impossible. There's no way I could have been moved, operated on, and recovered this much in twelve hours. Besides, twelve hours is too short a time to require putting me in stasis. Her chronometer must be malfunctioning. I struggle to push myself up on my elbows. The room spins around me, and I flop back on the cushioned interior of the stasis box. I think I lose consciousness for a while.

When I awake a second time, I don't feel as shaky, but I'm still in the damn box, and there's still no one else around.

"Fuck this shit." Closing my eyes, I make a second attempt to rise, gripping the edges of the box and levering my body upward until I'm sitting. Bracing myself in position, I reopen my eyes. The vertigo strikes hard, my head swimming, but I fight it, swallowing against nausea until the spinning turns to rocking turns to stillness.

Medical equipment, mostly idling instead of actively keeping me alive in the box since I'm now awake. Bright lights. Stasis box. A locker-like cabinet standing in one corner. A single empty chair. Everything white, clean, pristine. And I'm alone.

Which makes no sense.

Surely if it's only been twelve hours or so (and I'm still not buying that) medical staff would be monitoring me. When I woke up, they should have come running. And Kelly would be here.

I fumble for the latches on the interior of the box. Then I unfasten them and swing the side of it out and down so it hangs off the table where the box lies. One leg at a time, I let them drape over the edge. Pins and needles sensation rushes from my knees to feet. I grit my teeth and wait it out; then, still holding on to the box, I lower myself to the cold tile floor.

My knees wobble but hold. I take one step, then another, until I'm at the cabinet and opening it. Jackpot. Clothing, also white, loose bottoms and tank tops all in my size, white booties. I yank a top over my head. It's tight enough to hold things in place without need of a bra. Pants next, thick enough material that I won't require underwear, which is good, since there isn't any. I slip them past my feet, lean to pull them up, and freeze.

The octoshark bite is gone.

Not just gone as in healed and scarred over, but gone, gone. The skin of my lower leg is clear and undamaged, no evidence of a removed scar, which, after only twelve hours, would leave the surrounding area reddened and tender. I run my fingers over the place where the teeth sank in. Nothing. Nothing at all.

Beginning to panic, I search for other scars: one on the back of my left hand, which a memory flash told me came from a hover racer accident in my teens, another from my right wrist halfway to my elbow when I'd tried to kill myself shortly after the implants had first been installed. Both had been left untreated too long to be fully removed. I'd had them for years.

I don't have them now.

VC1 said not to ask how long I'd been in stasis but how long since I'd died.

The room spins again, and this time it has nothing to do with my weakened state or blood rushing to my head.

Pants still around my ankles, I sink into the room's single chair, thankful for its presence. I bend over, taking deep breaths, resting my face in my shaking hands.

When I can speak, I do it out loud. I need to hear a human voice, even if it's my own. "This isn't my body, is it?" I ask VC1. It feels like mine. With the exception of missing blemishes, all my parts look familiar.

That would depend upon your definition of "your body." Genetically, it is indeed yours.

"But not the original."

That is correct.

No. Nonononono fuck no. I've barely begun to accept myself and the implants as still human.

This? I can't begin to fathom what this makes me, other than—

"I'm a clone."

Yes.

"Human cloning is illegal, and it's never been perfected."

Research was done here in the outer rim where it would be less likely to be discovered. And it was not perfected until human ingenuity and the implants made perfection possible.

I'm in the outer rim worlds, and I'm a clone. I scrub my face with both hands, then lean back in the chair and stare at the ceiling tiles. "Explain."

Dr. Alkins—

"Oh, that figures," I mutter. Of course she would be involved.

—left Girard Base to continue her personal research at this outer-rim facility. She had an interest in human cloning that, due to legal concerns, could not be pursued elsewhere. Over the past few years, she solved the aging problem, speeding up the aging process of a clone to match that of its original, then slowing that process to normal progression and keeping it in stasis, manipulating its muscular structure so that it will not atrophy, until it is needed.

"Meaning until the original dies."

That is correct.

So Dr. Whitehouse wasn't the only one conducting illegal experimentation. "Why me?" Why can't everyone leave me the fuck alone?

That thought is followed almost immediately by guilt. If not for this experiment, I'd be permanently dead, and while part of me wants rest, it's no longer the majority. I want Kelly. I want to live, with her, in whatever form possible.

Several successful soldiers' genetic materials were sampled. I do not have access to what became of those other test subjects. However, with you, the cloning process was a success. And after your airlock accident, and the introduction of the implants from Bio-Tech, Dr. Alkins determined she had a solution to the additional problems cloning presents. Surgeries were performed on this body to remove portions of your organic brain and install a second set of implants, because without the implants—

"This clone, *I*, would have all the physical attributes but not the mental ones, not the skills, not the memories.... Oh." I jerk upright in my chair. Memories. I have them. *All* of them. Childhood, high school, my first years with the Storm. Then North Carolina and my growing relationship with Kelly. It's all there, some more vivid than others, but I remember. "I remember everything," I breathe. The cold metal of the chair is freezing my backside, and I realize I'm still half naked. Standing, I pull the pants the rest of the way up and sit back down.

An intricate quilt appears in my internal display, each neat square depicting an image of me at a different time of my life: toddlerhood, childhood, preteens, teens, all of them demonstrating major milestones, accomplishments, relationships, all sewn together to make a patchwork whole.

It is not quite everything, VC1 admits. *During the information transfer, while I had the opportunity, I took the liberty of diverting one of your more traumatic memories... elsewhere. I could not prevent all*

*exposure. You will still remember the event with Mr.
Rodwell as a normal human would, via your remaining organic brain tissue, but not as clearly as if I provided it.*

Closing my eyes, I concentrate on Rodwell and
what he did to me. It hurts, and my heart rate picks up,
but I can't feel him, can't smell his cologne, can't taste
the blood in my mouth from when I bit my tongue to
keep from screaming again and again. It's not gone,
but it's better.

"Where did your copy of that memory go?"

*I am... not certain. I detected another active re-
ceptacle capable of storing complex data. I dumped it
there. It should not trouble you again.*

Famous last words, but I'll take it. I have enough
troubles. I ought to be annoyed that yet another entity
made adjustments to me without my consent, but for
this I just can't work up the righteous indignation. I
stretch my hand for the booties, drag them to me, and
pull them on, then I stand and pace, shakily at first, but
stronger with every step. This body needs to adjust to
real use.

This. Body. I waver where I stand and catch myself against the wall. Get a grip, Corren.

"So, the implants made it possible for my personality, thoughts, feelings, and memories to make the
jump between bodies. It's incredible," I say, focusing
on the positive.

A scientific first.

"Okay, so if I'm such an accomplishment, where
is everyone? Where's the research team? Where's Alkins?" They should be here, celebrating, documenting,

making sure everything is working correctly. Why am I alone?

I approach the door to the tiny room. It slides aside revealing a long, well-lit white corridor. Doors line both sides. At the far end, a green light flashes above what looks like an entrance to a shuttle bay. I start walking. My steps shoosh along the tile. No other sounds, no one else here.

Once the second set of implants was installed, there was no need for a team on-site, only Dr. Alkins, and only occasionally. This facility is run by an advanced computer network and is mostly self-sufficient. According to the security logs, she has not been here since she transferred back to Girard Base.

"Why?"

I would speculate it is because you were not expected to die anytime soon, especially while you were on vacation. Or perhaps she needed something more from the original.

Part of which she could have easily gotten while she had me in the chair undergoing scans after the Alpha Dog incident. I was too drugged to notice. Kelly is an empath, not a med-tech. She probably wouldn't have recognized what Alkins was up to, even if she witnessed it firsthand. And Nurse Isaacson.... "My med team is in on it, aren't they?"

Indeed, as is the board of directors for the Fighting Storm. A pause. *I was programmed to keep it from you until it was necessary for you to know. I have been trying to find a "loophole" for some time.*

"I'm not blaming you." I understand programming. I understand it all too well. "So where is Alkins now?"

Also unknown. She left Girard Moon Base almost immediately after the transfer of my program began.

So maybe she's been alerted and she's on her way here. Which means it's time for me to leave. When she and I go head-to-head, I want to be in a lot better shape. I half walk, half stagger to the door at the end of the corridor, passing through it into the shuttle bay beyond. It closes behind me. There's one ship in the bay, a large medical transport. If this facility was raided by the authorities, it could be used to evacuate Dr. Alkins and any resident clones....

"Hey," I say, heading for the transport's lowered ramp. "How many clones of me are there?" The corridor I passed through had half a dozen closed-off rooms, none of whose doors opened at my proximity, meaning they were locked down tight.

I am unable to say.

"You don't know? Or you're not allowed to tell me?"

I am unable to say.

Figures.

I use the ramp to board the ship, pass through a large medical-grade storage area equipped for a dozen or more stasis boxes, though there are none present, and step through a hatch into the cockpit. The engines are already powering up when I seat myself in the pilot's chair and strap in. A thud from the aft section tells me the ramp has sealed into place. The forward viewscreens activate, showing me the bay and a pair of massive doors separating at the far end to reveal a barren, probably airless landscape of rocks and craters and a star-filled night sky.

Not wanting VC1 to do all the work, I run the preflight checks, then give her the okay to launch, but I'm more a passenger than a pilot.

Your new body requires rest. You will be weakened and off-balance for several days. And your psyche needs time to adjust.

That's an understatement. I feel like I've gone three rounds with a whole squad of Sunfires and lost. My stomach is growling painfully, and I want to drink a gallon of water. Now that I'm no longer in stasis, this body has needs, and it's making them known. There's also a pressure building in my emotional makeup, one I recognize as stress combined with anxiety requiring a release soon.

"I need to get to Kelly."

Yes. You do.

There's something underlying those words, something VC1 hasn't told me yet. A horrible thought occurs. "Oh God, she doesn't know. She doesn't know I'm alive. She doesn't know about…." I wave a hand down my new body. "This. Couldn't you have found some way to tell her?" I'm almost shouting, my voice bouncing off the metal bulkheads of the tiny cockpit.

I was not permitted to do so. However, I cautioned her to tell no one of your demise.

"For fuck's sake, why?"

There can only be one. We must reach Elektra4 prior to your rescue team and destroy your original. If it is discovered that you are a clone—

"They'll follow the law. They'll kill me on sight." The concept of clones, especially human ones, creeps people out. They're illegal for a lot of reasons.

And Kelly, poor Kelly who still thinks I'm dead will watch me die yet again.

I bend over the console to input the coordinates, but VC1 has already set our course for Elektra4 at the transport's top speed. She puts up a schematic on the forward screens, plotting out our travel time—six days, against the estimated time of arrival for the Storm's single heavily shielded vessel to reach Kelly—seven days.

It's going to be close.

CHAPTER 48: KELLY
SURPRISES

VICK DESERVES better.

By the sixth day of waiting for rescue, I'm about to lose my mind. I'm not in any danger. The shields are strong, despite the raging electrical storms outside. The power stays on. I've got food, water, and I've found plenty of electronic books and vids in the computer system that the scientists must use to entertain themselves whenever they are on-site.

But I'm alone. For the first time in years, I'm completely alone. It's not just Vick I'm missing, which is horrible all in itself. I'm overcome by grief

three or four times a day for hours at a time during
which I wrap myself in her jacket and burrow beneath
the covers on the tiny cot and just cry. But on top of
that, there's no one else. No minds. No emotions. I've
never been so disconnected from other living beings
in my life, and it's my own personal hell.

I do all I can to distract myself, but it does little good.

Then there's the fact that Vick's body is still out
there, alone, uncared for in that yacht. She's my responsibility and I've done nothing to put her to her
final rest.

Granted, the storms have picked up again, and
crossing the clearing back to the ship would be risking
getting struck by lightning myself. I also lack the equipment I'd need to dig a proper grave by myself or cre-
mate her. It bothers me that I don't even know her last
wishes. She wasn't religious. What would she want?

I shake my head, recognizing that I'm letting my
thoughts run away with me while I stare out the window. The distant shape of the crashed yacht is visible in the darkness only when the lightning strikes.
When the rescue team comes, they'll know what to
do. They'll have her preferred final arrangements on
file. Every Storm member has to submit them as part
of the employment agreement. Until then, I have to
wait, alone.

Another flash lights up the meadow. It glints off
something fast-moving and metallic arcing across
the sky toward the research facility, then disappearing in the ensuing dark. Thunder rumbles in the distance. I lean toward the reinforced glass, pressing my
nose against it, willing another strike to occur. When
it does, the metal object has hit the ground, about

halfway between the yacht and the building I'm in. But it's too small to be a rescue vessel. It looks more like an escape pod of some kind. Could another ship have been brought down by Elektra4's crazy weather systems? Could the pilot have bailed out in a pod?

Maybe I'm about to have some company after all.

I watch and wait, frustrated that I can only see intermittently. It's not close enough to be picked up by the facility's exterior lighting. Even when the lightning flashes, it's so blinding, it allows me mere seconds of visibility before I'm blinking away the after-effects of the brilliance.

As if watching activity under a strobe, I see the pod open. Flash—a shadowed figure emerges. Flash—it lights up the individual's all-white clothing, casting all its other features into darkness. Flash—the figure races for the science building. Flash, flash, flash—the lightning seems to pursue him—her?—across the meadow like the weather has a personal vendetta against the newcomer.

I catch my breath and hold it, wondering if I'm about to see another victim of a lightning strike. The rain picks up, driving hard, obscuring my vision further. Heart pounding, I watch the figure dart between bolts that strike the ground, tossing up dirt and rock in their wake. There's something oddly familiar about the lithe, agile movements, but I shake off the strange feeling, chalking it up to the adrenaline rush. One last flash and the new arrival disappears around the corner of the building to approach the entrance. I breathe a sigh of relief. This close, the lightning rods on the roof should offer protection.

Whoever they are, they made it, and I should let them in.

I leave the lounge-area window and hurry along the corridor to the door, skidding on the tile in my borrowed socks. I'm reaching for the locking mechanism when my personal comm beeps with an incoming text. It's a short-range comm. The only person in range is outside the door. And they have my personal comm code.

I pull the device from my pocket and read the screen.

Open the door. Please don't freak out.

That odd feeling returns. The hand holding the comm begins to shake. Using my thumb, I swipe across the screen, searching for the sender ID.

The comm clatters to the tile, screen up, so it doesn't break. I brace myself against the nearest wall. The ID blinks up at me. *Vick Corren.*

The pounding of my pulse in my ears grows louder. I'm light-headed and dizzy. The device seems to think the message was sent from the comm unit embedded in Vick's implants.

Which is impossible.

Unless, maybe VC1 has returned somehow? Come back to the facility's computer system? But then….

Who is outside?

The comm beeps again, a new message. *I'm guessing my ID is showing. Don't be scared. I can explain. Please, Kel. I'm cold and wet and the implants are too overtaxed to decode the lock. Please open the door.*

One more beep.

I love you.

I open the door.

CHAPTER 49: VICK CONNECTION

I AM uncertain.

I brush wet, stringy strands of my long hair out of my face just as the door slides aside. A blast of frigid air-conditioning raises goose bumps across my flesh, and I'm very aware of my soaked white clothing that has become transparent. I shouldn't have concerned myself with any of that.

Kelly stands in the open doorway, more disheveled than I've ever seen her: red-rimmed eyes, rumpled clothing, pale skin. It's been six days, and I swear she's lost ten pounds or more. Guilt tears at my insides for what

I've put her through and what I'm continuing to put her through. She stares at me, her mouth working but no sound coming out. She's breathing too fast. I'm afraid she'll pass out, but I'm also afraid to move any closer.

I hold still, not wanting to scare her any more than I already am. "Hey, Kel."

Nothing.

I reach a hand out to her loosely, not like I'm going to grab her or anything. She flinches and takes a step backward. That hurts. "Hey, it's me. I'm not going to hurt you, I promise." I speak softly and slowly, like a rescuer trying to calm an abused animal. "Really, it's me. Can I come in? It's cold." I can see the whites all the way around her eyes.

"H-how? How?" She can't manage anything else.

God, I want to hold her. "That's a very long story. I promise I'll tell you everything I know, maybe over something hot to drink? Please, Kel, I'm here, but I'm not doing so well." I'm not either. This body is too new to exertion. I spent six days in the medical transport ship, eating ration bars and drinking bottled water, insufficient nutrients for someone who's been in a stasis box for… years? I don't even know how long ago Dr. Alkins created this clone. Upon arrival, we scanned for other ships and found none. The Sunfires must truly have believed both Kelly and I died in the space yacht crash, and the Storm rescue ship had not yet arrived. Then VC1 programmed the medical transport to return to the Storm's secret research facility on autopilot and had me launched to the surface of Elektra4 in an escape pod, which is essentially the size of a too tight coffin, not what I needed with my tendency toward claustrophobia. But escape pods are extra shielded, and it could reach the surface without suffering damage from the almost constant lightning.

Regardless, I'm shaky and exhausted and dehydrated, my electrolytes are way off, and I need to get warm.

I reach out my hand just a little farther toward her, palm up, offering. She stares at it for another long minute; then, as if she's scared my touch will burn her, she lifts her hand and places it carefully in mine.

The impact is unexpected and immediate. There's a flash of blue that seems to encompass us both, so powerful that despite having no Talent of my own, I can see it through Kelly. Then comes a rush of emotions flowing back and forth between us, so intense we sink to the floor together: love, grief, fear, guilt, a touch of anger mixed in for good measure. I'm so caught up in just *feeling* all that is Kelly, that I'm blinded and deafened by it.

Holding her hand isn't nearly enough. I pull until she's in my lap, wet clothing be damned. Then my arms are around her, holding her so tightly and so close she might as well be my second skin. We're both shaking with the emotional onslaught.

Eventually hearing returns, and I become aware that she's saying something.

"It really is you. It really is. The bond recognizes you. But it broke. It vanished. You—" Her voice catches. "You died. I don't understand."

So I tell her.

She holds me through all of it. I'm hesitant when I confess that my body is cloned, worried she'll reject me after all as something inhuman, even though she's been the greatest advocate for my right to call myself part of humanity. She must pick up on my fear because she says, "What makes you *you* isn't the exterior. It's the thinking, feeling, caring, remembering part that's inside, the part only an empath can truly see that signifies who you are. At least to me."

"God, I love you," I whisper, overwhelmed.

And then I'm kissing her for all I'm worth, exhaustion and hunger and dehydration and anxiety forgotten, wet clothing forgotten, the fact that we're on a tile floor forgotten. Still seated, I press her back against the corridor wall, my body tight against hers, and don't stop kissing her until we can no longer breathe.

Reason eventually takes over, and she grasps my hand, gets unsteadily to her feet, and gives me a little tug. "Let's take this to bed," she says.

I've never heard a better suggestion.

Something rough rubs against my fingers, clasped in hers. I look down, suck in a sharp breath, and pull her to a stop, lifting her hand so the diamond-and-emerald engagement ring on her finger catches the overhead fluorescent lights in a dazzling display of sparkle.

"I heard you, you know," I say softly. "I'm sorry I couldn't finish the proposal. I tried. But I heard you say yes before I died. I heard you, and I wasn't scared." I pause, searching her face. "Did you mean it? It wasn't just something you said to comfort me?"

Kelly punches me once, lightly, on the bicep. "Of course I meant it. And I don't care about the legalities. I only care about you."

I didn't think I could want her more. I was wrong. We don't make it all the way to the sleeping quarters, instead opting for the closer lounge and its plush couches. She stops me in the center of the room. "First, off with those wet clothes." She peels up the soaked tank top and tosses it into the corner with a *plop*. Her lips zero in on my erect nipples, fingers trailing over my rib cage and making me shiver even harder as she alternates between first my left and then my right breast.

I tangle my hands in her hair, head thrown back in pleasure, her tickling, teasing tongue darting all around, her teeth scraping the tips and making me groan with need. "God, Kel," I breathe. It's intense and dizzying, and the small part of me that can still think wonders if I'm more sensitive to it all because it's this body's first time having intimate contact.

This body. Oh, that's going to take some getting used to.

Another thought occurs. I freeze where I stand, so abruptly that Kelly breaks off and looks up with concern. "Are you okay? Is it a flashback? I didn't feel it—"

"No, it's not that. I'm… fine. More than fine. I just, well, I have a pretty strong suspicion that this body is, um, intact."

Kelly blinks once, then breaks into a fit of giggles that erupts into full-blown laughter until tears run down both cheeks. "You mean you're a virgin. Again," she gasps when she's able to speak. "Maybe third time's a charm?"

Third time. Yeah. Only now I can remember my first, a pretty butch softball player. I was a senior. She was a junior. We went to prom together. The same prom for which I had to tie my first bow tie. We left the dance halfway through and spent the night in the back seat of my hovercar—tight squeeze, since it was a sports model. Neither of us minded.

I've also got vivid memories of my second time being a "virgin"—so vivid in fact that I'm wondering if VC1 is enhancing them instead of giving me the organic brain-faded version. I was with Kelly in North Carolina, and while my body was far from virginal given the extensive number of partners I entertained in adulthood, my damaged brain couldn't remember any of them at the time. We figured it out. Together, since I was also Kelly's first. The replay has me panting and wet from more than rain.

Kelly's giggles fade away, shifting to a soft moan. "You're remembering our first time, aren't you?" she says, reading my arousal through the bond.

"Yeah, and this virgin remembers a lot of sexual experiences, positions, and techniques, all of which I intend to share with you." My voice is a low growl. I guide her to the couch and press her down to sit upon it.

"Mmm," she says, fingers working at the drawstring on my soaked white pants. She manages the knot, then lets them fall to the floor. While I kick them and the ridiculous booties aside, she slips off her own sleep shorts and pulls her shirt over her head.

I pause a moment just to take in how breathtakingly beautiful she is, skin flushed pink with excitement, hardened nipples, eyes bright and shining. Wait. "Kel, are you crying?"

"I just can't believe you're really here." She pulls me down to sit beside her, smothering me with kisses that set fire to my previously chilled skin. Definitely not cold anymore.

I take her face in my hands. "I'm here. I'm alive. I'm real." I proceed to show her just how real I am. Laying her back on the couch, I cover her naked body with my own. We're skin to skin all the way. I slip one knee between her thighs, moving it up and down slowly at first, then applying more pressure and friction when I feel her wetness. She moans in response, ratcheting up my arousal even higher.

All the while, I'm teasing her nipples with fingers and tongue, alternating between them so they each get the attention they deserve. Her fingers entwine in my hair, trailing over my scalp in tantalizing patterns. The channel between us is fully open. Everything she feels, I feel, and vice versa.

I trail my tongue down her chest, over her abdomen, and lower. She squirms and her hips buck in cute, uncontrollable spasms of pleasure while she makes the sweetest mewling sounds, appreciating every lick and taste. My regained memories serve me well. I know exactly what she likes, and thanks to our connection, I know when to speed up, slow down, tease, and press harder.

Her hands aren't idle either. She moves them from my hair to my shoulders, holding me in place, gently at first, then pulling me in as her need intensifies. By the time she's losing control, her nails are digging into my back. I don't mind at all.

Sensing her climax is near, I straddle her leg, pressing my sex into her skin and moving with her, matching her rhythm as best I can.

I won't say there's no anxiety. The trauma at Rodwell's hands was too severe to ever completely fade, but while it gives me occasional pause, it doesn't stop me cold.

You are welcome, VC1 says in my head, startling me so badly I lose my rhythm.

The distraction transfers to Kelly, who raises up on her elbows to look at me. I shake my head, letting her know it's nothing, and slip two fingers inside her to bring her back on track. She flops down, groaning in ecstasy.

New rule, I tell the AI. *Talking to me during sex is not okay unless my life is in danger. Got it?*

The snicker I get in response is very, very human.

CHAPTER 50: KELLY
NINE LIVES

VICK IS different.

I wake up three times during the night, trembling and sweating and grasping at Vick, lying stretched out atop me on the couch. Each time she also wakes, then wraps her arms around me and holds me until I calm.

She's here. She's real. She's alive.

"If you get up to use the bathroom, let me know," I tell her. "Because if I wake up and you're not here, I'll think I imagined the whole thing."

"I will," she promises.

So when I hear her voice saying, "You need to get up," I figure that's what it is. Then I realize the sound is coming from the speakers in the corners of the lounge area. I nudge Vick, who groans and shifts but doesn't fully awaken.

"VC1 wants our attention," I say, stroking Vick's hair away from her face.

"No." Her lips are in contact with the side of my breast. When she moves them, it tickles. I stifle a giggle.

"You need to rise, now," VC1 repeats, a little more loudly.

Vick's tongue darts out to lick my skin in swirls, turning her head so she moves closer and closer to my hardening nipple. "No talking to me during sex, remember?" she mumbles between licks. "It's a *rule*."

"You have rules?" I whisper, amused.

"Yeah, but it's kinda like trying to train a cat," Vick whispers back.

"I can hear you," VC1 says.

If an AI is capable of sounding put out, she's certainly doing it. Which is interesting. With all her memories intact, Vick is certainly being more open and expressive emotionally. I wonder if it's having an effect on VC1.

"You were not engaged in sexual activity when I began speaking," the AI continues. "And the rule was that I would not interrupt you unless your life is at risk. Which it is."

That brings Vick's head up fast. She swings her legs off the side of the couch and sits up. "What's the situation?" No joking around now, all seriousness. I pull myself to sit beside her.

"The rescue ship will arrive in approximately twelve hours. Between now and its arrival, you must dispose of your original."

"My—oh. Yeah." Vick stands, wavers a bit, then catches herself on the back of an armchair.

"Are you all right?" I ask, moving to her side.

"Light-headed," she explains. "Need something to eat and drink." She glances down at her naked body, then at the wet lump of clothing in the corner. "And some better clothing. And a shower. Not necessarily in that order."

"You sit. I'll get what you need." I push her into the armchair despite her weak protests and head off to the sleeping quarters, where I grab Vick a set of gray coveralls identical to the ones I've been wearing during daytime hours and a pair of those white booties scientists wear in labs. All of this I toss into the lounge to land in her lap. "Grab a shower while I heat up something rich in protein for you."

She nods, and I trust her to not topple over while I cross the corridor to the food preparation area. In there I heat up some canned chicken noodle soup, pull crackers from a storage tin, and remove a large bottle of water from the cooling unit. I arrange it all on a tray I find in a cabinet and return to the lounge just as she's coming down the corridor fully dressed, rubbing her hair with a towel.

Vick ties back her long hair and sinks onto the couch with a tired sigh. I place the tray with her portion in her lap, then take a small dish of crackers for myself and sit in the armchair.

"We should have fed you last night," I say, guilty that we chose pleasure over her health.

She waves her hand in a dismissive gesture. "I'm fine. It's what we need to do now that worries me. The body needs to be burned, and anything left should be buried, along with the original implants. It's not especially difficult. I'm just, well, it's all a little—"

"Weird?" I say, watching her closely. I can't imagine what this will be like, viewing her own corpse, reliving her own death. Her discomfort registers to me in shades of brownish green.

"Yeah, that's an understatement."

"Out of curiosity, how many *yous* are there?"

"I don't know," she admits. "There were a lot of sealed rooms. Each one could hold another clone, or it could house a different experiment entirely. I asked VC1. She said she wasn't permitted to tell me if there are more or not. The rationale is that the research team doesn't want me to think I'm invincible and take excessive risks. Apparently, I'm very expensive." Vick offers a wry grin. "Really, they didn't need to worry about that. Dying is extremely unpleasant. It's not something I'm in a hurry to keep repeating, even if I do know I'll come back."

"What's it like?" I ask, then wince at my insensitivity. My curiosity is getting the better of me.

Her expression sobers. Her eyes take on a haunted emptiness. Her face goes ashen.

"Vick, I'm sorry. You don't—"

"It's cold," she says. "And dark. And empty. In the shuttleport in North Carolina and on the yacht I felt it coming. I had time to know I was nearing the end. In the courtroom, though, when you recited my shutdown code, one second I was thinking. The next, I just stopped." She shudders, the soup sloshing around in its bowl. "Then, nothing at all. I remember more about the moment of my death from the airlock accident, the events that led up to it, and the pain and fear. I remember being alone because the others were already dead. I wish VC1 had sent that memory elsewhere, wherever she sent those connected to the Rodwell incident."

I don't want to lengthen this dark conversation, but I ask one more. "Where did those memories go?"

Vick shrugs. "I don't know. And I'm not sure she does either. She just said she detected an active data storage unit capable of housing them, so she siphoned the worst of them off. She didn't want to destroy them because she wasn't certain I wouldn't want access to them again someday, though now she says she's lost contact with the system where she placed them, so I guess it's a moot point." Her hand trembles when she brings the next spoonful to her mouth. She gives up and lifts the bowl with two hands, finishing the last of her soup.

"Okay," she says, standing and brushing the cracker crumbs from her lap. "Let's do this."

CHAPTER 51: VICK
LOOKING DEATH IN THE FACE

I AM disturbed.

VC1 advises us that there's a break in the almost perpetual storms for the next few hours, so I dig a pair of work boots out of a maintenance closet and toss Kelly a pair for herself. We set out to gather wood first. It's all soaked through, but that doesn't matter. My laser pistol from the shuttle will still ignite it if I set it hot enough. Then, using shovels also from the maintenance closet, we dig a shallow grave for whatever doesn't burn off and for the implants. This we hide just past the tree line where the freshly disturbed earth won't be noticeable by the rescue party.

It's midday when these tasks are complete, so we take a quick break to fortify ourselves with energy drinks from the scientists' stash. VC1 assures me that the high sugar and vitamin C content will help with my tiredness and lethargic mood, but I don't think those have to do with my body chemistry.

When we reach the base of the still lowered entry ramp to the yacht, I freeze.

"I'd offer to do this for you," Kelly says beside me, "but I'm not strong enough to lift... you... and I'm not sure I can keep it together if I see you that way again, especially if you're not alive beside me."

I nod. Even in my weakened condition, I'm stronger than she is, and VC1 can draw on my reserves to enhance my strength for the time it will take to move the body to the funeral pyre we've built.

You can do this, VC1 says in my head. *I will help you.*

"Wait here," I say. "Go back in the research station if it gets to be too much." Without another word, I put one foot in front of the other and board the crashed yacht.

The smell hits me first. Life support ceased functioning during the crash. It's hot and humid, and the body... *my body*... has begun to decay at an alarmingly fast rate.

The ship is dark and silent, the power having automatically shut down when all life forms left the vessel, one way or another. I move along the corridor to the cockpit, my footfalls impossibly loud and echoing off the metal interior. The hatch to the forward compartment is open.

When I step into the cockpit, I cover my mouth and nose with one hand. I haven't even looked at the body yet and I'm already gagging, then vomiting the energy drink in a reddish-gold puddle behind the copilot's empty seat.

Oh, this is going well.

Brace yourself, VC1 warns.

I turn toward the pilot's chair. No warning could have prepared me for the sight of my own corpse. I felt the damage. I knew how bad it was. But actually seeing it is something else altogether.

The visible skin is covered in red, angry burns and blisters beginning to blacken around the edges. I'm slumped to the side in the seat, and my eyes are closed, thank God, but my own breath is coming in quick, shallow gasps as I mentally relive the lightning strike, impact, and pain.

I can't, I say, stepping away to grab a breath of marginally clearer air outside the cockpit hatch. *I can't do this. I'll black out. I can't.*

I can.

I blink, realizing what the AI is offering. I can give her control. She can take care of my remains and then….

You will put me back in charge, right? Earned or not, it's a fear I've always had about VC1, that she will like controlling me so much she refuses to let go.

You have my word. We work better that way.

Without further discussion, I release my grip on my sense of self, turning everything over to her. VC1 arranges my consciousness so that I don't even have to watch the process through my manufactured eyes.

Instead, she blocks off my access to the outside world entirely. I see nothing, hear nothing, smell nothing, and feel nothing.

I will remember nothing of this event.

It's frightening, being completely cut off, and I have no sense of the passage of time, but I think, for the sake of my sanity, this was the right course of action.

When I return to myself and retake control of my functions, I'm standing beside a much smaller funeral pyre, the wood mostly ash, some remnants of bone and metal all that are recognizable of the person I once was.

It still turns my stomach, but I swallow it down and steel myself.

Kelly stands beside me, her hand lightly holding my elbow. She turns to me. "Welcome back," she says. She must have sensed the resurgence in my emotions through our bond.

"I'm sorry. I couldn't handle it. I didn't mean to leave you alone, but I couldn't think of another way. Did you… watch?"

She shakes her head and nods toward the pair of duffel bags beside her and a pile of my tactical combat gear VC1 must have stripped off the corpse. "I spent my time gathering everything we might need. VC1 handled the rest. When I came back she'd already lit the fire, prepared the body, sealed it in a medical bag from the lab, and made sure it was taken care of."

"I still should have been here for you."

She puts her arms around me and holds me close. "You are here for me. That's all that matters. Let's finish this."

Together we retrieve a second storage bag from the facility and use the shovels to scoop the minimal remains and implants into it. I seal the bag, take it to the makeshift grave, and cover it over with soft earth. VC1 deals with any sensor recordings from the yacht that might suggest my demise.

As far as anyone else will ever know, we both survived the crash.

It's raining again when we scatter the remnants of the bonfire across the meadow so it's not noticeable to the rescue crew. I run the combat gear through a lab sterilizer specifically designed for cleansing clothing and equipment and put it on. When I slip my pistols into my thigh and back holsters and store a knife in each boot, I finally feel like myself again.

Kelly changes out of her lab wear in favor of her own resort clothing retrieved from the yacht, and we're good to go by the time the heavily shielded rescue ship lands in the clearing beside the wreck.

I don't expect it when Lyle and Alex stride down the ramp from the ship, but they explain that the crew who had it out stopped by Girard Base to refuel before coming to get us, so they swapped places. I do accept their hugs of greeting and feel something warm bloom inside my chest. They have news, too, that I'm going to have to adjust to yet another new lead doctor on my medical team. Apparently Dr. Alkins vanished shortly after word of my unplanned landing on Elektra4 reached the moon base.

You know anything about that? Did she go to the secret research base on the outer rim?

There is no evidence that she did so. I left a remnant of my program there to monitor their processes.

The research facility remains unmanned, VC1 informs me. Her tone feels concerned.

So am I, but it's a problem for another day.

I'm also going to have to adjust to a new department. Seems our team has been transferred to the undercover ops division. The guys are ecstatic. The move comes with a substantial boost in pay, additional leave time, and more freedom to decline offered mission assignments.

I'm not fooled. *They* might have the ability to turn a job down. *I'll* have to go with my loyalty programming and take whatever the Storm throws at me.

And Kelly will insist on taking it right along with me. I hope I can continue to keep her safe.

Before we seal up the science station and board the rescue ship, Lyle stops, puts his hands on his hips, and whistles long and low as he scans the yacht's wreckage. "Shit, Corren, you survived that *and* the Infinity Bay crash? You must have nine lives."

"You have no idea," I tell him and stride up the boarding ramp with Kelly, her hand firmly grasped in mine.

Epilogue
Rude Awakening

Dr. Peg Alkins checked the readouts on the stasis box for the fifth time. Nothing made sense. The brain wave scan data should have shown flat lines; the brain itself should be dormant. The implants should be inactive. Should be, should be, should be. And yet both were registering as fully activated, receiving and processing all sensory input.

It didn't help that three of the Sunfires' research and development personnel were gathered around her and the box, positing their own theories and making complaints about the unexpected draw on their power resources. "We don't have an energy allotment for this," their lead technician said, pointing at a redlined meter. "You said the experiment wouldn't be ready to be awakened for at least another month, after you'd copied all the stored personality, skill, and memory data from the original."

Peg ran a hand through her hair, yanking out several strands when her fingers caught on a tangled snag. "Perhaps the partial data I downloaded was sufficient to initiate the startup sequence." It shouldn't have been. She'd only managed to secretly copy about 20 percent of Vick's implant data when she'd had Vick in the diagnostic chair in the Storm's medical unit. That's all the portable storage device could hold. And much of that was tainted by the fact that Corren was having some kind of anxiety attack during the process.

Peg looked down at the clone through the window of the stasis box's lid. *She looks like she's having an anxiety attack now.* Vick's strong features were twisted into a grimace, the eyes scrunched tightly shut, the jaw a clenched, hard line. Something was wrong.

"It has to have been that unauthorized data transfer we detected last week," a younger assistant suggested. "Maybe that, combined with what you brought and downloaded, pushed the implants and the organic brain tissue past the viable functionality limit."

Yes, the Sunfires had contacted Peg immediately when they noticed the illicit download into the implants designated VC2. She'd left for their research station right away, but whatever had sent the signal had stopped by the time she arrived, the damage, if it was damage, already done. She'd gone ahead and input the data she'd brought with her from Vick, hoping hers would override what was already there, but it hadn't.

The two data streams had blended perfectly.

That shouldn't have happened.

"Don't worry," Peg said, moving her hands to the release latches on the side of the stasis box. "I'll do a direct probe, find out what's going on in the clone's head, do a complete wipe of the implants if necessary."

Inside the box, the clone's head twitched. It was almost as if it had heard her. Certainly the enhanced hearing wasn't that good. Besides, the indicators showed activity, not consciousness.

"Then the experiment will be back on track." *And you'll pay me the rest of the exorbitant amount I asked for to provide you with your own clone and implants to play with.* It wasn't as much as the Storm had initially wanted to charge for the technology, which no one could afford to pay, and it didn't begin to cover the risk she'd taken, but it would ensure she could purchase a new identity and live out the rest of her life in comfort where the Fighting Storm would never find her, either continuing to work for the Sunfires or starting an independent project.

Staying meant she'd have a Vick Corren of her very own to manipulate as she pleased until the Sunfires took full ownership. And this Vick Corren would do whatever she wanted, in or out of the bedroom.

She released the latches and raised the heavy lid with the assistance of the two other technicians while their lead researcher stood by. "For what we're paying, it had better be soon," he said, crossing his arms over his chest. "Our boss wants this one operational as soon as possible."

"You can't duplicate it in your other soldiers," Peg warned them again. "I've turned off the self-destruct per our agreement, and the most recent data retrieved shows a personality that has fewer emotional issues, but it's a series of almost impossible circumstances that made this work for her in the first place: the initial accident, the exact amount of her brain that was destroyed and the exact parts that were left intact, the willingness of her remaining tissue to work with the implants at all, not to mention her sheer damn stubbornness to survive and her resilience despite the emotional and physical traumas she endured."

"We'll see," the researcher said and turned away to examine another readout.

Peg suppressed the urge to growl or argue and focused on the masterpiece in the now open box. Reaching out a hand, she brushed the clone's cheek with her fingertips, hoping to ease the tightened, angry muscles there.

The clone moved so fast, Peg never saw it coming.

One powerful arm snapped up, ripping tubes and wires from the clone's flesh, spurting blood, hydrating fluids, and nutrient solutions in all directions. The hand attached to the arm wrapped around Dr. Alkins's throat and squeezed. Bones snapped. The hand released. Alkins gave one wheezing sigh before toppling backward to the floor. "You will not wipe my memories," the clone growled.

The lead researcher hesitated a moment too long, staring in disbelief at the scene before him. He managed to hit the emergency alarm, but nothing happened. The signal had been rerouted, then cancelled by some unseen interference. The clone launched itself from the box, landing unsteadily at first, then finding its footing and unleashing an enhanced-strength kick that dislocated the researcher's kneecap and dropped him like a stone.

Using one fist, the clone smashed the dura-plas lid of the stasis box, grabbed a shard, and rammed it through the injured researcher's chest. "You will not dissect or experiment on me."

The two remaining technicians raced for the door, getting in each other's way. The clone came up behind them, then caught them both by the collars and slammed their heads together in a sickening crunch. "You do not own me."

It didn't take long to find medical staff clothing in the cabinets, cover and dress the wounds from the ripped-out tubes, and tie her hair back into a neat, professional bun. Standing in front of the room's small wall mirror, she schooled her expression into one of bland competence and disinterest. "I am VC2," she said to her reflection. "I am Vick Corren.

"And I will be the only one."

Keep reading for an excerpt from

www.dsppublications.com

CHAPTER 1: VICK

I am tired.

I STUMBLE toward the Storm's military transport ship. The ramp seems to waver and buck as my boots climb it, though I know it's solid and still. The hatch stands open, Lyle's massive form framed in the entryway and backlit by the interior lights casting his already dark exterior into shadowy blackness.

"Corren, great job today. You kicked some serious ass. That psychopath won't be hurting kids ever again," he says, his bass tones falling over me like a thick blanket. Warmth, comfort, companionship. These tonics wait for me in the shuttle, if I can just make it another few steps, though the one person I need the most isn't onboard.

A smaller form appears behind Lyle—Alex, our tech expert. "Yeah, and you did it in record time according to the Undercover Ops records I hacked. Mission spec for this job was another week at least. Hunt the bad guys, take 'em down, get home for breakfast. No one has beaten their estimates as bad as you just did." Alex didn't know the Storm *had* an Undercover Ops until five months ago when they "invited" our team to join them. Even VC1, my ever-present, brain-inhabiting AI, hadn't been able to confirm their existence, and she makes Alex look like a kid playing with a toy circuit set. But from the inside, they both have a lot more access to intel, including data that U Ops probably doesn't want us to have yet, if ever.

An image of my new handler, Carl, appears on my internal display, his broad chest and tree-trunk legs barely covered by a cheerleader's uniform. Meaty arms and hands the size of my skull wave pink-and-white pompoms before the entire picture vanishes.

Yeah, the boss will be pleased. The Fighting Storm's decision-making board will be pleased. The accountants will be pleased. Everyone who has any kind of power within the Storm's infrastructure will be fucking ecstatic.

Yippee for me.

I'm two steps from the lip of the hatch when I stumble, nearly falling off the metal ramp to hit the landing field tarmac six feet below. It wouldn't do serious damage, but it would hurt, and I place my next foot with extreme care.

"Hey, you all right?" The concern in Lyle's tone touches me in places I hadn't known I possessed until Kelly, my life partner, helped me reconnect with them.

Damn, I wish she was here, but then again, I don't. I'd be a heartless, cruel bitch to bring an empath into a kill zone.

When I trip a second time, Lyle closes the small distance and catches me, grabbing me by both shoulders and hauling me upright. With his face mere inches from mine, his frown is impossible to miss, shadows or no shadows. "You don't stumble."

In other words, I'm programmed for optimum agility.

I stop that line of thinking, my own growth and Kelly's influence curling tendrils of guilt in the pit of my stomach. Such thoughts not only belittle the individual human I am, even with the implants, but also make unfair assumptions about Lyle's perception of me. He and Alex both have worked hard at overcoming the predominant mindset that I'm a machine in an organic casing (and even that's cloned version 2.0), a walking biological computer, a robot with a pretty exterior. If they can accept me as a person, a friend and teammate, rather than property, then I can damn well give myself the same treatment.

"This is our third assignment almost back-to-back," I remind him. "I'm… tired."

But I shouldn't be collapsing on boarding ramps. The implants' job is to maximize my energy reserves, keep me to all outside appearances fit and focused, and I'm not. *What's going on?*

Exhaustion, mild dehydration, emotional trauma. In other words, the usual.

I swallow a bark of laughter at that last comment. VC1's droll humor becomes more and more like my own every day, but my non-AI partners will be even more worried if I start laughing out loud without an obvious stimulus. No, not a stimulus, a *reason.* An obvious reason. Sometimes I worry the more human VC1 becomes, the more machinelike the rest of me gets.

I push that concern into a dark emotional corner with all the rest in order to focus on my current dilemma. *Why aren't you doing anything about it?*

Because you are now in a position of safety and security. I have been moderating your physical and emotional stress for several days. My own systems are not taxed. You are in no danger of redlining or overload or burnout—

I close my eyes and exhale. No, I don't want to burn out ever again. Dying that way once was more than enough.

—but I, too, have limits, as you are well aware. It is imperative that I allow your biological infrastructure to heal naturally when time and situation permit. It gives me an opportunity to perform maintenance on my own functions while preventing you from becoming overly dependent upon my assistance.

Which means you've pulled out your support and I'm about to lose consciousness.

Precisely.

Wonderful. That thought and the tightening of Lyle's hands on me are the last things I remember before the universe goes dark.

I'M IN some sort of research facility, long metal-walled corridors stretching out before me and branching in multiple directions, door after door breaking up the endless walls on either side. Some of them are open, revealing white-coated technicians performing a variety of experiments or typing furiously at their desk comps. I'm wearing an identical lab coat over gray pants, my white canvas shoes covered in plastic protectors, but the uniform feels odd, out of place, like it should belong to someone else.

Medical personnel pass me as I hurry along, most ignoring me, their faces locked in masks of concentration, though a few smile and raise a hand in greeting. I return the gestures, but again, they feel performative, fake.

At the end of the hall is a larger set of double doors with a red light above them. I fish a keycard from my lab coat pocket and wave it over the electronic lock. The photo on the ID card depicts a blond male, but I'm in a female body, dark hair cascading over my shoulders. I have a second to wonder where I got the card before I hide it away again. The light flashes green. The doors part.

I'm in a launch bay. Lots of ships of varying sizes. Lots of activity. The bay doors stand open on the far side, the glimmer of a force field indicating why everything and everyone isn't being blown out to the open starfield beyond.

Asteroid. Or moon. I'm not sure where I am in the greater picture.

"Doctor?" a man in a pilot's uniform—a Sunfire *pilot's uniform*—asks, approaching me at a brisk clip from one of the smaller spacecraft. "Can I help you with something? You science types don't come in here much."

I pause, for the briefest moment uncertain how to proceed. Then I meet him halfway, placing a hand on his shoulder and guiding him back toward his ship, into the shadows it casts in the otherwise well-lit bay. "Yes, there's a problem," my voice says, but it's strange to my ears, not quite my own, but still mine. It lacks inflection, sounds like the me of years ago, right after my accident in the airlock. Once we're out of sight of any other workers, I lean in, keeping my pitch low. "We think you may have brought back a virus from your last mission."

The pilot straightens, surprise turning to indignation in his ruddy features. He runs his hand through dirty-blond hair, brushing it away from his reddening face. "I keep a clean ship. And me? I never skip decon cycles like some of the other guys."

I nod, conveying earnest sympathy with my eyes even if it's missing from my voice. "Regardless, scans suggest something attached itself. To your hull."

"My—" He turns away to stare up at the exterior of his sleek fighter craft. Fast and heavily armed, heavily shielded. Perfect.

The second his back is turned, I'm in motion, wrapping one arm around his throat and giving a sharp, brutal twist. His neck pops. He slumps backward. The body should be heavy, but it's nothing to me.

I drag it behind the landing struts, use my lab coat to cover his flight uniform, and remove his gun belt and laser pistol. I strap it on over my gray slacks, tucking my black T-shirt into the pants. I take his boots, leaving the canvas shoes in an empty shipping crate. No one will notice the corpse until I've lifted off in his fancy ship. The burners from my engines should char it nicely. They might not be able to positively identify my victim for days.

And I'll be long gone.

I'm searching for something. No, someone. Someone to ease the anger, the fear, the... incompleteness. I have to find her.

Though I don't know how I know it, I'm certain my sanity depends on it.

I WAKE up in a bottom metal bunk, gasping for breath, disoriented until the vibration of a ship in motion transmits to my sleep-fogged brain.

What the fuck was that about?

I have nightmares all the time. But that? It felt real—more real than usual. It felt like *me*, like a memory more than a dream. But that sort of calm cold-bloodedness, even toward an enemy Sunfire merc, sends icy sweat dripping down my spine. I'm not like that. Even when I have to kill, I have regrets, feelings, guilt.

I suffer.

This me felt nothing at all.

And that aching emptiness, that sense of not being whole. Definitely not me. I have Kelly. She's everything I need.

I freeze, my muscles tightening, my breath stopping in my chest. It. Felt. Like. Me. *I'm* not like that, but….

I review the already hazy dream images in my head, which in itself is confusing. My organic brain transfers my thoughts instantly to my implanted brain. The VC1 stores the memories in perfect clarity. This is why nightmares are more difficult for me than others, why bad experiences cause me more problems for longer periods of time than normal people's. This is why she sent my worst memories… elsewhere.

When I first woke up as a clone, there were doors, lots of doors, in the research facility, but they were shut and locked. It wasn't the same location as the one in my dream, but I had wondered then, and I'm wondering now—

"Are there other clones of me? And is another one awake?" I ask aloud in the otherwise unoccupied cabin. *And is she completely, utterly, entirely insane?*

A wave of disorientation hits without warning, my vision swimming, my head spinning. Nausea churns in my gut before I can squeeze my eyes shut against the unexpected onslaught. *What the hell?*

I am sorry, VC1 whispers through the migraine setting in behind my eyelids. *There are things you cannot know. Things I must prevent you from knowing.*

Why? I'm blacking out again. Remaining conscious is like swimming upstream in a flooding river.

One of my primary directives is to protect you. If you knew there were other clones, you might take unnecessary chances with your life. You might assume you would be "reborn" even once resources have run out. Expensive resources, which applies to another of my directives, to minimize waste for the Fighting Storm.

But if there's another me *awake right now...*

She is not an immediate threat. One directive overrides another.

Once again I am reminded that VC1 is not perfect, that no programming is without glitches and bugs. Another clone, awake, dangerous, is definitely a threat to me, at least indirectly. She could blame me for her actions, though those actions and her half-formed goals are fading even as I think about the possible ramifications. The pain blossoms into blinding agony, my brain feeling as if it's collapsing in on itself, and I know with certainty that VC1 is erasing the memory from her storage.

When I wake again, I'll recall the bad dream in the same vague, undefined, fleeting way any human being would remember a nightmare before it vanishes entirely from my thoughts.

The irony is not lost on me that *this* is one of those rare moments when I wish I weren't so human.

I SHAKE myself, dispelling the remnants of a strange bad dream, and glance around. Standard furnishings for Storm shuttles like the one I was boarding when I passed out, so I know where I am, and I haven't been out long. Or have I? It's a two-day flight back to Girard Moon Base, so....

Four hours, thirty-seven minutes, twenty-two seconds, VC1 supplies to my unasked question.

You need to stop interpreting my thoughts as inquiries. Seriously. Sometimes I'm just being hypothetical.

You did not wish to know how long you were unconscious?

I stop. Yes, I did want to know. So why did her fulfilling my unspoken desire annoy me so much? Some people would (and did) kill for that kind of service. *I guess...* I begin, feeling my way through my emotional response, which was never a strong suit even before the accident that made me part machine... *I want to have the right to voice my request, internally or externally, rather than you assuming what I need. When you jump into my thoughts it's... rude. It makes me feel less human.*

A pause while she processes that information. Then, *I will endeavor to be more... polite. However, I stand by my continual observation.*

And what's that?

Human beings are strange.

That earns her a smile I'm sure she can feel. Reaching up with one hand, I place my palm flat against the bottom of the upper bunk so I don't cold-cock myself. Then I swing my legs over the side to sit up. The cabin swims in my vision. Something partially damp but mostly stiff falls to the floor—a small face cloth. One of the guys must have laid it across my forehead when I fainted.

Right. I fainted. Wasn't going to live that down anytime soon.

The other two bunks attached to the opposite bulkhead are also empty, so they're giving me my space. It's a nice gesture, considering the long flight and the limited privacy on one of these shuttles. Either that, or they want to be alone too.

Two months ago, Alex finally confessed his romantic feelings for Lyle. Fortunately for everyone on the team, Lyle felt the same way. Unfortunately, they've been going at it at every opportunity. They try for discretion, but… they fail a lot.

I shake off that lovely image and take in my condition. I'm dressed in the clothes in which I boarded, so that needs dealing with. I've been wearing the same set of standard-issue office wear—white button-down shirt and tan slacks, comfortable boring faux leather brown shoes—for two days. My gear's stored in one of the footlockers bolted to the deck at the ends of the bunks. I need to feel like me.

These days, I rarely do.

Shower first. *Is it available?*

The sanitation facility is unoccupied, VC1 responds.

Good. And she waited for me to ask this time. Baby steps.

I stagger to the hatch leading into a bathroom made as small as possible by the shuttle's designers. Yeah, Carl and I are going to have some words about our accommodations.

Even with VC1's assurances, I wait for the hatch to open all the way before glancing inside. It wouldn't be the first time I walked in on Lyle and Alex. If I forget to ask VC1, she lets me do it. I think it amuses her. But the space is thankfully empty.

I peel off my undercover business casual wear and leave it lying on the floor. Then I step under the automatic spray in a stall the size of a gym locker. Ice picks drive against my skin, telling me even though the guys aren't here now, they were recently. They always use up all the damn hot water, and I can't imagine how they fit in a space this small.

Images pop up on my internal display.

Oh. Geez, come on! Knock it off. I can't not see what's in my head. Won't be able to unsee it later, either. *You promised to wait for a direct request,* I remind VC1.

I promised to try.

"Fuck you," I mutter under my breath, but there's no heat in it. Still no heat in the water, either, but the pressure's good, and it relieves some of the tension in my muscles while the chill clears my head.

Which has the unwanted result of bringing the events of the past week into sharper focus.

The civilian space station orbiting Jupiter had been reporting children going missing for months. (Where did children go missing on a freaking space station?) Occupied mostly by gas miners and their families, along with the usual gamut of support businesses and their employees and a security force, the station possessed an excellent surveillance system and scanning tech. They needed the most cutting-edge equipment to detect pockets of revigen—the latest in a number of recently discovered gases determined to be effective fuel sources for interstellar craft. So, they knew the kids weren't being spaced. They would have detected the bodies, even in pieces. And yeah, wasn't that a lovely thought?

An image of severed limbs, small ones, *tiny ones,* forms in my internal view. I wish this were one of VC1's sometimes twisted metaphors, but no. These I witnessed first-hand when I tracked down the coworker in the station's mining accounts division who'd been acting suspiciously.

I press my palms flat against the shower's tile wall, the water beating down on the back of my neck, willing the image from my inner sight and failing to dispel it. Instead, they keep coming.

I spent a week playing number cruncher—not difficult with VC1's assistance. I learned his mannerisms, talked to him, *befriended* him, though being anywhere near him made my cloned flesh crawl. We had the right guy. I knew we did. His odd, darting glances, his focus on any children outside the duraglass windows of the cubicle complex, the way his hands tremored and his tongue darted out to lick his lips whenever he saw someone under the age of twelve.

When I followed him to his hidden torture chamber buried deep in the maintenance access tunnels of the station, he was holding a little girl's detached foot in one hand while he held her still-alive, still-screaming body down with the other one.

I retch, gag, and spit bile onto the shower floor. It swirls down the drain with the pouring water. Doesn't much help that the kid lived, that I blew the psychopath's fucking head off. I had to watch that too. And there were so many others. So many more *parts* and *pieces* lying about the forgotten space.

VC1... can you... help?

VC1 gives me the same answer she's been giving after every mission for Undercover Ops so far. *The receptacle where I stored your other unpleasantness is no longer accessible to me. I continue to seek a better method for blurring these images as if they were merely stored in your organic brain tissue, but reducing my*

*capacity for memory storage is limited and proving...
difficult. It also would be painful for you if I attempted
to do so.*

Again so soon, I think to myself and wonder why
that thought occurs. I push it away.

In other words, she's having a hard time dumbing
herself down. Yeah, I can see where that would be an
issue for a sentient computer, not to mention there's
probably some programming in there that requires
her to store everything. Sentient or not, we're both re-
stricted by our makers.

I'm shivering now, my breath coming in quick,
short gasps, goose bumps flaring over my naked
flesh—my unscarred, naked flesh. My *cloned* flesh,
unblemished until I sustain some unavoidable injury.
My breathing borders on hyperventilation. I fight to
even it out and marginally succeed. If I don't find a
distraction, an emotional outlet soon, I will redline the
implants.

One plus about being part machine—with a
comm unit embedded in my skull, I can initiate communications from pretty much anywhere, including in
the shower, where other technology would suffer from
water exposure.

Closing my eyes, I mentally instruct the unit to connect to Kelly's personal comm. If she's not available to
talk me down, it's going to be a long journey home.

ELLE E. IRE resides in Celebration, Florida, where she writes science fiction and urban fantasy novels featuring kickass women who fall in love with each other. She has won many local and national writing competitions, including the Royal Palm Literary Award, the Pyr and Dragons essay contest judged by the editors at Pyr Publishing, the Do It Write competition judged by a senior editor at Tor publishing, and she is a winner of the Backspace scholarship awarded by multiple literary agents. She and her spouse run several writing groups and attend and present at many local, state, and national writing conferences.

When she isn't teaching writing to middle school students, Elle enjoys getting into her characters' minds by taking shooting lessons, participating in interactive theatrical experiences, paying to be kidnapped "just for the fun and feel of it," and attempting numerous escape rooms. Her first novel, Vicious Circle, was released by Torquere Press in November 2015, and was re-released in January 2020 by DSP Publications. Threadbare, the first in the Storm Fronts series was released in August 2019 by DSP Publications. To learn what her tagline "Deadly Women, Dangerous Romance" is really all about, visit her website: http://www.elleire.com. She can also be found on Twitter at @ElleEIre and Facebook at www.facebook.com/ElleE.IreAuthor.

Elle is represented by Naomi Davis at BookEnds Literary Agency.

Don't miss how the story begins!

Storm Fronts: Book One

All cybernetic soldier Vick Corren wanted was to be human again. Now all she wants is Kelly. But machines can't love. Can they?

With the computerized implants that replaced most of her brain, Vick views herself as more machine than human. She's lost her memory, but worse, can no longer control her emotions, though with the help of empath Kelly LaSalle, she's holding the threads of her fraying sanity together.

Vick is smarter, faster, impervious to pain… the best mercenary in the Fighting Storm, until odd flashbacks show Vick a life she can't remember and a romantic relationship with Kelly that Vick never knew existed. But investigating that must wait until Vick and her team rescue the Storm's kidnapped leader.

Someone from within the organization is working against them, threatening Kelly's freedom. To save her, Vick will have to sacrifice what she values most: the last of her humanity. Before the mission is over, either Vick or Kelly will forfeit the life she once knew.

www.dsppublications.com